The White Noise Collective

The White Noise Collective

HELENA OELE

authorHOUSE®

AuthorHouse™ UK
1663 Liberty Drive
Bloomington, IN 47403 USA
www.authorhouse.co.uk
Phone: 0800.197.4150

Published by AuthorHouse 07/10/2015

ISBN: 978-1-5049-4587-5 (sc)
ISBN: 978-1-5049-4588-2 (hc)
ISBN: 978-1-5049-4589-9 (e)

Library of Congress Control Number: 2015910770

Print information available on the last page.

This book is printed on acid-free paper.

In loving memory
Of
Linda Oele, my inspiringly benevolent teacher, my mother;
Roland Oele, my gentle giant brother;
and Frank Oele, my kind and generous friend, my father

"You don't love someone for their looks, or their clothes, or for their fancy car, but because they sing a song only you can hear."
- Oscar Wilde

ACKNOWLEDGEMENTS

Lucianne Sythes for allowing me to use her original artwork on canvas for the cover and to William Burnett for his photography skills in transforming that artwork into a useable format, bringing out its depth and adding to its interest.

Cate Chapman for her editing skills and suggestions; whatever you think of this book, it is a far better one because of her.

Angela Saunders for believing in my ability to write and encouraging me to do it.

Vanessa Darley and Belinda Kemp for keeping me grounded with your realistic approach and inspiring me with your independent lives and challenging adventures.

Alison Renton for helping me find and believe in myself, again, and again. And for teaching me with your constant endeavour, to ward off life's difficulties, in the art of self-improvement.

Hilary Noble for her patience and kindness always. Your unwavering support and humour through difficult times is more precious than words can describe.

And to everyone else I know, your company and friendship brings joy, interest, knowledge and experience, lifting my spirits and enhancing my life, making any of my endeavours possible.

Thank you.

'Here's the church and here's the steeple
Open the doors and here's all the people
Close the doors and let them pray
Open the doors and they've all gone away.'

Anonymous – finger rhyme

Rushton Institute of Rehabilitation

Horace looked at the clock, Jake looked at the clock because Horace had, Gill checked her watch.

Horace looked at the clock, often; a white rimmed plastic affair in keeping with its place of residence. Rather than just moving his eyes, Horace lifted his whole head to bring the clock into view, his body regimented in white t-shirt and jeans accentuating his breadth and size; a body capable of lifting extraordinary weights. Rumour had it that he'd moved a car once, but a fatty food diet rich in dairy had layered his weary movements with extra weight, adding a psychological effort to the daily exercise of lifting his head. Jake looked at the clock because Horace had, inquisitive sparkling eyes peering out of his slender well-kept form. Jake eyed the clock thoughtfully, even though his compulsion to follow Horace's lead had been followed mindlessly. Gill, in her white coat that didn't fit all that well, checked her watch because Horace and Jake had both looked at the clock. Imogen shook her head and tutted under her breath: to her time had only periodic meaning; certain actions of the day were required at certain times but this did not – as Imogen saw it – require the constant clock watching of her strange companions. Boris never looked at the clock. Although silent to most of the others, the *tick, tick, tick* had fixed its constant faceless ticking motion on Boris, who had, for the moment, acquired a spot just to the left of the communal sitting area where the tick was loudest. Boris stood there for the best part of the day. Gill in her white coat (that didn't fit quite as nicely as another white coat) had not yet figured out what it was that held his attention, and so for Boris his days ticked on awaiting the *tock*. A low table marked with the ringed stains of spilt tea blocked any easy access to the television; perched on its veneer sat the half-drunk tea that Jake had left from breakfast, his fast paced glances avoiding the cup sitting still and cold, his name printed on its surface, the 'J' trailing down into an artistic twirl. His vivid blue eyes flipped between Horace and Boris instead: *Boris and Horace, brothers; Horace and Boris; Boris and Horace, brothers.* They *must* be brothers, it made sense. Their names entwined in a rhythmic dance, depicted their relationship: Horace and Boris, Boris and Horace, it seemed right. Jake looked away. Horace looked up at Boris; he had wild ginger hair, they were not brothers, Horace was sure of it. Horace's intensely dark hair and wide buff stature, still visible beneath the buttery mass, bore no resemblance to the averagely built Boris, an unnoticeable man behind his wild ginger mop: a man of average height, average build, average sense of presence. Horace was a tall, broad man with definition breaking through the bulk, his eyes quite enchanting, his tone calming, and the years (despite the aging wrinkles mapped to suggest a once happy face) had favoured Horace with a complexion still redolent of shiny adolescent vigour. He wore without exception (to remove any form of confusion) a white t-shirt and jeans, his daily routine easily executed without the confusing additions of decisions to be made, his body a simple hanging rail sporting Daz-white t-shirts. Horace looked up at Boris; he had wild ginger hair, they were not brothers, Horace was sure of it. Horace looked at the clock. Jake looked at the clock because Horace had looked at the clock, Gill checked her watch because Horace and Jake had both looked at the clock, Imogen shook her head and tutted under her breath, Boris never looked at the clock, but heard its tick. Horace lowered his head and imagined for Jake another Jake, a Jake called Quad. Jake's fluffy blonde hair flopped slightly, working free from its gel styling, and his sparkling sharp blue eyes knocked a few years off his actual age; at thirty-one his companions had placed him at twenty-eight, but Horace would often catch flickers of grey flecks streaking through Jake's surfy style: the Quad within. The name seemed to suit an inner dimension, a deeper wish for Jake: an intelligent, sensitive being lost in self-satisfied numbness. Quad opened up a world of personality to Jake, a complex, intricate soul. Gill wore a white coat and comfy white trousers. Jake often wondered if this was a uniform but the thought twisted away as the world had moved on; to release himself from the uncertainty of his existence it was now the 28th century to him, his cluttered mind whirring with unfiltered information: a tumult of images collated into an intricate montage of assumed memory, a dizzying mosaic of simulated involvement. His mind's life involved white coats, food free from the wall and a lack of money (which suited Jake as he didn't think he had any), everything here was provided for him, he was obviously important. Imogen checked the time: it was time for her mother's visit. Horace looked at the clock because Imogen had checked the time; Jake looked at the clock because Horace had looked at the clock; Gill checked her watch because Horace, Jake and Imogen had all looked at the clock. Boris ticked on. Imogen stood and went to her room.

Imogen crouched on the floor in her room. She had lit the candle. Now she watched her mother with legs pulled up, her arms wrapped around them, her chin resting gently on her knees. She felt herself breathing, tried to regulate it, keep it steady, floating on a breeze. This ritual Imogen repeated daily. The candle flailing about to its silent techno rhythm. Her mother, hunched by it, would never have associated its movement with techno, an unidentified sound she had only heard through walls or in fleeting moments whilst channel hopping; to her its erratic inconsistencies just strained her eyes. Imogen's mother's face tightened, the skin on her forehead bunched up, her eyes narrowed as if peering through a blinding light, straining to see the presence beyond. She closed her eyes without moving, the pain dispersed around her head, a slight smile flickered over her lips with the relief: peace, for a second. When she opened her eyes again the room seemed darker than before and the candle more annoying, the pain re-grouping, the ridge above her eyes where her eyebrows clung seemed heavy, pain collecting all around like ants at a large crumb. She dragged her book a little closer without lifting it up. Imogen leant back against the wall and looked up into the darkness, forgetting her thoughts for a moment as she watched the shadows and light change the room. Her mind had just begun to wonder, sucked into the techno party and its nervous energy, and the memory of something uncomfortable had just started to build its influence, shaping its quiet tension, pictures in the shadows, when a dark bulk swelled to block the flare, the shadows playing on the other side of the room. Her mother hovered, leaving the darkness in the air, the moment silent, the atmosphere waiting for her to move, to get out of the way.

Momentarily unsure why she had stood, Imogen's mother rested her left hand on the edge of the table and rubbed her eyebrow ridges with her right; the ants, disturbed, were running here and there about her face and brain. She sighed and squeezed her eyes first tight shut and then wide open as if surprised by the memory of why she had chosen to stand. She frowned, sighed again, and shuffled off to bed. She didn't need to shuffle, there was nothing wrong with her legs, hips, feet or ankles, but she liked to shuffle: it helped her express the tiredness within. Imogen waited. Silence. She listened; her eyes moved. She waited; her eyes rested. Her mother reached the bed and plonked herself down on the edge, blew out the candle and rolled under the covers, her feet clamped together, her hips and shoulder taking the weight. Imogen could no longer see her, the candle out, the shadows still, her mother gone, lost in the room and dark.

Imogen hunched forward to hoist herself up; once standing she tried to touch her toes to stretch out the cramp. She took a few paces in the direction of the table, felt around to catch the edge of it, guiding her way: *just over there, somewhere, is the door.*

Imogen, returning to the communal area, re-occupied the seat she had left vacant 20 minutes before and slouched back a little wearily. Another day's visit was over. Horace looked at the clock; Jake looked at the clock because Horace had; Gill checked her watch. The day ticked on.

Jake

Just a year before, Jake had stepped out onto his balcony, his soft pen-wielding fingers stretched out to clasp the metal frame of the railing. He allowed the steel to numb his hand; a long sleep from which he did not yet feel shaken doused his mood. Economic lifestyle choices streamed past on the road ahead, *'making retirement dreams come true'*, numbered lives going to or returning from a labelled job, financial survival, the human brain capable of so many things, something to do, what else *would* we do? The cogs of society working to ensure its tick. Jake's blonde fluffy hair and lively bright eyes evoked something distinctly boy-like, yet the combination of his fitted white shirt, enveloping an adult muscle structure, and morning stubble revealed a man, a man living out his own financial survival, a man clasping steel in his left hand, a mug of tea in his right. *'You shop, we drop'*.

His girlfriend had left him the day before, a lean woman of smart attire; sharp, dark, engaging eyes inviting you into her womanhood, a seductive invitation that had Jake weak at the knees. He had fumbled fetching her drink (that first evening), said something brash, thought he'd insulted her, but as a catch of sun can suddenly focus, like a lens, spreading reassuring beads of light, so a slight tilt of the head had softened her seductive gaze, lending the first touch of the childish playfulness, of lighter eyes that Jake had, over time, become more accustomed to; here was an innocent truth, a naivety, insecurity, a pretty girl.

Accused of only seeing her when it suited him, so that she was constantly rearranging her plans to fit in around him and him never considering her life, he had slept heavy and long. He had not argued in his defence, nor shown any motion towards understanding or even recognising her plea. His silence frustrating her further.

'Fine,' she had said, and left.

Rushton

Gill, in her white coat (a coat that didn't fit quite as nicely as another white coat, a coat that had mutated in and out of Gill's coat for about a week; same coat, changing face), turned on the television just in time for Jake's favourite programme, he was obviously important. 16 paces long, 10 paces wide: this is their space. The white coat so far had not let him down, except once: a long week when another white coat had arrived, a coat that didn't quite fit the same. Jake was sure that Gill was not there, he had asked Horace; Horace looked up and saw Quad, a complex, intricate soul; he looked down. The week passed and the original coat (which didn't actually fit as well as the replacement coat) was back. Jake watched the television, a black box flickering with amusements, laughter coming from an unseen but up-close audience. When his favourite programme finished Gill pressed her finger into the plastic surround of the screen; Jake watched, waiting for the inevitable day when only a stub of a finger would reappear, flesh consumed by technology. Quad didn't care (Quad didn't exist). Somewhere in the depths of his mind Horace remembered a question, a question that he was sure had been directed at him, when this had been and under what circumstance he did not consider; did he want large chips? These were his thoughts: *Do I want large chips? What does that mean? Longer chips? Fatter chips? More chips? Not sure if I even want chips? Do you get more chips? How many more chips do you get?* At the actual moment when Horace had received this question, he'd known what it meant. Did he say yes or no to the question? Horace did not consider. Horace looked up at Boris, he had wild ginger hair; they were not brothers, Horace was certain of it. Jake was sure.

'Boris... come say hello to your brother,' Jake waved a hand in the air as he spoke, goading Horace.

Jake: an intricate montage of assumed memory. Life outside involved white coats, food free from the wall and a lack of money (which suited Jake as he didn't think he had any), everything here was provided for him, he was obviously important. Imogen, who had no real understanding of what Jake's concept of 'brother' meant in this particular montage thought about her last walk to the shop… A guy had cycled by wearing a wool jumper *it has diamond shapes in white against a brown background he is wearing a white helmet and bicycle clips he looks like a wanker I go into a shop I buy something I interact I must do I have change I have left the shop I'm eating what I've bought I'm pleasant I do stuff you have to I'm in here waiting I'm looking at stuff just stuff things bench pavement rubbish there's stuff everywhere just stuff I can see them but I'm in here waiting just looking at stuff waiting I see clouds nice formation it moves me I know stuff lots of stuff in here I have all these memories of things things I used to do people I used to hang out with and all the things I'm doing now will be memories as well but I just don't feel its presence not really I don't really feel the presence of the moment just the memories of yesterday and the worry of tomorrow I'm waiting tick tick there's no tock not yet I'm freezing my legs shaking my face feels tight scrunching frowning I'm nervous dizzy there's a pendulum it's strong stronger than me I think I'm not sure I'm hanging on clinging stop the swing what happens when the tock comes I don't know what happens when the tock comes there's a tick a definite tick I feel nauseous I knew I thought I knew I felt focused sure but that was then this is now I'm freezing angst fucking angst frowning it's making my head hurt tick tick stop the fucking tick God what happens when it tocks I'm walking concentrating one foot then the other forward I'm moving forward I learnt to do this years ago I don't know how old exactly how old are you when you learn to move from the crawl become that little more independent that first step away from your parents that first step towards doing stuff growing up I'm not thinking but I'm thinking my mind's spinning but it doesn't feel like there's anything there I'm dizzy I feel dizzy what happens if I let go of the pendulum? everything feels so crazy I've got to hang on control the tock but it's pulling me my arms ache I feel weak I'm tired why can't I control this why am I unable to stop? Someone's talking I think they're talking to me I don't know I don't know that's the only thing I do know is that I don't know I cannot see I cannot see myself I don't know I thought I knew but that was then and this is now.*

Horace

It was 7.02am. Horace looked up at the wall directly ahead of him, the paper a dizzy swirl of patterns with big loops and waves, entangled light and dark shades of glittery silver-grey, the background white, the lighter swirls slightly elevated from the paper. Horace squinted at it as if willing a magic-eye image out of the madness. He stood waiting by the front door, his legs astride in a powerful stance, clasping the handle of his briefcase firmly in front of himself; his right index finger tapped the back of his left hand as he waited for his wife. He looked down at the briefcase, visualised its contents: a honey roast ham and thinly sliced tomato sandwich on low-fat margarine and granary bread; a brown envelope, containing absolutely nothing but addressed, sealed and stamped, first class; and a pencil, fairly sharp, HB. Rather than just moving his eyes, Horace lifted his whole head to bring the hallway into view and searched for his wife in the empty space: 7.06am. His podgy digit tapped more impatiently, the big toe on his right foot started to twitch, soon it would be tapping in time to the finger.

'I'm ready,' Horace heard a voice, his wife. That same woman sailed into the hallway and plucked her coat from the rack. His finger continued to tap as he watched the coat manoeuvred on, keys rattling in her hand. Then the door was open and Horace was following her out over the threshold, closing the door, giving it a little shove to test its security. The day was still, the blustery winds of the evening before had died down over night and the morning breathed with a light, quiet air. He gripped the briefcase with his left hand as if someone's life might depend on it, resting it securely on his lap in the car.

'Horace!' there was an elevated urgency in her voice as Horace's wife called his name.

Horace spun his head round to face her, a little startled. He had been thinking, day dreaming or remembering, Horace couldn't be sure. He had seen an image of his wife in the garden, tending to the artfully arranged planting, a spongy, plastic covered mat under her knees, soft flower-patterned gloves protecting her hands as she wielded sharp cutters towards a protruding twig. Horace and his wife had a daughter. She was 12. Horace smiled at her and she gave a gentle wave, her fashionable but practical clothing had not yet filled out with the forming body of adulthood. Her young innocence still radiated from her clear, soft skin. She skipped a little as she walked, her fair lightly curled hair bounced as she did so, one's early life still a happy dance. She gave him a tie each year on his birthday, and for Christmas; a different colour and pattern each time. In his reverie, he had seen his tie-giving daughter bounce out from the house, she had asked what time they were to have lunch, out on the patio – the patio on which Horace sat, lounging in a lazy garden chair, a book in his hand, distracted from the story by his wife, failing to concentrate on the unfolding intricacies of the developing thriller, the real-life one in front of him intriguing enough. His wife had replied with a gentle, 'Two,' to which the tie-giver smiled, called out a sing-song, 'Okay.' Then she was gone again, somewhere in the house, and Horace remained, lounging on a lazy garden chair, watching this woman tend to the garden.

'Right, you got your sandwich?' she looked across at him, checking him over for tidiness. Horace looked down at the briefcase and placed his right hand, fingers spread over its surface, visualised its contents: a honey roast ham and thinly sliced tomato sandwich, with low-fat margarine on granary bread; a brown envelope, containing absolutely nothing but addressed, sealed and stamped first class; and a pencil, fairly sharp, HB.

'Good,' she said, satisfied, 'have a good day at work.' She leant over, left arm up, trying to manoeuvre it around his neck somehow. So he kissed her and said something like, 'You too.' Then suddenly he found himself here: out of the car and facing an office building.

It had been 7.02am, then 7.06am, then ...07, ...08 and on. It's morning every morning. Waiting in the hallway for a wife whose only genuinely annoying habit was driving him to work every day – every day, every morning another morning – and ensuring he had remembered his sandwich, the sandwich he made for himself every morning before he waited in the hallway for this wife.

Horace strode with long paces as he marched into the office. Horace was a manager, but not of many: a middle man. As he placed his briefcase on the floor beside his chair and settled back into the bulk-buy faux-leather chair (*New Dynamic Office Seating, with Wheels*), he felt the full and uncertain weight of his middle man status: being neither here nor there. Stress levels rising as he strived to fulfil requirements, the boys above caring only about staff performance, the staff caring only for the rules inflicted by the boys above. The middle man, the messenger, the no-one. At moments like this Horace felt wearily average. He fondled the handle of his briefcase as it rested tight beside the chair, the *new dynamic office seating with wheels*, He looked out at all the people milling around the floor, his workers. *What a terrible scene.* Horace scanned the room counting the required number of workers that *should* be in attendance; all the terrible people were in. The office was complete. *Marvellous.* No cover work needed. He could get away with doing very little today.

He tapped his fingers on the veneer of his desk and listened to the repetition of the resulting dull thud, pondered on what to do with his day. He had a private meeting later (7pm at a secret location). He mulled over the contents of this meeting and structured its format, then, remembering the envelope, he caught up his briefcase with a swift but clumsy movement and banged it down on his desk. Eyes darted towards him from the office floor, 'Morning!' he announced in a general sense to the room. A united, unenthusiastic chorus of 'Morning,' was dutifully returned. Horace entered the three digit security code required to open it (currently 001) and unlocked the mechanism. In front of him lay a slightly bashed-up ham and tomato sandwich, parts of the cling-film squashed into the bread where it had bounced around the empty briefcase on his journey. Horace thought about tucking tomorrow's sandwich into a velcro-secured pocket. That should sort it. The brown envelope was safely slotted into its own slot (specifically designed to keep work flat) and the pencil (fairly sharp, HB) stood upright in its own allotted compartment. Horace plucked the envelope from its safety position, closed the briefcase, clicked the code back into its security mode and stood up. He would have to get a shake on to make the drop time.

Horace puffed out his chest and lifted his head, his nose in the air not with pretension but with pride and a sense of determination today. The post box was on the corner of the street, only two buildings' widths from the entrance of the office building within which he worked. At the post box's mouth he looked carefully at the brown envelope and then slotted it through the gap, his podgy hand disappearing for a moment as he insured its safe deposit. He strolled over to the pavement's edge, pressed a button and read the illuminated instruction: *wait*. Horace waited. After a short time the red standing man glowing at him from across the street magically transformed into a green walking looking man and the *wait* instruction went out. Horace strode across the street. On the other side it was only a short walk to a quiet, open, small park. Horace's bench sat empty, as always, adorned only with a remembrance in loving memory of Mr and Mrs Cunningham. An eloquent plaque, carefully engraved with slight swirls enhancing the loop of the 'g' in 'loving' and y of 'memory'.

Horace reached into his inside pocket to retrieve a smoke. He held it between his fingers, raised it to his mouth and sparked up a rather stylish silver lighter, quite weighty and highly polished. Horace looked over the park as he took timely drags on his cigarette, the scene was still: not a dog walker, not a child and mother, not a thing, except Horace sitting just to the left of the plaque. Somehow he felt it disrespectful to block out their names with his mass. Their names enjoyed the park and its stillness at times like this, and its activity at peak hours after school. They looked over it and Horace liked to sit with them.

Horace waited. He looked over the park: nothing. He waited some more. *Huff.* Horace stubbed out his cigarette in the grass around his feet a little impatiently, but retained the stub and rose to his feet without strain despite the weight that was being lifted, mumbling under his breath about the buffoons who organise these rendezvous, *it's just an information feed, how hard can it be?* As he passed the bin by the entrance to the park he dropped the stub into a discarded takeaway coffee cup and strolled back to work. *Huff.* The idiots had cocked it up again.

Back at work his staff were waiting in the conference room. Horace, confident and assured, leaned back in his chair, paused for effect, and raised a question, 'Why are we paying ten people to do the job of six?'

'Why are you being paid to sit in the park and smoke?' Jeffery, an efficient worker (on the rare days he actually bothered to turn up) liked to goad Horace. Charming and attentive to the other staff, he encouraged them to do the same, much to Horace's irritation. Jeffery's social ability, making him likable to his peers, did not go unnoticed by Horace, but it was not going to work on him and Jeffery knew it, so instead they played a tricky game of cat and mouse.

Fuelled by his dislike for Jeffery, Horace momentarily lost his patience and blurted out, 'Why are you being paid to be off sick for most of the year?' The atmosphere was strained, Horace quietly huffed in his subconscious. He could feel his authority slipping.

'You pay me because I'm the best person here, I do twice the work in half the time. I deserve to be off sick.'

'Perhaps you should go part time?' Horace suggested.

'Perhaps you should pay me more and sack a few others.' Shuffling and sighs from the other staff.

'You need to start turning up or we won't pay you at all.'

'I want to complain about the paper in the ladies.' Veronica, a tall, slender, beaky looking girl, interrupted. Horace had noticed that when eating a sandwich she would take small quick bites, as if indeed pecking at her food. Horace stared at her, but she continued, 'It gets all bunched up and you can't get single sheets, you have to stick your fingers up the dispenser and battle with the blasted thing every time you go.'

'Would it help, if, perhaps, it wasn't filled so tightly?' Horace applied his intelligence to the problem.

Veronica pouted slightly 'Do I look like a janitor?'

Horace stared at her some more, 'No, Veronica. Of all the things I think you look like, a janitor is not one of them and I think you'll find that it's a *caretaker* in this country.'

'Why can't we have rolls?'

'I'll find out.'

'I'll tell you why! It's cheap that's what it is! You think that if you give us rolls we'll use more paper or steal them or something.' As Veronica continued, Horace's eyes lowered in despair, his mouth now slightly agape. She was in full flow now, 'It's cost cutting, save a bit here, save a bit there, like why can't we have more than one stapler between us?'

'Alright!' Horace raised his hands to the air, their outstretched span almost obliterating the table light behind him and their presence ahead of his bulk silencing the maddening crowd. 'I'll look into it and I'll get you a stapler.'

'Can I have a stapler?' Jenny. Horace closed his eyes.

'Please finish up any loose ends before you go, let's not keep our customers waiting until tomorrow, okay!' With which Horace waved a giant hand dismissively and marched out, back to his desk where he immediately unhooked the receiver from the telephone's dialling body and called Claire, Claire who deals with all the stationary. 'Staplers,' he said.

'Uh huh!'

'We seem to have a shortage.'

'Uh huh!'

'Could you please have some, say maybe three if possible, sent up by end of work today?'

'Ah, it'll be tomorrow now, internal post boy has had to go home early, mum's not well.'

'I see. Could I collect them?'

'No, they get delivered, but the boy's gone home.'

'I see.' Slight pause. 'Could you bring them up?'

Heavy pause, 'I don't leave my desk, the boy delivers them but he's gone home, it'll be tomorrow.' The line went dead. *I see.* Horace's day ticked on.

6pm, and in a united school bell outing the office cleared in seconds, coats and bags having already been organised in the countdown minutes preceding the 6pm deadline. Horace perused the empty space and sighed, a little relieved. He put on his own coat, collected his briefcase, puffed out his chest and lifted his head, his nose not in the air with pretension, but with pride and a sense of determination. Horace left the building.

7pm at a secret location. Horace had a plant, it didn't grow lemons but when you rubbed its leaves between your fingers it smelled of them. It didn't need much care. Horace liked it. It perched on an undersized coffee table in the corner of the garage, a garage attached to his house and accessed by an inner door from the utility room off the kitchen. The garage had been renovated into an office, the walls plastered and coated in a biscuit matt, the floor a thick carpet, spotless. The biscuit walls supported classic paintings, prints of course, but not to Horace as he perused the original brush strokes of masters on his walls; his favourite was the Rembrandt, the crafty cover for a fake safe, specially installed (well specially painted on) and bearing a code only known to him. A wide oak desk dominated the space, flanked on the right by files of varying colours, always neat in ordered arrangement. Horace lent back in his executive high-backed leather chair and entwined his fingers. Rocking slightly, he raised his clasped hands to his mouth, lifting his index fingers to rest on his lips. *Here's the steeple and here's all the people.* Horace appeared deep in thought as he tapped his index fingers against his mouth. Then, almost springing from his seat (as if his high-backed leather chair was installed with some James Bond-esque ejector function) he walked, slightly unbalanced at first from his hasty stance but then quite deliberately, around the desk.

'It's a tricky job,' he said, plucking a file from the collection flanking the broad oak desk that dominated the space. He placed a grass green file in front of the empty chair opposite his own and lent into the air. 'We've been watching her for some time. Are you up for the job?' Horace lent in a little more, 'Are you?'

The space remained silent.

'You'll be informed of a rendezvous point after the job is done. No mistakes this time.'

The empty chair lent forward and an invisible hand flicked open the file, the grass green file that lay out on the desk, and a silent, 'No problem,' was announced by its invisible occupant. Horace was walking around the office space now, his head aloft, his manner important, his fantasy in full swing.

Horace's wife put out the place mats for dinner, a wood pigeon in full colour tapped at a tree on one, a blue tit in full flight soared across another and an owl *ter-wit-ter-wooed* from a branch on their daughter's. She arranged glasses, cutlery, then turned back to the stove, stirring the stew. Dinner would be ready in less than 20 minutes.

Horace took a cigarette from a box on the broad oak desk that dominated the space and lit it with his rather stylish silver lighter, quite weighty and highly polished. Pressing a button on a small remote Horace burst James Brown into the room, *'da, da, da, da, daaa, this is a man's world, this is a man's world, but it wouldn't be nothing without a woman…'*

'Dinner…!'

Horace pressed another button on the small remote, increasing the volume and waited for his wife to call again.

'…Horace, dinner!'

Horace looked at the door, *okay*. He pressed the stop button and placed the remote on top of the stereo, lining it up approximately one centimetre parallel to the stereo's edge. He strolled out of the converted garage and left the secret location, his private meeting postponed; Horace had excused himself, declaring that something important needed his immediate attention.

The tie-giver was already seated, the wife was placing heavily loaded plates on the mats. Horace picked a Merlot from the wine rank and fetched the waiter's friend for its opening.

'Wine?' She seemed surprised.

'Well, I thought as we're all here together and I got a promotion today…'

'Promotion?'

'Yes, not really in title or anything, just been given a bit more responsibility, they want me to look after a special client.'

Horace's wife rubbed his arm, the one holding the bottle as he continued to struggle with the not-so-friendly waiter's friend.

'Don't you already look after special clients?' Daughters, so easily open and honest.

'Well yes, but this is an extra special client.'

'Oh I see, extra special!'

'Yes,' Horace finished fighting with the Merlot and sat down. As he placed the bottle on the table his daughter reached to pour, but Horace placed a meaty hand over its neck, 'Needs to breathe.' Horace's daughter had developed a taste first for white wine after mistaking a glass for elderflower cordial when she was 10; a discussion on the next morning's journey to Horace's office had ended with an agreement that it wouldn't do her any harm, as long as they stuck by a half-glass-only policy. Her passion for red wine started after sneaking a sip when their backs were turned, a passion that was developing into a possible career choice, much to Horace's pleasure and her mother's apprehension, as they discussed grapes and good years. The tie-giver retreated her hand, knowing that her father was right of course, but eager to try this particular Merlot.

After dinner Horace dutifully washed the dishes while his wife chatted about things, stuff, some community problem with the town hall, a leak was damaging the far wall and (of course) this was the wall being designated for a local outreach project, a group of disadvantaged kids were to come and paint a mural; now (of course) it's all being delayed, and the disappointment, well, Horace just couldn't fathom but he was sure everyone was very upset. Horace scrubbed a pan as his wife moved on to a woman called Liz who she had bumped into at the shops, having some sensitive issues with her husband, he'd started drinking a little more. Horace glanced at the wine, his wife had had a single glass, the tie-giver only half a glass, the rest, well, that was for Horace.

'Maybe he's just having some extra pressures at work,' Horace offered.

'Yes, I'm sure you're right, nothing to worry about.'

And so on. Horace nodded, seemingly attentive.

9.14pm. Las Ketchup burst into the garage and Horace shook his booty.

10.20pm. Horace snuck into bed, his wife already asleep, her book (a booker prize winner) still on the bed, the side lamp still burning. Horace retrieved the book and placed it on the side table, switched off the light and manoeuvred himself under the duvet and into comfort. He lay for a moment, the activities of his day resting on his mind, annoyed at the no show of the rendezvous at the park, Horace kicked himself now for being distracted at the meeting with his staff because of it, a secret message may have been missed, and his demotion into house keeper irritated him: *toilet roll and staplers!* Surely these meetings were designed for more constructive discussion, perhaps even about the job they were paid to do. But this evening's meeting had gone well, Horace smiled gently to himself, his abilities were too good for the banal world of insurance and the imbeciles he governed. Turning to his side Horace closed his eyes and allowed himself to sleep, his confidence restored.

Rushton

The day ticked on. Imogen was tired but afraid to go back to her room, her mother was there, her mother now asleep, now dead this third year. Horace looked at the clock, Jake looked at the clock because Horace had looked at the clock, Gill wasn't there. Jake wondered where the white coat was; he was obviously important, but neglected. White coats lived *out there* amongst the everyday, while Jake lived with two brothers (he was sure they were brothers) and Imogen. He lit a match. Gill, the white coat who had mutated into another white coat for about a week, appeared in his space. Her hand extended itself from the white coat that didn't quite fit as well as the other white coat that had mutated in and out of Gill's coat, snatching the match from him and shaking the tiny stick free from its flame. Horace looked at Jake but saw Quad, a complex, intricate soul. Quad sat staring at his fingertips, the feeling of the match still very real to them. Gill looked at Imogen. Imogen lifted her sagging dulled pink jumper from the shoulder in an attempt to shrug. Jake had not listened; Quad (a complex, intricate soul) would have understood, but didn't exist. The day ticked on.

Imogen

Imogen's earliest memory was of a little her colouring in a large, or seemingly large, colouring book. She remembered vividly being careful not to cross the black outlines of the picture that lay out on the floor in front of her. She took her time, swapped pencils often and showed the first signs of the anal retentive aspect of her personality. When it was finished she rushed to her mother's apron and tugged. In a soft, encouraging voice, o's and l's emphasised, her mother simply said, 'Oh yes, that's lovely dear.'

Years later in a cupboard sort out (after her mother had announced her desire to leave their family home and move out into the country on her own), Imogen uncovered, in a frantic disapproval, the colouring book of this memory. As she examined the scratchy streaks of messy lines that shot across the page, she realised that her mother had lied. The encouraging tenderness of her mother's natural, approving remarks were lost to Imogen as she clenched her thoughts and considered the consequences of white lies, progressive over the years. What if someone told you that you looked good in something; would you wear it more? What if they had lied? How many white lies does it take to alter the course of your life, as you buy wardrobe after wardrobe of hideous rags? How many lies had her mother told her? How many untruths of this nature had caused her to believe that she was good at something? How many of these had remained nurturing, shielding her from unnecessary distress and how many had served as a continual hidden embarrassment?

The Diary of Rose Heather Roberts

I have this fantasy.

I take a gun from the inside pocket of my jacket and hold it to the temple of my enemy.

I pause.

Bang.

But I'd never do it.

Rushton

Quad waved his arms above his head as if swaying to a ballad. Quad didn't exist. Horace looked at the clock. Jake looked at the clock. Gill checked her watch. Horace looked up at Boris: he had wild ginger hair. They were not brothers, Horace was certain of it. The day ticked on.

Horace was allowed to go to the shop. He strode on. *Umm*. He followed the pavement, the yellow brick road would direct him. *Urgh*. Although not so yellow. *Umm*. Horace had an 'Umm', not a tastes good kind of umm, a nasal umm. He umm'ed. There were leaves on the not-so-yellow, not-so-brick, not-so-road, pavement, must be autumn. He strode on. *Urgh*. Horace had an 'Urgh', different from that of the 'Umm', it was throaty. Horace Urgh'd. He liked the vibration. The 'Umm' and the 'Urgh' had a vibration, a throat and a nasal vibration. The 'Umm' indicated a thought process, not of any particular scale of depth or type, just thought. The 'Urgh' generally proceeded a discomfort or a string of words that Horace deemed disagreeable. Horace liked it. He Umm'd. He strode on. He passed a man, outwardly an average kind of man, but Horace noted colour extending from his arm. He Urgh'd. He strode on. The man pulled at a bright red lead and a tiny yelp followed by a whimper caught Horace's attention. He Umm'ed and Urgh'd almost in unison. He reached the shop. He purchased... a loaf of bread, a four pint carton of full-fat milk, some chocolate and a can of soup from the bargain bin. He strode on. His mother had always had semi-skimmed but as far as Horace could remember he had never been given a reason why, therefore it didn't matter that he now purchased full-fat. He strode on. There were leaves on the not-so-yellow, not-so-road, pavement, must be autumn. He strode on. Horace carried his shopping in two bags, one in his right hand, the other in his left. The right-hand bag contained the four pint carton of full-fat milk and the loaf of bread, the left hand bag contained the chocolate and the soup from the bargain bin; it was not weight or size distributed, it just *was*. Horace reached the door and put down the right hand bag, the bag containing the four pint carton of milk and the loaf of bread. He opened the door. He picked up the bag (containing the four pint carton of milk and loaf of bread) with his right hand; the door was closed. He put down the right hand bag and opened the door. He picked up the same bag (containing the four pint carton of milk and loaf of bread) with his right hand and the door was closed, the automatic magnetic pull faster than Horace as it swiped his entrance away from him. Horace Umm'd. He put down the bag (containing the four pint milk carton and loaf of white medium sliced bread) from his right hand; he picked up the same bag (containing the four pint milk carton and loaf of bread) with his left hand and opened the door with his right. He strode on. The left hand bag, the bag containing the chocolate and soup from the bargain bin had never been put down. He now carried both bags in his left hand. As far as everyone knew this was how Horace always carried his shopping. A white coat that no-one knew the name of took the bags from Horace's left hand and strolled off to the kitchen. Horace followed. The white coat was familiar. Horace Urgh'd. A girl who didn't wear a white coat but always intervened entered the kitchen. Horace knew it was a girl because he'd once seen her naked, a strange day when Horace had accidently wondered into the women's shower room instead of the men's (located directly opposite), a misunderstanding in his mind as to which side represented his left or right, depending of course in which direction along the corridor he was travelling. His confusion over this misunderstanding only occurred to him when this girl popped out of a cubicle and stared wide eyed at him while throwing her hands and arms around her body in an attempt to cover herself up. He Umm'd. A girl who by some strange deduction had once concluded that her eyebrow was exactly the same length as a regular non-applicator tampon.

Jake

Jake's soft blonde hair danced slightly in the low cold breeze that skirted round his corner balcony. He was much of a muchness. Jake had been *cogged* and he knew it, one of many cogs, social cogs, the cogs of society working to ensure its continual rhythmic tick. The collar of his fitted white shirt, enveloping his adult muscular structure, brushed gently against his morning stubble as he felt the thrust of life jolting him somehow. He clutched the steel frame of the balcony in his left hand, a mug of tea in his right.

The rising stress of the mundane engulfed him in an ever increasing circle of mistrust and betrayal. He remembered a game he used to play at school, a circle of friends. Darren whizzed through his memory cells, sparking little mini explosions in his head: the dark haired, dark eyed naughty kid that his mother had made him play with. Darren was slightly shorter than average but by no means short, and had been one of the first on an ever increasing list of offenders who had helped snowball Jake's emotions. Darren ate a lot and nutritionally badly, but due to extensive sporting activities was never out of shape or over his recommended body weight. As a baby he had cried relentlessly, weighing down the images of his parents in photos of those early years with constant dark shadows beneath their heavy eyes. Jake, on the other hand, had been a beautiful infant, allowing his parents plentiful sleep. His mother, proud of her son's early achievements, had bragged of her restful child-rearing experience, causing Darren's mum to unconsciously sneer behind her noisy offspring's back. That dull resentment towards her son soon faded when a wide-eyed, puppy-dog cute boy finally emerged from the tears.

As years transformed these babies into boys and eventually into men, the wide-eyed, dark haired naughty kid stood in stark contrast to Jake's blonde and blue eyed flair; they unwittingly grew together. First playing with plastic sticky building bricks during that innocent age, the protected circle of babies, living a child's life never to be remembered: that voided zone of time that neither boy nor man could conjure from the depths of his mind, the memory not powerful enough to make sense of a time before real sentences could be devised, as if language is the only way in which we can formulate our memories into postcards of our past. Their mothers remained supportive companions for each other as baby became child and child became teenager, each boy learning to decipher the mechanical complications of toys. Their mothers insistent on activity toys designed to build the mind, encourage its developing abilities. So then inevitably the boys would attend the same schools, hang out with the same crowds and eventually fight over the same girls, as toys were transformed from their plastic exterior into real life experience.

A flash, a memory, of seeing Darren all tongues a-clanging with Jake's first proper girlfriend at another 'mate's' party tightened Jake's chest. The first heart wrench of many a beauty who would betray him to 'mates'.

But the term 'mate' was not just four letters thrown together, it did not introduce itself into Jake's life simply as an alternative greeting, but bonded his once 'friends' into a growing masculine brotherhood. A brotherhood of boys sharing their escapades, their early trials and tribulations, their growing competition; the boy becoming the man, the toys becoming the game of life. 'Friend' seemed too adolescent a term, too sappy, too remembered as your childish little friend; the term 'mate' opened a new dimension of cool, a new sense of combined individuality, a new era where 'mate' defined the bond of blood, while each did the other a secret injustice, a nudge on the shoulder, a pat on the back, 'We're mates, aren't we?'

An abrupt gust of winter chill swept suddenly and forcibly round the balcony as Jake's hand clenched the steel.

As time developed him from boy to man, definitions had circled back. The later years moulding his 'mates' back into 'friends' as they pursued dinner dates, giving the same syllables an edge of maturity, identified by sincerity, the coming of age. Faced with the dining friends they had become, still engulfed by life – its ambitions, the demands of others, the expectations, the trials and tribulations that mapped out competition and directed life – he saw little change, just alternative definitions. He had never forgiven his mates for their crimes, still haunted by his past, by the grief that his mates had inflicted on him – did age really make all the difference that time was supposed to heal? The pain remained just as real, although the deeds were long ago. Darren had not given a flying fuck about him when he'd kissed thingy at that party all those years ago, a stray hand wedged up her top, and hadn't he cared any more when he so obviously flirted with Catherine on his 25th Birthday.

An intricate montage of emotions swamped Jake's heart, a bitterness of past and living betrayals infused anger with resentment. A darkness cast its unnerving shadow overhead, easing its way through the intricacies of Jake's mind. Self-pity had transformed itself into a wall of protection, a self-consumed void amongst his own and only thoughts.

Rushton

Horace lived with his brother, although it was not his brother, he had wild ginger hair; Quad, a complex intricate soul; a girl who didn't wear a white coat but always intervened; a white coat that no-one knew the name of; Imogen; and Gill, who did wear a white coat but also had a name. Vincent was a visitor. He didn't wear a white coat and he was always shown in and shown out. Jake noted this. Vincent had dark hair and wore a variety of different outfits that always looked the same. He was familiar. He said 'Alright, Horace,' often. Jake would say 'Alright, Horace,' just as often. Quad didn't speak (Quad didn't exist). Horace looked up. *Umm*. Imogen, having vacated the same seat she had left and returned to before and after going to her room (her mother was there) stood up. The familiar visitor, also known as Vincent, nodded, 'Alright, Imogen.' Imogen lived with her mother; a white coat who no-one knew the name of; Jake; Boris; Horace; and Gill, who wore a white coat but also had a name. The familiar visitor was her brother, but Jake refused to believe it as their names didn't make sense. *Imogen, Vincent. Vincent, Imogen.* The names didn't match. The brother was a phony, Jake was sure of it. How could he wear so many different outfits but always look the same? Why was he familiar? Why didn't he wear a white coat? Jake didn't like him. A vivid tumult of images collated into an intricate montage of simulated involvement, life outside involved white coats, food free from the wall and a lack of money (which suited Jake as he didn't think he had any), everything here was provided for him: he was obviously important. Imogen's brother, also known as Vincent and familiar, sat down. After a few moments of silence he jumped up and strolled across the space, manoeuvring himself quite easily around the spilt-tea-stained table that blocked any easy access to the television, and changed the channel. Jake looked over, his will shooting pins, thousands of them, embedding their stinging little needles into the brother's flesh.

He waited for Gill. Gill walked over in her white coat that didn't fit quite as nicely as the other white coat that seemed to mutate in and out of Gill's coat (this transformation had only happened once and lasted about a week). Gill lived with a man called Bob, a child called Jenny and a cat called Bertie. None of them except Gill wore white coats, although Jenny had once put it on. Jake didn't know this. Gill changed the channel back and whispered something into the familiar visitor's ear. Jake was a smoker but he didn't remember. If he had remembered he might have wanted one about now. Imogen sat down in the same seat she had left only once to go to her room and back. Vincent never went to Imogen's room. Imogen's room was down the hall on the left; as you entered there was a small corridor type thing, bit boxy, with the bathroom to the right. Imogen was the only one to have a private bathroom. Should anyone have known this, there could have been riots; Horace in particular hated using the communal bathroom especially after certain others. Imogen never used her bathroom. Had anyone known this, there could have been riots; Horace in particular hated using the communal bathroom and had always secretly wanted his own private one. Should he have known that Imogen (who he currently liked) had a private bathroom that she never used, he may have found this rather frustrating. Imogen, however, had never opened the door to her bathroom, so it could be that she just didn't know it was there. As the room opened out there was a bed to the right in its own alcove, to its left in the centre of the room was a table like the table in the middle of a kitchen, only there was no kitchen. Imogen didn't look at the walls. On the table was a brass candle holder with a small handle, in it was a burnt down candle. Next to the brass holder with a small handle was a box of matches. When these matches ran out Imogen would sit outside beside her bedroom door (where, behind her, lay the bathroom she may or may not have known existed) until Gill, in her white coat that didn't fit quite as nicely as the other white coat that came mutating in and out of Gill's coat for about a week, would bring a new box of matches. Imogen would give her the empty one. The longest time Imogen had ever had to wait was during this mutating week, when Gill was actually lying on a beach in Spain. Jake had once looked at Horace with some depth: a complex intricate soul. The day ticked on. Gill, who did wear a white coat but not quite so well as another white coat that mutated in and out of Gill's coat (this had happened once, for about a week, while Gill lay on a beach), was good at time keeping. Horace looked at the clock, Jake looked at the clock because Horace looked at the clock, Gill checked her watch. Jake lived with brothers (although it wasn't his brother, he had wild ginger hair); Quad, a complex intricate soul; a girl who didn't wear a white coat but always intervened; a white coat that no-one knew the name of. He was sure there used to be another girl who didn't wear a white coat but always intervened, he was sure he liked her. These were strange times. A vivid tumult of images collated into an intricate montage of simulated involvement, life outside involved white coats, food free from the wall and a lack of money (which suited Jake as he didn't think he had any), everything here was provided for him, he was obviously important. Jake lived with these people and with Imogen and Gill (who did wear a white coat but also had a name). Vincent was a visitor, he didn't wear a white coat, he was always shown in and shown out; Jake noted this, he was obviously important. Vincent had dark hair and wore a variety of different outfits that somehow always looked the same. He was familiar. He said 'Alright, Horace,' often. Jake would say 'Alright, Horace,' just as often. Quad didn't speak (Quad didn't exist). Horace looked up. *Umm.* Imogen, having vacated the same seat she had left and returned to before and after going to her room (her mother was there), stood up; the familiar visitor also known as Vincent said 'See you, Imogen.' He scampered off, hand twitching in the air as he waved his sister goodbye. Vincent, the brother and familiar left. Rather than just moving his eyes, Horace lifted his whole head to bring an ill-fitting black suit into view. The man in the black suit was large, but even so he swamped Horace only while standing in such close proximity while Horace sat. In a standing position Horace triumphed in height and size against most competitors. Aware that he held only a momentary advantage for the brief time before Horace rose to his feet, the doctor encroached into Horace's space as massively as he could. Horace peered around the figure in its cheap untailored suit, trying to see the clock. Jake looked at the clock because Horace had looked at the clock; Gill rushed over. Horace looked down. A powerful, godly voice (although Horace was quite sure it wasn't actually God) projected his name, 'Horace!' Strong looking digits, unfamiliar, intruded the air between them, breaking through the invisible protection of his space with a snap. 'Come on Horace', God spoke again, the voice peremptory. Horace looked for Gill, Gill stood back. Horace didn't like Gill. Horace's mind ticked, what was he doing here? Jake pointed and looked at Gill, Gill looked at the clock, Jake looked at the clock because Gill had looked at the clock, Imogen pulled her knees up to her chin. The day ticked on.

Horace

Horace was often romantic; he loved his wife, he was sure of it. He had seen her first at a party, well, more of a gathering perhaps. A friend of hers and colleague of his were having a 'do'. What precisely the 'do' was in aid of no-one was quite sure, but as they mingled, glass of wine in one hand, hors-d'oeuvre in the other, no-one really cared. Janis stood by an expensive, ugly-looking lamp, conversing with April. Horace knew April, she was the wife of another colleague with whom he had cause to interact fairly recently over the photocopier. He had met April (as he had met most of the staff and spouses) at the Christmas party; a drab hotel reception hall, lined on one side with a paper plated sausage-and-stick buffet, in which a slender girl and chubby boy decanted wine into plastic cups laid out in rows of white, red and rosé. He had not spoken to April for long, he had not spent that much time bantering over the photocopier with her husband either, but he had met her, they had conversed and so he could legitimately go over. Janis had eyed Horace with an intriguing gaze as he stepped into the frame, he had eyed her back, a contact which caused April to shuffle slightly and make a polite exit. Left to their own devices they talked extensively about nothing in particular, their eyes each flickering over the other's, more and more intrigued as the evening drew on. He asked Janis if she would like to meet again, perhaps for a drink or dinner, and gleefully she had nodded, shining eyes expressing a definitive yes. As time passed and dates ensued, they married and had a child. Horace was happy; he loved his wife, he was sure of it. He enjoyed her company, her manner, her charm, her.

6.25am. Horace was in the kitchen spreading low-fat margarine on four slices of granary bread. A pack of honey roast ham and ready-sliced cheese sat still by the plate, awaiting their turn to accompany the bread to create Horace's sandwich. When complete, he wrapped it in cling film and entered his three digit security code (001); the sandwich to be deposited, as always, in Horace's briefcase.

6.58am. Horace was waiting by the front door, legs astride in a powerful stance, hands together, clasping his briefcase's handle firmly in front of his body. His right index finger tapped the back of his left hand. He was waiting for his wife. He looked down at the briefcase, visualised its contents; a honey roast ham and sliced cheese sandwich on low-fat margarine and granary bread. *Yum?!* No brown envelope today; a pencil, fairly sharp, HB. Instead of simply moving his eyes, Horace lifted his whole head to bring the hallway into view and searched for his wife in the empty space, now 7.02am. He looked back at the wall, the paper a dizzy swirl of patterns with big loops and waves of entangled light and dark shades of glittery silver-grey, the background white, the lighter swirls slightly elevated from the paper. Horace squinted at it as if willing a magic-eye image out of the madness. His podgy digit tapped impatiently, the big toe on his right foot started to twitch; soon it would be tapping in time to the finger.

'I'm ready!' Horace heard a voice, his wife again, as she sailed into the hallway, unhooking her coat from the rack as she swished past. His finger stopped tapping as he watched the coat get manoeuvred on this time, keys rattling in her hand. Then the door was open and Horace was following her out over the threshold. He closed the door, giving it a little shove to test its security. The day was breezier than the day before, the blustery winds of the other evening which had died down over night were rebuilding their strength and the morning breathed a chill. He gripped his briefcase with his left hand, resting it on his lap in the car. This wife of his was quiet today, far away from home in her mind, worrying about the town hall and such like. Horace thought about staplers, toilet roll, Jeffery. It had been 7.02am, then 7.06am, then 7.07, then 7.08 and on and on. It's morning every morning, waiting in the hallway for his wife. Every day, every morning, another morning. *Staplers. Toilet roll. Jeffery.*

'Right, you got your sandwich?'

'Yes,' Horace said, quite abruptly. He looked down at his briefcase and placed his right hand, fingers spread, over its surface.

'Good, have a good day at work,' and she leant over, left arm up, trying to manoeuvre it around his neck somehow. So, as always, he kissed her and said something like, 'You too.' Then out of the car to face an office building.

Horace strode with long paces as he marched into the office, his chest puffed out, his nose not in the air with pretension, but with courage today. Horace was a manager but not of many, a middle man, and as he placed his briefcase on the floor beside his chair and settled back into the *bulk buy new dynamic office seating with wheels*, he felt pretty unimportant, felt the full weight of his middle man status: being neither here nor there. He picked up the receiver from the dialling body of his phone and called an internal number. *Claire.*

'Morning!' Horace announced.

'Morning,' Clare repeated with a slightly more subdued tone to Horace's elevated welcome.

'About those staplers, I wonder has the post boy come in today?'

'Not due in till ten.'

'Ah, I see. Could you have him bring three staplers when he arrives?'

'Won't be till this afternoon, he's got a list here.'

'Right. But please ensure that it's today.'

'Not promising.' The phone was dead.

Right.

The stress levels rising as he strived to fulfil requirements; the boys above caring only about staff performance; the staff caring only for the rules inflicted from the boys above. The middle man, the messenger, the no-one. Yet at monthly meetings with his direct manager he would be told of the importance of his position, how he was the glue that held the two sides together and kept the communication in flow. He liked this idea, being the glue, but knew that his position was not irreplaceable. He looked out at all the people milling around the floor, his workers, *what a terrible scene!* Horace scanned the room, counting the required number of workers that *should* be in attendance. All the terrible people were in. *No, wait. Jeffery. Damn him! He's not getting a stapler.*

'Morning, Mr Conway,' Jenny said brightly. 'Any luck with the staplers?'

'You'll get more staplers when the company is good and ready to start handing them out!'

Jenny stared at him, disbelief cruising her face with flickers of contempt. Horace waved Jenny away with his massive paw and switched on his computer. He drummed his fingers on the veneer of his desk as he waited for it to boot up. Once booted, he logged in to Jeffery's files and scanned the information for any work that needed dealing with today. He spotted three things, which combined would surely only take a concentrated half-hour. What were all these wretched people doing?

Clicking a few icons, he duly sent them over to Camilla with a thank you note, then rested back in his *new dynamic office seating with wheels* and folded his arms. Horace's work was done. *Toilet roll? Right!* He picked up the receiver from the dialling body of his phone and called an internal number. Claire.

'Do I look like a janitor?'

'I have no idea, I can't see you. And that's *caretaker* in this country.' Stony silence. *Beeeebb.*

Helpful. Pause. Horace dialled another number. Maintenance.

A gruff but kind voice greeted him, 'Hello?'

'Yes, hello. I'm calling from Great Insurance.'

'Can see that, got a lighted list here.'

'Right. I wonder if you know why we don't have toilet rolls?'

'What?'

'Yes. I'm getting complaints from my staff that the paper dispenser gets jammed and would it possible to have rolls instead?'

'Can't say about rolls, but can have a look at the dispenser.'

'Great, that would most certainly be a good start.'

'Okay, I'll try and get up there today.'

'Great, thank you.'

'No problem.'*Beeebb.*

Right. Toilet rolls. Horace rose to his feet, his destination Mr Blanchett's office. He knocked gingerly, a light tap with the knuckle of only one finger.

'Come in!' Mr Blanchett had an unexpected voice, a funny sort of dignity in it, a strength of sorts, good education in essence. Mr Blanchett was a skinny, weathered-looking man, but tall and reasonably presented. He had strong hair, much like Horace's, still redolent of shiny adolescent vigour. A small and neat moustache covered his top lip, he seemed old-fashioned, transported from another time.

'Good morning, Mr Blanchett.'

'Horace.'

Horace looked around the office, it smelled musty.

'I...'

'I'm glad you're here, got a job for you.'

Horace's eyes perked up and then he remembered that that would mean him having to do some work. *Toilet roll.*

'I wonder, Mr Blanchett, if the ladies could have toilet roll instead of a dispenser?'

'What the hell you talking to me about toilet roll for man! Here's a job that needs sorting,' a folder wavered in the air above Mr Blanchett's desk. 'Well take it!' Horace took it.

'Yes, right, thank you, sir.'

Mr Blanchett looked up at Horace hovering and eyed him curiously. Horace looked down at the folder, 'Yes, right on it, sir.' *Shake on.*

Back at his desk Horace opened the file and stared. *Data entry*, he gave Mr Blanchett's office a side glance.

'Jenny!' Horace called her name clearly and directly. Jenny looked up. Horace waved her over with the palette of his aeroplane signalling hand. She stood by his desk, jigging slightly, as if the toilet roll situation was becoming just too much and she was holding until she got home. Horace handed her the file from Mr Blanchett's office, 'Toilet roll is a perk,' he said, looking her right in the eye, 'the harder you work, the better the toilet roll gets.' Jenny stared at him, disbelief cruising her face with flickers of contempt, for the second time today.

Horace's work was done. Then Camilla was at his desk.

'I can't cover Jeffery's work as well as my own, can it be spread about a bit?'

A concentrated half-hour.

'I'm sure you'll cope, it's only for the day.'

'But he gets loads of phone calls, clients ring all day.'

'Really?!'

'And it seems that they all get re-directed to me,' Camilla pointed quite sternly at herself.

'What kind of calls?'

'Client calls, checking on updates and questions, endless questions about the small print. I think his clients are a bit thick.'

'I beg your pardon? *Thick?!* Insurance is quite complex, you should endeavour to answer all customer questions. Now get back to your desk, there'll be more to do now you've wasted time hanging around here.'

'But *my* clients don't ring all the time.'

'Well maybe you're not highlighting the important details that need answers.'

'Maybe I have high premium customers who understand the information!'

'Everyone needs insurance… and a job.' Horace stared at her, with slight disbelief and a flicker of contempt, for the first time, ever.

'He's not even sick, he's never actually sick!' her voice trailed off as she made her short journey back to her desk. *Jeffery.*

'I NEED A STAPLER.' Jenny.

3.02pm. Horace picked up the receiver from the dialling body of his phone and called an internal number. Claire.

'Claire,' he announced, 'if the post boy is unable to deliver three staplers today, I'm coming to get them myself.'

'No-one's allowed to get stationery themselves, there's a system: it gets signed out and delivered by the post boy.'

'Claire… please, is it not just a little ridiculous? I just need three staplers.'

'There's a news agent on the corner that sells them if you can't wait.' Horace sagged. Claire went on, 'The post boy's flat out, but it's on his list; he'll get round to it.'

'Right. Thank you.' Horace could sense the receiver at the other end moving away from Claire's ear.

'Claire—' he called after her and the receiver returned to its muffled ear-pressed hum, 'seeing as though there is a system of such organisation, would it be possible to get three staplers of different colours? It would help identify whose is whose.'

Claire sighed 'There's only black ones, you want something specific, have to put it in on an order form.'

Horace sighed. The receiver clicked off. *Beeebb.*

6pm. Horace watched as his collective body of workers lifted their tired and aching bodies from each chair, hauling themselves up to leave from a hard day's work. *Wretched people.* This evening Horace was to walk some of the way home. There was a little detour he wished to make. He walked with confidence, a slight frown the only indication of uncertainty. He approached his passing-point destination cautiously, his massive presence not really the best for discretion. *There she is.* Horace twisted his wrist to expose his Rolex replica. He made a mental note of the time, repeating it over in his mind, and then ducked down an alleyway which would lead directly to the correct bus stop for home. Once there, he placed his briefcase under the broad oak desk that dominated the garage and flicked open a mustard yellow file from the ordered and neat collection that flanked the desk. Plucking a pencil from the pot, he noted *6.33pm.* He scanned the information: two days ago it had been 6.28pm. *Good traffic day.* He would check again in three days' time, three consistent days should be evidence enough of a pattern. *Charlotte's home arriving time, done.*

34

'Dinner,' Horace's wife called from the kitchen.

The tie-giver was not there today, out at some friend's or other that her mother had driven her to earlier in the evening. Horace sat opposite his wife, no wine today, a glass of water from the filter jug sat awaiting him instead. A wood pigeon in full colour tapped at a tree in front of him, Horace stared at it.

'Good day?' his wife enquired.

Horace nodded. Shrugged a little, 'You?'

'Yes, met up with Mrs Granger today, you know the dotty rich one from the Neighbourhood Watch committee. Had tea and cake at that lovely little new café on George Street, lovely new place,' she repeated eagerly, passing Horace his plate. 'She's going to donate £1000 to the town hall, isn't that wonderful?'

Horace nodded. Shrugged a little.

'That should fix the leak and stretch to a new lick of paint.'

Horace looked at his wife quizzically, 'Wasn't the wall being designated for a local outreach project or something, disadvantaged kids and a mural?'

'Yes, yes it was, but since the leak the council have given them an outside wall... Oh Horace! It's going to be lovely, they're going to paint that ugly stretch of concrete along the by-pass.'

'They'll have to close the road to traffic if they've got kids wielding paint brushes up ladders on a main 50mph road.'

'Only one lane, oh but it'll be worth it, concrete's so horrid don't you think?'

Horace nodded. Shrugged a little.

His wife clattered on, Horace could hear the noise but not the words. One mouthful at a time, he devoured his pork chops, potatoes and vegetables with dedication. After dinner he washed up and cleared the table, his wife retreating into the lounge for a seemingly endless timetable of soap operas. Horace swooped into the garage, pressed a button on his little remote and poured a glass of cognac; the 'Dolphin Dance' started to ooze out of the speakers. His invisible guest today was female, elegant and within his grasp for extracting information. He would play this one coolly.

10.07pm. Horace was perched on the edge of the large oak desk that dominated the space, his invisible guest looking wide-eyed and indulgently at him from the empty chair opposite his own. Herbie Hancock burst with joy as he jazzed out 'Watermelon Man', Horace closed his eyes to a section of trumpet.

Tap, tap. Tap, tap. Horace's wife knocked gently on the internal garage door that linked it to the house.

'Yes?'

'Going to bed now,' a pause, 'you coming up soon?'

Horace nodded. Shrugged a little.

'Horace?' a tad louder.

'Yes. In a minute. Be right up.'

He couldn't hear the foot shuffle but knew that his wife's slippers were brushing smoothly over the utility tiled floor as she walked away. He sipped at another glass of cognac and smiled at his invisible companion.

'There's a rather urgent matter that Russell needs me to attend to. Could we resume this meeting at another time?'

The chair politely responded with affirming words, a gentle tilt of the head and a reassuring soft smile, encouraging Horace that he was making headway with this one.

'Good,' he said, 'I'd like to contact you myself, secretaries are so impersonal and I think – hope – that we might be beyond that.' He raised his glass and returned a soft smile. So with the meeting adjourned Horace necked back the remainder of the cognac in his glass, checked the room for orderly straightness and shuffled off to bed.

Rushton

Gill (in her white coat) turned on the television, just in time for Jake's favourite programme; he was obviously important. Vincent was a visitor. He didn't wear a white coat and he was always shown in and shown out. Jake noted this, he was obviously important too. Vincent had dark hair and wore a variety of different outfits that always looked the same. He was familiar. He said 'Alright, Horace,' often. Jake would say 'Alright, Horace,' just as often. Quad didn't speak. Quad didn't exist. Horace looked up, *umm*. Imogen, having vacated the same seat she had left and returned to before and after going to her room (her mother was there) stood up. The familiar visitor, also known as Vincent said, 'Alright, Imogen.' Horace was feeling decidedly peculiar. He looked up: Jake was watching TV; Quad was missing, Quad didn't exist. *Gill.* Gill, who wore a white coat but also had a name: the white coat that switched the TV on and off; the white coat that brought over drinks and left them on the little oak table by Horace's chair; the white coat that bought a new box of matches to Imogen when she waited outside her room (the private bathroom that she did or did not know that she had lying quietly behind her); the white coat that brought food at 9am, 1pm and 6pm; the white coat that checked her watch when Horace looked at the clock; the white coat that once became an impostor for a week. The white coat that watched. Horace looked down. Horace felt decidedly peculiar. *Imogen.* Horace looked up. *Imogen.* Horace looked down. The white coat that brings pills. *Urgh.* Horace looked at the cup, a small paper cup containing his pills. He took the cup. He had taken its contents every day, for how long? Horace looked at the cup. Gill waited, her hand twitching, her nails uneven and slightly soiled under the tips. Horace felt an urgency tapping its impatience as he stared at Gill's canvas shoes standing silent and motionless. He returned the cup, its contents now resting tightly between his back teeth and gums. Gill (in her white coat) strolled off, the swishing motion of her garments silent to all but her. Had they given him the wrong pills? Why could he think? Horace looked up. *Gill*. He felt he didn't like Gill. Why didn't he like her? Horace had a longing, but for what he could not be certain. A flash. A memory. A feeling. How long had he been here? What was this place? Why all these questions? *Who am I? What do you want?* Horace felt a wave of panic, he went to the bathroom. He spat out the pills and looked at them in his hand. 'What do you want?' he asked them. The pills did not reply. Horace pulled his hand closer, re-adjusted his focus and looked at the pills more earnestly. 'What do you want?' he asked again. In tiny black print Horace made out the letters, *lx*. He shuffled them around in his hand, his thumb and little finger twitching with nervous energy. 'What about you?' he asked, focusing on a different one. He peered closer still, orange letters, magic-eyeing their way through the redness of the pill, *re4*. Horace dropped them to the floor and pressed his right foot into them, dispersing the pill powder, their colour and tiny letters, their poison or help now assisting or hindering the tiling. Silent chemical brothers in arms, changing people, their destiny altered, their purpose crushed, their point changed. *lx* and *re4* now an identity, now Horace's pills. Horace shuffled back to the living area; he didn't need to shuffle, there was nothing wrong with his hips, legs, feet or ankles, but he liked to shuffle: it helped reflect the tiredness within. He looked at the clock; Jake looked at the clock because Horace had looked at the clock. Gill looked at her watch because Horace and Jake had looked at the clock. Horace looked down. With his head lowered he glanced up, lifting his eyes without moving his head to bring Jake into a strained view. He watched Jake. Jake, a man who talks nonsense, containing the potential or echo of Quad, a complex intricate soul.

Imogen

'Oh mate, she's hot isn't she?' Mark nudged Vincent with his elbow and waved his thumb to their left. A leggy blonde lent seductively across the bar. Long bouncy locks spilled from her head. Vincent could almost see the advert, a flick of the neck sending the revitalised silky flow across the screen, making you wish for or desire upon the hair that can be transformed by whatever product... none came to mind. Grabbing a hand full of the hanging light brown drab that had excreted itself from Imogen's head, Mark scrunched his face, 'Not like this.' His own hair, dark brown and cropped, ruffled with budget wax.

Imogen forced back her drink, drowning dialogue that tipped on the edge of her pink flappy friend, unamused by Mark's scrunched up expression as he held and twisted her long and natural hair.

'Looks like she could have an accent,' nudging Vincent again he continued with a playful *boys will be boys* inflection, 'how sexy is that?!' Not really looking for a response, Mark chuckled to himself and re-arranged his seating. Imogen got up to go to the bar, offering a round as she stood.

'Pint for me,' Mark requested without looking up.

Vincent half-stood, 'I'll come with you.' He directed his voice in a low clear diction towards his sister alone.

At the bar Vincent lent in, inviting Imogen into his trust. 'What are you doing with him?' he wanted to wave a disapproving thumb in Mark's direction but held it tight in his fist, aware of the urge.

Imogen ordered their drinks, changing the vibe in her tension, trying to create a carefree feel, *forget this stuff, it's fine*. 'He's lasted more than a week,' she giggled to herself, but Vincent could read her face, the subtle lip indents in the adult face of his childhood companion.

'Are you trying to find excuses to be pissed off with yourself? The guy's a jerk and it's not your fault or your problem! Dump him.'

Imogen handed Vincent Mark's pint to carry. 'He's kind to me sometimes,' she whispered, catching her brothers eye and projecting a flurry of information as she did so – *its fine, it's my life, I kind of like him, so leave it alone.*

Vincent sighed, his heart heavy.

The Diary of Rose Heather Roberts

Steam and lung air, that strange chemical thing when warm meets cold, allowing you to see the functions of your breath, mixed together as I gently blew across the rim of my mug. Hot, hot. My hand clenched to the handle, my knuckles white, my bitten nails sore.

'What are you doing out there? It's too cold, come in, you'll catch a death,' my friend Janet hollered at me, her head just visible, folding itself round the back door.

'Sure' I said, but I liked the air, the crisp winter freshness. I could feel it warming as I sucked it in. My lips chapping. My eye lids freezing. I wasn't without my protection, I had put on a cosy jumper especially and it worked: my body felt warm, safe in the jumper. I wasn't a fool, I wasn't going to actually freeze out here, nor was I going to catch a death. How does one actually catch a death? Aren't we dying already, did we not catch it at birth?

I have this fantasy.

I take a gun from the inside pocket of my jacket and hold it to the temple of my enemy.

Bang.

But I'd never do it.

41

Rushton

Horace lived with his brother (although it wasn't his brother, he had wild ginger hair); Quad, a complex intricate soul; a girl who didn't wear a white coat but always intervened; a white coat that no-one knew the name of; Imogen; another girl who didn't wear a white coat but always intervened; a man of rather larger proportions, sometimes; and Gill, who did wear a white coat but also had a name, a white coat that was once missing, thought to be mutating in and out of a white coat that didn't quite fit the same. Vincent was a visitor. He didn't wear a white coat. He was always shown in and shown out. Jake noted this, he was obviously important. Vincent had dark hair and wore a variety of different outfits that always looked the same. He was familiar. He said 'Alright, Horace,' often. Jake would say 'Alight, Horace,' just as often. Quad didn't speak (Quad didn't exist). Horace looked up. *Umm.* Imogen, having vacated the same seat she had left and returned to, before and after going to her room – her mother was there – stood up. The familiar visitor, also known as Vincent, said 'Alright, Imogen.'

'Twat.'

She didn't look at him, her face remaining impassive. Horace looked up. Jake sniggered. Quad was missing (Quad didn't exist). Gill made a phone call. Vincent went to the bathroom. Horace felt a desire to follow him. Horace felt decidedly peculiar. It was time for Jake's favourite programme. The white coat that did have a name, namely Gill, switched on the TV, pushing her right index finger into the black surround of the screen. Jake watched, awaiting the inevitable day when only a stub might reappear. Horace looked at the clock, Jake looked at the clock because Horace had looked at the clock, Gill glanced at her watch. Vincent was early. Horace looked down. Horace wondered what he was doing here, *there is a path to be trodden, a destiny, a life.* Horace wondered what he was doing here. He whispered to his angels, he felt as if he were waiting for something. He wondered how long he'd been waiting. Had he spent his life waiting for it to start, missing the seconds turning into days, shortening his life? *Imogen. Umm.*

Jake

Jake sipped at his tea, his left hand still clenched to the balcony's smooth rail. Unsure at this point whether to blame them or himself he remembered again a game he used to play at school, throwing a ball amongst his 'friends'. You had to throw on fast as if trying not to have touched the surface of the ball at all. You had to think quickly, pick out the kid not looking and fire without time to aim, the reflexes of the fast-working brain. He imagined now his consciousness like that ball, with him the only player, throwing himself as quickly as he came, away to the next state of mind, the next Jake. Happy in the turmoil, in its shadowy mist, his soul felt alive. A quest fronted him, just as an immediate past followed, a circumstance in which he could find countless excuses to talk about himself to himself, to think about himself, to feel something for himself. To feel. Self-pity building a protective wall, shooting arrows through the gaps, blaming, accusing, *not fair, not fair, not fair,* but after a while the wall became foreboding, the gaps filled in as he blocked more and more with cement and mud. Tired of blaming, judging and re-judging. There was an obvious design flaw as Jake searched for windows, the darkness closing and the happiness once found in self-pity became dark and depressing. He stopped throwing the ball, held it instead, studied its structure, its size and weight, the way in which it had been sewn together, the labels and warnings printed on the surface, the hole into which you pump more air. He held it for ages, at first gripped tightly, almost hugged by both his arms, nervous that it might escape him, its fast routine so instilled, so commonplace, a habit. But after a while Jake eased his grip, held it out in both hands, sometimes lightly passing it from one palm to the next, then between his fingertips. Finally he bounced it, to see how it would feel to let it go and as it hit the ground Jake was glad to see it bounce back to him. He cut out some holes, put in a window. As he peered through the bullet

44

proof glass, he wondered whether it might be safe to put just shatter-proof in or even plain glass that could be opened to let some air through. Jake peered hard, poised to duck under the frame, safe again behind the wall. The view was beautiful and calm, a beach on a hot day, the wind slight and the sea clear and beckoning. Jake started to long for it, to be free from the encompassing wall. The ball left his hand, thrown somewhere aimless, but another Jake jumped to the side, intercepted it, held it and then threw it up over the heads, over the wall. Someone had to go and retrieve it. The agile, fitter Jake put up his hand with an adolescent confidence, 'I'll go' and started the climb to the top of the wall.

Rushton

So sat three individuals: one looked at the clock; the second looked at the clock because the first had looked at the clock; an outsider but insider all at once (the presumed sanity amongst them, a monitor, a non-sitter at this moment) looked at the clock because the other two had looked at the clock. The third sitter sat in the same seat she had left vacant only once to go her to room (her mother was there). The day ticked on. Vincent was a brother, he was shown in and shown out. He wore a variety of different outfits that always looked the same and had a slightly sharper nose, a more determined, slightly formidable edge to his profile compared to the softer, rounder features of his sister. He looked at Imogen, his sister: she was skinny, a petit frame carrying over layered, oversized t-shirts and jumpers about its snap-able delicacy. Her brother wore fitting, clean, tidy clothing (chosen mainly by his wife) that always somehow looked the same. Imogen's slightly rounder, softer face came from her mother's side; inherited weight had moulded itself into facial features over the generations as the body slimmed and slimmed. Her light brown hair hung unwashed, uncared for. When managed it highlighted green engaging eyes, transforming Imogen into a sparkling delight, a sight that Vincent recalled having witnessed only twice, her 21st Birthday and his wedding, two days in a lifetime of company. Those two days held themselves as the predominate picture in his mind, his sometimes beautiful sister. Vincent glanced at her; how beautiful she had been on these two occasions. He looked for the darkness, the frustration, the force of life that had led his sister to find her peace in such a drastic way. She seemed dulled of all that she once was, the life sucked from any choice of existence. Was that the point? To be, but not to be. Yet he read a faint contentment in his sister's languorous eyes; she seemed fulfilled somehow. He knew his mother not to be the best; teachers had tried in their limited way, amongst their own transforming lives, caring enough to push as best they could the prospects of the talents of their charges. They had noticed the non-attendance at evenings that required his mother's attention, had made an effort to be positive about the future that lay ahead, encouraged the limited talents that this sibling duo displayed. But despite this, he felt sad that Imogen had not looked beyond herself, had not seen that this mother, having ignored them both, had still been kind.

What strange worlds exist beyond the known, the mind so complex, so free to summon its own intricate montage of collated images. Vincent felt altered, certainly, but largely unperturbed by the effects of his mother's grief. He had married, had kids, got a job that supported his life; not especially excelled himself, but got on. He would grow to be a jolly fellow, 'A nice chap,' as his colleagues would say. Happy and considerate, he was a nice chap; many who had known him associated this quality with his father before him. A kind, un-boisterous manner, a fundamental goodness that stretched beyond all that life could throw at him. Vincent's hereditary Santaesque kindness drew his attention to all that was good in his world, releasing the ugly, letting go. He was sad for his mother, sad for her sadness and sad too for Imogen's. Vincent was a little older; he could remember snippets of his father and yes, he missed the unit that his presence had completed. His sister was right in the sense that the family was never really a family again. But he knew he was missing something that he'd never had, not memories of a man missed but a fantasy of a life un-given. His mother, lost to them after his father's death, their childhood trials and tribulations missed somehow. As he looked upon his sister he thought of his father and how sad he must feel to see the results of his tragedy. Vincent was sure that he wouldn't have wanted his death to have caused such ongoing despair, his daughter lost and his wife missed by his children while she still lived. If he could conjure the slightest hint of arrogance he might feel pride in his own existence, in his own achievements, in comparison to have come so far. But instead he felt sadder still, sad that they had chosen simply not to function anymore. Perhaps he would have achieved more, perhaps he would have been happier, *perhaps, perhaps,* but this is what life had chosen for him. At the very least he felt that one should endure and get on, for there was nothing that could now change what had happened. Life was his to make of what he could. Perhaps that's what they did, he pondered, made what they could and endured enough to still live at all. People's limits involved varying degrees of resilience.

He mulled it over, thought of points and compared them to others. Vincent was a logical man, he reasoned with his life and after much deliberation decided that blame served no purpose. Vincent believed himself predictable by the influences of his past, the consequence of birth, schooling, the beliefs of guardians and the behaviour of friends – even the past of yesterday, the past of today and of tomorrow when the day is done. He was, like everyone, the product of his life, with injustice and unfairness helping mould the confusion of what people become, but he felt it important to take responsibility for himself and to let go of any blame that had influenced him. To live a life consumed by it seemed to him to add a new injustice; he felt no need to carry the burden of others.

Vincent reached for his can of coke and as he tipped the aluminium up, over his lip, around his teeth, tingling his tongue and fizzing down his throat, he reckoned that Imogen was properly barking. He could still remember her, his sister: always a welcome addition to an invite list, she rarely disappointed with the amusements that she brought to lift a night out. He'd had fun with her, talked with her, not known this about her. One friend in particular had enjoyed her company so distinctly, perhaps due to Imogen's inner self-obsession, detracting from the usual attention that she herself would have to endure over the years; Miracle found comfort in someone who couldn't care less for her beauty. For Miracle was beautiful, Vincent had fancied her himself, who hadn't?! She had had that *je ne sais quoi*, but she had also been the only friend to have extended a friendship to his sister without back-biting issues, without attitude or motive, the only friend that genuinely found Imogen interesting beyond the antics of her amusing pub scenes, and yet the only friend who would eventually feel the true force of Imogen's capabilities. The friend who would highlight the true darkness that lay silently awaiting a click in Imogen's mind that would one day turn a fun, sassy, slightly annoying person into a killer.

Imogen was a tired-looking character. Vincent was a visitor; he was shown in and shown out.

Horace

Charlotte was not without her flaws, she had some irritating habits. She stirred her tea in a complex three to the right, two to the left sequence, followed by a quick push through the middle, ending with a tap on the outer rim. This enthusiastic stirring created a challenge which a number of delightful hand-crafted cups had lost, cracked or chipped out of use. But she was certainly a likable girl, pretty. Independently single, a life lived for oneself while one only had oneself, that romantic melancholy diary desire always lingering. A life filled with mini tests, excitements and failures. A life where nothing too extreme had ever happened to her, until Horace strolled around the corner. A bit of a dreamer but a realist; life, society, the functions of things were all fine as they were. Things could always be better or worse. No complaints, not in comparison to those stories she heard on the street from people with clipboards or those portrayed in adverts and charity events. No complaints, by comparison. She liked her job with the local council, working with good people, trying to make a small difference. She had friends she hung out with at the weekend, a few close friends in particular that kept in touch throughout the week. A likeable girl, pretty.

A Friday night would often be complete with a man or two using their confidence (softened, perhaps, by a pink shirt or tie) to sway her their way. An offer she sometimes explored further, sometimes not. Her desire, although dreamy, was informed, learned and understood within herself, the man she desired and the life she could foresee. Content for the moment in the one she currently lived, its happy tick and functional breath. And then Horace strolled causally around the corner and asked her the time. She was a size twelve, Horace could tell. She shopped at Next and had chosen for today a blouse and skirt combination from last season's collection; many of the size twelve items had been in the sale that year. It was a combination Horace liked and he had been surprised and intrigued to find it so abundant in the sale. He made a comment. Initially, not surprisingly, she was slightly disturbed by this detailed knowledge of women's clothing but was then quickly embarrassed, as clothes bought in seasons were supposed to be exclusive, as if she wore designer cloth. Friends had even said how much they had liked it, enhancing its individuality. The acknowledgement of the Next label had embarrassed her. Horace noticed the coy eyes and went on to compliment the outfit, how he knew it to be Next because he had liked it so. An unusual man. She gave him the time, curving her slender wrist around to reveal the watch face that ticked out the information required, she smiled. Charlotte's gaze flickered over his frame, he was slimmer then but by no means slim, his broad stature capable of lifting incredible weights (rumour had it that he'd moved a car once) prevented him from ever being that slender hunk, but still it bore a softness, a male quality, a strange bulky trust. Along with enquiring eyes he portrayed comfort; the paying-attention gaze so sought after in the dating scene was alluring and his broad, well-built stature protective. Having fulfilled the answer to his question, she paused, not quite ready to move away from him just yet.

Having learnt the time, Horace feigned missing his last bus and invited Charlotte for a coffee. Relaxed by the idea of coffee over alcohol she agreed and recommended a place just around the corner where she knew the waitress. Horace, fussy about his bean, gestured towards a place he liked, a reassuringly spacious, busy all night café, dappled in Elvis memorabilia and various knick-knacks of the 50's era. There Horace chose an inconspicuous table where neither of them would be remembered by the evening's passing trade.

Inspector Jacob Rodgers

Inspector Jacob Rodgers caressed the page of his book as he stared down at the words. He had picked up this particular novel on many occasions, but was yet to finish it. A single malt rested on his side table, two cubes of ice floated on the surface. He tried to relax, he read, *As Martin wondered along the side walk, a thought hit him...*

'About time!' Jacob conveyed out loud, sweeping the tumbler off the side table with a magician's elegance. He lent back into his sofa, rested the novel in his lap and sipped from the tumbler, the ice gently brushing against his top lip. He sighed inwardly, the novel not hard work due to its intricacy or insightfulness, but simply boring and frustratingly obvious. Placing his drink down to the side, he hoisted the novel back up into view. Not wishing to be defeated by the obvious he read on, awaiting the twist.

Several hours later and only ten pages on, Inspector Jacob Rodgers gave up, marked the page and folded it closed. Reminiscing, he recalled his mother's criticism as she watched him fold the corner of the page over to marks its place. Every Christmas amongst the chocolate bars and soaps-on-ropes, a bookmark would be unwrapped, and as the years progressed the bookmarks became ever more elaborate until the day it even came equipped with a light, a bendy tube you could manoeuvre in all directions, an insect or alien eye peering at the words with its spotlight.

It had been an odd week and the inspector's inability to involve himself in the story of the novel was not solely due to its inadequacy; there had been a discovery. A garage that had been insulated and decorated as an office sat with neat and ordered attention next to a semi-detached home in the outskirts of the town. A frightened and slightly confused woman had called in the police using the local number, the same woman who had met them at the door and showed them in. The wife of the garage user. In it the police had found files full of information that was deemed potentially incriminating. Inspector Jacob Rodgers was called.

Rushton

Horace looked at the clock, a white rimmed plastic affair in keeping with its place of residence, the time was 4.30. Horace considered, *am? pm?* Horace looked down. Jake looked at the clock because Horace had looked at the clock, Gill checked her watch. The day ticked on. Horace looked at the clock, the time was 5pm. They had not eaten yet, he had not slept after breakfast and lunch yet, Horace was certain of it. They ate at six. He'd look at the clock, he knew it would be six. Was he mad, or was he going mad? He had just returned from the bathroom. A new trend had slipped into his routine, each day after taking his pills Horace would go to the bathroom. It was a new trend that had not gone unnoticed, but as time passed small alterations to routine were expected. Each day while in the bathroom, having just lodged his *lx* and *re4* tight between his lower right teeth and gum, Horace would manoeuvre them free and stare at them, increasingly impatient, awaiting the day when they might reply to his questions. As the days passed Horace became more aware, increasingly he noticed various traits in his day. Looking at the clock: Horace did this often and although he was unsure why he felt a need to continue the repeated clock watching of his existence. Too many alterations to his routine might give Gill cause to question. He was aware of the change each day as he lifted his mass from the same chair he had rested in yesterday and last week, last month, the last four hours. It was not customary for him to require the bathroom after his pills and although Gill had not made any gestures of concern, he felt that the clock might be of a higher significance. But now, conscious of his clock watching habit, he tried to figure out the pattern, paranoid that he might be looking at the clock at the wrong time. Was there a time? A sequence? He didn't know.

Imogen

They sat in a café opposite each other gazing into nowhere, breathing heavily to take in the freshly baked bread and coffee aromas. Imogen liked to dream of these things. She felt sure that these were good things to linger over, a comforting memory of sorts, fresh bread and coffee, the casual joys of life, the simplicity of things. They sat for some time. Jazz hummed in the background. Imogen/Louise/once Samantha/but usually Rose sharpened the air, a cloud hovering over the table; she pictured this dense mass of energy as a physical form over their heads. She irritatingly kicked the leg of the unoccupied chair next to her, gulped wine, smoked, still tense from the night before. Imogen's/Louise's/once Samantha's/but usually Rose's head felt fierce, pounding. She winced at Miracle (whose name always remained the same), trying to teleport her anger, wanting Miracle to know the unidentified sin, to apologise before she had to point it out. But she didn't. Miracle smirked. *Witch.* A waiter brought Miracle's lunch over.

Imogen/Louise/once Samantha/but usually Rose put out her cigarette, screwing it into the ashtray, courteous to her friends at all times. Miracle looked up. 'Okay?' she asked. Perfect nails delicately handled cutlery, slicing lettuce into strips and the tomatoes into tiny pieces as Miracle arranged her salad for consumption. Imogen/Louise/once Samantha/but usually Rose watched open mouthed at her precision, aware of the rhythm of her breathing.

'Why did you do that to me?' Imogen/Louise/once Samantha/but usually Rose spoke softly, not wanting Miracle to get to her – she didn't want Miracle to know – but her tongue tipped on the edge of temper, flapping about inside her mouth without speech, irritated even more by Miracle's eating habits.

'Why what?' Miracle asked with a smile, knowing full well. Imogen/Louise/once Samantha/but usually Rose sprang to her feet, no longer able to contain her pink flappy friend. Miracle smiled again. Imogen/Louise/once Samantha/but usually Rose screamed, slamming her hands down on the table and accidentally hitting her fork; it pinged up flipping over onto the floor, clanged sharply as it bounced on the tiles.

Miracle's drawn in eyebrows remained perfectly positioned, inexpressive of her frowning. 'Please, Rose, you've dropped your fork, sit down… Rose, your fork. Please, sit down.'

Imogen/Louise/once Samantha/but usually Rose stood silent and still for a moment and took a breath as if to speak. She sat down.

'It was a joke,' Miracle said.

Imogen/Louise/once Samantha/but usually Rose cut off her speech by raising her hand, 'I don't want to know actually, it's all so… it's probably best if we pretend it never happened, just as long as you know that it wasn't funny.'

Imogen/Louise/once Samantha/but usually Rose said nothing more and lit the cigarette she had been waving about her. She regarded Miracle. She was beautiful. On the outside anyway. The room was full of it. Eyes lingering at their table. She wondered if Miracle knew herself.

Imogen had been bouncy and prolific. Popular on the outside.

They had found Miracle buried in a hole surprisingly deep for a girl of Imogen's size to have dug. A network of mutilated trees stabbed at by a knife had been the grounding for a mathematical plan, indicating the site of burial. A crude target cut into the bark of one particular tree had centred in the design of a final map. Police had found a notebook with ruler drawn lines connected by dots, seemingly random but clearly devised. Experts from the highest stations of the policing network had agonised over the drawing in an effort to decipher its meaning.

Imogen's petite frame had struggled with the hardened dried-out summer soil, a household spade hacked at the ground, dispersing stones and surface grass about the area where she worked. After digging a good seven feet down Imogen replaced the soil meticulously, touching up the edges with incredible precision; no evidence displayed itself upon the surface, no jogger or dog walker would ever have visually acknowledged the disturbance of the night before. Many users of the common were so familiar with the area that a mild winter moonless night would not have caused them to have lost their way, but they remained clueless about the body that lay freshly buried and sorely missed by friends and family beneath the ground over which they passed daily. Eight months passed, every hour decomposing evidence, every minute haunting Miracle's family.

Imogen sat in a café, taking in the coffee aromas; the dots and lines of the notebook map, connecting tree to tree, darted about her mind. Light brown shoulder-length hair sagged from her scalp, memories building layers of insecurity frustrated her; the so-called mates who had picked on her at middle school, truanting and misbehaving through secondary for her mother's un-given attention, the boyfriend who had betrayed her, then the persecuting friend in her first real place of work. Imogen's constant effort to improve herself, striving ever forward to become a better person, had resulted only in further disillusionment: the next friend that would rip her off; the next boyfriend and the next and the next. The years of building hatred, pushed aside time after time as she tried to overcome the depression that haunted her, the thin darkness that clouded her vision, its thickness ever increasing as she lived out her life.

The Diary of Rose Heather Roberts

This guy I knew once said, 'Life's gifts are what you make of them. This job is a gift, I'm working.' Well, I thought, what an incredibly positive man. The half-full kind of man. 'How quick people are,' he would say, 'to make their lives more difficult for themselves. How it is our tendency to acknowledge the hardship of things before we recognise their fruits. Life's little gifts.' I have remembered these words and to some degree tried to live my life to their rule, but I still wait for the day that the acknowledgment of hardships feels like a calm realistic recognition after a smile at the ease of life as I appreciate its gifts. The down heart of things still hits me first.

I have this fantasy.

Taking a gun from the inside of my jacket and holding it to the temple of my enemy. Bang.

But I guess I'd never do it.

Rushton

Horace looked at the clock, he looked down; Jake and Gill followed suit as they always did. Horace was allowed to go the shops; he thought about this trip that he made once a week, every Thursday. It was his compulsion to look at the clock, surely he must do it every time before he left for his adventure out into the streets and he must look again on his return. Yet he could not recall ever having calculated how long it took. How much time did he have free from his daily routine? What would Gill do if he was gone longer? Did he even have to be here? Why was he here? Did it matter if he just got up and left? But there was something about the routine, something about the atmosphere, it wouldn't do to just walk out. Horace was sure that someone would stop him. And what would he do? Where would he go? Where was he? Who was he? *Horace.* A name. A name and an identity within *lx* and *re4*. He decided to take it slowly. He had followed his routine as best he could, Gill's constant watch checking and pill giving the focus of events. Jake's TV watching, Imogen's visits to her room. These people were mad. White coats. Tough guys taking him away. Where did they take him? What did they do to him? He could not recall, those moments lost to him. Vincent watched the changing dilations of Horace's pupils. Horace noticed his gaze and looked at the clock; Vincent shook his head and turned to the television.

Jake

The agile Jake, having climbed the wall, searched for the ball, the trained psychological behaviour undermining the calmer, more balanced thoughts that throwing his fast paced mind away may have brought him. The need to hold on to the habits of his working mind. He saw the ball, his consciousness clear to him, he imagined it nestled in the sand. Only it felt a bit lost amongst the billions of grains watching the lapping surf. He forgot for a moment the rapid intensity as he passed his mind around and wished to have it back. He went to it, touched it and recoiled, the midday sun burning both its surface and him, warning him of its true maddening behaviour. But he couldn't let it go, he couldn't just leave it there, lost and alone. He wrapped it up and took it home. Put it in a cupboard and told it that he might need it again someday. It will rest there, in hope, content to know that maybe someday he'll play 'hot potato' again. His whispering shadow.

He had always wanted to go to the other school.

16 paces long, 10 paces wide.

His hand tightened around the steel, his balcony catching the brisk breeze that skirted round its corner, a constant platform for Jake's thoughts, the cold shooting through his nerves, inverting him frighteningly inward, the traffic now silent to him, their slogans a blur, awakening his muscles, exercising his mind.

What had he become? What had happened in his life to ensure that he would think of these people and know that he hated?

In the forward planner section of an adolescent diary a few weeks before, Jake had uncovered this: *'The future holds promises of fortune from the moment we are born, but the future relies simply on fate which holds no promises of fortune from the moment we are born. We are taught that fortune is in our control and that fate is therefore at the mercy of our hands, but how does one control mistakes made around us and therefore fate and its wicked hand?'*

Had fate bought him here? One Sunday afternoon, perched on a slightly wobbly wooden bar stool, Jake had shuffled a little to the left. Below him at a table sat an elderly gentleman with two other types that Jake could only describe as hippie backpackers. The backpackers had asked the gentleman a question: 'What would your advice be?' A question directed to a man who had been retired longer than the backpackers had been employed. A man whose age and manner of discussion had empowered him to be the voice of wisdom, given his life experience – fifty years longer than Jake's, possibly sixty years longer than the hippies. For life, what would your advice be? After much discussion defining the point, the retired gentleman had responded simply: 'Let go.' Jake had thought at repeated intervals what answer he might give. The responses are endless and open to any amount of elaboration, the significance of the answer – the one guide, the one thing that you would recommend as the guide for life – seemed overwhelmed by the singular significance of the question itself.

Let go? Let go of what? The pain of death? Let go abandonment? Let go betrayal? Does it mean to forgive? Let go your second mind, your monkey, your subconscious, your inner voice? Whatever it is that you call it, let go the tittle-tattle that it speaks of, the negativity and nagging that it barks or gently seduces you with. Let go the demands of others, the expectations, the trials and tribulations of others that map out your competition and direct your life. *Let go of what?* Jake's mind an intricate montage of his life, his life involvements emotionally scrutinised. The heartbreak of that first emotional confusion, Darren his Judas mate versus Claire, the first proper girlfriend who had betrayed his love. Swiftly followed by Derek, then them and them and them, the growing maturity of the outer body had not brought with it loyalty in age, as friend after friend and stranger after stranger tested his patience. Did it mean to forgive?

He unclenched his frozen hand from the rail to focus his racing thoughts, the cold clearing his mind as his hand soothed his forehead, releasing the pain like a doctor's reassuring touch.

What other advice might you give? Live a dream? Listening to his heart Jake knew what the dreams were by its insistent need for fulfilment; it hassled him, it knew what it wanted to be happy. But it did not wish to be hurt, it did not like to be broken. His heart inflicted fear to protect itself from the unknown and sent him into uncontrollable spasms of infatuation to fulfil its need for desire and attention. He questioned love. The love of knowledge, the love of oneself, of material things, the unconditional, the romantic, the passionate, the true and the hate. By giving he could feel good, but was that the intention? There is the love of giving and the openness to receive with thanks, the love of acts of kindness to others, without reward. The love of God. The love and passion of all things; he'd seen a guy once chained to a machine, and similar images many times in the news, people chained to a tree or railing, to protect something that will never give them personal thanks. The love of another, the unconditional and the true.

He turned to his head, kicking out the memory slide show – flashes of his mother, his girlfriends, random people… a women who he had helped to pick up her bag, having strewn her belongings down the pavement on a wet miserable day, and then a child stuck in a swing, when he hadn't gone to help. Instead he'd watched the struggle, his body still, his head full of intentions. His chest tightened, he felt his surroundings closing in, the crisp winter air heavy, polluted. The space that closes in under pressure, suffocating your spirit.

What of freedom? Jake had dumped girls for freedom but now, with Catherine gone, he still felt suffocated. Bound by his life. Taxes, financial survival, under the command of managers or own businesses. Scheduled by bus, train and traffic times and signals, dictated to by fashion and supermarket prices and choices of product. Suffocated by the majority's opinion of proper behaviour, fight against that that you do not approve. One man can be counted, but Jake felt that he might never be free from the fight. He had felt an experience of freedom, calling kids fucking bastards felt good. *Free to say what I like.*

He was freezing, his hand white, his tea cold, mind still whirring.

Nature, we are governed by nature, so vast and unpredictable that man will never overcome it. He imagined a hot beach far away on a desert island, free from the order and structure of the world within which he currently battled, but with it came a bond girl, sexy and bronzed, he could not hold the freedom image for long, he would not be able to survive, his lack of practical skills clear to him… the mind dreamt on towards dinner with the girl, a lush restaurant with good service appeared on the beach, a stunning dress with matching purse floating towards his table. The convenience and freedom of his local restaurant and supermarket suddenly became apparent, but even if he could learn the required skills to survive on a desert island, man cannot control when it rains or how often the earth will crack, we yield to the power and freedom of our natural universe. Jake felt trapped, he would never be free from the world within which he lived. His mind now his prisoner, the world an enemy. He tried to stretch out his mind beyond the fifteen or so square metres that would ordinarily constitute an average person's personal space, our interacting safe zone. Jake's space was more complex than the one we all hold around us, the space that determines our comfort zone. Jake's space incorporated his whole being. The space that dictated his clothes, how he acted, how he stood, breathed and thought. The personal space that closed in under pressure, suffocating his spirit. The space that his mind bounced around, rebounding back to itself over and over, the ball knocking on the cupboard door, *let me out, let me out.* The space that walked with him, ate with him and slept with him. The space that was his world. The space that consumed him. The space that was Jake.

Rushton

It had been decided by the administration to introduce fish to the ward. This had transpired after much discussion about the variety of pets available, a discussion over which Gill had particular influence (it was inevitably her who would care for the creature). Fish were purchased and placed in a large glass bowl in the centre of the communal area.

Boris stood in his usual spot just to the left of the communal seating area where the tick was loudest, considering the possibilities of his position. The endless all-consuming *tick, tick*, was becoming a little tiresome, so without too much deliberation he knelt on the floor and tapped the glass of the tank to the beat of the tick and for the first time worded his focus. Tapping, he silently mouthed *tick, tick, tick, tick, hey fishy, fishy*. As Horace looked at the clock and Jake followed his gaze, Gill checked her watch, as she had done every day, several times a day, for what had seemed like her entire life. She watched the second hand complete its circuit: each second clearly ticked by the tiny hand that jerked its way around the dial. Roman numerals marked each hour, the strap changed twice in the 20 years Gill had worn it, a gift from her father and his father before that. It held a great importance to her, a wartime keepsake still clinging to the very sweat of the brave man who had fought with it proudly strapped upon his wrist, only the watch remaining as a physical memory of his return from the field of battle. She felt her father's presence, his strength and comfort, as she watched it tick another minute away.

Turning on her heel in a gesture uniquely hers – heavy but strangely balletic – a realisation struck her. Gill picked up the receiver as she glided into the office that overlooked the communal area and requested a caretaker to attend with a ladder and screwdriver. He arrived promptly; she indicated the clock. No polite small-talk for the caretaker, just precise and clear instructions as he arranged his ladder in front of the office's spying window. Horace looked at the clock, ignoring the caretaker as he fiddled with the white plastic surround; Jake looked at the clock because Horace had; Gill checked her watch. Horace felt empowered, his self-knowledge of his awareness was starting to impress him; no longer trying to figure out what he was doing there, or how long he could be missing on his weekly walks, he was now enjoying his secret, content with his *lx, re4* and clock watching shenanigans. A remarkably childish, fun-like element entered Horace with his little glances of sanity amongst his crazy companions. He smirked to himself, in a way he would have remembered as a child playing a practical joke on his mother, or that particularly comedy moment when he put a snake in his sister's bed, if he could remember anything. He felt suddenly devious, he wanted to jump on a scooter and whiz round the wards... *wards*. He was in an institution! Gill requested the clock disconnected but not removed, her thoughts towards Horace's development, prompted by Boris's *hey fishy, fishy*, the current priority, as government pressure pushed for results. Horace would have to be tested. So with the clock still hanging, silent, frozen in time, Gill waited.

Horace

It was a clear, fresh day late in January, the sales were starting to die down and the excitement of Christmas was being replaced by Easter eggs. Another year progressing its way forwards, just like the last. Horace rested on a bench after an exerting climb up the park's hill, during which struggle he had passed a mutilated tree. Pausing to examine the damage (*little bastards, with their fold away army knives*) he pressed his podgy digit into one of the cuts, 'Kids!' he muttered. He worried for his daughter, *knives, crime, boys*. How safe was she in the world?

The bench where Horace rested overlooked a good portion of the common, dog walkers and joggers rushed across his horizon. The fresh day whisked up a light chill in the air and, resting now, Horace's body cooled quickly; the sweat built up from the climb sent a flutter of shivers over his skin. He peered out across the view of the common, the fresh, clear day causing him to squint slightly against the glare of the sun. A father kicked a football for his son, the boy scampered across the grass dribbling the leather quite dexterously with his nimble feet. Horace thought back to his own days as a boy: he'd not been much for sports. A mother pushed a pram and watched guardedly over another child trotting a little to keep up by her side. A jogger sprinted by, headphones clasped around her head, her exhalations and intake regulating her breathing. Horace could tell by the panting patterns with every exhalation that she was in control of her pace. She was wearing running gear by 'Nike', but trainers by a company he did not recognize. He took a mental note to investigate the make. Strapped to each wrist she wore light weights and a water bag with a tube adorned her back. She was clearly on an intensive fitness plan, he made another mental note. His eyes strained to see her sprint off into the distance, her pace quite fast but steady; she must do this often. He took another note of the time, he would return here and see her again.

Horace relaxed into the bench, the flutter over his skin had warmed as he had rested. He sank further into the bench, for the moment *his* bench; the day clear and fresh, the breeze slight, the moment still.

Horace arrived at his desk to find three staplers, still in their boxes, waiting on the veneer. Post boy working late or early, making up missed time. Everyone has to work. Claire on his case, Horace on Claire's case, Jenny on his case. Endless, pointless work. Staplers. What a terrible chain of utterly stupid events.

'Morning,' Jenny said chirpily.

'Ah, Jenny! A gift for you!' Horace held up a boxed stapler. Jenny reached out for it but Horace swiped it out of reach, 'I am assuming that with this stapler fiasco over, one can expect more efficient work from you, seeing as you will be wasting no more time searching for a stapler?'

Jenny eyed him with worn disbelief and slight contempt.

'Good,' Horace said shoving the boxed stapler into her awaiting outstretched hand.

'What about the toilet rolls?' Veronica could be heard from somewhere in the background.

'You can have a stapler if you stop going on about toilet roll!' Horace lifted his voice to reach wherever it was his words needed to carry, Veronica still not in view.

'I'd rather waste time finding someone else's stapler and have roll!'

Right.

'Well?' Veronica was standing over his desk now.

'Get on with your work,' Horace huffed.

A stifled muttering shuffled off.

'Jeffery.' Horace called, waving him over with the palette of his aeroplane-signalling hand. Jeffery stood, straight and defiant in front of Horace's desk.

'Where were you yesterday?'

'Ill.'

'Ill?'

'Yeah, ill.'

'And you're okay today?'

'Feel better.'

'Jeffery,' Horace paused, 'you continue this course and I'll have to start disciplinary action. I need an account of exactly what was wrong with you yesterday. On my desk by lunch time, typed, dated and signed.'

Jeffery stared at him.

'Go, get on with it!' and Horace waved him away, his giant hand blowing the top sheet in his in-tray.

Horace picked up the receiver from the dialling body of his phone and called an internal number. Maintenance.

'Hello?' the same gruff voice greeted him.

'Yeah, hi,' Horace suddenly casual, 'I was wondering if you'd had a chance to check on the toilet dispensers in the ladies up here?'

'Ah yes,' pause.

Horace waited.

'They're fine.'

'Fine?' Horace enquired.

'Yeah, I mean they work fine.'

'Ah!' *I see.*

'I mean they're not the best, rolls are easier to deal with sure, I see your staff's preference, but these dispensers are over the whole building and they work fine.'

Horace, quite stunned in some way that this caretaker had remembered his rather trivial and – quite frankly, boring – story of dispenser dismay, thanked him for his precious time and hung up the phone.

3pm: afternoon tea. A nice cup of cha with a piece of well-presented cake was just the ticket. Instead of just moving his eyes, Horace lifted his whole head to check the specials board. On the odd occasion a special had grabbed his taste buds and inspired him to order something more substantial, but today would be cake. His regimented dark suits and light shirts glinted slightly as the light caught their ruffles, today he had chosen a red tie with blue stripes, a gift from his daughter, though which birthday or Christmas it represented Horace couldn't be sure.

'Hello Mr Conway, how are you today?' A tall girl (or at least tall from Horace's seated position, forcing him to elevate his head once more) stood beside him. As he lifted his head he manoeuvred his eyes to take in every aspect of his waitress's bodily being, scanning every seam for an encoded message. Poised with pad and pencil for order instructions, Horace's waitress waited. As his eyes reached the pad he remembered his purpose there and ordered a cappuccino and slice of walnut sponge. She scribbled something down (presumably *a cappuccino and slice of walnut sponge* or the abbreviated version of those instructions) and turned on her heel, her black short skirt and white shirt creasing with the movement. Horace waited, mentally noting the secret message she had passed on to him in bursts of broken code, a conundrum indeed, but Horace had it all figured out before the sponge arrived and a response code was passed, equally fragmented to avoid detection.

The walnut sponge was beautifully bouncy and the steaming cappuccino, although in opposition to Horace's personal, 'save-traditional-tea-houses' scheme, was light and complimentary to the cake. Horace enjoyed it immensely and then strolled back to the office for the second round. And just as he had expected, round two began with Veronica and toilet roll.

'I've spoken to the real caretaker, who incidentally doesn't look anything like you, and he has informed me after much testing that the dispensers work perfectly fine and that the whole building uses this type, so rolls are out of the question.'

Veronica opened her mouth, speech just about to...

'So, that's the end of that, no rolls. Persevere with the dispenser, maybe you're just handling it wrong.'

Veronica opened her mouth, speech just about to...

Horace's giant hand, held lightly in the air, obscured her face from his view, 'No. No more, no rolls, deal with the dispenser.' He paused, then added as an afterthought, 'Here, have a stapler.' He wafted a still boxed stapler in her direction.

A quiet 'Thanks,' drifted into the distance as the stapler was snatched from Horace's finger tips and Veronica floated off.

'Jeffery, where's the explanation I asked for? Get it to me or bring a lawyer to work with you tomorrow.'

'I think you'll find that's *solicitor* in this country.' Jeffery mocked.

Smart arse.

A sheet of paper appeared on his desk. Horace examined its contents. Dated at the top and addressed to Horace in a letter format it continued to explain an ongoing sickness of inexplicable symptoms and unexplained dizzy spells. *Right.* Horace picked up the receiver from the dialling body of his phone and called an internal number. HR.

'Hello?' a fairly chirpy, young female voice answered.

'Hello,' Horace repeated back, in an equally chirpy response, 'I wonder if you could help me with procedures, dealing with eye testing. I have a member of staff who seems to get unexplained headaches and I would like to eliminate his computer usage at work from being the cause, or if it is the cause, to do the appropriate thing to assist him.'

'Call medical and make him an appointment for an eye test, they'll assess him and let you know, glare screens are usually all you need.'

'Right, okay.'

'When was the last time you had a risk assessment done?'

Horace paused. *No idea, if ever.* 'Think we're probably due.'

'Right, I'll send someone up next week, say Wednesday? All your staff need to be in and they'll go round and check everyone's seating, lighting, screens, etc. you know?'

'Yes I know. Okay, should I book the eye test as well?'

'Might as well, better to be safe than sorry, especially if these headaches are affecting the ability to work.'

'Yes, of course.' *Everyone's got to work.* The phone clicked off and Horace dialled another internal number. Medical.

'Hello?' a slightly more sombre voice, the end of the day in sight.

'Hello, can I book a member of staff in for an eye test?'

Shuffling of paper, 'Next Thursday 2pm?'

Horace considered, Jeffery would have to make it to work two days in a row. 'Perfect, Jeffery Donald from Great Insurance.'

'Okay.'

'Great, thank you.'

The phone clicked off, Horace had no idea these departments were so useful.

6pm: everybody out. Horace, a little hasty himself today, marched off right behind them to make his small detour. Check out the home arrival times three days in a row, just to make sure, and then the continuation of his elegant meeting from yesterday evening.

Horace twisted his wrist to reveal his Rolex copy: 6.29pm. On the bus he thought about Jeffery having his eyes tested, then shook it out of his mind. *Everybody has to work.*

At home he unnecessarily rearranged some of the files flanking the broad oak desk that dominated the space. Horace was waiting for his wife.

'Dinner!' Right on the mark.

Horace sat opposite his wife, the tie-giver sat to the right of Horace and the left of her mother.

'How was your day?' Horace's wife's soft tones directing their kindliness and genuine interest towards the tie-giver.

A shrug, 'Okay.'

And then the gaze flowed round to Horace. 'Okay,' he said also.

A united tie-giver and Horace cast their eyes on the mother/wife in a collective, 'And you?' And as the story of today's social journey began to unravel, the tie-giver and Horace shared a glance. A glance and a slight tender smile. Dinner ended with a summary of the day's events and then Horace cleared the table and washed up as usual, the-tie giver unable to dry today, homework. Horace dried and put everything away without complaint or indeed any inkling of frustration towards his family for delaying his forthcoming elegant meeting, but as the last plate clattered to its resting place with the others, Horace smiled. Hanging the towel on the rack, he raised his head and strolled to the garage.

'Good evening,' he began. Horace loosened his tie in a notably casual way, having only just tightened and straightened it before entering. He floated over to the cognac, offered a glass (which was duly accepted) and poured a good measure into his own tumbler. Holding the tumbler lightly in his animal hand he floated a little more around the room, his mind talking casually about something sophisticated, a subject of which he actually knew nothing about, so the words stayed inside, the fantasy living on. Having not only captured her attention but enraptured her with his intellect and dazzling analysis of the topics at hand, wrapped in a faultlessly charming manner, he slipped into his position on the edge of the broad oak desk that dominated the space to perch over his company, sitting on the chair opposite his own. His left hand wafted in the air, emphasizing various points in his silent conversation. Horace ended with a short list of book recommendations, listing their titles and authors as if he lunched with them, but unable to conjure imaginary believable titles quick enough he mumbled his way through. His guest thanked him for his time, complimented him on his genius and then ever so beautifully, breathtakingly, seductively, told Horace her hotel room number. A professor at a conference, a different kind of fantasy today. He checked over the room with a quick but focused scan and followed his invisible guest out, locked the door behind him and went up to his wife, the ending to this fantasy a surprising treat for Mrs Conway.

Rushton

The dull smell of disinfectant oozed its way through the nostrils and down the throat. Inured to its weekly infliction some didn't notice, but others twitched their noses and rubbed the drips away with their hands, not wishing to clear their airways with a good blow in case it allowed the stench to poison them somehow. The mottled cream with brown lino stretched out over the floor, meeting the scuffed, once-white walls, encasing them in a box of ugliness. The furniture was of varying styles, each piece losing its independent stance as each plastic seam united it to its plastic brother. Supplied by a furniture charity, each piece brandished its giver's logo, a reminder of helpful work and unselfish people. A low table marked with ringed stains of spilt tea blocked any easy access to the television. Perched on its veneer sat the newly added glass bowl and fish that had so captured Boris's attention.

Horace looked at the clock; Jake looked at the clock because Horace had; Gill, as always, checked her watch. She studied Horace, had he noticed? Horace looked down, unsure what to do, the clock had stopped, was he supposed to notice? What should he do? He avoided glancing at Gill but desperately wanted to. Over his excitement and childish inner freedom Horace now tried to formulate a plan: he needed to know how Gill felt about the clock. He looked around him, *they're all mad*. What difference did it make what he did? It was unpredictable, it was all crazed. He settled back and awaited his pills. Despite the lack of tick counting out his day he knew what the time was.

Boris sat in a newly assigned chair next to Imogen, his mind clear, his brain in motion; he glanced at Horace, he knew Horace, knew his type, he knew Horace was faking, he knew they were in an institution. Gill brought Horace's pills, as the ritual dictated. Straight after wedging his *lx* and *re4* between his back teeth and gum, Horace hoisted himself from his chair and made his way to the bathroom. Boris followed.

Tap, tap. Horace looked around his cubicle, *lx, re4* resting in his hand. 'What?' he asked.

'*lx* and *re4*,' a voice whispered through the door, 'they mess with your head, used to give them to my girls.'

'What?' Horace asked again, his tone lighter, his frown crunched.

'Your pills, they mess with your head, keep you sedated,' the voice seemed closer than before, the words easing their way through the gap between the divide and the door, Horace could almost feel the breath coming into his space. An uneasy breath, a dark, disturbing carbon monoxide – oxygen mix, infused with evil.

'What?' Horace repeated, a little more urgently.

'The pills man, get a grip! Crush the pills.'

'What?!' Horace's voice lifted an octave, he felt nervous. He placed the pills on the floor and pressed his left foot into them and rubbed them gently to disperse their powder. He felt like a child again, a teacher outside the door, the evidence being quietly and discreetly destroyed. 'I'm not doing anything!' he wanted to say, but the room had fallen silent.

Horace returned to his chair, his little oak table sitting next to it with his glass of water missing only the mouthful needed to feign his swallowing of the mysterious and very uncooperative *lx* and *re4*. His head down, his back slightly bent, he shuffled on to rest again. He looked at the clock, Jake looked at the clock because Horace had, Gill checked her watch. Boris stared at him. Horace could feel his glare, the air between them suddenly thick. He breathed heavily trying to find the oxygen he needed. *Turn the fucking clock back on.*

Horace looked at the clock again and then again, as if trying to will it into motion. Boris stared at him. A slight wink caught the corner of Horace's eye. Boris started to laugh, a noise no-one had heard for a fair while, paranoid and shifty. The last time a group of white coats had said something funny it had resulted in the Level 1 Blue Team's building uncertainty, nervous laughter amplifying itself into a neurotic frenzy. Horace looked at Boris, saw his teeth glinting, his evil emitting an uncomfortable enmity. Horace looked at the clock; Jake shuffled in his seat and looked at the clock because Horace had; Gill checked her father's watch (roman numerals marking each hour, the strap changed twice in the 20 years she had worn it) and made a call. Imogen got up and moved her chair an inch further away from Boris. Nobody liked him. The room had changed, the atmosphere thicker, harder than before. Craziness had encroached into their space, strangeness even beyond their own, a new level of formidable madness. Horace thought about what day it was. *Wednesday.* Tomorrow he would go on a walk to the shops. Perhaps tomorrow he wouldn't come back. Gill bought Jake's pills over. Horace looked at him and, swinging his arm around, knocked the nearly full glass from his little oak side table, only the half mouthful missing required to feign his *lx* and *re4*, then (having distracted Gill) he embedded his eyes into Jake's. He looked at the clock, Jake followed suit, then looked at his pills, Horace looked at the clock again and again. Jake seemed confused, his pills still in their small white cup. Gill mopped up the water from the floor and collected shards of glass into her hand as another white coat (that no-one knew the name of but who always intervened) brought a dustpan and brush. Gill and the other white coat that no-one knew the name of fiddled about around Horace's little oak side table. Horace stood up, blocking Gill from Jake's view, and shook his head. Jake looked at him and then at the cup. Horace wanted Jake on side, he didn't know why, but he seemed a better option than Boris. If they were going to go, he was taking Jake with him. Boris wanted to blurt it out, 'He's trying to stop you taking the pills!' but he didn't say that, he didn't say anything. They stared at Jake.

Jake shuffled around in his chair like a child needing the toilet but not wanting to say, then threw the pills to the back of his throat. Horace sat down. Jake looked at him, so he looked at the clock; Jake looked at the clock because Horace had; Gill checked her father's watch (roman numerals marked each hour, the strap changed twice in the 20 years she had worn it) and then glanced at the small white cup. She looked at Jake and then the cup again. Boris flicked through a magazine. Horace looked at the clock; he had decided amongst all this confusion just to do so every time the altering shadows of things around him caught the glimpsing corner of his eye, an instinct generated by the changing waves of things around him. Should anyone within his vicinity move, Horace would look at the clock. Catching Jake follow his lead and then Gill's response to Jake's movement, Horace was confident that this unformatted schedule was correct, the randomness of things seemed organised, as if movement was the key trigger to his behaviour. He had at first been concerned that he might be over-noticing the things around him, but now he relaxed into the idea; Gill showed no signs of concern.

Imogen

Imogen's tired eyes lay flatly on a figure seated at a table across from her, a handsome man, composed and successful looking. He sat confidently amongst his colleagues. A slight smudge on his tie caught her eye. A dream of a life that had escaped her flickered and then flared into a sudden yearning, before plummeting swiftly and harshly into the emotional realms of her deepest self. He would have looked over if Miracle had still been here, all eyes smiling at her and then darting across to Imogen and wondering why such a beauty was sitting with a scruffy nobody. Now she was just a scruffy nobody, and their odd glance told Imogen that this seemed justified to the audience: *who'd want to be friends with that ugly scruff?* What had she done? What had happened to her? What had happened in her life to ensure that one day she might look at this figure and know that she was lost? A girl broke her view as she sidled past, Imogen caught a glimpse of her attire without averting her eyes and her butterfly mind responded, unasked: *I do not like sleeves that are too short on me.*

She looked at her hand, its aging wrinkles starting to alter her, time catching up. She knew very vividly that it was hers, that this hand belonged to her. She turned it over, turned it back, moved one finger. It was a part of her, the person within, the soul living out its life within this body, the puppeteer. Only her. Who gave a fuck what other people thought?! She had a right, a destiny. She looked at her hand and knew it was her. She had done this as a teenager and known then that it was her; she could wiggle a finger – just one, one at a time – as her mind desired. *This is me and there is only me at every moment of my life.* Waking up with herself, having breakfast, brushing her teeth, not necessarily in that order but dear God! Who was this person who moved her hand and craved for coffee and cigarettes, or whatever, every day, every second? Each moment looking at her hand and knowing it was Imogen.

As a teenager she was afraid of it, the isolation, the loneliness, *only me, just a confused little me to cope with the world*. But despite the fearfulness, she needed to know that she was real. In later years she would look at her hand and be strangely excited by its possibilities, by there being only her, having a choice. But she wanted to know why she did not know what she was doing. How it was possible that her mind might live her life without her. That she did stuff every day, just *stuff*. Her body moved, she smoked, drank, ate, walked, did stuff. Yet her mind was not thinking about these activities, her mind was in the past or the future. More often than not her mind was nowhere and everywhere, the world going on around her like a film. She would often wonder how it was that she lived every day without herself. How her body knew before she did, how the language of the body and face spoke before her. It was *her* mind, *her* body, why did she not know it? Her arms moved, her body talked, her mouth expressed words and the lines on her face would show a question or surprise or any kind of feeling, shown to its audience before she had caught up, before she knew how she felt, before she knew where her arm had moved to. But there was only her, just Imogen; she controlled these things, yet she did not. Her mind lived out a life without her. In an effort to understand these thoughts she concentrated, monitored everything – every thought, every movement that she made – and discovered a feeling and reality of living in the moment. The only thing that seemed real was each second as it came, all other thoughts were memories of the past, dreams of a future, or fantasies of another life. The only reality was right now; a whole lifetime could pass by, very rarely (if ever) knowing reality, for the mind, she felt, was almost constantly in another time.

Walking down a street, she saw a girl pushing a pram. She asked questions, in a second she had asked: *Is she a single parent? How old is she? Where does she live? Is it her only child? Is it her child?* A hundred questions in a single second and then the answers came in the fantasy of her mind and in a few more seconds she had written the story of this stranger's life with several alternative scenarios. Then a guy walked by and the process began again. She popped out to buy some shampoo. When she got home she was exhausted; unbeknownst to her, she had just written, pictured and almost experienced at least 20 films in a matter of minutes, it had only taken half an hour to walk to the shops. The screenplays had come and gone so fast, only a vague recollection of seeing a few people on the journey filled her head. Her mind was not walking down the street, her mind was not with her body as it placed one foot easily in front of the other, opened doors, found money, carried a bag. Her mind lived out her actions without her, while her life...?

Her mind lived a dream, a collection of fantasies, worries, memories, expectations and hopes, she was not living, not really, just dreaming. She did not know that she was there, moving and doing; she did not know how she looked, how her body walked; she could not see herself, she was not herself.

The Diary of Rose Heather Roberts

I have this fantasy.

Taking a gun from the inside of my jacket and holding it to the temple of my enemy. Bang.

But I'd never do it.

What am I doing? Sitting here a nervous wreck.

Never ask permission to do anything, he has no right to grant approval.

I have this fantasy.

Taking a gun from the inside of my jacket and holding it to the temple of my enemy. Bang.

But damn it, I'd never do it.

Rushton

The morning bell rang. In the early days it echoed down distant corridors of their minds, deepening into a dull kind of thud for some or a ringing maddening shrill for others, consuming their morning awakening either way. Confusing them, hurting, pounding round their heads, the bell a daily ritual, like so many things, in fact all things. But today they simply woke up and got up. Horace hauled himself forward and up into a seated position and rubbed his sleepy morning eyes. Jake bounced from his bed, threw on his jeans, rummaged around a drawer for a clean t-shirt and scampered out of his room to breakfast. His slender usually well-kept self felt excited today. Imogen awoke and leaned over to her bedside lamp switch. Fixed lights hovered over their heads, activated by a plastic coated switch always placed to the right of the bed above their laying minds. Imogen was the only one that used it. The light burst into action, startling her into a day's beginning. Every morning it surprised her. Boris woke with a half-smile etched onto the morning stubble of his face.

Thursday morning was light and fresh, as if spring had entered the room, one of those bright, clear days that entice you to clean as the sunlight highlights layers of dust across every surface your eyes rest on; a day for chores, a day to get on. The mottled cream with brown lino danced with dappled shadows as the light played in a heavy breeze, the breakfast stodgy and thick. The usual plastic sectioned trays moulded into rudimentary plates landed in front of each occupant, brought round by the ones who didn't wear white coats but always intervened. Gill made her usual notes regarding punctuality and attendance, ticking them off a list columned with time and date information. As they ate their breakfast Gill would tick further columns to record which food and drink had been consumed by whom. Horace took a sip of orange juice, the thick plastic beaker always tasting a little odd, the juice altered by it somehow. Gill bent down and shuffled with a pen. Horace put the beaker down and stared at it. A girl who didn't wear a white coat but always intervened strutted her determined ostrich-like gait past Horace's back, 'Drink up your orange juice, Horace. It's good for you: vitamins.' He turned his head away from her and caught Boris watching him, sitting diagonally opposite him across the table. Gill checked her watch.

As breakfast was completed and the occupants re-established their usual places in the communal sitting area, Horace looked at the clock. It was time for his walk to the shops. Gill stomped over. It was an unusual stomp, but an earlier fight with her husband about the hours she was working had made her resent these rehabilitating criminals this morning. An excellent stroke of luck for what Horace was about to ask: 'Can Jake come with me?' Horace's voice was firm but enquiring.

Gill thought for a moment: the less of them there were the easier her morning would be. 'Yes, yes, take him,' she announced, waving her left arm behind her as she marched off to get on with her chores.

Boris catching her indifferent mood jumped up, 'Can I go?'

'Yes all go, there's a list on the side of what you need to get.'

And so it was this newly acquainted threesome collected the list and strolled off towards the door to their freedom. The not-so-yellow, not-so-brick, not-so-road pavement had transformed into a grey concrete chipped path, manoeuvring its way around remarkably empty roads to the convenience store on the corner. They passed a man, an unremarkable man. Horace turned to follow his step, *have I seen him before?* A fleeting thought, quickly lost in distraction as his companions marched on ahead and without him. They reached the store and purchased the items from the list. Stepping back out onto the street, they stopped and looked at each other.

'Let's go that way', Boris indicated with his thumb to go right, their entrance door back to the communal area was left. They strode on. They passed a post office, a hairdresser's, a row of housing and a small park with newly tended, closely-cropped fresh bright grass, as if sculptured onto the flat. The smart and shiny swings seemed almost haunted, as if untouched by the children for whom they were intended.

'Does anyone else feel weird?' Jake looked around him, the emptiness of things seemed strange: no dog walkers in the park, no grannies shuffling along blocking the pavement. The post office without a queue, *that never happens.*

Boris pointed with an outstretched arm, 'Look, a pub. Let's go and have a drink.'

Horace and Jake coyly glanced in each other's vague direction – both wanted to go further, to keep walking, far away from here – they shook their heads.

Boris spoke up, reading their thoughts, 'We've got to go back, you can't just walk out like that. We're still in the complex! Look at this place, it isn't normal. Come on, we'll have time for a pint before they come and fetch us. There's enough change from the shopping isn't there?'

Horace and Jake looked across him to each other more directly this time, coyness replaced with inquiry. Shrugging in unison they lifted and twitched an eyebrow at each other to indicate their agreement.

They stepped into the public house and a strangely familiar feeling embraced them.

'Good job boys,' Boris raised his glass in a toast, 'you're not as pathetic as I thought!' A gentle smile cheekily rearranged his face, his eyes alive, the curve on his lips natural.

Jake sipped at his pint, the cool flavour and refreshing froth reminded him of something: a time gone by; a life lived but forgotten. Horace preferred wine and although he didn't remember this snippet of information about himself the beer was wrong somehow: at the very least it needed to be in bottle, Horace was sure of it. Horace looked up at Boris, he had wild ginger hair: they were not brothers, he'd always known it.

'What are we doing here?' Horace asked as if Boris were his doctor, the knower of things, the creator of this infliction.

'We're all killers.' Boris said casually, as if he were noting an unimportant but curious fact, like they were all Sagittarians, yet voiced with conviction and a certainty, as if it were a truth too obvious to question. Horace looked at Jake, Jake looked at Boris. *Urgh.*

'No I'm not!' Jake sputtered.

'Yes you are,' Boris pronounced. 'We all are. Why do you think we're in here?'

'Maybe I'm depressed,' Horace enquired.

'Don't be an idiot! It's not the 1960's, they don't put people in places like this for that anymore! You killed someone, maybe more than one. I know your type, I can tell – *women*, Horace – you killed some, I'm sure of it. Don't know about him though,' Boris waved a thumb towards Jake. 'He seems a bit of a soft boy.' Horace sighed.

Jake twitched, he didn't want to be a killer but he didn't want to be a soft boy either.

'Maybe I did kill someone, chopped their limbs off,' a soft tone pronounced each word clearly, a comparative question, another perspective offered up for debate. Jake shook inwardly with tension.

'Maybe you did,' Boris raised his drink to salute Jake, 'limbs or not, you killed someone.'

Jake tried to remember people; who might he have killed? Who did he know? 'How do you know?' Jake turned with accusing disbelief, his eyes trying to fix onto Boris's, but Boris's eyes darted around his head, avoiding Jake's eyes, and his neck had a funny bouncy wobble as if a thin spring was encased inside his vertebrae.

'Tick, tick, tick, tick,' Boris ticked in a whisper, the rhythm in time to the second.

Horace and Jake stared at each other. An acknowledgment flickered between them: from all the different tests of trust that each had ever experienced, remembered or not, they equally and unanimously did not trust Boris.

'How do we get out?' Horace finally voiced the question that had been hanging on his lips, pressed to the side of every corner of his thought, clock watching.

'The only way out is to be rehabilitated. They want you to leave here and get married, have children maybe, live happily ever after, you can't even raise your voice to someone, need to have found your balance and be as calm as a fish.'

Jake and Horace thought for a second.

'Fish have a tendency to panic,' Jake informed the group.

'Alright, a crocodile then!' Boris jested.

They thought again.

'Aren't they, like, perfectly evolved, the perfect killing machine?' Jake argued.

Boris smiled.

'I don't think there are any,' Horace joined in, 'any that aren't predators, I mean.'

'A sloth,' Boris intercepted as if recalling something required for a quiz question, 'or a koala, they look pretty chilled out.'

Jake and Horace sighed.

'Look,' Boris began, 'life's not that fucking complicated, *tick, tick, tick, tick*, each second is the only truth, reality, you know?' Horace and Jake didn't know, but Boris continued anyway: 'Christ!... Okay! Like Imogen's taking all this shit on, like her mother's still in the bedroom, even though she's been dead for years, years of stuff building in her head you know?' He didn't wait for a response. 'She takes it all on, then kills someone. Maybe she killed her mum, I dunno.' He paused and took a gulp from his pint. 'I've killed people, and in the moment, it is a *real* moment, the only kind that exists. You can take event after event of stuff and carry it around with you or you let it go and live the moment.

'Look, if you take on each pain, it manifests: grows bitter and twisted, like me, then something else happens, then something else and then... Bang! You kill someone. I liked it, so I did it again. Don't care about all that stuff anymore.'

Jake and Horace stared at him in disbelief.

'Look,' Boris continued, 'you have to understand what you've done, so that you can control it. I wanted to keep my head, you know?' Horace and Jake did know. 'Maybe you think that by stopping the drugs you're keeping your head, but your heads are all messed up; that's what got you here, messy heads. Just because you are thinking now, doesn't mean you're normal.' Boris raised his glass again and knocked back the remainder of his pint.

Jake looked up from staring at the table, clearly the smartest man amongst them, and finally stated, 'I am normal.'

'Shit!' Boris said. 'You're not! That's what I've been saying: you snapped, found your moment.'

'Why didn't I just take on Buddhism?' Jake asked, thinking how profound Boris was being, but did Boris even know it? Jake wasn't sure.

'I don't know, maybe you should have, but you killed some people instead.'

'Some people?' Jake seemed startled. 'You said some*one*, that's one person, not some people.'

Boris pointed to Jake's half remaining pint, 'You want that?'

Jake looked at it, 'Yes,' he said.

'Look, I don't know how many, but I bet between us it's quite a number.'

'You're fucking mad.' Jake downed his drink and walked out of the pub. Waiting at the entrance stood Gill with her arms folded and her foot tapping, like his teachers used to do. 'You're late!' they'd bellow as he dragged his feet towards the classroom.

'Do you fancy a drink, Gill?' Jake jested.

'Don't get your hopes up, it's not alcoholic. Come on! And you two!' she lifted her voice over Jake's shoulder, 'Let's go!'

Jake

Darren, Jake's longest friend and growing-up buddy had lived out his childhood dream of becoming a fireman. The pursuit of this desire had encouraged his extra-curricular sporting activities and made good the best of his abilities; still fit and strong he had put up a good fight in his defence, but Jake's complete body weight overthrew Darren's defences as he gasped for air, pushing upwards against Jake's force and the rushing water. Jake had left him to float down river. He'd packed up the camping gear that they had carried split equally between them over the green of the hills, recently revitalised after an earlier week of rain that had delayed their venture and thereby given Darren (unbeknownst to him) an extra week of life. Leaving what he could not fit into his own pack, he trudged off to the nearest town and reported his friend missing, the first to feel Jake's wrath.

Jake had executed this weekend with confidence and had chosen his hands as weapons. Although a strong man and able to swim, Darren had not been a strong swimmer. Jake had relied on this for accidental death when up against kayaking the extremities of the gushing river. A defining fact that had proven its efficacy: no doubt was cast on the happenings of this tragic and sad death and Jake lived unquestioned, unsuspected.

Rushton

Horace looked at the clock, he didn't know what else to do. He needed time to think. What an odd walk to the shops it had been, Horace wondered if it had been real. Jake looked at the clock because Horace had; Gill checked her watch. The day ticked silently on. Vincent was a visitor, he was shown in and shown out; Jake noted this, he was obviously important. He did nothing different from them, they did nothing different from him. Horace looked at the clock; Jake looked at the clock because Horace had looked at the clock; Gill checked her watch; Vincent glanced at Gill and then at the clock.

Horace

Horace brushed his hair at the bathroom mirror, six strokes varying in manner exercised his arms. Horace was a geezer, *Sha!* Straightening his collar and shaking off any stray threads clinging to his attire, Horace prepared himself for work. Striding with long paces he marched into the hallway, his scent altering the air.

6.58am and his wife glided into the hallway. 7.01am and Horace followed her out over the threshold on his way to work. A slight lipstick smudge remained on his lower lip from having being accosted at the doorway, where a shocked Horace had gripped his briefcase uncomfortably between himself and his wife, unable for an untimely moment to shake off thoughts of Jeffery's forthcoming eye test and the office health and safety check. His wife thankfully didn't notice, the magic of Horace the night before untarnished by his missing presence at this moment. She drove as if today were a day free of time constraints, the sun beating down her back on a perfect morning somewhere expensive. She pulled in to the curb outside Horace's office but did not battle with the headrest this morning, instead she smiled and wiped the lipstick from his lower lip, 'Have a good day at work.'

'Good luck at the council meeting.' Horace just got better. His wife's smile broadened and the battle with the headrest commenced.

Into the office: 'Morning, Mr Conway!' Jeffery raised a hand and a smile. Horace glared at him.

'Was wondering if I could have one of those staplers you're handing out?'

'If you can turn up to work for five days in a row I'll give you a pack of re-fills; if you make two weeks, you get the stapler.'

Jeffery glared back at him.

'After that, who knows! Fresh pack of blu-tack, new easy flow pens… attendance wins you prizes.'

'How did you get this job?'

'I turned up,' Horace was looking directly at Jeffery, eyeing him with a new fire in his heart and determination in his eyes. Jeffery felt the competition, but competition is always winnable; he eyed Horace back with obstinacy.

'Jeffery,' Horace called him back just as Jeffery tried to take his rebellious eyes away. He turned mid-step and faced Horace cautiously.

'You have an eye test on Thursday at 2pm with the medical department,' Horace waved the account, letter formatted, that Jeffery had supplied him with loosely in the air. 'Your *unexplained headaches*,' he recollected from the typed words and placed the sheet on his desk, securing it with a firm spank of his giant hand. 'Even if you are unwell on Thursday you are to come in for this test. Only death will excuse you, do you understand?'

'Only death, got it.'

Horace nodded seemingly absent minded as he pretended to fill out a form, new easy flow pen in hand, 'Good,' he said, but Jeffery was already gone.

Horace's in-tray was looking a little bulkier than usual. Mr Blanchett had dumped another pile data entry his way. Camilla was good at it, evidently, but her work load was reaching unfair proportions. *Jenny*. Redemption for the stapler fiasco. Although Horace was willing to admit that the staffs' search for staplers had been a huge time wasting activity, he was surprised that they had made such a fuss to get some more. Time wasting was surely one of their favourite things, and the stapler situation had provided an ongoing excuse. *Veronica*. The staplers had done him a favour, the toilet roll versus dispenser however...

'Veronica!' Horace bellowed, the big bad gruff.

Veronica glanced up and the day ticked on.

7pm and Horace was inspecting the Charlotte folder, checking all the times, dates, dots and dashes. He scrutinised the components for accuracy and neatness while studying the content, memorising the details. If he was to complete the mission successfully, every aspect must be remembered correctly.

'Dinner!' Horace's wife, right on the button.

Horace closed the file and placed it back with the others that sat always in neat and ordered arrangement, flanking the broad oak desk that dominated the space. He pushed his hands down on the desk to help lift himself from his executive chair, the broad oak desk sturdy and heavily legged, his weight no match for it, not the slightest wobble as he pushed his mass into the wood. Another dinner, another day, another life.

Inspector Jacob Rodgers

Inspector Jacob Rodgers picked up his ringing receiver and clipped out his name. After a short burst of speech from the other end he replaced the receiver and sat back in his chair. A cold cup of coffee tilted precariously over a pencil, tipping it towards a pile of paperwork to hover over the destiny of work sketching out more death. He straightened the cup and replaced the pencil in its rightful position in the holder, then took it up again, whizzing it through the electric sharpener, his name etched into its metal shiny side. The sharpener had been gift from his colleagues after his constant requests for hand sharpeners or new pencils had moulded itself into the office joke, the *ho-di-ho*, the *he-di-he*. He straightened a few more things around his desk unnecessarily and then stood, put on his coat and started his journey to the Rushton Institute of Rehabilitation.

Imogen

Catty chattering, crazy noise, the drone, the high pitched squeals, the clattering of voices shaping out lives, the fucking annoying manager, the colleague, the friend, 'To be honest... blah, blah.' Noise, fucking noise, the bitch, the degraded, the *it* and the *and*. 'Look at her, did she just grab whatever rags she had lying about the floor and throw them on or what?' One country screams gold, the other Ikea. All bitching because that guy over there doesn't *have it*. A hand stretches out, a signet ring proudly displayed upon its skin, loosening of the shirt reveals a thick chain, pride, a vivid tumult of images collated into intricate montage of simulated involvement.

The Diary of Rose Heather Roberts

What's happening? Do you think everyone goes through this? I'm no weirder than anyone else. Ask me, the whole population — the entire human race — is messed up.

Have you ever wondered what it would be like to be someone else? Do people ever really know who they are?

They don't approach you the way you want, so you behave differently to react in their 'way'. It's all you, but only a side, one side of all the possible reflections which could have been. Reality relies on interaction, the responses of others determine what you display. But hang on, am I not one of those others?

I have this fantasy.

Getting a gun from the inside pocket of my jacket and holding it to the temple of my enemy.

Bang.

But DAMN IT, I'd never do it.

Rushton

Inspector Jacob Rodgers was shown in, he didn't wear a white coat. Jake noted him. Horace looked at the clock, Jake looked at the clock and as always Gill checked her watch. Jacob stood in the communal area, a slight air of depression tickled his nostrils as the disinfectant eased its way from the cream with brown lino that stretched out to meet the once-white walls that encircled the space and the plastic, mismatched furniture of the room made him uncomfortable. The guests sat quietly. Jake watched the television. Horace stared at the floor, Boris read a magazine and Imogen was visiting her mother. Gill glided over to greet the inspector, her comfy white trousers and coat swishing against her skin in silence to all but her as she almost sneaked into his space.

'Inspector,' she held out her hand.

'Yes,' he said, 'and you must be Gill.'

'Yes,' she returned. She bowed her head a little to the left, indicating for him to follow her. She held her arm and hand as if wishing to interlock with his as she moved out of reach. She stood proudly next to the television and used her hands again to introduce each member of the Level 1 Blue Team. Imogen, she explained, was in her room. The inspector said hello as each name was told to him.

'This is Inspector Rodgers.' She announced his title with the same diction she had used to himself.

Boris flinched and averted his eyes from the inspector's gaze. Jake and Horace nodded slightly, shrugging the information off as irrelevant to them. The room waited for an 'and'. After a long and slightly uncomfortable pause Gill put her best foot forward, 'This way, Inspector.'

Gill marched off towards the corridor and a room on the right. Jacob followed. In the room sat a beefy man. Fat, yes, but different somehow, beefy, like he ate a lot of cow. His cheeks were red, flushed, as if he had a heart condition and his suit sagged uncomfortably around his bulk. Gill turned on her heels and left the room without any introductions.

'Inspector Rodgers,' a powerful, almost godly voice echoed round the room.

Inspector Jacob Rodgers smiled gently, 'Yes, and you are…?'

'Dr Henry Washington,' his hand extended over the table that separated them, urging Jacob to come forward. Jacob paused for a second, took in the atmosphere with which the other man had filled the room, trying to find his space, his part in it. The doctor's hand was clammy, beefy.

'Take a seat,' the doctor gestured towards a chair pushed far to the left of the table. Jacob looked around himself and pulled the chair to meet the doctor face to face across the wood.

'How can I help you?' Jacob asked.

'Yesterday,' the doctor began, 'Jake, Horace and Boris went for a walk.' The doctor sat tense, hoisted upwards in his chair.

'I see,' the inspector remarked, not having any clue why this information might be important to him.

'You know these characters?' the doctor asked.

'Well,' the inspector paused for thought, 'I know *of* them, as an investigation.'

'It appears,' the doctor went on, 'that Jake might be cured, of sorts.'

Silence fogged the room. *Cured?* The inspector twitched a little, his memories of Jake clear as yesterday; the time lapsed nearly five years. 'I see,' he repeated.

'They went to the pub and had a conversation within which Jake demonstrated a true normality; that is, he didn't know that he was a killer and more than that, he didn't like the idea that he might be.'

'I see,' the inspector returned, lost for any other response.

'We'd like you to take a look at him, see what you think, see if there's any reminiscence of the man you…' the doctor mulled some words around in his head before selecting one, '*investigated.*'

The inspector stared at his companion, the words *I see* hummed on his vocal cords but he could not bring himself to say it again. Instead a silence ensued, which the doctor broke without the slightest acknowledgment of the inspector's uncertainty. 'I'll bring him in, you can have a chat.'

The inspector's eyes rolled around the room. 'Perhaps,' he interjected, 'it might be better if I just go and sit in the living area,' his hand waved about him, trying to think of something kind to say about it. 'I'll hang out there for a bit, see what I think of him.'

The doctor thought, tapping his fingers on the desk, he wasn't impatient, just unsure. 'They don't do a great deal,' the doctor paused on the edge of a recommendation, *the right medication for the right illness is always necessary.*

'Perhaps,' the inspector began to suggest, 'you could bring in a spy...'

'We are the spies,' the doctor placed both hands flat on the table as if about to hoist himself up. 'Cameras everywhere, this place and the town are very much covered, Inspector, hence how we know of the conversation. If Jake is lying to his fellow inmates, he will lie to a spy.' The doctor paused to allow the inspector some time to digest this and then continued, 'We were just curious as to how you might find him; go sit in the communal area if you please and let me know what you think.' His beefy hands rushed with blood as his weight pushed down on the desk, his fingertips white, the table unsteady. The doctor was standing now, the inspector looked up at him a little bemused. 'Come,' said the doctor, indicating towards the door.

Back in the communal seating area Boris tried to rouse the others, 'Do you know who he is?' Boris asked his rabble. Jake and Horace looked at him and then at the clock. 'Oh for the love of...!' Boris sighed and turned back to his magazine.

Horace wanted a symphony to explode into the room, a magic infusion of musical art. Jake wanted a vodka. Boris wanted to kill someone. The inspector wanted to go home. The doctor wanted Jake to be a miracle, *his miracle*, the defining medical moment of Dr Rushton's idea: the cured, the corrected, the rehabilitated killer, the one who would put his name in the archives, his memory into the future, his beefy self on the map. The inspector sat amongst them and watched the television with Jake while Horace stared at the floor and Boris flicked nervously through a magazine, over and over again. Imogen returned from her room and sat in the same seat she had left vacant 20 minutes before. Horace looked at the clock, Jake looked at the clock because Horace had looked at the clock, Gill checked her watch. The inspector followed them through this ritual.

'Do you like it here?' the inspector asked, seemingly to the room in general. The rabble looked about them, unsure how to respond, they'd never been asked a direct question of this sort before, not like this, not out in the open. He turned to Jake and looked directly into his vivid blue eyes, unconsciously leaning forward, drawing closer to him. Inspector Jacob

Rodgers studied his own reflection shining back. 'Do you?' the inspector questioned more earnestly.

Jake's blues asunder, 'No,' he said, 'the cream and brown lino and once-white walls are vile, I don't know where I come from but I'm sure it has more class.'

The inspector maintained his gaze, *yes it does*, he thought. 'What are you doing here?' the inspector pushed.

'Boris says I killed someone,' Jake physically wobbled as if a shiver, an entity, had passed through him, 'maybe more than one…' his ending to the sentence trailed off. Jake broke the gaze and looked soulful, his mind trying to recall the tragedy of what Boris had suggested, 'Did I?' he asked.

The inspector looked away as Jake redirected his eyes to recapture his. 'I don't know,' he almost remarked, the thought rushing through his mind, *I don't know what I should say*, so he made a quick decision not to comment. Jake looked down and then at the clock as Horace's head lifted in the corner of his field of vision.

'Who are you again?' Jake asked the inspector.

Jacob thought for a moment, trying to formulate a lie, but decided it best as he had been introduced earlier to be direct, 'Inspector Rodgers,' he paused to allow Jake to take it in. 'From the police,' he clarified.

'Do you know me?' Jake questioned, as if he'd never seen this man before.

'Yes,' The inspector responded, 'I do.'

Jake turned away, as if not willing, not wanting, to take on what that might mean.

Boris's eyes dropped, his ears twitching, burning. Jake got up and left the space. 16 paces long, 10 paces wide. The inspector wanted to go home, where a single malt awaited him. He almost jumped from his seat as Jake strolled away, the thought and taste of the whiskey overpowering his senses, and made his way the few steps across the cream and brown inflicted lino to the office overlooking the space to accost Gill.

Without words, Gill nodded and directed the inspector towards the exit. Opening the door and stepping out of his path, she motioned for him to pass through the air between them and leave. As his right foot touched the concrete of the supposedly outside world, he turned to look at Gill, her white comfy trousers and coat identifying her, giving her an authority: a Level 1 Blue Team authority. He shook his head as if trying to remove a fragment of annoyance, that irritating nudge in the mind's eye, *white coats*.

Jake

A knife flew with precision, a commando precision perfected with care. Several different lengths, shapes and weights had been tested. Several trees had been mutilated in his endeavour to discover the perfect thrust. He would swagger over, twist the knife a bit, give it a shove. From the corner of the room a killing confidence would embrace him, Darren's pointless frantic defence empowering him. Slouched, comfy, in a chair purchased just for the occasion he'd watch his girlfriend – ex-girlfriend – fiddle with the wardrobe contents, locked in a decision repeated daily, *do I wear this one or that one?* Her mind ticking on, bound by the 'you shop, we drop' convenience that had filled the wardrobe to its capacity, shoving Jake's smart (and, he might add, far from cheap) suits and shirts required for his work ever further into the walls of the cupboard, reversing the hours of hot steam with which the Renaissance Clothes Care Company had so meticulously ironed his attire. He had practiced in the park, a target cut crudely into the bark of a tree. Once decided on type, he had purchased several knives to avoid the consent exertion of retrieval and perfected an accurate, Olympic-standard throw.

Rushton

One large building stood proud at the edge of a village, Blue Block, where the rabble resided, surrounded by acres of fields; a row of distant trees marked only the first boundary of the land. Blue Block was headed by Dr Henry Washington, it stood as the headquarters. Via a tunnel beneath its structure lay Orange Block, headed by Dr Jeremy Jefferson. Covert and underground, it invisibly marked the hub of Dr Rushton's idea.

Jake stood silently, arms by his side. Dr Henry Washington and Dr Jeremy Jefferson sat at a table in front of him. Gill stood back in her white coat, not quite as well fitting as another white coat that had arrived in its place for about a week, while Gill lay on a beach in Spain. She checked her watch, the pill round was in ten minutes. Her job was their care, the daily ritual of organising their meals, their pills, their routine. Her canvas plimsoll tapped gently on the mottled cream with brown lino that stretched into the office and into every room of the building. As she lifted her wrist again, Dr Washington waved his beefy hand and asked if she would prefer to get on with her chores. Without verbal response, Gill turned on her heels with a swish and left the room.

Dr Washington questioned Jake, 'How are you feeling Jake?'

Jake shrugged.

Dr Washington continued, 'You have often talked of your discontent with society, how are feeling about that?'

Jake met Dr Washington square in the eye and said, 'I think I miss it.'

Dr Washington suppressed a smile, 'What do you miss about it?'

'Living.' Jake lifted his arms up and out to indicate the broader possibilities of life. *16 paces long, 10 paces wide.* 'I think I need something to do,' Jake stated, his arms still in the air.

Dr Jefferson shifted slightly in his seat. He was a neuroscientist and the tech brains of the outfit. He wore a long white coat over his corduroy jeans and ironed shirt, his hands were clean and nimble. He held his body with ease and brought a calm to the room over Dr Washington's sweaty beef. Dr Jefferson's head was down as he scanned the open file in front of him, he flipped over a page and then another. Jake stood, arms still in the air, frozen in time, waiting for the moment to change, for someone else in the room to propel the situation forward so that he could put his arms down. Dr Jefferson slid one of the pages he had been discernibly gazing at over the table towards Dr Washington. Dr Washington put his beefy right hand on to it and nodded.

Dr Jefferson finally spoke; Jake released his arms from the air. 'Jake...' he began, with a soft instructive informed tone, 'How would you like to work, Jake?' he asked, changing the octaves to an inquisitive stance.

Jake still stood, his arms limp by his side, Dr Jefferson continued without waiting for a response, 'It won't pay very much, but it would keep you busy, save you from just sitting around watching television.'

Jake half nodded, he was certainly bored of the television. Dr Jefferson went on, 'All the jobs here are of a manual type – landscaping, gardening, shop assistant, bar work, that kind of thing – not what you're used to coming from an executive position, but it will give you something to do, be more active, help you feel a little more normal.'

Jake tilted his head and gazed into the air, his mind blank, his posture a man in thought. He nodded, absent minded, and so it was done: Jake was to work, the next stage in his rehabilitation, the next step towards his cure.

Horace

Horace's right arm swung, brushing against his mass to the rhythm of his bounce. His wife's car had faulted the evening before and was now parked on a forecourt awaiting the doctor of engines to revive its spluttering hulk back into life. His wife had driven him to work every day for fifteen years. He had not seen the point in this ritual himself, despite the fact that the lengthy alternative journey on this day would stride him into work 15 minutes late. His wife insisted on time each day together, although they journeyed mostly in silence unless a gas bill or their daughter was up for discussion. But it was important, his wife needed to remember him, to know he was still there.

Having not paid the premium cost to grant him a replacement car during its treatment, Horace now marched to the bus stop 200 yards from his house. Instead of just moving his eyes, Horace lifted his entire head to bring the bus information and times into view. He was dressed in one of his regimented dark suits with light shirts, sale-bought and never fitted, their monotony broken by the random selection of a different tie each day, mostly gifts from his daughter to cover Christmas and birthdays for the past 12 years. His suit stood proud around his bulky body (capable of lifting extraordinary weights) which supported the head from which his eyes scanned the information for his transport needs. His unwavering left arm, from the end of which his hand gripped a black leather briefcase, felt hot. Feeling its presence Horace listed the bones in his head, *ulna, radius, humerus*, moving up to the shoulder he concentrated, trying to envision the skeleton picture he had studied, *scapula, clavicle*.

Arriving at the office 15 minutes late, he was surprised and irritated by his boss's glare through the door's gap; Mr Blanchett's beady head peered round the veneered cheap office installation. Horace had underestimated the bus travel times during this busy period of the morning, it was true, he was late; tomorrow he would leave earlier, catch the twenty-to. He manoeuvred himself around his desk and placed his black leather briefcase next to the *new dynamic office seating with wheels* and felt less important than he had only seconds before during the journey in.

After settling in, he picked up his black leather briefcase from his sitting position, placed it on his desk and opened it using his three digit personalised code (currently set as 003). Horace stared into its emptiness, rummaged around in the space and closed it again, clicking the three digit personalised coded lock back into its safety position. Horace perused the room, ticking off an attendance record in his head, all his staff were present. No wait, *Jeffery, always fucking Jeffery!* Where the hell was Jeffery? He clicked the button on his desk phone to activate an orange flashing light which indicated the taping of a message. Horace picked up the receiver and listened. Jeffery's weary voice mapped out a day-off plan of ill health. Horace's mind snapped a little, *you don't know who you're fucking with you insolent little prick.* He slammed down the receiver, then picked it up again and flipped open his desk diary to the back and scanned the list of employee home phone numbers, pausing at Camilla's he glanced up to see what she was wearing that day, then dialled Jeffery's number. A chirpy Jeffery voice opened the call with an uplifting 'Hello?' Horace paused, the crackling of the phone line engaging his attention. Horace was starting to feel angry this day. Filling the silence that crackled down the phone line, Jeffery repeated his hello but this time his cadence lifted the trailing end of what suddenly seemed like a long word, as if asking a question. Horace waited. Jeffery became agitated and asked again. Horace returned his receiver back to its clicked position against its dialling body and smiled.

'Good morning, Mr Conway,' a cheery acknowledgment echoed around Horace's brain, he shook his head. 'Not a good morning, Mr Conway?'

Rather than simply moving his eyes, Horace lifted his whole head to bring the embodiment of the voice into view, 'No... car's in the garage.'

'Oh, just a service I hope?'

'No...'

'You alright Mr Conway?'

'Yes.'

'We're going for drinks after work if you fancied? Might make the day seem better.'

'Yes.'

'Right... well, I'll grab you at five.'

'Yes…' *Er, no,* the word had been uttered without thought of its consequences. Horace shook his head again, more deliberately this time, lengthening the pause to allow him time to think of an excuse or perhaps he'd go, not sure. Feeling his thought process too long Horace nodded, 'Okay.' He'd remember a commitment later.

Horace erased the message from Jeffery and sat back in his *new dynamic office seating with wheels.* Tapping some buttons Horace scanned information to see what Jeffery (*fucking Jeffery*) was supposed to be dealing with today and emailed it over to Veronica, she'd hate that. *Toilet dispenser.*

At lunch Horace went out, a Mediterranean deli he knew served the best olive and sun-dried tomato bread in town. Horace went there and purchased a mozzarella and basil sandwich to take away and then jumped on the number 6 bus to Jeffery's house, his fresh hand-made sandwich bouncing around his black leather briefcase alone. Horace was 47 years old, 13 years away from his free bus pass, which he would receive five years before he would retire; he had calculated how much this would save him already and looked forward to the day. Despite his wife's insistence to drive him to work each day, she did not often collect him.

Inspector Jacob Rodgers.

Jake Hamilton had used the local common as a target test ground in preparation for his girlfriend's (ex-girlfriend's) murder, practicing on random trees; he'd even cut a crude target into one particular tree which centred the others. Inspector Rodgers remembered Jake well, his blasé attitude and unprepared, un-thought out protection for himself had left the inspector with an easy catch. Cocky and revengeful, Jake had planned to simply pick off his friends one by one. Getting away with the initial murder of his oldest friend Darren Parker, he'd moved swiftly on to the planning of his next victim. Caught for his girlfriend's (ex-girlfriend's) murder, Derek Faulkner (the collar up, finger-clicking twat) was saved from becoming the next victim. An outline of his demise was found on scraps of paper.

Jake had talked about Derek at length during his compulsory visits with a psychiatric physician. Angry and ready to make Derek the next, he had talked bitterly of his friend, while his voice spoke in an uncannily calm and controlled manner, relaxed in his environment as if he swaggered around on a lazy Sunday afternoon, totally at odds with the words that framed his hatred and planned the destiny of people who knew him.

Jake had hated the lies and considered the consequences of even the supposedly innocent, kind, white ones, as another friend betrayed his trust. What if someone told you that you looked good in something, would you wear it more? What if they had lied? How many white lies does it take to alter the course of your life, as you buy wardrobe after wardrobe of hideous rags, paint a picture that everyone laughs at or write a book that no-one understands? How many untruths remained, nurturing, shielding him from unnecessary distress, and how many served as a continual hidden embarrassment?

At interview Jake had admitted the intention of several more killings to come, giving the inspector an easy path to court. He had been able to prove this intention to the jury with a mound of evidence that Jake himself had admitted, but despite years of service and many confrontations with dangerous men, Inspector Jacob Rodgers cringed slightly, faced with a man bearing his own name. The inspector had found Jake disturbingly calm and unnerving. A matter of fact attitude while describing the scene as Catherine squirmed away from his twisting knife. Only five years from this moment had passed and they were already saying that he was nearly cured, *cured?* How was this possible? He seemed only not to remember, so far as the inspector could tell.

Imogen

Imogen crouched on the floor, her knees pulled up to her chest, her arms wrapped around them. If she had allowed herself the freedom, she might have rocked slightly. With the curtain open a spooky orange light focused the room, dingy and hazy as if Imogen had smoked very recently. The room's furniture could be mapped out, its contents bulky lumps around the space. She scanned it as if waiting for a predator to appear from the darkness, clasping her legs as if her life depended on it. The shadows she cast rotated the room, as if a lighthouse spun its circuit outside the window, creating flickers of a ghostly presence. She pulled her knees in tighter, her heart beating against her leg. Her eyes welled up as the pressure behind them, deep in the mind, fought its way forward. The shadows beckoning her out of herself, the room light and aired, the darkness within.

Someone had once queried, more wondered perhaps, in Imogen's presence, how many roll ups you get from a 50g pack of tobacco. Imogen smoked roll ups but didn't know. She waited. On the opening of a fresh pack she relieved a paper from its packaging and rolled herself a cigarette. She opened a notebook and drew a vertical line on the page. *One.*

The Diary of Rose Heather Roberts

Life's a bitch. Then you are one.

I have this fantasy, drawing a gun from the inside of my jacket and holding it to the temple of my enemy. Bang.

But I'd never do it.

I've made a decision. To live. Now, before it's all over, before I reach 30, before it starts again at 40. Before it's too late.

Rushton

Horace, Boris and Jake were to visit the pub again. A handwritten letter had found its way to the highly organised desk of Nurse Gill. She studied its contents, brief and to the point it stated that Horace, Boris and Jake were to attend the pub again. Clapping her hands in an unusual fashion she marched into their space, whisked them up, handed Horace some money and sent them out the door to the pub.

They shuffled there, almost in line and in time, arrived at the pub, purchased a drink and sat. Suspicious, they sat silently, struggling to find something to say.

Inspector Jacob Rodgers talks to
Dr Henry Washington about Jake

Dr Henry Washington relaxed back into his *new dynamic office seating with wheels*; across from him sat Inspector Jacob Rodgers, the slightly irritating, scruffy looking policemen that had visited him often, too often in recent weeks. The doctor's executive oak desk seemed bulky and dividing, separating the men as if to protect them from one another; his files flanked the broadness, always standing in neat and ordered attention. An ornate pen pot caught the inspector's gaze as he scanned the room, it reminded him of something, a holiday tourist gift perhaps. Inspector Jacob Rodgers removed a notebook from his inside pocket and held it up along with his pen, nodding it at the doctor to confirm approval. Dr Henry Washington sipped from his water glass, a strangely comfortable but pregnant silence sat between them. Dr Henry Washington checked his watch, then glanced at the clock hanging on the wall to the left of the desk.

'So, Doctor,' the inspector began, 'tell me about Jake.'

The doctor had been waiting for this question, and launched into a monologue, accentuating his words with expressive hand movements, 'Well, where to start... Jake's smart. He always took care of his appearance, not exactly cheap shirts and suits for work. His clothing expressed an intricate part of his frustration and confusion about life.' The inspector squinted and scribbled in his note pad – *annoyed by attire*. Dr Henry Washington went on, 'He was happy with his existence, in the sense that he was happy to exist. Being alive was not the issue, it was the world in which he found himself living that upset him.

'He talked about a ball bouncing amongst different parts of himself, an insightful and self-aware analogy, about his consciousness being passed around his own head as he tried to figure out his thoughts. But the more he thought the more angry he became, forced to be this suited man that made deals, made money. He struggled with the definition of *friend* and *mate*, having been let down by them both. This led to questions like "what does it mean to let go, let go of what?" The meanings and personal experience of fate, love and freedom, nature and its unpredictable uncontrollable power, man's ignorance and greed, which in turn (as the mind explored deeper) made him feel...' Dr Henry Washington's eyes wondered up as he rattled his mind for the right word, 'suffocated,' he announced resting his gaze once more on the inspector. His gaze lingered for a moment, before he continued, 'His personal space seemed to close in under pressure, suffocating his spirit. He struggled daily – hourly – with his urban surroundings, yet found himself uncomfortable with nature, not an earthy man.

'He understood the advantage and the convenience of the things around him, yet hated them. Understanding them was not the way to find peace with them. He had been political, an attempt to have a say, to make a difference to that which he did not approve, but the fight in itself was the problem, the constant disapproval. So many people, so many ideas! Jake couldn't find a way to be content against this battle, but conversely to remove himself would leave him alone and lost in nature, too powerful and unpredictable for him, too much to learn... to fight with nature would be just another fight, as creatures eat his crop and the weather ruins his plans for future growth.'

The doctor took another sip of water, then continued without leaving any room for interjection, 'He watched sci fi; Star Trek spurred a dream for him, a world free from these things, a world where money had no meaning, where food simply appeared to you out of the wall. The idea of the exploration of other worlds provided him with an endless fascination. Worlds far from this one. He could not imagine for himself the ideal world, Jake is not a sociable, kindly man, so a world of happy-clappy peace wouldn't suit him any more than an angry war driven one. To explore the galaxy and its changing sociological patterns offered a chance, a chance to find his place. But he did not believe that man – even in the distant future – would ever be at such peace with itself to be able to serve the galaxy with the compassion demonstrated in his favourite television programme. This left Jake in a void, a void that meant his existence had no future. No Buddhist philosophy of re-birth, no sense that goodness in this life would help him in a future one; his small existence seemed to make no real difference to man's self and the harmful power he exudes. One day he would be dead, and so? The consequences of such an act seemed neither here nor there to Jake, "So what? What difference does it make what I do?" He even considered the compassion required for his future to exist, his rebirth to be amongst the Star Trekking future; he considered the idea that if we are ever to explore with such compassion, then we must start the process today, compassion can be amongst us, that we must choose our traits of path. "Be the change you want to see in the world" and all that… But on reflection, he thought that the best change is to rid the world of these hideous people. A belief that now taints his own life, held too by the jury that convicted him and by the harmless voting public who wished to feel safe in their neighbourhoods…'

Dr Henry Washington twitched with pleasure, leaning back in his *dynamic office seating with wheels*. He felt proud of his speech, very comfortable with his analysis of Jake. Inspector Jacob Rodgers crunched his mind, wishing he had the educational background to deliver a counter argument that the doctor would respect. There was something else, something more to the calm, direct nature of Jake's intentions and two completed murders.

'Clever boy.' he remarked, bringing his pen down on the pad in an emphatic full stop.

'I'm sorry, Inspector, what did you say?' Dr Washington lifted the 'you say' in his speech, trying to sound indifferent but polite about the inspector's quiet comment, Believing it to be praise to him.

'Thank you,' Inspector Jacob Rodgers extended his hand as he stood to leave, 'thank you for your time, Dr Washington.'

At the door, Inspector Rodgers turned and, sounding as if he were scratching his head, asked, 'Are you saying, Doctor, that Jake killed simply because he didn't think that it mattered?'

Dr Henry Washington relaxed back in his *dynamic seating* and entwined his fingers, 'Yes. Darren fondled Jake's first girlfriend, betraying him when he was 15.'

'15!' the inspector repeated in a soft tone.

'Yes, 15. He held on to his anger all his life, one rage building into the next, eventually bleeding into life itself, into its structure. Then he finally figured that it didn't matter what he did, because the world was crap. Jake's mind an intricate montage of his life; he's a clever man, just very self-obsessed and self-motivated. Jake is a ball of anger, manifested over years of tiny incidents, rolling like a snowball, collecting more and more – small annoyances, little let downs – building and building until it became too big and he had to release it, and then bang! He went camping with Darren.'

'I see,' the inspector's mind turned in thought, wondering if Jake was not actually trying to *be the change* as he killed those who he thought were spoiling the world somehow. Which meant, surely, that it did matter?

As if reading the inspector's mind Dr Washington interrupted his thoughts, projecting his voice as if the inspector was suddenly further away, 'Ridding the world of these people mattered, but it was Jake's world, his personal upset world – these people were not dangerous or generally horrible in any way – he was not creating a change for the betterment of our future, the future of mankind, in this self-motivated revenge. The rules of society no longer mattered to him, he didn't and doesn't respect it, and that includes us. He thinks we've got it all wrong, he thinks we're mad.'

Dr Washington paused, thinking for a moment, 'His revenge towards his friends was personal,' he continued, 'his hatred towards society just enabled him to justify his actions, although it was the betrayal of his friends that lead him to hate society. It is a circle of events, Inspector, a vivid tumult of images collated into an intricate montage of simulated involvement.'

'I see.' Inspector Jacob Rodgers stared down at his open notebook, his head still being scratched. A little hesitantly he posed another question, 'In your professional opinion, Doctor, do you think that Jake – giving consideration to his hatred towards society – that he might have been a threat to it?'

'You mean, when his revenge list of friends ran out, would he have started to plot against society, to blow up parliament for instance?' Dr Henry Washington composed his sentence as a question but was not looking for an answer, 'It is possible,' the doctor paused and nodded to himself, 'I wouldn't put it past him.'

'I see. Thank you, Doctor.'

'Inspector, Jake is a clever man. That intelligence provides him with the ability to deceive us, we are aware of that, but it also provides us with an opportunity to teach him, help him to adjust the perspective he carries on life, re-train his mind. He has the intelligence to understand.'

'Intelligent enough to believe himself right, Doctor? Intelligent enough to believe there is nothing he could learn from you that he doesn't already understand?'

'Intelligent enough to find his peace, Inspector, to understand his own way of thinking. Intelligent enough to re-establish right from wrong.'

'Whose right, Doctor? Whose wrong? Whose ideals are you asking him to follow, society's?'

'There are many questions, many, that do not carry a right or wrong answer, many ways of doing or thinking about things. It is not important that Jake likes or dislikes society, he has a right to his opinion. But you cannot dismiss the fundamentals, Inspector, of whether or not murder is wrong. This we can teach him.'

'I see. Thank you again, Doctor,' and with that, Inspector Jacob Rodgers left, his head still itchy.

Rushton

Horace looked at the clock, so Jake began the ritual of following suit. It was his day off. Having asked the doctors if he had attended a gym in his former life and with the answer a nodding affirmative, he had opted for something extra physical to get himself back into shape, two days a week: landscaping was Jake's new line of work. But on this day, at this moment, clock watching on his day off, his focus caught Gill as his eyes manoeuvred up towards the white rimmed plastic affair attached silently to the wall, above the office that overlooked and monitored the activities of this space, 16 paces long, 10 paces wide. He steadied his focus and regarded Gill, an enquiring tilt of his head softened his intensity, but it still caused Gill to shuffle a little under his gaze. Since the pub and the inspector's enquiring eyes and ears, Jake had taken more care over his appearance, *I belong in more class.* He was still wearing the same clothes but they seemed arranged differently, his adult muscular structure revealing the man behind the madness, his soft blue eyes and slightly fluffy hair flopped free from its styling gel. Jake was a fine looking man. A little embarrassed, Gill glanced at her watch, but didn't notice the second hand jerking its way round the dial to complete its minute; she went to fetch the afternoon pills.

Horace

It was three o'clock. Afternoon tea. A nice cup of cha with a piece of well-presented cake was just the ticket. Rather than just moving his eyes, Horace lifted his whole head to check the specials board, on the odd occasion a special had grabbed his taste buds and inspired him to order something more substantial. His regimented dark suits and light shirts were shop bought and never fitted, yet they did not strain at the seam or sag lose over his frame. Today he had chosen a blue tie with red and yellow flowers, a gift from his daughter, though which birthday or Christmas it represented Horace couldn't be sure. He lifted his briefcase onto the round café table. Horace always visited traditional tea rooms, Starbucks could go back to America, Horace was British and with that national identify came a sense of tea room pride. He liked the wholesome girls that worked in them, traditional tea rooms that served the elderly and refined. His black leather briefcase dominated the table area, a quick shuffle of condiments and its emptiness was manoeuvred into position. After his quick visit to Jeffery's house the day before, he had adjusted his three digit security coded lock to 004. Clicking it back into place, the new code set, he lifted his black leather briefcase from the table and arranged it tight to his leg on the floor. Letting go of the handle, Horace rested back into the wooden country style chair and awaited service.

'Hello, Mr Conway, how are you today?'

A tall girl (or at least tall from Horace's seated position, forcing him to elevate his head once more) stood beside him. As he lifted his head he manoeuvred his eyes to take in every aspect of his waitress's bodily being, searching the cloth folds for messages – a slight pull on the skirt, a loose thread indicating a code – Horace took a mental note. Poised with pad and pencil for order instructions, Horace's waitress waited, as his eyes reached the pad he remembered his cover purpose for being there and ordered a Lady Grey tea and a slice of Victoria sponge. She scribbled something down (presumably *a Lady Grey tea and slice of Victoria sponge* or the abbreviated version of those instructions) and turned on her heel, her short black skirt and white shirt creasing with the movement, the loose thread lifting slightly in the air. Horace waited.

Rushton

Gill decided to re-connect the clock, just to see. A caretaker was called. No small-talk was offered as he arranged his ladder in front of the spy window that overlooked the space, 16 paces long, 10 paces wide. Horace looked up. He wanted to look at Gill but knew that she would be looking at him, so decided to avoid any confusion by looking at the clock, above, around, and through the caretaker who stood on his ladder fiddling with the white rimmed plastic affair. Jake looked at the clock, or at least what he could see of it, and Gill checked her watch. The caretaker got down from his ladder, folded it in half and strolled off. The clock ticked, one second, then another. The thin sweeping hand that counted out the once all-consuming *tick, tick,* jerked its way round; 15 seconds, 30 seconds, a minute passed. Horace looked at the clock, Jake looked at the clock because Horace had, Gill checked her watch again, but for the first time wondered, *why?* She stood in the doorway of the office that overlooked the communal area (16 paces long, 10 paces wide) staring at her watch, wondering why. She watched the jerking second hand sweep its way round the circle of roman numerals printed on its face. *Tick, tick.* Boris looked up from his magazine to fix his eyes on Horace, the clock behind him.

Inspector Jacob Rodgers talks to Dr Washington about Imogen

Inspector Jacob Rodgers was back. Dr Henry Washington took a deep breath.

'Tell me, Doctor, why did Imogen do it?' Inspector Jacob Rodgers was settled back in his chair, he put down the notepad he held in his hand and rested his pencil on its surface.

With the inspector poised in readiness to listen to his educated and intelligent evaluation, Dr Washington wet his lips in preparation for his embellished analysis. 'Well,' he began, almost modestly, 'Imogen had searched for happiness, expecting more and more things to make her happy. Demanded it – not always verbally but most certainly inwardly – from the people around her. She had believed that you can only know happiness having first experienced despair. She believed that there was boredom in paradise, if everything was fluffy and nice she might go crazy for excitement. She thought of a time, but couldn't recall one, when she was happy. Perhaps this time had only been for a fleeting moment, but in that moment there had been no room for boredom, no need for bigger and better material possessions. Happiness had come from within.'

Dr Washington paused, struck by his own turn of phrase, 'Happiness had come from within,' he repeated. 'This led her to believe that it was her mind that controlled her, but she knew her mind and "Imogen" were in it together: they were the same thing. So she wanted to learn how to tap into herself, how to feel in control, how to stop being a spectator. She wanted to stop her mind's endless thinking, as if thought itself was in control. This process included in its complexities the removal of thought and the reaction to emotion, trying not to think too much, trying to be a part of her emotions. But despite her efforts she felt a darkness ever increasing, frustration ever more the drive as she removed thought and replaced it with raw emotion. Anger and jealousy became the new engulfing embodiment of her world... And then, Miracle!'

Dr Washington paused again, leaning back in his chair, 'Imogen explained how, as she struggled with the hardened summer soil, all her world made a bizarre sense. She was transfixed by the unquestionably *reality* of the moment, the fantasy lived, the past and future, now.' Dr Washington leant forward, took a sip of water and looked questioningly at the inspector, quite sure that his companion wouldn't fully understand.

Inspector Jacob Rodgers picked up his pad and pencil and lent back again in his chair. 'I see,' he said, simply. After a pause, Jacob tapped his pencil against his top lip, feeling the contact between himself and the worn down rubber on the end, and asked almost as if thinking out loud, 'Did you ever direct her towards Buddhism, Doctor?'

A little perturbed that the inspector had understood more than he had anticipated, Dr Washington found himself seething slightly that a scruffy policeman might find the audacity to recommend a course of action. 'Counsellors recommend religion, Inspector. I administer help.'

Jacob nodded, *I see*. Dr Washington snatched his glass and then, remembering himself, sipped gently from its rim. Inspector Jacob Rodgers took refuge by looking around the room; a heavy sideboard in fine condition stood proudly against the wall, its fixings highly polished, its sturdy wood unblemished and dust free. He asked the doctor how much he thought he might get at auction. Dr Washington twitched his head as if trying to avoid an annoying fly buzzing around his face, 'Somewhere in the region of six hundred pounds, I'd imagine.'

The inspector examined the wood and fixings a little more closely, 'I would have thought you'd get more, Doctor. You should get someone else to come take a look at it.'

Dr Henry Washington stared at the sideboard, *aren't we a clever boy today*. 'Was there anything else, Inspector?'

Inspector Jacob Rodgers had moved his eyes and thoughts away from the sideboard and sat quietly, as if in his own private study, contemplating the world. 'Why does she visit her dead mother?'

Dr Washington sat back and took a few moments to collate his response, 'Her mother...' he began, as if stating the magic reason behind all things, as if he had just had an inspiration, as if he (rather than the inspector) had tabled the question. 'Well, Imogen's father had worked hard for his family,' Inspector Jacob Rodgers settled back in his chair, sensing the length of the answer to come, 'he had made best the skills and opportunities afforded to him. Imogen and Vincent's father had been the light of the family, the Santa at Christmas, the financial provider, the jolly at the weekends, the source of love and affection, all that brought a soft light flickering to the corners of the darkest room. A light that has become erratic and engulfed with sadness, its usual soft and calming nature now a pain transcended from year to year. Imogen uses a single candle to light her visits with her mother, she has talked of this, and of her father.'

Dr Washington reached for his water and took a sip before continuing, 'His tragic death left a void in the hearts of those that remained. Her mother, of course, feeling the wrench more acutely than others. But as years progressed, the wrench inflicted a void in his daughter's world, as her mother's loss infiltrated all that Imogen tried to be.'

Dr Washington took another sip, enjoying the suspense he felt the pause create, 'Too young, perhaps, to appreciate the depths of her mother's broken heart, she hated the attention that was lost to her,' he continued. 'Her mother's love belonged to a past that she could not remember, when she needed it here and always now. From this point onwards Imogen related each and every difficulty to the last, building endlessly, each one adding another reason to be angry, another damming trend in the world that hated her. Her mother's deteriorating health over the years had served only to add – as Imogen saw it – yet another strain to her already challenging life.' Dr Washington raised his eyebrows and gave a half shrug, 'She had no real memory of her father, but his figure, in spirit, haunted her growing years and consumed her adult ones. And all the time her mother's disconnection to her children's worlds became more and more of a painful issue to her.

'Unsympathetic, as I said, to her mother's loss, Imogen resented the attention a dead man's past had removed from her living present. Those early years of confusion helped to shape the totally inward connection that Imogen had developed with herself alone. An attention seeking child, she grew into a self-consumed adult. Her motives and thoughts always a vision generated from the Imogen within; the outside world a motion picture of timeless space and inconsiderate people.'

The inspector tried to list back the points, skipping over parts where the Good Doctor had repeated himself or become grandiloquent. 'Does she visit her mother because of guilt?' he asked finally.

'I don't believe she killed her mother, Inspector.'

'That's not what I asked. Guilt over her anger towards her, maybe.'

'No,' Dr Washington was determined to be the smarter of the two men, 'she visits her mother because without her she has no-one to blame.'

'I see,' the inspector tapped his pencil on the side of his notebook. 'What of her two names?' he asked tentatively.

A surging irritation started to leak its way out of the doctor's pores, Jacob was clearly pushing Dr Washington's patience up towards its limit. 'Imogen was like a nickname, something your mates would call you. Different names can make you feel like a different person; it gave her confidence. She never had a split personality in the traditional sense; she knew what she was doing, who she was. It was just a way of being something else. Rose wrote the diaries, as her true self (so to speak). It was Imogen who went to the pub and Imogen who killed Miracle, but Rose who expressed her fantasy, her anger. She was never more than one person, she was always both – in fact I'll re-define that – she was always Rose; Imogen is just a name, it was never a personality distinct from Rose.'

'I see.' Inspector Jacob Rodgers nodded slightly and jotted in his notebook.

'It's like a compliment, the name Imogen. If you left this room and one of the nurses passing you in the corridor commented that you looked good today or that they liked your tie, wouldn't you feel slightly more confident as you left the building, as opposed to how you felt leaving my office? The name Imogen made her feel better about herself in the same way, like a compliment, that's all.'

'Why attach a surname to it?' Inspector Jacob Rodgers flipped through his notebook, he knew the name but felt the need to portray the policeman thing, to stall the doctor, to bumble a little, to help the doctor realise that nothing is forgotten. Why, he wasn't sure, he didn't know, but he didn't much trust the doctor, didn't much care for him at all. 'Baker, Imogen Baker. She had post addressed to her under this full name. Why do that, Doctor?'

'I think it's fair to say, Inspector, that Imogen took things to their extreme extents. The name became a part of her inner obsession and confusion, leading of course to Miracle's death.'

'I see.' The inspector paused, not happy with this limited explanation but deciding to push on. He flipped a few more pages, landing on a page that reminded him to check the records for Jake's driving licence, a check long since completed. 'In her diaries she repeatedly writes of a fantasy where she shoots someone, but she didn't use a gun for Miracle…' the statement hung in the slightly stale, musty room without the need for a direct question.

'Perhaps she couldn't get one,' the doctor shuffled a little and clearly eager for the inspector to leave, offered a quick response. The Inspector Roberts had been called in to assist in the evaluation of Jake (it would not be possible to release him without police involvement) but questions about Imogen? The inspector was meddling now.

'I see... It isn't possible then,' the inspector continued, as Dr Washington sighed, almost repressing a yawn, 'that this fantasy was meant for someone else?'

'Yes it's possible. But she's never mentioned anyone else.'

'I see. Thank you once again for your time, Doctor.'

The Diary of Rose Heather Roberts

Why? Ask it till you're sick of it.

Everybody has dreams, fears and anthropomorphisms. Do you think I'm antagonistic? Why am I asking you? You're me.

When do moments like this begin to feel like always?

It's strange isn't it how you can be in a room full of people and feel really alone, but stand in a field with no-one for miles and feel overcrowded?

I have this fantasy. I take a gun from my jacket and hold to the temple of my enemy. Bang.

Rushton

Horace looked at the clock, a white rimmed plastic affair seemingly in keeping with its place of residence. Gill checked her father's watch, the baby hand jerking its way round the dial, past the roman numerals marking the hours and the little lines indicating each second as it clicked from one to the next. Jake was planting a rhododendron in a pot in an attempt to pretty up a concrete floored square near the post office. It wasn't always landscaping, it was sometimes building work too, replacing paving or fixing a fence. Jake worried about his hands, his soft pen-wielding fingers were becoming rough and hardened.

An assortment of tools were laden across the back of the van, the van into which Jake climbed two times each week at 8am precisely. A man with a van collected him. Spades, trowels, shears, hammers, pliers, tools, wire, wood posts, a reel of plastic garden fencing. Stuff. Jake stood staring at it.

'You're not planning on doing anything crazy with any of that are you?' the man with the van asked, a veiled instruction.

'What's the gun for?' Jake enquired.

'Shooting rodents.'

'Rodents? Right, you get a lot of rodents?'

'No, not many, but if you see one got to get rid of it or there'll be plenty more.'

'Don't you have some kind of poison for that sort of thing?'

'Yeah, but I like to shoot 'em.'

'Right... Are you like me, I mean... you know... in this place?'

'Do you think if I was like you they'd give me gun?'

'No, I suppose not... but if you weren't like me, I'm not sure you'd be shooting rodents... with a hand gun.' Shooting rodents with a hand gun, *a hand gun*, crazy fucking people. Jake scratched his head.

'Here,' the man with the van shoved a sandwich into Jake's newly roughed and hardening right hand, 'cheese and tomato.'

'Great,' Jake eyed his sandwich with distaste: cheese and tomato. Jake was sure he had more class, where was the Parma ham and rocket?

'And here, I got you a water holder, attaches to your belt,' the man with the van shook it at him, 'seeing as you drink so much water.'

'Thanks.' Jake took the holder with his rough, hardening left hand and nodded gratefully.

Jake drank lots of water for two reasons, the first was his health, he was sure (and the nodding doctors had confirmed) that he would have been the type to have gone to the gym, and types that go to the gym were also types who cared about what food and drink they put into their bodies. Water was good. Essential. The second was to help flush out the drugs they probably added to his food and other drinks. It didn't occur to him that they might add it to his water, but if he had considered it he would have thought four things. Firstly, that the man with the van drank the same water, decanted from a large plastic container with a tap in the back of the van, and he had a gun and therefore was not one of them. Secondly however, it would have occurred to him, moving on from the first thought, that poison may well be more dangerous than a gun – it could be added without notice – and if the man with the van was one of them, maybe he'd used poison in his former life and was safer with a gun… this place worked in mysterious ways after all. Given the second possibility to be true (although it was the less likely of the two) Jake would be left unsure whether or not the water was safe, so the third consideration would have been back to basics: does it taste funny? It would have then occurred to him, while swishing, gurgling and slapping his lips in a wine tasting manner (he was sure he came from more class) that if he drank enough water, 'they' might worry about over-dosing him, thereby reducing or removing the drug anyway. Four considerations ending in the conclusion that the odds were on his side – the water was safe and to drink lots of it was safer.

Inspector Jacob Rodgers

Inspector Jacob Rodgers settled back, relaxing into his sofa. In his hand a fine single malt swirled around clinking ice. He took a breath and tried to focus his thoughts, but the only words that came to mind in repeated motions, dancing to their own rhythmic tune were these: *What's going on?!* Images of Jake projected onto the walls of his mind, images of Jake's story, of the investigation… his thoughts outlined their history of murder, and with them came the answer to Jake's question: *yes, you did kill someone; more than one.*

Rushton

At the New Wave pub Boris sat opposite Jake. It was another day release ordered by Dr Washington and ushered by Gill, who wore a white coat that didn't fit quite as exactly as another white coat. A wide table, bulky and wooden, filled the space between them; a candle holder sat to one side, but no candle rested (either burnt down or new) within its cradle. Prints of great artists adorned the walls around them. Each man held in his grasp a pint. Each man's eyes remained averted from the other's, flickering from wood table to pint, to candle holder, to pint, to wood table, the silence strangely comfortable for two men so estranged. Boris began, 'Nice here isn't it?'

Jake nodded and looked around him, his reaction positive, but his mind elsewhere, 'What do you think of Horace?' Jake asked, as if enquiring after a friend recently introduced.

Boris raised his eyebrows, 'Weird. He's never killed anyone you know.' Boris wasn't asking, Boris was stating an informed fact.

'So what's he doing here then?' Jake sipped at his pint, seemingly unaffected by this new information.

'Well he's mad isn't he?! He *thinks* he has, *thinks* he's killed people, proper nuts is that one. I mean I know we've killed people, but to think you have when you haven't, well it's just nuts isn't it?' Boris flipped his hand in the air, 'I understand if you have killed someone and don't remember – blank it out if it's too much – but to think you have when you haven't, well it's just not real is it?' but Boris wasn't asking, Boris was stating. 'He kept cut outs, pictures and internet stuff, loads of info about women. The potential was there. His wife called them in you know,' Boris wasn't asking, he was stating an informed fact, 'snooped round the garage or something, found all this stuff, the cut outs, pictures and stuff and called the police.' Boris took a swig of his pint. 'Thought he was a geezer, was right cool was old Horace, but he's not your made it man. He wanted to be you, Jake, someone like you: good job, smart suits, smart car, nice watch. Bet you always wanted a wife and kid, that'd be right! He's got a daughter you know, but never hurt her.' Boris looked out into the room, his pint in hand.

'But wasn't there a girl?' Jake asked.

'Yeah, stalked her, weird. I mean to be fair to the girl, a man Horace's size loitering outside your bedroom window, you'd be shitting it too. He is a bit creepy, but he never meant her any harm, he was just gathering information for his fantasies.'

Jake pictured Horace in his head, *was he creepy?* 'Fantasies?' he asked.

'Horace believes he's some sort of undercover spy or something.'

Jake raised an eyebrow, *interesting*. 'I heard there was a guy as well?' Jake enquired.

'Oh yeah! Got on a bus and went to his place, wrote something on his garden wall, but he's never killed anyone I'm telling you. Carried an empty briefcase, they reckon that the number code he used to lock it represented the amount of people he'd killed, I bet he told them that; nuts.' Boris twisted his right index finger into his temple, 'Nuts! I'm telling you.'

Jake put down his pint as he leaned forward, 'Why wasn't I just a bit nuts, a bit weird? Why did I have to kill someone?' Jake's mind floated off away from Horace, he didn't really care if Horace had killed or not.

'You don't want to be any weirder Jake, you just want to be less angry, then you'd be alright. I mean these people you killed...' the remainder of the sentence, lifted at the end to introduce a coming question, waited. 'Why were these people's opinions and behaviour so important to you, Jake?'

'Who said they were?'

'You killed them, you killed them. You could have walked away – I mean ultimately you just wanted them to disappear. Does it matter now? Does it? Whatever it was they did. I mean, you could still be living your high flying life.'

'Who said I lived a high flying life?'

'You got nice clothes, designer stuff, you're not a Primark shopper are you and you've got a beautiful watch.' Jake looked at his watch, twisting his wrist to catch the light.

'Why didn't I walk away?' Jake's voice was soft, the words a whispered thought.

'I don't know, anger I guess. You needed your power over them. Your own importance over the importance you attributed to them.'

Jake's eyes darted up, 'People are wankers!' His voice was elevated, impassioned by this statement. No particular memory evoked it, but something, something irritated it, made it itch, 'You need to be a wanker to compete or win out.'

'That's great Jake, just what the world needs: more wankers!' Boris paused to sip at his pint and as he lowered it back to the wood he announced a simple sentence, 'The betterment of things.'

Jake shuffled his pint, twisting it round in his palm, the cogs of his mind whizzing, his consciousness almost visible. Regret? No, just thought, the breaking down of Boris's words, the strange wisdom that Boris had a tendency towards mulling over in his mind.

'You mean that I should strive to be better than them?' Jake asked as if for a reading, the forecast of his future.

Boris looked at Jake with a soft but earnest gaze.

'But then I sacrifice myself.' Jake went on.

'What?' Boris snapped, 'Your ego? The only thing you have sacrificed, my friend, is your greatness and wisdom. Not that Horace had any of that, he's just weird.' Boris necked his pint and slammed the empty glass on the table.

'You're not my friend,' Jake looked at Boris directly, the words seemed sure of their own truth, but a softness in his face made it almost a question.

'No, guys like us don't have friends, and to be honest it's better for me if we're not: you have tendency to kill yours.'

Jake's mind wondered a little back to Horace, the tendency to kill his friends still floating around the cogs of his *tick,* 'Jesuusss! This isn't rehab, this is a mental institution!'

'It's an experiment. Come on, let's go.' Boris stood, collecting the two pint glasses from the table and returned them to the bar.

On the stroll back, Jake thought about Boris's last words, *an experiment.* That meant there were no rules yet, no set policies or standards; experiments are open to challenge and change, they didn't know what they were doing. Boris had said he was angry; Jake knew what he needed to do.

Horace

Although hefty enough to move a car (so rumours had it), Horace had not been dextrous enough to manipulate their working parts and so was not adept enough to follow his father's profession as a motor mechanic and thereby turn a single generation's career into a family legacy. Instead, given his average attempt and success at exams, Horace endured insurance, a middle man resting in his *new dynamic seating with wheels*. His father's business, never to be extended to *Conway and Son* remained a singular named *Conway*, and along with the local post office and grocery store it reflected the hub of a town, the local heartbeat, the essential cog that constitutes the very being of a working community. Horace had never in fact even driven, the car an unnecessary machine in a town with a bus route on his doorstep and a direct train to the city. His wife however, through Horace's insurance company, insured a compact neat little car that carried their daughter to clubs, him to work and on occasions to *things*. But tonight it would motor along weighed down with the monthly shopping burden of the joint credit card expenditure. Parked on the driveway, the garage door bricked in, the compact little motor sat quietly awaiting its monthly outing.

Horace glanced at it as he made his way to the front door, key in hand awaiting the lock that would require his concentration – just for a moment, his full concentration – as he manoeuvred the key into place and turned it anti-clockwise till it clicked the latch free. As he glanced, he felt a momentary desire to drive it. A memory snatched his thoughts, his wife's car mutated into a different model, an older car – a Ford, he was sure of it – the old style more boxy than the rounded Fords of today. He recalled his father's passion for his work, his pride, his community obligations and earned respect. His father's overalls, dark blue and dirty, smudged hand marks across his hips, oil and grease, rust and paint. He remembered the smell of diesel, the smell of grease and manual labour. What had he become? What had happened in his life to ensure that he would one day glance at his car and remember? That he would one day realise that he had wanted more, that he thought his dad a loser? Horace was going to be bigger. Horace had his fantasies that separated him from them. Horace had power. Horace was a geezer, *sha!*

Rushton

The fish swam round the bowl, their three-second memory reconnecting to the drab cream with brown lino that stretched out to meet the once white walls that encircled their space, over and over. *Tick, tick, tick, tick.* Time passed by them as the residents went to bed, got up, watched television, read a magazine, stared at the drab cream with brown lino that stretched out to meet the once white walls that encircled their space. Horace looked at the clock; Jake looked at the clock because Horace had, his mind full of questions, his interaction with Boris at the pub had left him feeling a little peculiar and the day's events only added to the strangeness of things. The room seemed empty: Imogen was gone and Horace was nuts but not a killer, *what the fuck is going on here?* Gill automatically glanced at her watch as Horace and Jake looked at the clock, but didn't register the time. The second hand jerking its way round, past the roman numerals that mapped out the face, hour by hour, intercepted by tiny dashes marking the second motions, counting every 60 to the minutes, as another hand swept its way, dash by dash, to another hour.

A single shot had seen to it that Rose Heather Roberts and Imogen Baker were dead. The memory of Miracle Romandas, although having been already dead for some time, was free to settle; somehow now she was truly dead, her murderer dead with her, her revenge dead. And finally, very truly, Imogen's mother was now lost in the room and dark, the techno-irritating candle now forever out, without the matches to kindle it, without Imogen to live it.

Vincent was once a visitor; he didn't wear a white coat. Jake had noted this. He had always been shown in and shown out and wore a variety of outfits that had somehow always looked the same.

Inspector Jacob Rodgers reads the Diary of Rose Heather Roberts.

Inspector Jacob Rodgers had been called to the scene of Imogen's death; a quick conclusion had determined that she had taken her own life, but an investigation into where she had got the gun was under way. He had tucked her diary into his oversized coat pocket as he searched her room for any indications towards the gun's original home. Now back at the station he leaned back in his chair as he always did; in his left hand rested a leather bound diary, a pen twirled between his fingers in his right. Undated and random the pages scribbled out thoughts across the paper, entwined with added notes, arrows and lines pointing towards corrective additions of text.

My name is Rose by the way, my mum said it's because it's the most romantic flower, but that she also anticipated that I might grow a little prickly. Now the question hangs in the balance: did I become prickly because she anticipated it, there by nurturing it into me somehow; or was she just right.

I'm having lunch, it's nice, tuna sandwich with salad garnish, two slices of chunky tea house granary, cut into four perfect little triangles. I add salt to the slices of cucumber and eat them on their own, away from the rest of the garnish. Behind me, at the next table there's a group of girls. They seem pleasant enough. They talk a lot. Right now they're talking about how great their mothers are: working, running the household, bringing them up and their younger or older siblings, how great their mothers were when their friends came round, how well they had dealt with their first loves and the trauma that had evolved with it and a variety of teenage things, events and problems. Their fathers were mentioned once. Sailing. And then, inexplicably, there it was... 'I think its women's nature to want to find a man to look after you.' The next slice of cucumber had just touched my tongue, the salt refreshing, light and moreish. I was enjoying my cucumber before it spat itself back onto the plate. Did I miss something? Had you not just been discussing how your mother held down jobs, looked after the house and its finances, how she raised you and your siblings up, how she dealt with your friends and problems? And then she needs who to look after who? You said it, I heard you, your mother doesn't like sailing. Are you serious? Can you not hear your own words? Can you not see the pictures of your life and there, always, working, smiling... YOUR MOTHER? Eventually I guess, when you find this great man who's going to look after you, this person you talk about, this person is going to be you. Now I'm going to rant... I bought this magazine, on the front its selling point: 100 ways to GET your man. Then there are the 20 top tips to losing weight, the top ten make-up recommendations and the fashion pages, the recipes, the glowing white teeth, each with a list of tips. Why? Because its women's nature. Does any of this sound natural to you? It is women's nature, in part, to nurture. 'Peace is for women and the weak,' so they say. Does that, in its passivity, make us the underdog, simply because we care? I'll show you weak, you scrawny little fuck, I'll take my gun, I'll hold it to your temple. Bang, fucking bang, you fuck. Then they go on, comparing these tips, with the promise of the perfect body, with perfect skin and trimmings, to find, keep and excite your man. Is this perfect being natural, is it even actually possible? The dimensions don't seem consistent with reality. I bet they stretch to a video, squeeze into that number, comb, bleach, straighten, curl, plait, colour, fuck up your hair. Wax, paint and remove, cover all those natural signs of womanhood. Are you serious? Can you not hear your own words? Can you not see the pictures of your life?

Finishing on the left side of the book the text stopped there, the right side blank. Jacob turned the page, moving his head unconsciously to the right and down, trying to see the page before it was workably visible to him. Eager? No, nervous, as if the page might come alive, might bite him.

And if I hear one more time that it is man's nature, with his stupid penis, the red blooded male, the Neanderthal, I will... I don't know, fucking bang; I have this fantasy, of putting a gun to your head and pulling the trigger, pulling the trigger, pulling the trigger. Beyond your stirring member you are evolved, you are an intelligent being, are you not? Maybe I'm giving you too much credit, but you have changed the face of the earth with engineering and technology, philosophy and poetry. Be better than your throbbing member. It betrays you, lets you down. It is your madness and your undeniable weakness.

I hate you all. You stupid fucks.

Jacob shuffled uncomfortably in his seat and looked a little woefully towards his own member. Unsure whether or not it could take the pressure of responsibility, he reflected on the text and concluded in his favour, that the edge in the tone suggested the writer's judgement to be based in an experience, an experience which had not involved his own respectable and natural attachment, and although generalised he was sure its intentions were towards a 'type', a kind of member to which his own did not belong. Jacob averted his eyes from the words. Thoughts of a writing analyst flickered through his consciousness and then settled on the text again.

Effort: Some people dream of worthy accomplishments, while others stay awake and do them.

Jacob read the sentence again. *Effort: Some people dream of worthy accomplishments, while others stay awake and do them.* Worthy accomplishments? Stay awake? Jacob's eyes bored into the text, asking it, willing it to give answers, to talk to him.

I'm Rose by the way, I'm 5' 6', it's an okay height; I have green eyes which are endearing (apparently) and brown hair which I have never dyed. I have a tendency to lie, or at least that's what the doctor told me. He says I have an unhealthy reflection of the world which serves only to make my life harder. I think – but I could be lying – that the world sucks and that it's unfortunate that I find myself in it. Perhaps that's an unhealthy outlook, but I took it upon myself to discover some point in it, and so I find myself a member of the Rushton New Wave of Rehabilitation. 'Where you from?' people will ask, 'Oh, Rushton', I'll say. 'Oh, where's that?' they'll say, and I could respond with 'Middlesex,' or 'Yorkshire,' doesn't really matter.

'Where are we anyway?'

The Diary of Rose Heather Roberts

You're not angry at me. You're just angry.

You do nothing different from me, I do nothing different from you. Just like me under your skin.

I have this fantasy of drawing a gun from the inside of my jacket and holding it to the temple of my enemy. Bang.

But I'd never do it.

Would you?

Rushton

'£1,200.' The antique dealer ran his hard hands over the top surface of Dr Washington's sideboard and nodded inwardly, 'I can take it away today if you'd like, Doctor.'

Dr Washington stood back, his original quote from a family dealer that his brother had recommended had just been doubled. The sideboard, his father's finest piece of furniture, was only in his keeping; his brother was the true inheritor of its perfect condition and fine polished fixings. He pursed his lips slightly. 'No, thank you, I was just curious about its value.'

'Okay, well just let us know if you ever want to sell her, Doctor,' as the dealer pronounced the word 'doctor' his tone raised a little, slightly more breathy, more tired.

'I will, thank you.'

Inspector Jacob Rodgers

Jacob cleared his throat before launching into his explanation. 'The Rushton New Wave of Rehabilitation was a concept designed by Dr Rushton and is now executed by Dr Henry Washington and Dr Jeremy Jefferson. The details of exactly what they do is unclear, but there is an indication that they introduce the world to the programme's residents in a new way, eventually transforming mad people into ordinary social people, who could be released without fear of re-offending.'

Jacob paused, the moment silent. 'Slow introductions,' he continued, 'to the outside world and its everyday behaviour would ease the patients into a normal way of life. Horace's walks to the shops would eventually develop into a job of sorts, adding to his social skills, slowly allowing the mind to adapt to the basic principles of life: those residents, for instance, who didn't wear white coats but always intervened had been given just such an upgrade, reintroducing them to contributing and functioning as a normal working part of the whole.'

Inspector Jacob Rodgers lent back in his chair as his speech trailed off to indicate the end of his explanation. A gentle sigh encapsulated his unsatisfactory feelings towards the conclusion of this cycle, this charade in which he had found himself entangled.

His companion, an archaeologist and lecturer of history, shook her head in sympathy with a deep, tender disbelief. She thought for a while, what other options were there, what was to be done? 'In Georgian time, 18th century...' she began her response with a sentence that, should Inspector Jacob Rodgers ever find himself attending a lecture of this nature, might cause him to start nodding off a little, eventually and embarrassingly ending in a dull snore. But on this occasion Jacob was focussed, as he would be if he were listening for evidence, the crucial details that lead to a truth, the pieces of a misshaped puzzle forming a picture from the chaos. Each piece still not quite flush to its neighbour, the picture still bitty and incomplete, he was curious to hear anything that might relieve him of a nagging uncertainty about the crimes around which their conversation skirted.

'Poaching was fair game,' his companion continued, 'the fair distribution of wealth.' She gazed out the window, the clatter and discussions of the tables around them formed a light wash of sound, an un-distracting ocean wave. 'Gentry land was an open market, but as the gentry made the laws, they soon figured out that laws could make wealth and so poaching became subject to the penalty of death.

'At Tyburn, which is now Marble Arch, they hanged 24 people all at one time – I mean they designed rigs that could do that. The full sentence passed upon those convicted of High Treason up to 1870 was "That you be drawn on a hurdle to the place of execution where you shall be hanged by the neck and being alive cut down, your privy members shall be cut off and your bowels taken out and burned before you, your head severed from your body and your body divided into four quarters to be disposed of at the King's pleasure." Awful isn't it?!' The inspector's companion was looking directly at him, the words quite frightening. Jacob nodded, the law of a time gone by. She continued, 'As the years progressed to 1948 the judge would say the full name of the prisoner followed by "You will be taken hence to the prison in which you were last confined and from there to a place of execution where you will be hanged by the neck until you are dead and thereafter your body buried within the precincts of the prison and may the Lord have mercy upon your soul." And now, of course, we don't hang at all, we've changed a lot,' the inspector's companion added chirpily, swigging a mouthful of cappuccino (no chocolate). 'Do you believe in capital punishment, Inspector?'

Jacob felt momentarily muted, did she want him to believe in it? He sat for a moment, considering the question, 'No, not really,' he finally allowed himself to admit.

His companion, after pausing to hear his answer, went on, 'As the years go on we continue to remove the law's harshest punishments; the law must be above the actions of those we condemn as our collective morality changes, re-develops. Perhaps it is time, Inspector, for a new wave of rehabilitation.'

The inspector thought, his mind considering, but in sweeping motions one memory kept coming back to him: Jake sitting calmly, considered, as he described the actions of his murders, and this image coupled with the seemingly shaky notion of re-introducing Jake to the outside world by simply getting him to plant a few perennials as a grounds gardener. Inspector Jacob Rodgers excused himself from his company, eager to get back to Rose's diary. His companion had a point, but he needed more convincing that Rushton's idea was the next step in our evolution.

Rushton

Horace looked at the clock, Jake didn't; Gill checked her watch and then looked at Jake. She waited. Horace looked at the clock. Jake didn't. Gill was still watching, her arm aloft awaiting her glance to check the sweeping arms, the roman numerals intercepted by the tiny dashes indicating the time. Gill turned, averting her eyes to move directly from Jake to the entrance she was about to cross. She sat in the *new dynamic office seating with wheels* (recently upgraded with the yearly budget supplement), and pulled out the day's record from its allotted slot on the wall shelf. A desk sat under the viewing window; Gill's eyes just peered over the frame. A high chair towered behind her, from which you could scan the whole space (16 paces by 10) without obstruction; the chair perched by a high bench suspended from the rear wall. Gill never sat there. She made a phone call.

Inspector Jacob Rodgers talks with Dr Washington about Horace

'Can you tell me what might have happened on a particular day?' Inspector Jacob Rodgers tapped his pencil against his pad, a light rhythmless thud filled the pause, 'I mean to ask, what might have happened on that day, the day it started?'

Dr Washington sighed a little as he began his analysis of Horace, but soon bounced into the rhythm of his expertise, 'Horace tended to stand back, like a spectator of his own life. He judged and interpreted the workings of his environment and interacted with them, for fun, knowledge, companionship, many, many reasons – not even consciously recognised as reasons, just life – while all the while he remained inside, looking out, as if his mind were in a separate bubble distanced from the physical world.

'There is a lot to be said for spectating. Take sport: it's fun, interactive, exciting, social, it has the power to conjure all emotions from anger to tears of joy. The buzz of being at a match, the intensity of watching your team winning and the anguish of them losing. But Horace felt that he would never truly understand the game unless he was in it, he would never see the stadium from the pitch, he would never feel his true skill in making that pass and the play of his competition. He would never be as happy or as gutted when the match was over. Horace had wanted to join in, but as his days ticked on an ever increasing frustration overwhelmed him. Paper cuttings, photos, books and fantasies stretched out the seconds day by day, adding years to his life, a life that he felt had not yet begun. Inspector, it was any day, every day.'

Dr Washington relaxed back in his chair, as he always did after saying something he thought profound, impressive, even perhaps ingenious: something that pieced together his education and training infused with the very heart of himself.

'I see,' the inspector mustered from his throat. 'It's not likely then, that something in particular may have occurred to spur him?'

'It's my belief, Inspector, that something happened every day to spur him, eventually and inevitably, to the result.'

'The result?'

'His new home, Inspector, his residence here at Rushton.'

'I see.' Jacob drew tiny circles on his pad. 'Was there not a childhood thing?'

'A childhood thing?'

'Yes, something in his childhood that may have caused this behaviour.'

'Inspector, there is *always* a childhood thing. Horace's insecurities around not being practical like his father is most certainly one of them.'

'I see.'

'Do you?!'

Inspector Jacob Rodgers looked up from his spiralling circles, 'Yes I do,' he said confidently. 'Doctor, what was Horace doing with the files found in his home office?'

Dr Washington sighed, 'He used them to live out his fantasies, he would pretend, for instance, that he was someone high up in politics or MI5 and use the files as props.'

Inspector Rodger's hand paused and then dashed over the page to circle the word *spectator*, as the doctor continued, 'He went to a lot of effort to create the files, the information in them was for the most part true to the people he had followed. It was part of his fantasy, collecting the data was part of the practice of whichever character he was being on any given day. He needed real people to follow so he could live out his fantasies beyond the garage.'

'I see.'

'Inspector, is there anything else? I do need to get on.'

Inspector Jacob Rodger wistfully glanced out the window, as if taking a long and dedicated drag from a cigarette. 'No, I think we're done for today.'

'Today?'

'I may think of something else.'

'There is this amazing technology called "the telephone", Inspector. I assume you do have one of those?'

'I'll call in again if I think of anything more.'

'Right.'

'Good day, Doctor.'

Dr Washington twitched, 'Good day, Inspector.'

Rushton

Gill, who wore a white coat still not quite as well fitting as another white coat that had seemed to mutate in and out of Gill's coat for about a week, peered over the frame from her *new dynamic office seating with wheels* in the office that overlooked the space, 16 paces by 10. Jake sat a seat away from Imogen's chair, the indents from her body fading from the cover and padding as others, usually doctors, had rearranged the creases to fit the mould of their own bodies. Watching the television, Jake's behaviour more and more exhibited the definitive *yes*: Dr Rushton's New Wave of Rehabilitation was working. Dr Washington had called in further doctors to analyse Jake's movements; he could not afford a mistake, he would need the ability to blame a different authority should Jake be faking. Jake was clever, the doctors knew that: he had excelled in his tests, he had excelled at school and had earned the wage to reflect it. But he was not as clever as them. Jake sat back and picked up his book; Gill peered over the frame. Horace looked at Boris, Boris was looking at Horace, the moment felt awkward; Gill stepped in and ushered Jake away.

Jake stepped into Dr Washington's office. Dr Washington's files neatly flanked the broad oak desk between them. A chair awaited him, a simple but definite gesture flowed from the doctor's arms as he silently instructed Jake to be seated. 'Mr Hamilton, thank you for coming to see me.'

Did I have a choice? Jake considered.

'Would you like anything? A coffee, perhaps?'

'No thank you, I'm just fine,' Jake responded, resting back in the chair that Dr Washington had gestured towards, although inwardly he did quite fancy a coffee. The chair was comfortable; he hadn't thought before how uncomfortable the communal area's chairs were, the chair he had sat in every day for however long.

'Very well,' Dr Washington moved some papers across his desk and then looked up to face Jake directly for the first time during this encounter. 'Jake...'

Dr Washington's interaction was intercepted as Jake interrupted, 'Doctor, can I ask you a question?'

Dr Washington didn't like interruptions, especially when he had already poised the words ready for speech, and beyond this he didn't want his authority to slip (he needed always to stay in control of the situation) but opening his palms as an expression of welcome, he simply said, 'Yes. Go ahead Jake.'

Jake entwined his fingers and relaxed a little more into the comfortable seating (no wheels). 'What advice would you give?' Jake was still looking at the doctor directly, earnestly, quite seriously and yet the tone and manner of his voice projected as a question to the room. 'For life; what would your advice be?'

There was a tense silence. Dr Washington was uncertain, but he maintained his outward composure and filled the time with an equally earnest gaze back. He looked as if he were musing the question and then stated, as if he were advising his son, 'Be true to yourself,' and then realising that Jake was not his son he added, 'that's what they say isn't it?'

And then, there it was, Jake's response: 'Was I being true to myself when I killed those people I'm told about, or was it a projection of anger and unbalance?' Jake paused, but was not waiting for an answer, his hands untangled now. His body was quite still yet somehow gave the impression he were leaning forward, leaning in, 'I overheard that question being asked to someone once, an old guy, being asked by some young hippy backpackers – he said the thing to do was to let go. Let go. And interestingly enough, Doctor, the more I let go, the more true to myself I feel. I don't remember what you say I've done, I don't quite believe it but I wouldn't be here otherwise, would I? I'm guessing here – you're the expert – that my behaviour had something to do with an internal anger that I had, escalating on some ever increasing scale to total blindness. It's an anger I don't understand. I'm sorry, I'm truly sorry for the people I have been informed were victims of this blindness. I wonder if I could remember though, whether the anger with the memory would rebuild... what do you think, Doctor?'

Dr Washington was so caught up in Jake's words that he did not take time to realise their full significance, could Jake have thought of the question if he hadn't felt that such a memory would rebuild the anger? Dr

Washington concluded that in this particular case a noncommittal answer was suitable – it was 50/50 – but added that as Jake was able to recognise the possibility for himself, that the chances that he'd be able to manage any emotions arising from the memory were good, and that with guidance and help he would be able to control the feeling and not go back to the man he had been.

And so the process began for Jake's fast track rehabilitation towards release.

Clever boy.

Inspector Jacob Rodgers continues with the Diary of Rose Heather Roberts

Inspector Jacob Rodgers flipped open Rose's diary. Although unable to find a consistent narrative to follow in any particular order, Jacob read the diary page by page; there wasn't a word he wanted to miss.

I sit nonchalantly amongst my incarcerated companions. I'm potentially lethal, like a sharp knife being wielded in anger or a dinner guest invited to an occasion that Poriot might attend.

I have this fantasy.

Inspector Jacob Rodgers folded the book closed and breathed heavily. He settled back in his chair, the diary of Rose Heather Roberts gave him hope, an observational narrative that might, just might, unfold a truth to help him answer the nagging question that Dr Washington had placed at his feet: was Jake transforming? Was the Rushton Institute of Rehabilitation working? An expensive whiskey swirled round his glass, the ice clinking against the four-for-a-fiver tumbler clasped in his hand. A whiskey gifted on his 20 year service anniversary from his partner at the time, a gift he treasured more than the gold clock assigned to him by the Policing Association. Now at the edge of retirement, early retirement, and held by this constant question stirred up by the memories of these killings, the whiskey had been opened, each sip relished. The expense of it was not lost on him, the purity of the spirit allowing him to keep that distance from his thoughts as it broke each pause with flavour. Inspector Jacob Rodgers flicked open the diary once more and scanned its pages. *Jesus,* he thought, *what am I doing? What can one mad person possibly tell me about another mad person?* He read another paragraph

You stupid fucks, what is the point of all this anyway? What does it matter if I'm out there or in here? Who cares? They say they care, they care if I kill someone, they care for that one, that person, but for all you know they could have been a wanker, could have been a real wanker and I could be lovely. So now they care for me, so they say, in here, trying to cure me, fix the twist, the prickly bit that killed someone, but they don't care they just control, want to control everything, everyone, but who the fuck are you, who are these people who make the rules and put me here, who are you compared to me?

Jacob tipped his tumbler towards his lips again and relaxed while the sting and flavour engulfed him. Rose Heather Roberts, sister to Vincent Roberts, killer of Miracle Romandas had a fantasy, to take a gun from the inside pocket of her jacket or coat and hold it to the temple of her enemy. On the 5th May she put on a jacket and sat back in the seat she had left vacant through the previous 20 minutes while visiting her mother, her mother now dead this fifth year. Two hours later she returned to her room and lived out the fantasy, placing a gun to the temple of Imogen Baker and Rose Heather Roberts, firing a single shot at zero range through her own head.

Speculation as to where she had acquired the gun lived on, her brother Vincent was interviewed, the security of the Rushton Institute questioned, but no light even flickered to reveal how she may have got such a thing. Sadness but relief released itself in a slow collective exhalation as Gill imagined the carnage if anyone else besides Imogen had obtained such a thing. Jake and Horace passed a knowing glance between them with the very same thoughts, only in their case the carnage was *wanted*, their freedom inches away from them inside the coat pocket sitting there (just there!) only minutes before, if only they had known that Imogen had had such a thing.

Inspector Jacob Rodgers, with his thoughts spinning and the question unanswered, wished the world had never known such a thing.

The Diary of Rose Heather Roberts

Art – '*Human creative skill or its application; the branch of creative activity concerned with the production of imaginative designs and expressions of ideas.*'

A rock with a meaning.

A blob created by a thought.

I have this fantasy, I reach into my pocket and draw a gun, I point it to the temple of my enemy. Bang.

Would I do it?

Rushton

"'Be true to yourself,' that's what they say. Blimey, Jake, fat lot of good that is! Horace here rapes and kills women, I killed a family and you killed your friends. Maybe it's not good for us to be true to ourselves, you think?' Boris sat forward, his magazine suspended open in the air.

Horace looked a little numb; no-one had mentioned rape before. He shook the thought from his mind with a hefty jerk, twisted his head to turn his attention to Jake and the unfolding conversation. With Horace and Boris both now looking at him, a new question searched for an answer. They looked through him, the answer in him, somewhere deep beyond the surface. Jake had suddenly become the man with answers. Gill made a phone call. Jake closed his book and looked into the air, 'You know, I miss women.'

Horace silently agreed but immediately searched his feelings: *rape?* He thought only of his wife, and never in such an attacking way; he simply didn't believe it.

This is punishment now, this place. 16 paces long, 10 paces wide.

Gill sat in the office, Jake's file open on the desk. Her phone call had been fobbed off, she had been told not to worry. She watched the three men, their eyes flickering through each other, a nervous yet controlled glint passed between them.

Jake

Jake stood at the checkout waiting for his four items to be bleeped past. He watched his three bottles of silver-award-winning 2005 Vintage Merlot roll down the slope that directed his items to the packing area. His box of truffles would follow, but rather than hanging on to it until the last moment so that it didn't roll and crash, the truffles were shoved a little as the cashier mindlessly manoeuvred item after item along the revolving belt, past his bleeper and down the chute to the bagging area. Jake waited patiently as the cashier re-arranged his seat and fiddled about under the till. After the bleeps had passed and his four items lay in the shoot, plastic bags dangling two inches above the surface, Jake waited to be offered a wine box to carry his purchased items away. The queue began to shuffle as the thick air started to make everyone uncomfortable; one woman tapped her foot, like his teachers used to as he ambled his way towards the classroom. Jake decided to request one.

The cashier answered with a head wagging sigh, 'We don't have any, you'll have to double bag.'

Each irritation, building brick by brick the bullet proof protection of Jake's inner bubble.

Rushton

It was Autumn again and although the sun was shining an early winter chill was ripe in the air. Jake rearranged his scarf and then pulled his coat closer around his neck, the brisk wind still catching his ears. He shivered a little.

'Need some weight on you, like old Horace here,' Boris slapped Jake on the shoulder, a contact that Jake didn't care for much, but he nodded politely while slowing his stride to drop behind his companion. As they weren't heading for the shop, the not-so-yellow, not-so-brick road (which was actually a pavement) had been abandoned for a shortcut down an alley to the pub. At its entrance the warmth of the enclosed space forced Jake to loosen his scarf and undo his coat as he stepped over its threshold. Boris went to the bar, snatching the cash from Horace's light grip. Horace looked at Jake for a seating decision; Jake nodded at a table by the window.

'Well lads, here's to Imogen, a month today.' Boris's pint already aloft, Horace and Jake raised their pints to support its gesture.

'Damn shame, she was alright. Clearly nuts, but alright.'

As the pints hit the table after their first gulp of the day they relaxed into their chairs and glanced around, as they always did despite knowing this pub as well the 16 by 10 paces space to which they were so accustomed.

'That picture's different,' Horace pointed at a painting across from them. 'It was a Monet before. Now it's a Rembrandt.'

Boris and Jake twisted round to examine the work of art under suspicion. Boris nodded thoughtfully as he looked through the painting, not really caring much for its style, or artist. Jake agreed, 'You're right Horace,' he said. They took another gulp from their pints, releasing the painting from their minds.

'Where did she get the gun?' Boris twiddled his pint glass around in his palm, watching the froth swish gently, 'I mean, we are in an institution after all: an institution for the dangerous.'

Jake looked towards the floor in thoughtful calculation. *Where might she have got the gun?* His brow questioned. He bit his lip as he considered several possible scenarios, the truth passed over his mind. He returned to his pint and re-joined the group, his companions, his cell mates, and offered up one of his thoughts, though not the one he believed most possible. *Shooting rodents.* 'Maybe Vincent brought it in for her,' Jake somehow no longer felt suspicious of Vincent, of whether he really *was* Imogen's brother.

'Surely they check visitors?' Horace questioned, pretty sure that even the innocent, lawful people living on the outside would not be admitted without at least a metal detector entrance or something. Boris and Jake nodded.

'Maybe Gill gave it her.' Boris remarked, quite dead pan.

The boys looked at him, 'Don't be mad!' Jake retorted. 'But maybe it's that girl that doesn't wear a white coat but always intervenes, she's a weird one.'

Horace thought. He knew it was a girl because he'd seen her naked, she was the one that had by some strange detection discovered her eyebrow to be the same length as a non-applicator tampon. She was definitely odd.

'Can't be,' Boris lifted his pint to take a sip. 'She's one of us, you know,' but he wasn't asking, he was stating. 'It's part of rehab, get her functioning, it's like life training.'

'Why don't we do stuff like that?' Horace enquired, why was Jake working and that girl serving, while he just sat around looking at the clock?

'We are doing that, we're here, at the pub; that girl gets to go out, your walk to the shops Horace… it's all a part of the process.'

Horace thought about the process. How long had he been here? How long had he been doing this? Going to the shops, taking and then not taking his pills, how long would this all go on for? The boys finished their pints and rose to their feet, once again donning their warm attire for the brisk cold air outside, they arranged their clothes and left the pub. Horace marched ahead as he always did, Jake strolled taking the scene in and Boris watched the two them, his mind ticking over the Imogen question: *how did she get that gun? Who could she have got to bring a known killer a gun?*

Horace

Horace had been a middle man for 20 years. Each day Horace would brush his hair at the bathroom mirror, six strokes varying in manner. Each day Horace would look at his own reflected image and believe himself a geezer. *Sha!* Each day he would straighten his collar and shake off any clinging threads from his attire; Horace was preparing himself for work. He would march into the office carrying his demeanour of businessman importance, his scent altering the air. Horace was a manager. But for 20 years he had never managed more than ten people, for 20 years Horace had been a middle man of no more than ten people. He would place his briefcase on the floor beside his bulk buy supposedly *new dynamic office seating with wheels,* and no longer feel as important. His middle man status: being neither here nor there. His stress levels rising as he strived to fulfil the company's requirements, the boys above caring only about staff performance, the staff below caring only for the rules inflicted by the boys above. Horace felt invisible. The messenger. Yet at monthly meetings with his direct manager he would be told of the importance of his position, how he was the glue that held the two sides together and kept the communication in flow. He liked this idea, being the glue, but knew that his position was not irreplaceable. Horace had his fantasies, thoughts, secrets that separated him from them.

Rushton

Horace thought more and more about his predicament. Was he ever going to get out of here? And did he know what waited for him beyond? He wasn't even sure what he had done and yet he felt something, a fantasy, a life not yet begun, something... He was waiting for something, he just couldn't put his finger on what it was. He started to pace his room. A man on monitor duty watched him on screen through the night vision tones of the gloom, the contrast distorted, his eyes seeking out a predator in the darkness. His podgy digits picked up a pencil and noted by Horace's name, 'pacing'.

Over the next few days, Gill watched for signs of agitation during the day, anything that might reflect the pacing recorded by the digits at night. Then one night, apparently chosen at random, Horace paced out of his bedroom door and down the corridor. It was 9.50pm. The digits watched, pencil poised.

Gill sat in the office that overlooked the communal area, 16 paces long by 10 paces wide. She was organising files and filling in last minute information about the occurrences of the day as Horace paced into the room. Marching in with long strides, his scent altering the air, Horace was a geezer, *sha!* He strode into the office, towering over Gill as she sat at the desk, the viewing window in front of her. He looked at her directly, his gaze steady. Gill breathed gently in, preparing herself for speech but before her words could be realised, Horace raised his arm and with a single blow knocked Gill's body from the *new dynamic office seating with wheels* to the floor. The wheels spun in the air aimlessly as the chair flipped over on top of her. He strode over and pushed the chair away from her. Gill lay unconscious but alive beneath his formidable frame. She was still breathing, but in an irregular gasp, shallow and effortful. Without thought, and perhaps even without intent, Horace raised his arm again and powered it down, crushing the life from Gill's now quiet body. And then, as if he had done nothing abnormal, he eased the *dynamic seating* out of his way and stepped over Gill to reach for his file, which rested in its ordered position on the shelf to the left over the desk. Plucking it from its station, he flopped open the file and scanned the pages. As he flipped the sheets a terrible urgency built up in his mind and heart: days, weeks, months, years of nothing passed on the paper. *Nothing.* Nothing of murder and nothing, as Boris had suggested, of rape. He spun around and placed a wide hand on the file that had been open on the desk before his arrival, the file Gill had been updating only minutes before. Jake's profile lay spread out before him, a killer of two: an ex-girlfriend and a lifelong friend. Horace had killed no-one, until this moment, here in the Rushton Institute of Rehabilitation.

Mayhem ensued. The digits had pressed the red emergency button while simultaneously trying to dial three numbers at once, not sure who to call first. Inspector Jacob Rodgers stood somewhere in the scene. Forensics, dressed in their ill-fitting white jump suits, taking swabs and placing things in bags, worked around the upside down *new dynamic office seating with wheels* and Gill's body which lay, twisted and bloody, on the floor. The files lay open on the desk. Inspector Jacob Rodgers had seen the tape that had been quietly recording the events as the owner of the digits had stared dumbstruck at the actions unfolding on his watch. Well, Horace had said he wanted to join in.

Dr Henry Washington dimmed the room as his presence blocked one of the spot lamps illuminating the carnage. 'Inspector,' he acknowledged.

Jacob twisted his head to view the doctor directly, 'He's all yours, Doctor. I'll inform you of the results from these tests but I think we can be sure of what they'll tell us. I take it you've seen the tape?'

'Yes.'

'Good. Well he's already here, so I guess he stays here till the trial, so that he can be sentenced to come back here, and with any luck you'll all bloody well die here!'

'Inspector?!'

'Sorry, Doctor.' Inspector Rogers passed a weary hand through his hair.

'Actually, I've been informed that he's to go with you – I don't mean you personally, Inspector – but with the police... he's to be taken to jail until the trial.'

'Super.'

151

'After Imogen… Rose's… suicide, and now this, I'm afraid this institution is under some fire and although I've convinced them to allow me to continue Horace has to leave, as do a few other patients who are not considered stable.'

'Stable? Is there anyone here that you would consider stable, Doctor?'

The doctor shook his head impatiently, 'It's a different kind of stable, there are specific criteria of stability.'

'I see.' Jacob didn't see. He glanced around the office within which they both stood, 'Would Horace have been one of these unstable types? I mean, based on your *criteria*, should this have been done by someone else, Doctor?'

'No.'

'Good. Then I'll undoubtedly see you very soon with another incident.'

Inspector Jacob Rodgers finishes the Diary of Rose Heather Roberts.

Inspector Jacob Rodgers picked up the diary of Rose Heather Roberts. He had read it urgently, searching for clues, help. He concentrated on the final page.

I see Horace looking at me, his eyes pass through me as he raises his head to look at the clock and he looks at the clock often, he's nuts, he's one of those proper women-killing nuts, I know he's looking at me, I know he's nuts.

Inspector Jacob Rodgers held Rose's diary in both hands, his elbows on his desk, the bottom of the binding resting on the wood.

Jake's cute. I love his surfy hair and sparkling blue eyes, he's been dressing smarter recently, same clothes, same cleanliness but somehow he looks different, like he's thought about how he looks, like he's checked himself in the mirror. Been going out more and when he comes back he seems thoughtful. Been reading more. Stopped looking at the clock because Horace looks at the clock. I know Gill's noticed. She makes phone calls, I can see the office reflected in the television. I can see her eyes peering over the frame, can see the way she moves, I know she's on the phone, it's brief and functional. It's like a film in here, like we're all zombies or something, emotionless and functional. It's cold in here. But it's cold out there. It's cold everywhere.

Inspector Jacob Rodgers paused to sip from his forgotten cup of coffee, his face tightening as the cold bitterness touched his tongue. He placed it back to his right and considered the writing; the next sentence was slightly different, a different emotion had possessed the hand as it wrote the words, a different time, a different space in the mind, the room still 16 paces by 10.

I have this fantasy. I take a gun from the inside pocket of my jacket, I'm gonna stick to a jacket, I don't have a coat. I hold this gun to the temple of my enemy and then bang. Why don't I have the courage to do it?

Jacob rested the book flat on the desk and leaned back in his chair. She had found the courage, she had taken a gun from the inside pocket of her jacket and held to the temple of Rose Heather Roberts and fired a single shot through her own head. Her enemy. The diary ended there, the last entry, asking herself why she had not the courage to do what she did, perhaps the following day, or that afternoon. *Where had she got the gun? What was going on?* Inspector Jacob Rodgers held his head in his hands, two people were already dead, he needed to find out what the Rushton Institute was really about.

The Diary of Rose Heather Roberts

You know my fantasy. I draw a gun from the inside of my jacket and hold it to the temple of my enemy. Bang.

Rushton

Nobody spoke. The day stretched out endlessly. Tension and confusion suffocated the air. Jake stepped outside and breathed purposely in, expanding his lungs to bursting.

The white coat watched Jake, fluffy hair bouncing as he walked then flicking back as he threw his head to breathe in, pulling the air deep into his lungs. The white coat placed a thoughtful and caring hand on last night's report. Jake had shuffled in his sleep, a single bead of sweat had manoeuvred its way across his forehead, ducking and diving the obstacles of his frowning wrinkles and then tucking itself under his eyebrow as it raced across his lid and trickled tearfully from the corner of his eye across his temple. A man on monitor duty watched him sleep on screen through the night vision tones of the gloom, the contrast distorted, his eyes seeking out a predator in the darkness. His podgy digits had picked up a pencil and noted by Jake's name, 'crying in sleep'. The white coat gazed at the report, three misreported words missing nuance and context, all she saw was 'crying in sleep.' Her heart felt heavy.

Inspector Jacob Rodgers

Jacob lent over to retrieve the bottle of vintage 2011 Merlot from the centre of the table; pouring from the bottle with a slight twist he re-filled his companion's glass.

'They're going to release Jake, you know,' Jacob sighed a little, white coats flickering across his eyes. 'Despite their blunders, or maybe because of them, they're going to release him.'

'What will happen to him?' Jacob's companion was curious but wary, her voice wavering.

'I don't know, he has a parole officer type thing who he has to check in with, and he has to attend psychotherapy – he'll be meeting with a psychotherapist once a week for the first 10 weeks, then once a month for however long is deemed appropriate.'

'Is it safe?' Her eyes seemed a little glazed, her worst fears clouding their usual shining spark.

'I don't know, you'd hope they've put all the right precautions in place, but look what happened with Horace. I don't know.' Jacob shook his head, his thoughts reaching out to worse imaginings than his companion was able to envision, his experiences over the years eating into his core.

'What happened with Horace?'

'Awaiting his trial,' Jacob twirled the stem of his wine glass gently between his fingers.

'What do you think he'll get?'

Jacob raised his eyebrows, 'I really don't know. There are so many options these days, so many different kinds of institutions and prisons and rehabilitation centres, who knows what they'll try next. I mean the man was a bit strange, but he didn't kill anyone until he was at Rushton; his defence has every opportunity to blame the therapy, try for a verdict of diminished responsibility. But I don't know if they'll send him back, it clearly wasn't working for him.'

'Do you think his wife will sue? She sent him there to fix him and it made him worse, he went from a strange, unusual kind of husband, to a murdering kind of creepy husband. I'd sue.'

Jacob smiled, the tone in his companion's voice light and entertaining, 'Strange and creepy… she must love him: she sold the house to pay for his treatment. I guess if she's smart, she'll think of suing.'

'I guess it depends how the court finds it; if the Rushton Institute gets blamed then she's won already. It'll be nice if someone gains from all this craziness.'

'Jake's going to gain, I've got this really odd feeling… if he's playing a game, he's winning. Six doctors, three of them psychologists, one behavioural expert, a GP and a guy who writes reviews about the institution, though I don't even think he's ever been there, are all collaborating to get him released. I think I'm the only one saying we should give it more time. But who am I?! I don't even know how the institution works, I don't know what they're doing to these people, how they make this change happen. What frightens me most is that I'm not sure they do either. It's like some crazy experiment.'

'It won't be your fault if he's released and offends again.' Jacob's companion placed a tender hand over his arm, the arm attached to the swirling wine stem fingers.

'It's not going to be good enough to be able to say I told you so. If this is a mistake someone is going to die, and if Horace became a killer what the hell is Jake going to do?'

Jacob's companion's hand squeezed his arm gently, there was nothing she could say, there would always be the question awaiting a news report answer one day. An ordinary day, with the sun shining through the kitchen window perhaps, one spring morning while making breakfast the news will come on and the reporter will say the name *Jake Hamilton* and someone will be dead. She wanted to say: *but what if it works? What if Jake is cured?* But the *what if* still left the question hanging, the question awaiting that news report answer one sunny spring morning, perhaps. Her reassurances would be pointless, its motive just to have something to say; they would only know if it had worked or not when the news report came on. Until that day, every day that Jake remained a law abiding citizen, every day before the news report would be an uncertain one, they would never know for sure, never believe it had worked. They would only know if it failed.

Rushton

It had been a strange year; Imogen's death had shocked and confused everyone. Boris had wondered why, perhaps it was inevitable that a member of an institution such as Dr Rushton's would attract characters quite capable of murdering themselves, since they had felt the need to kill other people, and yet it had hit him too. And where had she got that gun? And then there was Horace: the slightly more confusing actions of a man who had not, previous to his stint at the Rushton Institute of Rehabilitation, been capable of murder.

Boris poked his head around the door; Dr Washington sat behind the broadness of his oak desk, his files flanked as always in orderly and neat attention, the ornate pot that kept his pens in tidy easy reach sat slightly to the left of him. Boris stepped in and stood framed in the doorway.

'Have a seat,' Dr Washington gestured towards the chair to his right of the desk, as he always did. Boris stepped forward, turning briefly to close the door behind him, and then sat down without moving the chair, unlike Inspector Rodgers who always scrapped it across the lino to the centre of the desk to face the doctor directly.

'Jake.' Dr Washington paused, his voice a little unsteady, 'Tell me your opinion of Jake's status.'

'You're not telling me that you're going to release a patient on the recommendation of another patient, are you?!'

'In the light of Horace's actions, we have to find a success story. We need Jake to be released.' Dr Washington lent forward, placing the pencil he had been holding carefully onto the surface of the desk, 'Boris, you are our greatest success story to date, but you can never be released. The irony, of course, is that you are such a success story *because* you can't be released: your awareness of the possibilities and your determination not to act on them are quite a success story in any rehabilitation program. If I had to, I could argue it and win.'

Boris tensed. He understood what Dr Washington was saying but feared that he was acting rashly, 'It wouldn't be enough, Doctor. People don't want their killers to be enlightened, they want them to be punished and then rehabilitated. Rehabilitation hasn't completely worked if I can't be released.'

'Talk to me about Jake.'

'I'm not sure.'

'Why are you not sure?'

'Sometimes I think he's lying. I can't be sure.'

'Your chats with him, I've been watching them. He doesn't seem to be lying.'

'Doctor, if I hadn't told you the truth, would you have released me?'

'It was too early to say. Your honesty preceded any start towards that kind of decision.'

'But you weren't in such a rush then, were you? Not so much pressure from the sponsors and government and whoever presides over this thing. Maybe if you had more time, gave it as much time as you did me before you started asking these kind of questions, Jake might be just as honest. Maybe you've discovered an alternative to rehabilitation, maybe you've discovered a new answer: a compromise between what people deserve in the sense of keeping dangerous people off the streets, and the human rights of the killer. I mean, if they can honestly regret, if they honestly know what they are, if they can live a useful life helping reform others… We could grow food for the local community or something wholesome like that – be useful – but I don't know if we should ever be released. Maybe I am your success story after all, Doctor: maybe this is the best result and the only result.'

'Most killers get released one way or another Boris, either from hospitals or prison. At least when they're released from here, there is more chance of a change in behaviour.' Dr Washington picked up the pencil he had placed down earlier and made to resume the paperwork he was attending to before Boris arrived.

Boris stood up and strode to the door, where he paused, 'Doctor, give Jake more time.'

'Thank you, Boris.' Dr Washington didn't look up.

Horace

Horace watched a Debenhams bikini stroll past, his wife in her Marks and Spencer number lay beside him. His daughter, about five at the time, played in the sand, her neck and face almost ghostly with sunblock. He put down his romance novel (a peculiar habit, his wife had always thought) and hauled himself up into a kneeling position before starting the climb to stand. His wife opened her eyes, his mass was blocking her sun. She peered up at him, the man she loved, and the sudden shade sent a chill across her arms.

'Want something from the shop?' he asked.

'Ice cream!' came his family's united request.

Rushton

Jake slouched back against the wood frame of his chair, pint in hand, trying to get comfortable as Boris waffled on.

'In our democracy we are free to vote, complain, have our say, but we can never be free to be or do as we ultimately want. There are so many of us, so many ideas of how that should be and a minority who kill – once, maybe twice, maybe more – and paedophiles, fraudsters, rapists... any number of crimes that we fear. Our protection is essential and so we have the police, the army and around those forces a structure within which we live to monitor both them and us, to identify those at risk and those on whom suspicion falls. And this structure needs to be organised, trained, cared for and financially viable.' Boris paused to sip at his pint while he thought, his gesture demonstrating his consideration, his reasoning. He worked through the process of bringing his glass to mouth, drink to throat, words waiting on his lips, ready to burst into action.

'Whatever we think of these people – organising, controlling – they are merely a part of society's function; you could yourself (should you be motivated enough) be one of them, because it is all a part of the whole, a part of the process, a part of our lives, a part of our protection.' Boris dropped his head, the thoughts slowing with their increasing intensity; the need to translate them clearly took a hold and each word became more carefully articulated, 'And all of this has to be paid for. We have to work, and in order to make that feel worthwhile we have to shop, fill our homes with nice stuff, buy a home, live a good life – individually equated of course – in order to make it worthwhile. But ultimately we are paying for our protection.

'Anyone can apply to paper push; you could work in any of these organisations,' Boris's hand wavered in Jake's direction, light and elegant, it expressed the idea with ease and certainty: of course Jake could if he wanted. 'Anyone can be a part of the process, we are all a part of the process. We decide. And there are people like you, who think they can see it for what it is, see the function and see it as ultimately pointless...' Boris was leaning in now, as if trying to physically reach Jake with his words, '...believe it worthless; kill because it doesn't matter, because what else would you do? What dream do you have? Any dream of life requires the technology and privileges that society has created, of what society can offer you in your comfortable dream. We all live and feed from it, we are all a part of its rule and evolution. Each one of us plays their part, *tick, tick, tick...*

'It is society's fault that we cannot walk on a pavement without fear or greed. Whose fault is it if I trip on a loose stone in a community park? Barriers, signs, rules and restrictions: they are all our own doing, suffocating our spirit, closing in under pressure. Society creates pressure and who is society made up of? You and me, Jake. Blame, blame, blame: it's everyone else's fault and yet it is all our fault, that includes you and me.'

Boris pointed at himself and then at Jake, his finger waggling at each of them in turn, out of time with his words. 'Collectively we make changes – generational changes for instance – the 60s, 70s, 80s, 90s all have their distinctive era, their mark, their stand, each one a reflection of society's thoughts, fashion, guidance... With so many people and so many ideas, it is hard to muster enough common ground, enough unity, to deliver a trend, you would think,' Boris tilted his head in a sudden jerk, 'and yet it happens! The feelings of people direct society: organic food; environmental issues; the care and protection of children, old people; humanization; the goodness in things surround our greedy society...we care while we spend, a new generation re-harmonizing old ones perhaps. The 60s and 70s pledged these ideas while high on a concoction of drugs, but now those ideas are developing into a real change as the 60s generation become a mature part of the tick.

'Your turn will come, your change in the making, your future defining. Be wise to your choices.' Boris paused to gulp from his pint, the string of words flowing from him without breath drying his throat, and then continued, 'I know when people hurt you it can feel like the world's against you, when even a shop assistant smirks or is short with you, you want to lash out, punch the world and all the wankers in it, but you know when you do that you become a wanker yourself, which makes you wonder... maybe the shop assistant had a bad day, had a bad life, maybe someone was rude to them so they lashed out and were rude to you, what does that do, Jake?

It just extends the badness – we're all wankers – because that person was a wanker, that person: one person, Jake! One!' Boris held up an index finger to accentuate the oneness, 'If that person wants to be a wanker, then let them be a wanker, let them be miserable and bitter, let them have a crap day, but why let them spoil your day, your life? You become a victim by reacting, by not letting go.'

Jake paused for a moment, Boris could feel Jake's thoughts in the air. *Let go.*

Jake responded flatly. 'You've said all this before, Boris.'

Jake's words killed it, dispersing Boris's thoughts with a quick and decisive put down.

'Oh... well, it was just running through my head, that's all.'

'Right,' Jake nodded his head in acknowledgement, 'I don't feel angry anymore, Boris, I don't quite know how I do feel but it doesn't feel like that anymore.'

Boris paused, he didn't remember Jake using his name quite so often and he wasn't sure if he liked it, 'Well... good, Jake, I'm pleased for you.'

'Do we have enough for another?' Jake held up his empty pint glass and waved it a little in the air.

'Yeah, I'll get them.'

While Boris was at the bar Jake sat forward. Twisting his body he reached into his inside coat pocket, his hand rummaged around an empty space; he could feel the seam plucking the cloth together to create his pocket. Boris sat back down opposite him, reoccupying the seat he had left vacant only moments before to visit the bar.

'Boris, did I used to smoke?' Jake removed his hand from his inside coat pocket and reached for his new, full pint.

'I don't know, Jake,' Boris shrugged. 'Maybe... why?'

'I don't know, it doesn't matter,' Jake shook his head as if to shake off a thought, his mind switching to recent events. 'What was up with Horace then?'

'Think Gill might have fancied you a bit, Jake.'

'Doesn't matter now.' Jake sipped at his pint. 'Don't you think that it was a bit odd, killing poor old Gill like that?'

'Horace was a bit odd, well, guess he still is. I told you.'

'But you said that he hadn't actually killed anyone.'

'He hadn't, but he *thought* he had. Do you really not feel like that anymore?'

Jake looked up and at Boris directly; Boris was intent, already poised to take on his gaze. 'I feel the same as you. You say this stuff to me as if you were trying to convince me of it, but I already know it. Only I don't feel as angry about it as you.'

'I'm not angry,' Boris felt strange that this man might be about to say something more reformed than himself.

'I wouldn't need to air it, that's all. Makes me think you need to get it out somehow, like it still bothers you.'

'I see. Maybe I was just seeing where you were at.'

'Why?'

Boris felt a bit stumped, why would he be doing that? 'I don't know, maybe just checking in, see how you are.'

'Maybe or were?'

'Maybe or were what?'

'Checking in, maybe you were just checking in, or were you checking?' Jake's voice rising slightly, suddenly threatened.

'Not actually sure, who knows why we do anything!' Boris tipped the last few inches remaining at the bottom of his glass down his throat, 'I dunno. Let's go.'

The walk back was quiet, the two men strolled at a gentle pace towards the space they had come to know as home, 16 paces long, 10 paces wide. They passed a man, a man they had seen before. It seemed to be his job to wander around all day pretending to be a civilian just out and about.

As they stepped onto the mottled cream with brown lino that stretched out across the floor, a new white coat (that did fit slightly better than the old white coat) ushered them in from the cold. The office overlooking the communal area was still taped off, out of bounds while they awaited results back from the lab. Horace's and Imogen's chairs sat still and cold at either end of the semi-circle of seating. The table still stood, blocking any easy access to the television, in front of Jake. Today it was wiped clean of its usual spilt-tea stains. Wiped clean too of the ring left by the goldfish bowl that had woken Boris all that time ago, the fish long gone, the bowl stored in a cupboard somewhere in the building, awaiting a new fish one day. As they sat, the white coat that fitted a bit better than the previous white coat turned on the television. Jake was no longer engaged by his favourite programme and no longer awaited the inevitable day when only a stub might reappear as the white coat's finger pressed into the plastic surround of the screen. The television was being activated for the enjoyment of a new inmate, a new favourite programme watcher, a new guest to be rehabilitated.

Simon seemed long: his legs stretched out as if there would never be quite enough space to accommodate them. He sat uncomfortably in a cramped sort of way. Simon was slim and didn't wear a white coat. Jake noted him. The day ticked on.

The Diary of Rose Heather Roberts

A limit crossed, the invisible boundary, re-marked, adjusted time and time again. I'm already weak, I don't express the strength that I feel and go over in my mind. I don't demonstrate my potential.

I have this fantasy. I take a gun from the inside pocket of my jacket, I hold to the temple of my enemy.

Bang.

'Here's the church and here's the steeple
Open the doors and see all the people
Here's the parson going upstairs
And here's the parson saying his prayers.'

Anonymous – finger rhyme

Rushton

Jake had been called in shortly after his conversation with Boris at the pub. A nodding and excited Dr Washington had almost hugged him as a meeting concluded that Jake was to be released. Jake packed his t-shirts into a small bag, the years at Rushton had not increased his possessions and he looked around his room for anything that he might want to take with him, but saw nothing of interest. He breathed a long dedicated breath in through his nose. He would always remember that smell.

Boris sat watching the television with his new companion. Simon's legs extended out across the cream with brown lino that stretched out across the floor, his feet tucked under the table that blocked any easy access to the television, its spilt-tea stains cleaned away along with the ring mark left from the fish bowl (now stored in a cupboard somewhere in the building awaiting more fish one day). Simon took his pills when required and spent most of his day waiting for his favourite programme to start; the new white coat that fitted slightly better than the previous white coat was always timely, efficient. Boris waited. The days ticked on.

Jake

A few months on and Jake strolled along a street. Should he have remembered, he would have known this street quite well. It was not, however, the street on which he used to live; 'they' had sold his flat to help pay for his keep and care. Rushton's New Wave of Rehabilitation also exerted a new wave of financial rights over its occupants. But it was a street where a friend had lived, a friend he had not planned to kill. Jake strolled past a deli where he had once purchased a fine mix of olives, sun dried tomatoes and peppers in a sweet virgin olive oil marinade. As he passed it a minor glimmer of recollection swept over his mind, his taste buds tingling, alerting him of a favourable culinary option, but he did not stop to take it in. Jake strode on.

Jake pushed open the door to the King's Arms, the pub where he was to meet the Rushton representative with whom he had to check in every week. He scanned the layout, looking for his drinking companion for the next half hour, and spotted him seated at the far right corner table, already with a spare pint sitting opposite him, awaiting Jake. Jake strode over and sat in the seat earmarked for him.

'Hey, Jake. How's it going?'

'Okay, yeah, good.'

'The job?'

'Good.'

'Any problems?'

'No.'

'Dating anyone?'

'No.'

'Anything to share?'

'No.'

'Made any friends?'

'Yeah, a few. Some people from work, been out a couple times, it was good, I like them.'

'What are their names?'

'Erm... Jerry, Rachel and Edward.'

The Rushton representative looked up at Jake, urging him to elaborate.

'They invited me along one day for a drink after work, and I went. They invited me a couple more times after that... it's nothing really.'

'How are you liking this area, I mean to live in?'

'Are you always going to ask me the same questions?'

'Yes.'

'I like it here. It seems a little familiar, makes it feel safe even though I don't recognise anything. Well, I guess I'm starting to recognise it by living here, it becomes more familiar every day.'

'Have you had any specific memories or recollections?'

'No.'

'How are you getting on with your psychologist?'

'Fine.'

'Have you changed any of the décor in your flat?'

'What?'

'Have you changed – altered – any of the décor in your flat?'

Jake looked at the representative with a slight tilt to the head, 'You helped me learn my way around, got me a job, showed me the way so to speak, so what is the point of all this now? Haven't you done your job?'

'Just got to check in with you, Jake.'

'Well, it's a free pint,' Jake lifted his pint and raised it towards his companion. 'Nice coat by the way, new?'

'Yeah, got it the other day.'

'Nice.'

'Thanks.'

Jake finished the last few remaining inches of his pint, 'Is that it then?'

'Yeah, that's it. Thanks for coming.'

'Do I have a choice?'

'You always have a choice, but showing up is certainly the right one.'

Jake strode off, back down the street that if he could remember he would know quite well, past the deli with its flicker of recollection and up the stairs to his flat.

Rushton

Mary, in her white coat that fitted slightly better than the previous white coat, swished over and pressed her index finger into the plastic surround of the screen; it was time for Simon's favourite programme. Boris looked at the clock. Simon looked at the clock because Boris had looked at the clock, and Mary checked her nurse's watch, lifting it from its usual position pinned to her chest like a brooch. A mottled cream with brown lino stretched out across the floor to meet a once-scuffed white wall, recently redecorated with the refit to the office that overlooked the communal area, 16 paces long, 10 paces wide. Simon stretched out from Jake's old chair while Boris tried to lounge in his, positioned slightly to the left of the table that blocked any easy access to the television. Boris looked at the clock; Simon looked at the clock because Boris had. Mary, in her white coat that fitted a bit better than Gill's old coat, glanced at the nurse's watch that hung from her bosom.

Horace

It was 11.30 on a Sunday morning. Horace's wife had already prepared breakfast, taken the dog – Alfie – for a walk, and was now preparing a Sunday lunch for her family. Their daughter, Laura, was 12. She had gone over to her friend Emma's house, but was due back at 2pm for the meal that Janis was preparing. Horace sat in his garage, *his garage*, a garage not used for cars, bikes or any kind of transport needs; Horace's garage had been insulated, closed off, locked. He sat there for some time, perusing his folders, always in neat, orderly arrangement, flanking his desk: a broad oak desk, executive and domineering.

Rushton

Boris looked at the clock; Simon looked at the clock because Boris had; Mary checked her watch. A curious quiet hung over the space, 16 paces long, 10 paces wide. Simon's half-drunk tea sat on the stainless table that blocked any easy access to the television. It was left over from breakfast, in a mug with his name on it; the 'S' curved in a little swirl around the mug. His legs stretched out, his feet resting half under the table, his arms were folded, his light blue t-shirt scrunched under them, jeans pulled up a little, socks exposed. Boris sighed inwardly.

Simon

Simon climbed into the cab of bus number 643. He hung his assigned uniform coat on the hook provided to the right of the seat and shook his head; the coat's left arm billowed out the window. He zipped up the coat's inside pocket to protect its contents; pot holes were a constant reminder of both the seat's discomfort and the ongoing risk to his pocket's belongings. He fiddled with the dynamic seating bars, the dials and levers, his long legs an ongoing practical conundrum: his legs always a little bunched, the steering wheel always a little too far away for his arms. Simon checked his watch and compared it first to the ticket machine and then the GPS System: his watch read 2.43pm, the ticket machine 14:37, the GPS 14:44:13. He fiddled with various buttons on each side of his watch to bring it into line, just in time for the GPS System to spin out, flashing *error 2463*, or something, and then switch itself off. He checked his duty schedule, then his watch again: *damn it*. The whole palaver had taken 3 minutes and 15 seconds. He checked his mirrors, closed the doors, released the hand brake and pulled away from the curb, now late running.

The traffic lights ahead changed from orange to green, but nothing moved. Simon leant forward and sighed, his lay over time at the end of his round trip was being eaten in to, dwindling away as the seconds ticked on his watch, his break shortening. He checked his duty schedule again as his passengers began to chatter, 'Be quicker to walk...' The lights went through another cycle – red, orange, green – *and we're off!* A minute later Simon pulled into the next stop, the need to do so indicated by a walking stick being waved into the road. A collective sigh filled the lower deck with carbon dioxide as he slowed to stop. As the bus came to a halt an old but not ancient gentleman shuffled toward the step of the bus; Simon pressed the kneel button to lower the step to the curb.

The Diary of Rose Heather Roberts

It really needs more lettuce, own brand coffee sucks and the living room's back to how it was before I started moving it around.

I have this fantasy.

I'm right handed, so I'd get the gun with my right hand from the inside pocket of my jacket or coat and I'd hold it to the temple of my enemy.

Bang.

Rushton

The smell of disinfectant mixed together with the lingering paint fumes from the recently redecorated office overlooking the communal area. The smell washed over Boris. The paint was a new addition. The disinfectant was a normal everyday smell, one that Boris never liked. He felt a little giddy. Boris looked at the clock; Simon looked at the clock because Boris had; Mary checked the watch that hung at her breast. The girl who didn't wear a white coat but always intervened was sitting with them, the girl who had (by some strange deduction) discovered that her eyebrow was the same length as a regular non-applicator tampon. She sat passing the time with a girly magazine, looking remarkably normal, if such a thing as normal existed... Boris wasn't sure anymore, wasn't sure what normal was, normal in comparison to what exactly? Normal for here was anything possible; normal out there... he could hardly remember. He eyed Simon and wondered how Jake was getting on.

Mary had organised an outing to the park, a picnic had been thrown together with a few items that Boris had collected on an earlier walk to the shops; the girl who didn't wear a white coat but always intervened was to join them. They marched to the park, Mary in her white coat, blanket under arm, the girl who didn't wear a white coat beside her, Boris carrying the picnic bag and then Simon, who had been passed a bottle of lemonade to hold. Together they strode on towards the looming fence that marked the outskirt of the park. They passed a man, an average kind of man: Simon noted him; Boris had seen him a million times before. A slight smile flickered between him and Mary. No recognition passed between him and Boris.

At the park, Mary marched on towards a specific spot, an unremarkable and seemingly random spot, nowhere in particular given the vast expanse of grass that faced them. But a specific spot nonetheless, a place where the cameras could see them best, where the sound picked up the slightest ruffle, a falling napkin. Mary billowed out the blanket and instructed the group: Boris was to unload the picnic bag; Simon to put down the lemonade; and the girl who didn't wear a white but always intervened simply to be seated. 'There,' Mary pointed at the ground next to Simon. Silently they perched on the blanket, munching the thrown together sandwiches and cold sausages rescued from the fridge, one day left on the best before date. 'What a lovely day,' Mary announced, sighing mildly and leaning back a little in relaxed enjoyment of the moment. Chairs would have been good. She swung her left arm back and propped herself up with it, head tilting towards the sun.

Jeeesus, Boris thought, *if I regretted killing anyone before, for their sake, I regret it now for mine.* The days ticked on.

Jake

Jake sat in his newly assigned living space, his flat. One arm draped over the end of the sofa, the other clasped a glass of water. Why had Boris told him that he was a killer? Jake leaned forward and placed the water on the table that blocked any easy access to the television across from him, its dark face staring blank and empty back at him, the reflections of the room making him uncomfortable with their distorted shades of grey and nothingness. *Why didn't they just leave me without the memory? Wasn't that the point, that we wouldn't remember anything and thereby somehow start a new life as if the old hadn't existed?* Why had he been given this question, hanging endlessly over him?

In the far corner of his bedroom stood a packed and untouched cardboard box, delivered shortly after his arrival. Jake went to it and shuffled it forward away from the wall. He broke the flaps free from their taped holding then folded them over and creased them flat against the box's body. He lifted out a strange variety of objects: a tupperware container with lid; a bedside lamp with an adjustable angle neck; two flat glass candle holders wrapped in pink tissue; a hole punch... Jake paused at a large brown envelope. He stepped back and sat on the edge of his bed. He eyed the envelope cautiously, turning it over several times before opening it. He untucked the envelope's lip and retrieved an address book. Flicking through it he perused names, addresses and telephone numbers that he did not recognise, all neatly listed under their appropriate letter. When he reached the end he started again, slowing his search and scanning each page more carefully for any recollection. The names seemed known to him, some distant part of his mind knew who these people were, only his current brain processes excluded them from him. He searched past the letter B, through E and stopped at F. Jake stared at the page: Derek Faulkner's name, address and telephone number rested gently in his hands. Jake retrieved the cloth marker from the inside cover and laid it down the centre of the F page and sat silently for a moment. Snapping the book closed in his left hand, Jake stood and strolled over to the sideboard in the hallway. Easing open the top draw he placed the address book inside and closed it smoothly but purposefully, put on his coat, and headed out to his car.

Rushton

Simon thought about his trip to the park, beyond the walls of his imprisonment, the outside world of the park. He had thought it strange that there weren't that many people around. He looked at the clock, following Boris's look at the clock, an indicator for Mary to gaze down at her breast, at the nurse's watch hanging from her bosom.

Horace

Horace liked flowers, but not being a green fingered kind of man the garden was left to his wife. As she was not much of the gardening persuasion herself, the garden was arranged to be neat and easy. Seeded spring flowers bordered a vividly green lawn, revitalised yearly with the latest chemical product designed to *green up and weed out your turf.* But still, Horace liked flowers: he enjoyed them at the park, liked towns that made the effort and enjoyed his neat bordered garden. He watched his wife in the garden, just as he would watch strangers in the park, only here he'd be lounging on the garden furniture with its removable cushions instead of perched on a hard wooden bench. His wife would catch his gaze and wave absentmindedly from her crouched position, tending to the odd weed that had found its home among the seeded flowers. Horace would return to his book, but glance up again as she turned away, trowel in hand. At lunchtime Horace's wife would bring out to the garden table an offering of cold meats, salmon, bread, iceberg lettuce with cucumber, coleslaw, potato salad. Their daughter would join them. All sitting together in their neat and bordered garden, they would enjoy a sunny Sunday afternoon in suburbia. And then, while his daughter and wife cleaned it all away and tidied up, Horace would go for a walk, go to the park, go somewhere in his other world: the world that would eventually take him to the Rushton Institute of Rehabilitation.

Rushton

Simon was allowed to go the shops. He strode on, elated, a gentle bounce in his stride elevating him even beyond his own ridiculous height. He smiled to himself, a sense of the outside – fresh air, freedom – encompassed him. He bounced on. He passed a man, an average kind of man. He took a second glance, remembering how quiet the park had seemed, how absent of people. He bounced on. He reached the shop to which he had been instructed to go and purchased the following: a medium sliced loaf of white bread and a carton of milk. Skimmed or full-fat was up to him, so he stared at the choice and picked out the green capped one (green meant go, meant good, red was a danger colour and blue was no colour for food). He nodded happily with his decision, picked out more items. A can of soup from the bargain bin and then chocolate: a bar of dark for himself; milk for Boris; and white for Mary. He had asked about the girl who didn't wear a white coat but always intervened (the girl who had joined them at the park, the park that was strangely quiet) but had been told not to worry. Maybe she was allergic. He bounced on, bouncing right into the communal area that was overlooked by a window; 16 paces long, 10 paces wide.

Simon

It was the Thursday after the Thursday before. Simon looked at his hands, the roughness built up over the years by manual labour, the working man, the grafter, the underdog, to some the wanna be – but not to Simon, he had never 'wanted to be'. He was. It was Thursday: the Thursday after the Thursday before. He looked at his hands, rubbed one over the other, interlocked his fingers; as he crushed them together he watched the tips flood with blood, his nails pushing. One by one they might pop off.

Changing company over the years (with their varying faces and personalities) had not influenced Simon, he remained true to himself. A quick yet striking memory flashing in his head released his hands. He remembered being outside a pub with one of the changing faces of friends, having just punched – no, beaten – another man for saying something off-hand, inappropriate. His friend had stared at him, mouth slightly open, eyes slightly glazed, slightly tearful, slightly drunk, the voice a desperate, 'You're out of control, man!'

Simon smiled to himself, as he had done that evening, his eyes clear and penetrating.

The Diary of Rose Heather Roberts

I have this fantasy, but you know that. I take a gun, as you know, from the inside pocket of my jacket or coat – I'm still waiting for you to decide which – and hold it to the temple of my enemy.

Wait.

Can you feel it?

Hold the gun.

Go on I dare you.

Hold a gun in your hand, right now.

Hold it out.

Now…

Wait…

BANG.

Rushton

Boris looked at the clock; Simon looked at the clock because Boris had; Mary checked her watch, lifting it from where it hung at her bosom. Simon turned his head back to the television screen, arms folded, legs stretched out under the table that prevented any easy access to the television, the spilt-tea stains long removed, along with the ring mark left from the fish bowl (now stored in a cupboard somewhere in the building awaiting more fish, one day). Boris looked at Simon, his wide blue eyes transfixed to the screen, his light, almost white blonde hair reflected the strip lights of the room, turning it slightly (only ever so slightly) yellow. His eyebrows were thin and almost invisible, maybe they would have been invisible if it wasn't for the lights reflecting, bouncing off them. A sharp nose and thin lips, pale; so pale a skin that Boris thought him almost dead. His arms crossed, tucking his left hand under his right arm, the right hand resting on his left. Long fingers clasped around his arm. Skinny arm. *Funny,* Boris thought, *skinny, but capable of so much strength.*

A godly voice (although Simon was pretty sure that it wasn't actually God) spoke over him, the man's mass casting a shadow across his outstretched legs. A hand protruded into the space between them, a chunky hand, beefy. 'Come on, Simon,' it said.

Simon drew his eyes from the television to bring the speaking hand into focus. He stared at it, waiting for it to speak again, to see the mouth open from the palm, the space between laughter- and life-lines. Instead other hands lifted him from the shoulder and before he had recognised his own position he was standing, then marching across the cream with brown mottled lino that stretched out across the floor to meet the white, once-scuffed walls, down the corridor, past his bedroom, past Imogen's old bedroom (the only one to have a private bathroom, still unknown to anyone), past Dr Washington's office and onward to a place he never remembered.

Boris looked at the clock, even though Simon wasn't there. A habit now. He looked again taking it in this time. How long had he been sitting here? He looked across the 16 by 10 paces space, for a moment expecting his eyes to find Gill, but there stood Mary, her hand clasping the nurse's watch lifted clear from her bosom. Boris looked away, his heart a little heavy, his life caged, his mind clear, his motives good – for the moment at least – for he knew himself and knew the restrictions that that created.

Jake

It had been a long time since Jake had driven. He wasn't even sure, in the moment when 'they' had handed him a set of keys and indicated him towards a red Ford Escort, if he had ever driven. If he had, he was quite sure it would have been a different make and model, in a different colour, but as he took the keys and held them, his hand fit around them with a familiar confidence. Nodding reassuringly he bounced the set of metal, joined by a silver ring from which hung an odd choice of key ring: a yellow man with a fat stomach and a speech bubble enclosing the word 'Doh!'

'They' had taken him round the town a few times to see how he would fare, how he felt and how – above all – he drove. On the way round, 'they' pointed out various sites of interest or use: the supermarket, the library, the post office, various bus stops for varying destinations. At the end a voice spoke in a monotone dullness, 'Well, you seem fine. Steady and safe enough. No need for any recap lessons.'

So now, Jake started his car and refreshed himself with the feeling of the steering wheel in his hands. He took a light but calculated breath and released the handbrake.

Rushton

Simon stared at the television. His favourite programme had been on for 20 minutes, but he had not really taken it in. He had been aware of Mary pushing her index finger into the plastic surround of the screen, a distant voice had told him to expect only a stub to reappear one day; he had been aware of Boris looking at the clock as Mary made her way to the television to push her index finger into the plastic surround of the screen; he had been aware of the nothingness before she appeared; time working backwards, his memory now resting 20 minutes ago. But since his favourite programme had started he had lost himself and the space. He pulled his legs towards his body, clearing them from under the table positioned to block any easy access to the television, its stains long removed. He put each of his hands down beside him to rest on the arms of his chair, Jake's old chair, and pushed them down, lifting him from his seated position. Once standing, he paused, considered: what was he doing? Why was standing? Boris eyed him with a silent question: what was he doing? Why was he standing? Simon shuffled a little to his left, edging past the table that blocked any easy access to the television, the television that was broadcasting his favourite programme. He didn't need to shuffle, there was nothing wrong with his legs, feet or ankles, but he liked to shuffle, it helped him express the tiredness within. He shuffled off.

Boris followed, the journey ending in the communal bathroom. Boris stood outside the cubicle that was occupied, occupied by Simon, and put his right ear to the door. Boris knew he had made mistakes with Horace, whether or not his actions had directly influenced the events that followed was irrelevant – he was not going do anything the same. So he did not tell Simon to bin the pills, or share his own past. With Horace he had explained, 'Used to give them to my girls.' But in this moment he just listened, waiting for Simon to make his own decisions. Simon stood motionless in the cubicle, unsure quite what to do. He had sat in front of his favourite programme for 20 minutes; the pills were all soggy and stuck around his mouth now, the taste quite horrible. He gagged a little as he thought of it. He moved his fingers around his gum to release the sodden debris of his pills and flicked the remnants into the toilet bowl, wiping his fingers on the paper roll and chucking it in. He flushed and opened the door. Boris stood in the frame. Simon stared at him. Boris bowed his head and shuffled off; he didn't need to shuffle, but it helped him express the awkwardness within.

Horace

Horace hovered outside number 24. Charlotte peered around the curtain in her bedroom, clasping the cloth of one drape with her left hand while supporting herself against the wall with her right. The solidness of the wall helped her feel safe: safe behind the wall. Horace paced up and down on the other side of the fencing that fronted her home; his hands seemed to be chatting with each other, communicating with their silent talk, his head down; like a shy small boy with an infatuation. She'd had coffee with him, this was a fact, she knew it to be real. Did she regret it? No, not really, it had been a nice event in her life, a random detour from her life's usual ritual, but why was he pacing up and down her fencing? She watched him, his hands talking their silent talk, as his mass paced the width of her home, over and over. Horace looked up towards the light of the window; Charlotte ducked, releasing the curtain, her hand still pinned to the wall as she moved out of view. Horace stood still, backlit by the dappled orange street lamp on the other side of the street, his mass massive. Charlotte carefully peered round the curtain she had released a few moments before and considered Horace with a softness in her heart; she had noted the ring on his left hand during their late coffee encounter and felt sure that his wife was lovely, sure that his life didn't need this. What was he doing? She had no idea of the grass green file Horace kept about her and it's lack of any real significance to her life; how their late night coffee encounter had not been by chance; she had no foreknowledge that Horace was destined to be a resident of the Rushton Institute of Rehabilitation, or of anything beyond.

Rushton

Boris looked at the clock. Simon looked at the clock because Boris had. Mary checked her nurse's watch. Boris and Simon had looked at the clock just to see her look at her watch: a silent smirk passed between them.

Eva noted their exchange. A new inmate/companion/resident had arrived: a girl called Eva. She had strolled in, plonked herself on a spare chair and stared at the empty television screen, the blankness reflecting the room in dull tones of grey. She chewed at her mouth, rotating it, as if gum were being manipulated. Eva was lean, athletic, her long dark hair pulled up leaving bits free at the front; she flicked them to cover or reveal her eyes as she desired. Mary marched over (it was time for Simon's favourite programme) and pushed her right index finger into the plastic surround of the screen. Eva giggled, waiting for only a stub to reappear. As the television flickered into action and characters emerged into focus, Eva reached into the top pocket of her light summer jacket – a jacket she wore indoors, outdoors, all the time – to retrieve her glasses, glasses she needed for watching television. She put them on using both her hands to manoeuvre them over her ears and into position. Simon and Boris watched, a little opened-mouthed, a little bemused, a little in love, the nurse's watch forgotten.

Simon

Rebecca's clear eyes watched Simon with an emotional certainty, 'I don't want to be someone you just pop over to see for a few hours before going out.' The sentence was delivered straight up, no pauses, with her eyes fixed on him, her emotional certainty certain, 'Or even someone you pop over to see before I go out.' Rebecca looked away from him, her fingers from one hand found her fingers from the other, they talked their silent talk, played with each other, communicating. 'The only thing I'm sure of – and I don't know why – is that you're not popping round to see anyone else, another girl I mean,' her words broken up, pauses introduced, her emotional certainty emotional, 'but it's not normal, whatever that means, it doesn't *feel* normal, you know, like the adverts,' Rebecca smiled.

Simon smiled, he knew what she meant. The adverts. And no, there wasn't any other girl that he popped over to see. There wasn't any other girl that wasn't straight out of the adverts, the movies, the expected. The norm.

Simon felt caged: caged by life, caged by his surroundings, his flat, his car, his job, his life. His freedom was to pop round and see a girl he liked, a girl called Rebecca. A girl who wanted to live a life filled with tenderness, fun, love, stuff, other and beyond the daily routine of the rest of her life, a girl who wanted Simon to give her freedom, time out from the world around, happiness. Simon nodded, his rough hands finding their own communication, entwining themselves, chatting their silent chat (the roughness built up over the years by blue collar occupations, the working man, the grafter, the underdog, to some the wanna be – but not to Simon, he had never wanted to be. He was). She needed more from him, she needed tenderness, she needed him to make her feel loved, to forget, to lose the world in the moment, to be free from it in the moment. But what she didn't know – and what Simon did – was that if it became more than 'popping round' their time would join the rest of the world, would blend a little and then a lot, until life was us and the rest all at once. And then the freedom in it would be lost as this other world, the world with this girl he liked, this girl called Rebecca, would become the same as the rest: all at once, all together, all caged.

But what Rebecca knew – and Simon did not – was that freedom (in the sense of escape) could be longer than the few brief hours when he popped round; that she too felt a little caged, a little frustrated, a little lost in a world full of rules and adverts, and that to be with him was also her freedom. And that when their time joined the rest of the world – blended first a little and then a lot, until life was them and the rest all at once – it would be freer: that life would be better and fuller. *The cages of the world feel better because I'm caged with you, loving me.*

The Diary of Rose Heather Roberts

Came out like a bullet, that's what my mum told me, fast and furious I was, couldn't wait to get out into the world. Now I'm here and I wish I hadn't been so keen, a few less days out here and a few more in there and I might not be so tired, might not be so me.

I have this fantasy. The inside pocket of my jacket or coat has stored in it a gun, what kind I'm not sure, don't really know much about guns, wouldn't know what type I had if I had one. But I know you have to cock it, then you pull the trigger... bang.

Fuck it. Let's do it.

Rushton

Boris looked at the clock. Simon looked at the clock because Boris had. Mary checked her nurse's watch. Boris and Simon eyed her as she lifted the watch up from her breast to check the time. Boris looked at the clock; Simon looked at the clock; Mary checked her watch; Boris and Simon giggled. Eva watched them all, forehead creasing, her eyebrows folding, her mind ticking.

Jake

Either they didn't make cars like they used to or Jake was in the wrong car. The gear box was clunky and it barely seemed to move when he eased one foot up from a pedal and down on another in an attempt to pull away. Also, after the first time winding his window down by hand, he was sure that there should be a button. Jake pulled into his office car park and felt like he should be gliding between the lines; instead he hopped and spluttered into the space he had chosen. Beside him was a BMW 6 Series Coupe; Jake stared at it, *now that's a bit more like it*, but no, not quite. Jake stepped out of his car and scanned the car park. *There!* Jake almost pointed, and as he got closer he reached out to touch it – he almost wanted to kiss it – a 5.0 V8 510PS Supercharged Jaguar XKR, with 20" Nevis alloy wheels, high performance braking system with red callipers, sports active exhaust with quad tailpipes, Bowers & Wilkins 525W surround sound system, suede cloth premium headlining, Jaguar Smart Key system™ with keyless start and keyless entry, heated and cooled front seats, heated leather steering wheel, auto-dimming exterior mirrors, heated windscreen with timer, 6 disc in-facia CD and so much more… Jake took a deep breath, how did he know all that? The car washed round his head, this was defiantly more like it, but he'd been at Rushton for how long? He couldn't be sure, maybe an older model, but definitely more like this one. Jake strolled back over to the rusting red Ford Escort that sat in his space, next to the more appealing (but still not cutting it) BMW and put the key in the door to lock it. Jake was sure there should be a button for that too. In the office he went to his booth and scanned the office floor, as he had done in the car park, searching for more that might make sense to him.

Rushton

Dr Washington ushered Boris in as he always did, his hand waving towards the seating to the left of the desk: his left hand would wave, his right remaining poised with a pen, hovering over the paperwork in front of him, his head down scanning the information. As Boris sat, he would look up and place his pen gently on the desk.

'What do you think of Simon?' Dr Washington asked this time, quite naturally, quite calmly but cutting straight to the point.

'He's curable.' Boris spoke absentmindedly, as if he were fiddling with a loose thread on his cuff, or one that had manoeuvred its way free from the leather upholstery, a seam coming loose. Dr Washington stared at him for a few seconds, his mind racing. Boris continued, more directly this time, 'I think Simon is the one, the one you can fix, the one you could release back into the wild without fear of him re-offending, I think he's curable.'

'Jake?'

'I told you to give him more time, I'm not sure what you've released; worse, I'm not sure Jake does either.'

The doctor's eyebrows pulled in with some emotion (concern, fear, realisation?).

Had he acted too hastily to prove a point? No, who was Boris to tell him about the workings of the mind! He was a doctor; Boris was an ex-murderer. But still he paused and considered. He hadn't been entirely sure about Jake, perhaps it was time to call him in for an evaluation, respite. *Yes.* Then he'd be seen not only providing ongoing care to the community via Jake's meetings with Steven, but also via official checks carried out personally by himself; then the release of Simon, the actual cured, the real McCoy... The system works.

'Jake has been behaving very well so far.' Dr Washington announced, justifying his decision, reassuring Boris and himself.

'Good.' Boris declared, glancing down at his own hands, folded in his lap, 'Good.'

Horace

Horace had a plant, it didn't grow lemons, but when you rubbed its leaves between your fingers it smelled of them. It didn't need much care, lucky for Horace. Horace liked it. It perched on an undersized coffee table in the corner of the garage. A garage that had been renovated into an office. A wide oak desk dominated the space, flanked on the right by files of varying colours, always neat in ordered arrangement. Horace lent back in his executive chair and entwined his fingers. Rocking slightly, he raised his clasped hands to his mouth, lifting his index fingers to rest on his lips. *Here's the steeple and here's all the people.* Horace appeared deep in thought as he tapped his index fingers against his lips. Then almost springing from his seat he walked quite deliberately around the desk.

'It's a tricky job,' he said, plucking a file from the collection flanking the broad oak desk that dominated the space. He placed a grass green file in front of the empty chair opposite his own and lent into the space. One hand poised on the desk, the other on the back of the other chair. 'We've been watching her for some time. Are you up for the job?' Horace lent in a little more, 'Are you?'

The space remained silent.

'You'll be informed of a rendezvous point after the job is done. No mistakes this time.'

The empty chair lent forward and an invisible hand flicked open the file. A silent, 'No problem.' was announced by its invisible occupant. Horace was walking around the chair now, his head aloft, his manner important. His fantasy in full swing.

Horace's wife put out the place mats for dinner. A wood pigeon in full colour tapped at a tree on one, a blue tit in full flight soared across another and an owl *ter-wit-ter-wooed* from a branch on their daughter's. She arranged glasses and cutlery around the mats on the table, then turned back to the stove, stirring the bolognese. Dinner would be ready in less than 20 minutes.

Rushton

Simon was called into the boardroom. Dr Washington, Dr Jefferson, a GP and the review writer all sat at a desk facing the door. Simon strolled in, Mary with him.

'Please sit down, Simon,' Dr Jefferson put his hand out and indicated to the chair ahead of the desk. Simon sat down.

'How are you feeling?' the GP asked. Dr Washington and Dr Jefferson glanced at him.

'Good thanks,' Simon responded, quite relaxed.

'How are you finding it here?' Dr Jefferson enquired, his head a little tilted, his eyes soft.

'It's alright, bit boring.'

'How would you like to work?'

'Doing what?'

'Well, there are several things you could do, let's see...' Dr Jefferson flicked over the top page of the paperwork that was laid out in front of him. 'Landscaping, odd job kind of position, how would you feel about that?'

Simon shrugged and twisted his mouth in consideration, then his eyebrows lifted and he nodded, 'Yeah, that might be cool.'

The review writer injected, 'You used to be a bus driver didn't you? How did you find that?' Dr Washington and Dr Jefferson both looked at him, they hated the fact that these two other imbeciles had to be there.

'Yeah I did.' Simon shrugged, 'It was easy, you know, didn't have to think about it. I mean you have to concentrate of course, otherwise you'll run lots of people over, but you don't have to think, not really. And people are nice – you know, "Thanks, driver" and all that – it's pleasant.'

'But you were brought up on several violent charges while bus driving weren't you?'

'Ah yeah, well, then you have cyclists and other road users you see.'

'So a job where no-one gets in your way would be good?' it was posed as a question, but he wasn't really asking; the review writer waved a pen in the air.

Simon smiled, 'Yeah I guess.'

Dr Washington and Dr Jefferson were getting increasingly agitated, 'So you're good with landscaping, odd jobbing?' They tried to announce at the same time, but Dr Washington's powerful voice stole the show.

Simon nodded.

'Good. You'll be collected twice a week at 8am outside the communal area's side door. Tuesdays and Thursdays. Today is Wednesday, so you will start tomorrow. Is that good with you, Simon?'

'Yeah, whenever.'

Dr Jefferson looked over his shoulder at Dr Washington, 'Was there anything else?' he asked him softly, a communication between the two men and the two men only.

Dr Washington placed his beefy hands on the desk. 'No. Very good Simon, you must let us know how you get on, or if you have any problems. Say you wanted to do something different, anything, don't hesitate.'

'Okay.' Simon felt a little perplexed. 'Okay,' he said again, his head lowering, his confidence draining, uncertainty building, Dr Washington's voice quite overwhelming.

And so it was done, Simon's next step towards his rehabilitation: he would be collected by the man with the van at 8am tomorrow morning.

Simon

'I know you like hanging out with your mates,' Rebecca sighed a little wearily, torn between her needs, by her yearning for loving companionship, and Simon.

'There's nothing wrong with that is there?!'

'No, of course not…'

'Guys do that! You know, hang out with their mates.' Simon interjected, his defences building.

'I know, Simon, girls do that too, but that's not what I'm getting at…'

'Jason does it, Andrew does…'

'Simon,' Rebecca's voice rose, trying to capture his attention, 'it's not the hanging out, it's the mind-set that accompanies it. It feels to me like Jason's life is his work and his girlfriend – same with Andrew – his life is elsewhere and they come out to hang with you. But your life is your work, Jason and Andrew, and then you come round to see me. Jason and Andrew don't do that. Do you see the difference?' Rebecca emphasised her question by holding her hands out, palm up towards him.

Simon paused and thought briefly about his life. Yes, he did do that. They were his life and Rebecca part of a wider life, perhaps even a different life, but all his, all his life. Silence infused the space between them, creating a strange invisible chemical chart around them, the molecules, compounds, equations and compositions all drifted above their heads, floating between their bodies, seemingly trying to calculate them, to join them, to rebalance their lives.

But despite it being, all in all, his life, Simon's core was – in his head – *out there*. His mates didn't ask questions, didn't dig too deeply, didn't need him to do anything except get another round in. That's why they hung out too, he knew that, but when they went home it was complicated: their lives were complicated. Simon didn't want that, complications. He liked Rebecca a lot, could even push himself to love (he thought) but he didn't want a life based around her, a life that involved thinking, doing, being, because when their time joined the rest of the world – blending at first a little and then a lot, until life was them and the rest all at once – it would suffocate him. He went to work, then hung out with his mates and got wankered; it was simple, straightforward, and his. Because what Simon knew and Rebecca did not was that it was all about survival. He spent so much time with himself, he'd wake up, check the time on his watch that he had laid on the bedside table the night before (he never slept wearing it), then he'd lie back down for a bit, gather himself up to start his day. He'd get up with himself, have breakfast, sometimes shower, sometimes not, get himself ready for work. He'd go to work, he'd sign in, get a coffee, take himself outside for a smoke, drive a bus. He'd do all these things, all the while remaining *in here*, in his head, minute by minute. He'd come home for lunch sometimes, sat in the canteen other times, ate a meal, lived his life, always in his head, always with himself.

Rebecca was different from him, he liked that because it didn't reflect him, though he didn't know it. He had no real idea of who he was when he was with her, there was nothing of him in her; she was like a rest, a break from himself. This was why he craved her, why he got stressed sometimes if he hadn't seen her in a while and also why they couldn't spend too much time together before they needed to be apart, needed to find themselves again – or rather, before Simon needed to find himself again. He needed to lose himself and then re-find himself in a continual cycle in order to keep balance with himself. He spent all this time with himself, all these minutes! When he was with Rebecca that person was gone, resting somewhere in the subconscious, taking a break. He didn't want her to be his life, he needed her to escape it.

But what Rebecca knew and Simon did not was that freedom, in the sense of escape, could be theirs, together, that when their time joined the rest of the world, blended a little and then a lot until life was them and the rest all at once, it would be freer, that life would be better and more full. Life would feel free, the cages of the world would feel less oppressive because she'd be caged with him.

A conundrum faced him now: if she became his life, who would he be? But then, if he didn't have her in his life he could never escape it, never rest from himself.

'I...' Simon tried to speak, to explain, perhaps even to plead a little if required, he needed her to keep the balance between himself, but he could never allow her to be his life: how would he rest, where would he go?

Rushton

Boris looked at the clock; Eva looked at the clock, then watched Simon look at the clock, quickly followed by Mary. She put her magazine down on the table that blocked any easy access to the television and went outside for a cigarette. Jake and Imogen had also smoked occasionally in their previous lives, but neither of them had smoked in here. Eva's mind had retained this little snippet of behaviour, this pattern in her life, and so she went outside for a cigarette. Through the communal seating area's side door there was a smoking area, covered by corrugated plastic sheets; she sat at the picnic table provided. The gates that allowed the man with the van to pull up were closed and bolted, a padlock hung from a short chain wrapped around the two gates, holding them tight together. A man strolled past the other side of them, it was the same man she had seen when Mary had taken her to the hairdressers. *Creepy*, she thought.

She was plucking a stray bit of tobacco from her lip when Mary appeared in the frame, pill cup in hand, 'Do you have water out here with you?' Mary asked.

Eva looked at her and then at the table, 'No,' she said. Mary disappeared again, returning promptly with a glass of water and the pill cup and held them out to Eva. Eva re-lit her fading roll up, put the lighter down, took a few more inhalations, stubbed it out, then finally took the pill cup and water. Mary waited. Eva threw the pill cup up to tip the contents into her mouth, held the glass up to Mary in a cheers gesture and took a gulp. Once swallowed, Mary took both cups back and marched off. Eva rolled another cigarette. The days ticked on.

Eva

It was a cool day but a bright one; people were out in their skimpiest, regardless of the light breeze chilling their arms. Eva sat at an outside table in front of an independent coffee house, a large cappuccino frothy and steaming in front of her. She leant back in her chair and rolled a cigarette, her hair was loose and it flicked and settled to follow her movement. As the lighter reached its destination, her eyes moved out; she hated that crossed-eyed feeling as she stared down her nose to meet cigarette with lighter.

A young woman of around Eva's age bustled by, buggy ahead of her, an intrepid off-road mountain pushchair to negotiate the city's obstacles, a cute and silent child happily watched the world unfold in front of him, projected forward through space. As the buggy skipped over an orange juice carton lying in its path he turned, just for an instant, and eyed Eva up and down. A smile passed between them, then he looked up and over to find his mother, her approval confirming his safety while communicating with this stranger. His mother smiled too, first at him and then at Eva. Satisfied, the boy child smiled more broadly and went about his day. Eva slouched back and folded one leg across the other.

'Hey, what happened to you last night?' Michael/ Mickey/ Mike (Eva preferred Mickey), sat down at the chair opposite her, 'You were with Chris weren't you? Where is he? Can't find him anywhere.' Mikey was a guy she knew, not well, but out and about. He perched on the edge of his seat, bouncing slightly.

'Don't know.'

A strange silence hovered above them as Mickey looked anxiously out into the world, scanning the people for his friend. 'What happened last night?' Mickey asked. Eva liked Mickey best.

'I don't know. I left about midnight, not heard from him today.'

Mickey drummed his finger tips on the table, 'Right.'

Eva sat looking out across the road towards a group of lads on the other side, her cappuccino no longer steaming, the froth retreating. She turned to him and smiled, 'You still going to the Arms later?'

'Yeah... look, I've gotta dash; let me know if you hear from Chris, yeah?'

Eva nodded, 'Sure,' she said, knowing that she wouldn't, knowing that nobody would.

As Mickey scampered off Eva followed his bouncing progress down the street, until a young guy strolled past catching her gaze, a handsome chap. He gave Eva a second glance over his shoulder as he passed and she looked up at him, gave him the once over, *quite hot* she thought as her eyes flickered over the contours of his frame. Eva screwed her cigarette into the ashtray and lent forward to make a move just as an old man shuffled up and pointed to the empty seat opposite her with his walking stick, Eva waved her right hand towards it, 'Sure,' she said and settled back down, rolling another cigarette.

The group of kids that were hanging out on the other side of the street had caught the attention of the old man, their secret dialect projecting itself across the traffic, cocky and boisterous. He huffed and puffed a bit as he arranged himself in the seat, all the while talking about the youth of today. Fearful but determined not to be afraid, he put forth a confident persona. Eva listened, respectful of a life's practice and knowledge longer than her own. How was he to know that the nice young girl he was sharing a warm midday coffee experience with was more dangerous than the youths they were discussing. Eva tapped her cigarette gently on the edge of the ashtray next to him. Her eyes soft, her interest genuine. She looked across at the youths, 'How old do you think they are?' she asked. The gentleman considered, '14,15,' he pointed, his arm straight out, 'but that one, he's 18 or 19, should be more of a role model.' Eve followed the arm's pointing and settled her eyes on the older boy. 'Perhaps I can teach him a thing or two,' Eva smiled through the words, lighting up her face. She stood and made her way across the road.

The Diary of Rose Heather Roberts

I have this fantasy... I hold a gun to the temple of my enemy. I can feel the trigger, the power of a strangely simple invention that rests in my hand awaiting death.

Bang.

Rushton

Boris looked at the clock, Eva looked at Boris, Mary checked her watch. Simon planted seeds in rows, as instructed, to fill a near-perfect circle of dug-over earth at the edge of the park. Landscaping. The man with the van stayed close, but not too close. He didn't appear to be guarding, just watching over his shoulder as he planted seeds in another carefully dug-over circle at the edge of the park. The two men worked throughout the morning until the man with the van waved a gesture of time out, the index finger of his left hand pointed straight up, the palm of his right banging flat on its top.

Simon sat on the back bumper of the van, the doors open, the back laden with tools, fencing, other useful objects needed for their work. He glanced them over as he ate his sandwich: cheese and tomato.

'What's the traps for?' Simon asked pointing a little with his sandwich.

'Rodents,' the man with the van said.

'Get a lot of rodents?' Simon enquired.

'No, but when you see one gotta get it, else there'll be plenty more.'

Simon nodded, stuffing the last remaining corner of his cheese and tomato sandwich into his mouth.

Jake

Jake marched into the office, his head held high not in pretention but with an air of confidence today, but as he placed his briefcase on the floor beside his *new dynamic office seating with wheels* he felt less important than he had walking in. He looked around at all the people milling across the office floor: *what a terrible scene*. What an odd cycle of events the world had to offer, *tick, tick, tick...* but where's the *tock*? People, cars, things, all moving around, interlocking in an ever increasing cycle of, well, what exactly? Cogs in the whole, rotating and working to keep the machine ticking over, to keep society in order.

Jake twitched and held his head in his hand as a rush of pain swept over his brain and a memory flashed before him, an argument he had had with a bus driver. Jake did not catch buses often, rarely if ever really, but on this day it had been the easiest and quickest way to make a meeting, not far across town (which town and for what he couldn't remember). Not knowing the bus system all that well he had asked questions of the driver and been confronted by an impatient, brash response, igniting Jake's hair-trigger intolerance. Jake had taken the driver's name, threatening action, but really threatening *him*, Jake wrote it down: S-I-M-O-N, 'Simon what? he'd asked.

'That's all you're getting, it's just Simon.'

Jake recalled it now, Simon had been on Jake's death list. Jake had also been on Simon's and if – just for a moment – they had stopped to talk, both men would have realised that they were edging towards death, both on each other's list for the same reason.

Rushton

It had been decided by the administration to reintroduce fish to the ward. A bowl appeared on the table that blocked any easy access to the television. Eva strolled in and sat down, 'Oh God,' she stared at the fish bowl, 'bloody animals.'

'Fish actually,' Mary corrected.

'I hate pets, especially fish. I mean what's the point of them?'

'They're calming,' Mary enforced.

'Not bloody calming to me, find it quite stressy, swimming round and round and round… God, it's enough to drive you mad.'

Mary sighed, 'Would you like me to move the fish?'

'Yes, you stupid tart.'

Mary ignored Eva's tone and picked up the fish bowl, the fish swimming round and round and round within its shape. 'I'll put it in the office.'

'Don't care where you put it.'

Boris looked at the clock; Mary, putting the fish down in the office, glanced down at the nurse's watch at her breast. The original introduction of fish had been an excuse Boris had used before to relieve himself from the *tick, tick* cycle, *here fishy, fishy*. But now he didn't care for them much either, swimming round and round and round, a tiny parody of the residents' own lives in their infuriating motion.

Simon strolled in from the communal area's side door, his hands grubby, his knees muddy. Mary flew in and ushered him off. Boris looked at the clock, Eva sighed, Mary checked her breast again. Boris considered… How did Mary do that, be everywhere at once? Gill was the same. *Witches*.

Horace

It was raining the morning Horace was born. A light rumble snapped through the humidity and blossomed into rolling thunder, bringing with it torrential rain. His mother's screams of childbirth in sync somehow with the claps and drones of the sky. The midwife smiled, the head visible, each birth a miracle of 'man's' nature. His father paced the corridor. The grease and grime from his day sweating off his hands. He rubbed them into his overall.

At 11 lbs 1oz, Horace dominated the hospital cot assigned to him. The other babies (some premature, it's true) were dwarfed by his size as they all lay side by side, row by row, in the maternity room for newborns. His father stood at the glass window overlooking the spectacle, his wiped but still grimy hand pressed against the glass, embracing his son.

Rushton

Eva wondered around her room; a bed nestled in the alcove, a lamp attached to the wall above the head. A table sat in the centre of the room with one chair tucked under its wooden surface. The window had a black blind that rolled down to block out all the light, the room black, black when it was down. Eva hated it. She looked up at the walls: no pictures. There was something depressing about this room, she didn't care much that she had a private bathroom, she wanted out, something haunted her.

She marched out to the communal area (16 paces long, 10 paces wide) and banged on the window that overlooked the space. Mary looked up from her seated position below the window to see Eva peering through the glass, her hand aloft, ready to bang again. Mary pushed her *dynamic wheeled seating* back and lifted herself up to stand and meet Eva outside the office, but even as she started to move Eva was already there in the frame of the doorway, waiting. 'I want to move rooms,' Eva announced.

Mary was about to ask, *why, what's up with it?* but Eva answered the thought before she had a chance to speak. 'It's creepy,' Eva continued, 'something weird in there.'

'Creepy?' Mary enquired.

'Yeah, creepy. Don't like it in there, I want a different room. I need light and pictures… I want a cheery room, that one's depressing.'

'We could get you some pictures?' Mary suggested.

'I want a different room.'

'I'll see what I can do.' Mary turned to shuffle through some paper work unnecessarily, appearing to be seeing what she could do.

'Make it snappy.' Eva turned and left the communal area for a cigarette.

Mary made a phone call. Boris looked at the clock, Simon looked at the clock, Mary missed her place in the queue, Boris noted this.

Simon

Rebecca shied away from him. She loved him. She wasn't sure why, but she loved him. Simon hadn't said anything at their last encounter, the silent chemicals had dispersed and the moment had gone cold as he had decided that he didn't need her – wanted her, sometimes, usually when he was a bit drunk and horny – but didn't need love, didn't want to be tender, didn't want to be loving. He didn't need that. Simon had left and re-joined himself: he could take it or leave it.

Rebecca had been left without herself, alone and wanting. She knew then that this thing they had could never fulfil her, could never be the companionship that she desired and wanted, and so one evening late in the autumn, Rebecca told Simon it was over.

Simon went to the pub and got a round in.

Rushton

Eva was moving rooms. A non-descript person whose name no-one knew was to take her place in the room that, as you entered, featured a small corridor type thing, bit boxy, with the bathroom to the right. As the room opened out a bed tucked into its own alcove behind the private bathroom, a bathroom that today everyone knew existed. On the left in the centre of the room was a table like the table in the middle of a kitchen, only there was no kitchen. The window had a black blind that rolled down to block out all the light, the room black, black when it was down. The walls were blank, pictureless.

The non-descript carried in a box, Eva carried a box out, they passed in the boxy corridor, squashing themselves against the pictureless walls. Boris and Simon watched; Mary attempted to organise, but was really just an onlooker with the rest of them. Eva marched proudly towards her new room, a room that overlooked the gardens, the gardens she hadn't known existed. 'Why can't I smoke out there?' she enquired with defiant irritation, pointing out the window.

'Get unpacked,' Mary instructed, 'it's nearly time for lunch.'

'But why?!' Eva shouted after her.

'It's not a holiday camp, Eva.'

Eva

It was a hot day early in June and despite the building breeze whipping up into a wind, Eva removed her jacket, a black jacket with many, many pockets. A young man lounged on a park bench nearby. He eyed her with some intent: some curiosity, but mostly desire, her black wavy hair and slender athletic well-kept appearance thoroughly attractive. Her jacket slid off her shoulders in a way he might have removed it himself (given the chance) to reveal a tight ribbed white vest top and the exposure of a Celtic tattoo on her upper arm, an unusual work of art, beautiful and intricate, not the standard tattoo shop kind. The young man lowered his sunglasses and squinted at her more carefully. The white ribbed vest top met a pair of comfy brown trousers, which met soft sporty shoes. There was something unique about her, slightly dangerous even, the black jacket had made her look a little severe, the tattoo carried on the trend. He liked that, a feisty one perhaps, a rock and roll girl. Eva flicked her hair unconsciously and swung her jacket around her waist, tied a knot, low and loose at the front. The young man manoeuvred over for contact. He sidled up to her, a nervous use of hands fiddled with his face, 'Hi,' he said, quite kindly, quite simply.

Eva didn't respond, removing a tobacco pouch from her jacket's top pocket (nicely in reach at her hip) and silently moved away.

'Wait,' the young man urged, raising an arm after her.

'What you want?'

He scampered towards her, 'Want to get a drink?' Eva looked at him, took a drag of her cigarette and smiled. His gaze soft, a little glazed even. She liked the way he looked at her, a little naive, a little cute and very gullible.

The Diary of Rose Heather Roberts

I have this fantasy. You know it...

Bang, fucking bang.

Rushton

Simon eyed Eva with curiosity, his head facing the television, his favourite programme projecting itself across his retinas. His eyes flicked (with what he imagined to be subtlety) between Eva and the television.

'What?' Eva finally aired out loud.

Simon turned his head to her, 'What do you mean, "what"?' he replied, a little cocky, a little embarrassed.

'I'm sure you think you're being subtle, but your eyeballs are all over the place, TV, me, TV, me.' Simon pushed his head away from her and kept his eyes fixed to the television.

'You're bit stupid, aren't you?'

Simon's eyes darted left, right, left, right, thinking, covering, 'No,' he finally reassured himself.

Eva smiled at him. 'Want a cigarette?'

'Don't smoke.'

'Then keep me company.'

Simon followed Eva out to the smoking area and sat opposite her across the fixed park bench, by the bins.

Eva pinched him.

'Ouch!'

'It's the first of the month.'

'So?'

'Want me to punch you too?'

Simon nodded while rubbing his arm, 'Oh yeah, "pinch, punch, first of the month," what the hell is that all about anyway?'

Eva shrugged, 'What you looking at me for?'

Simon shrugged.

Jake

Jake had made a few friends. Jerry, Rachel and Edward. They worked in the same office and had invited him, not long after starting there, for a drink. Jake had gone along, this drink had turned in to other drinks and it would be fair to say that they were now friends.

Jerry fancied Rachel, he had told Jake this; Edward fancied this other girl called Clare, who also worked in the office but avoided drinks with them, sometimes at great length – the last excuse had involved an elaborate tale of family intervention, where Clare and her brother were getting together to come between their sister and a new friend whom they didn't much like. Jake tried to steer Edward away from Clare, thinking that all that intervention was none of their business and that Clare was, frankly, an annoying old cow. Edward however saw great tits and good clothes. Jake quite liked Rachel, but didn't tell either of them.

Rushton

Simon looked at the clock because Boris had. Unusually, he counted: *one, two, three, four.* Four seconds to move his eyes down from the clock to their resting place, a comfortable height about a metre up from the mottled cream with brown lino that stretched out across the floor, his eyelids half closed. He noticed how he always sighed once his eyes had returned to this position, he noticed too that his eyes weren't focused where they rested, his gaze diffused. Another second would bring his head round to view the television, across from the table that prevented any easy access. Boris looked at the clock; Simon looked at the clock because Boris had, losing his train of thought; Mary checked her watch, hoisted up from her breast.

Horace

It had been a while now since Gill's death and Horace sat in room not too dissimilar from Rushton's 16 by 10 paces space. Only it felt different. Horace squeezed his eyes tight shut, it smelled different too. Where was he?

Horace paused for thought, his mind an intricate montage of fantasy, a life not lived but imagined, a life beyond himself, beyond reality itself. He sat quite still, stunned by his own thoughts, his mind ticking out the moments of his life. He looked at the clock and waited for anyone to follow suit, but they didn't. He slowly bought his eyes to rest quietly on the floor, a little lost, a little sad. *What had happened?*

Rushton

A dull hum that had been droning on for the best part of the day suddenly and unceremoniously stopped. The drainage work (replacing old copper pipes with brightly coloured plastic tubing) ceased for the day. The occupants of the Level 1 Blue Team gazed up in united recognition of the sudden silence, having not noticed the drone throughout their rituals of the day. While their eyes wavered about aloft, wincing slightly against the harsh florescent lighting of the communal sitting area, the drainage people arranged a maze of orange plastic fencing, weighed down with sand bags, around the holes they had dug.

Simon

Simon had found an Emma, a nice girl with not too much going on. He popped over to see her. He hated it, for Simon always went with him. What was it that Rebecca had done? How was it that she lost him, so that he could be free from himself? Wherever else he went, whoever else he hung out with, he was always there. It had been the fear of this that had stopped him from allowing Rebecca to become more to him, but now – lost in the world with nowhere to hide from himself – he reflected on her thoughts. Had she been right, could he have been happy in a life with her? For he'd still go out with his mates, he'd still go to work, he'd still have to be with himself. The minutes passed, piling on top of each other into hours and then days. He grabbed his head, fingers tugging at his hair, he needed a rest, a break. Emma talked, making a flippant comment. Simon didn't really hear what it was, he wasn't listening, he was in here looking out. She spoke again and again, circles of noise, fucking noise. *Shut up, shut up, stop talking, squealing*! Where was Rebecca to take him away from this? But the band played on and as the squeals echoed round and round, his arm lifted, his hand tightened and his fist met Emma's head. 'You're out of control,' he could hear his mate, the pub scene, the bloke he'd bashed, as his fist met her head again and again. *Shut up, shut up.*

Rushton

Boris looked at the clock, its rather loud tick counting out the mechanical workings of a *tock*-less time machine, ticking out the seconds into minutes, minutes into hours, hours into days, days into months and months into years. No-one knew exactly how many of each had passed and no-one asked the question, not even to themselves.

Eva seemed somewhat immune to it all, bouncing around in her own little world. She watched the clock-watching ritual with some interest, watched Boris: there was something about Boris. She scratched her head, shook it a little, shaking her thoughts; where she was, what she was doing, life's little turns. She plucked a cigarette from the top pocket of her jacket and popped it into her mouth. She did this every time, poised herself as if to light up in the communal area. Mary watched, awaiting the day she might light it where she sat. Spotting Mary in the corner of her eye Eva smiled a little, hoisted herself up, and strolled out to the courtyard.

Eva somehow managed to sit firmly while giving the impression of perching. She rested her right elbow on the table, her left dangled beside her, sometimes tapping a tune on the bench wood. Simon bent his legs a little, pushed them out further than usual with each stride and with clear purpose snuck over and sat directly at the table, both his knees facing Eva. A comfortable silence rested in the air. Eva waited.

'I don't want to speak out of turn,' he began, 'but I've noticed that you use an unnecessary amount of toilet roll.'

Eva's eyes darted right. 'What?' Her cheeks puffed a little, as if the irrelevance of Simon was becoming a bit too much to bear.

'It's a ripple of events, you know: it's not just you using too much toilet roll, you have to acknowledge the wider consequences of what you do. Because of your excess, you've wasted time: someone has to go to the shops and get more, more often than truly necessary, then there's wasted money purchasing more, wasted resources used manufacturing the product itself and made the fat cat owner of the product richer, all because of your excess, because you insist on using more toilet roll than you actually need and slap more cream on – because I bet you do that too – than your skin actually requires.'

There was a pause. Eva continued to smoke her cigarette, head held aloft as if Simon wasn't there.

'What if you could only afford two toilet rolls a week, would you use it like you do now and just run out and have none, or would you use less to make it last?'

Silence.

'Okay, would you smoke all your pack in three days or ration to have at least one cigarette every day?'

Eva twisted her lips in thought, then nodded, 'Probably smoke all at once.'

Simon's palms faced upwards, his fingers twitching, 'But why? Surely it's better to have something all the time than nothing half the time?'

'What are you saying?' Eva tapped her cigarette against the edge of the ashtray, a mini ball of grey ash dropped in, 'Do I want to live half my lifetime as a millionaire or my whole lifetime poor?'

Simon shook his head, 'No, that's not what I'm saying. I'm asking why you would want to use more toilet roll than you need, which means you're not even using it, and then potentially have none? Whether you are a millionaire or poor, the principle is the same, it's not how much of it you have, it's about how much you actually need, and what is the point of wasting it, what purpose does wastage have?'

'Oh God, you're one of those environmentalists aren't you!' Eva waved a finger at him, her eyes squinting.

'It's not logical, we don't waste things we value. Take money, say: we count it, save it, ration it, store it and don't unnecessarily waste it – I mean, that's not to say we don't indulge, but that's different – but you know what I'm getting at, we do all our money counting while leaving the tap running.'

'Look, I value each and every one of my cigarettes. See,' pointing at the filter, 'I smoke it right to the butt.'

Simon lowered his head a little, shaking it a little, almost tutting a little and spoke to the table, 'You're so negative.'

Eva took the last toke of her cigarette and screwed it into the ashtray, 'Seems to me that you're the one that's being negative, worrying about the consequences of wastage. Live a little, fuck the consequences.'

'Even if the consequence is being in here?' Simon lifted his head to bring his face into Eva's view as she rose to leave the courtyard, 'I don't want to be in here.'

Eva turned to him, paused in thought: *this place, in here.* She breathed in, sat back down and lit another cigarette, 'Don't worry, it's in the budget.' She clicked a flame into action and sucked hard on the filter, inhaled deeply and placed the lighter on the table in front of her and between them. 'You didn't waste toilet roll to get in here surely?'

'No,' Simon's head lowered again and breathed into the wood of the table. 'There's a consequence to everything we do, that's all. Everything. We can pass someone on the street, someone we may never see again, but if they had to move a little to the left to get out of your way, or if you're in a queue with them, the queue's longer because you're in it, because you're there, changing things.'

'Bloody hell! What drugs they giving you?'

'Don't you see, everything you do has consequences: everything you touch, everything you say, everything you do.'

'I don't know what you did, man. I guess you're a bit emotional about it, feeling the consequences, people you hurt and all that. You want to feel bad, crack on, but I don't care about toilet roll, I don't care about consequences. Lighten up, man! Come on, it's not so bad! We could ask Mary if we could have a party, invite some of the real weirdoes from the other block.'

Simon looked up, 'What weirdoes from the other block? What other block?'

'Oh mate, you've got to get out more!'

Simon shuffled on the bench, wobbling it slightly. He wasn't much interested in the weirdoes from the other block or the other block itself, 'How come you remember stuff?'

'I don't know, maybe they want me to remember, maybe they want me to regret and you to forget.'

'Why?'

'Because I'd do it again and I know it… like Boris. If that's right, I'm going to be in here for the rest of my life. Boris totally lives here, he's almost a part of the process, must have been years… Still, make the most of it eh, don't want to be negative!'

Simon looked up at Eva's face, looking into her eyes like peering through a blinding light, trying to see the presence beyond, trying to find the truth.

Eva

A clear ball point pen with a blue tip protruded out from under Jeff's jaw. As Eva watched, the clear plastic filled with blood. Jeff's eyes wanted to speak, but the pen denied him. Eva spoke instead, 'Met this one guy, he survived, smart bloke, I liked him… you're in shock, come and sit down,' Eva took his arm and guided him to the sofa, Jeff sat. Then without delay Eva walked around the back of the sofa and produced a penknife she had bought on the journey and lifted it aloft. She paused a moment to consider the situation, had she covered every angle? Had she protected her back? And then she plunged the knife into Jeff's heart. Just like that: no mistakes, no consideration for the man for whom the penknife was destined, straight to the heart. Jeff was dead.

The Diary of Rose Heather Roberts

The shadows flicker across the room, an eerie feeling around me, around me but not really within, not inside. My mind busy with all kinds of esoteric activity. I am calm in this space, but then I stand and leave the room and the feeling comes, a feeling I knew somewhere else, somewhere beyond this place. A fantasy. Bang.

Rushton

Autumn, and the leaves lay strewn across the garden, glowing with an eloquent beauty, oranges, reds, yellows and gold. Enrapturing and exhilarating, they filled the view from Eva's new room, the low morning light sparkling from the dew. Eva fought with the window's locking mechanism, but only the small, very small top window allowed any give. She punched the glass with a tightened fist, an unusual desire had momentarily consumed her, she wanted to put her arm out, feel the day, breathe the air.

Inspector Jacob Rodgers

Inspector Jacob Rodgers fiddled with a pen, twirling round and round and round between his fingers. His back rested against the support of his chair, but his body was tense with thought. Inspector Jacob Rodgers had been given a list of the objects returned to Jake with his move to a new flat and home outside the complex in which he had found a 'cure'. One item struck Jacob as frighteningly risky: an address book, listing within its pages not only his family and general associates, but also his victims and Derek, the next on his list. If there was any truth in the reincarnation of this man, how would this book affect him? To what lengths would he go to find out about himself and, vicariously, the people listed within it? And more, if there was no truth in it, if the rehabilitation wasn't for real, then might those lengths become something else...?

Unable to bear it, Inspector Jacob Rodgers made a phone call. Dr Washington was needed to help him understand the meaning behind this decision, the decision to offer Jake an insight opportunity. Perhaps there was something – a psychological something that the doctor had thought of – a reason that eluded him.

Rushton

'What did you mean the other day, when you said you were never getting out of here, because you were just like Boris?' Simon fiddled with his hands, partly nervous, partly cold. The autumn seemed to have appeared overnight: the day before had been summer, the air light, the day still and sunny. Time was losing its connection, the chill on his hands came as a surprise.

'Aren't you supposed to be gardening, or whatever it is that you do, today? There's loads of leaves out the other side that need hovering up!' Eva fiddled with her hands, partly agitation, partly cold, as the sudden autumn breeze skirted round the building to rush over their seating.

'Man's ill,' Simon stated.

'Man? Doesn't he have a name?'

Simon shrugged.

lx, re4.

Simon stretched out a shaking hand across the table, the question lingering in his mind, 'What did you mean the other day?' he repeated.

Eva shrugged, 'He's part of the system.'

Simon frowned, 'What does that mean? You don't strike me as someone who would want to buy in to any system, so why are you like that?'

'Look,' Eva straightened up and stretched out her arms, so that their hands were only centimetres apart, 'I know what I am and I'd do it again, but you can't do it in here or you end up like Horace. There was this guy, Horace, stayed here before us, probably in your room. He killed the last nurse, the one before Mary, some bird called Gill. Now he's in a place where the patients wear white coats and foam from the mouth. That's not going to be me.' Eva pointed to herself, blowing out air in a quick burst as she did so, *that's not going to be me.*

'What do the doctors wear, if the patients are in white coats?' Simon asked.

Eva stared at him. 'Does it matter, man?! The point is that this Horace character might as well be dead, he's on so many drugs that he's wheelchair bound and foaming at the mouth. Makes no fucking difference what you're wearing when you're like that, does it? They're all in white coats, only some can speak and move around and the rest just drool!'

'That would suck if you suffered from prosopagnosia, not even having the personality of the clothes someone wears to help identify them.'

'What the fuck is prosopagnosia?' But of course Eva knew perfectly well what prosopagnosia was: Eva knew everything.

'It's a condition where you can't recognise people by face, sometimes not even your own family, or even yourself if you saw a picture, bonkers.'

'Is that true?'

'Yeah, my aunt or someone had it.'

'...Or someone...' Eva smiled.

'How you know about this Horace and stuff?'

Eva shrugged, smiling at Simon with her eyes.

'Here,' Eva passed him a cigarette, 'if you're going to sit out here with me all the time, you'd better start smoking. I don't want *them*,' Eva nodded a head towards the building, 'to think we're friends or anything.'

Simon took it, holding it between his thumb and forefinger. He twirled the cigarette around, considering it.

Eva held up a light. And so it was, on this autumn morning with a chill on their hands, that Simon became a smoker.

Jake

'So Jake, how's it going?' Jake's post-institution supervisor poised a pen over the pad in front of him, the pen hovering under the printed question, *how are things going?* The first section, of this, his third monthly visit questionnaire, was headed *General*.

'Good,' Jake pronounced.

'Just good?'

'How many people do you know that might be more than that? How would you say you were doing? I think "good" is pretty good, wouldn't you say?'

Jake's post-institution supervisor wrote the word 'good' under the question and moved on to the next, 'Have you made any friends?'

'Yes, I told you about them before.'

'How's that going?'

'Good.'

'How's the job working out for you?'

'Good.'

'How do you feel about your life?'

'Good.'

'Any worries or thoughts?'

'Sometimes I find myself locked in a difficult decision between Marmite and Vegemite, not quite sure which one, if either, I prefer.'

'Which have you decided on?'

Jake stared at him, 'Neither, I went for Bovril.'

'Do you feel that there is too much choice?'

'I want a better car.'

'Well, you're earning money, save up and get one.'

'Can I trade that red Ford thing in or do I have to give that back to you?'

'You'll have to give that back, it belongs to Rushton.'

'It's rubbish.'

Jake's post-institution supervisor smiled, 'Well, it's economical and practical. What kind of car would you like?'

'Something with more style. There's a promotion coming up at work, can I go for it or am I locked in a stage for supervision?'

'You're locked into that company, but not the position. If you feel you can do it, go ahead.'

'Do it?! I could run the building.'

'Do you know that or just feel it?'

Jake thought for a moment, 'Both.'

Rushton

'What are you?' Simon took a cigarette from Eva, not yet adept at making his own.

'What?'

'You said before that you know what you are, what is that?'

'Blimey, when did I say that? I dunno.'

'Few weeks ago; you told me about a guy called Horace.'

'Who?'

'Horace!'

Eva shrugged.

'And Boris… you said you were like him and I asked you what that meant.'

Eva stared at him through the smoky haze of exhalation.

'Shit, girl, this is nuts! Do you not remember?'

'I know I sit here a lot, listening to you waffle on; you got a lot of questions for someone who's supposed to be sedated.'

'I'm not foaming from the mouth yet.'

'Not yet, but they're coming to get you.'

'What do you mean?'

'What do you mean, "what do you mean"?! Figure it out and stop asking me stupid questions!'

'They're not stupid questions.'

'Christ, what are *you*? That's the question, what the fuck are you doing in here? You're so fucking right on and straight.'

'So you do know what I'm talking about.' Simon smiled a little.

'Manipulative as well. Are you really clever or just canny?'

Simon shrugged, 'Pushy, maybe.'

'Look dude, I'm just trying to get through one day then the next. You look at the clock, watch the same television programme all the time and then come out here and ask questions like you're fine: it's all nuts.'

'What? I do what?'

Eva stared at him, quite earnestly, 'Never mind, don't worry about it, I'm just being sparky.'

'Sparky. That's a nice expression for you.'

Eva rolled them both another cigarette, 'It's warmed up again, don't you think?'

Simon nodded while taking in the air. He hadn't noticed, but yes, it had, 'Good for this time of year,' he replied.

Horace

It was raining the morning Horace was born. A light rumble snapped through the humidity and blossomed into rolling thunder, bringing with it torrential rain. His mother's screams of childbirth somehow in sync with the claps and drones of the sky while the midwife smiled: the head visible, the birth a miracle. His father paced the corridor. The grease and grime from his day sweating off his hands. He rubbed them into his overall.

At 11 lbs 1oz, Horace had dominated the hospital cot assigned to him. The other babies (some premature, it's true) were dwarfed by his size as they all lay side by side, row by row, in the maternity room for newborns. Horace's father stood at the glass window overlooking the spectacle, his wiped but still grimy hand pressed against the glass, embracing his son.

White coat, white coat, white coat, slurp, *white coat, white coat.*

Rushton

Boris looked at the clock. Simon looked at the clock because Boris had. Mary checked her watch then swished over in her white coat, a coat that fitted slightly better than the previous white coat, and pressed her index finger into the plastic surround of the screen. It was time for Simon's favourite programme. Boris looked at the clock; Simon looked at the clock because Boris had looked at the clock; Mary checked her nurse's watch, lifting it from its brooch position, pinned to her chest. A mottled cream with brown lino stretched out across the floor, meeting a once-scuffed white wall, redecorated with the refit to the office that overlooked the communal area (16 paces long, 10 paces wide). Simon stretched out from Jake's old chair while Boris tried to lounge in his, positioned slightly to the left of the table blocking any easy access to the television. Boris looked at the clock; Simon looked at the clock because Boris had. Mary in her white coat (that fitted a bit better than Gill's old coat) glanced at her nurse's watch that hung at her bosom. Eva never looked at the clock. Eva shook her head and tutted under her breath, to her time had only periodic meaning: certain actions of the day were required at certain times, but this did not – as Eva saw it – require the constant clock watching of her strange companions. She rolled a cigarette.

Simon

Simon hated shopping. The crazy crowds rushing in and out of every shop, the battle over a single rail that several people want a claim on at once. That hideous shirt in the window display and the ill-fitting ones he tried on in dismay. Nothing quite fitted, his frame tall and skinny, the arms or legs too short, the chest and waist too big. Not quite tall enough for the special *tall and big* section, but still too tall for the average section, he blundered on in vain, searching out a new item to replace the blood stained one he had burned. Several films had shown him the way to remove evidence: the burning of the clothes was an important bullet point. Simon's garden incinerator had been a most valuable purchase, although Simon was quite sure (once he'd got it home) that he could have made one out of an old metal dustbin himself. Little feet and holes punched in the side were the only difference.

Rushton

Eva liked her new room. The poky, dark, depressing room she had come from haunted her a little. In the old room the bed was fixed into an alcove whose wooden surround had come loose on one side, prised up and open. Behind it Eva had found a diary, on its cover funny swirls in various coloured ink, and on its first page the words, *'The Diary of Rose Heather Roberts – The Truth'*. Imogen/Louise/once Samantha/ but usually Rose had written two diaries consecutively; one now sat on a shelf at the home of Inspector Jacob Rodgers, the other lay gently in the hands of Eva. The addition of the words *The Truth* to the title of the second book had been added to inspire Imogen to write more thoughtfully, a different pace was initiated and this diary was always picked up after the other. Nonetheless, despite her intentions both diaries ran consecutively as a mirrored outpouring of immediate thought. Eva held it now, sat in her new room. In the old room the wood surround of the bed, fixed into its alcove, had been pushed back, the depressing room left as she had found it minus a book, a book with the title *'The Diary of Rose Heather Roberts – The Truth'*. Eva read.

Eva

Eva had once known a man she didn't kill. A brief encounter, a coffee, the slightest tender brush of contact during the polite air kiss on the cheek pushed breath over her skin. Sometimes she remembered him, sometimes struggling to remember the details, peering through the air, trying to conjure his features and feel the breath on her face. Sometimes she saw him as if he sat beside her now, the exact rhythm of his intonation, the flick of hair slightly out of place with the rest, the sleeve of his shirt, the shape of his nails, the wear on the soles of his shoes; Eva knew how he walked because of them, the slight lean to the inside of his feet.

The Diary of Rose Heather Roberts – The Truth

Horace hasn't killed anyone, he's never done anything. That's not to say that he's not a little strange. He's defiantly a little strange. I like him though. Capable of lifting extraordinary weights; moved a car once, they say. He makes me sad. And sad is not good for me. Well that's silly, is sad good for anyone? All in moderation, all in moderation. I'm smiling now, I remember that saying a lot growing up, 'all in moderation'. Can you moderate sadness? Will I go to the inside pocket of my jacket or coat, will I hold it to the temple of my enemy, to the temple of my own head, because it's all my fault, it's me, I'm a fucking liability. I know I do this to myself, I know, but here it is. I like Horace, but he makes me sad. Had files they say, stalked some girls, one in particular and kept files on her, but he's not a bad man, his wife called them in, must have been very distressing for her, to find all those files, what would you think? Poor woman, sold the house to pay for his rehabilitation, it won't work, this place will be the death of us all. Got to go, my mum's coming.

Rushton

Simon waited by the gate, the gate that opened up from the smoking courtyard. Eva sat at her usual place on the bench, casual elbow on table, watching Simon wait by the gate. There came the clang of a chain, the pop of a padlock, and the gate swung open. Eva's eyes darted to the other man, the man with a white van. He was well built with a morning shadow; she could almost feel the dark bristles scratching her skin, her mind feeling for his hand and pulling it around his back, her pen knife poised under his ear. *Wait.* She looked back at Simon, the moment passing quickly, the men climbing into the white van. Could it be she had met another man, a man she did not want to kill? Simon's skinny body curved through the door and into the passenger seat. As he leaned out to pull the door shut he glanced at Eva, a smile twitched between them. The other man, the man with a white van, now pushing on the gas and rolling the white van away was, in Eva's mind, already dead: the moment's imagining brief but irrevocable. Simon's twitchy smile was the only thing she thought of now.

'Come on, take them,' Mary waved two cups at Eva, one of water, the other an unknown concoction of chemical-based powder, compressed into tiny round pills.

'You and Simon seem to get along well,' Mary smiled.

'Don't speak to me.'

'You know, Eva, it's not a bad thing to find a friend in someone.'

'What are your friends like?'

'Well...' Mary sat down. Eva flinched, *Oh my God!* She was actually going to tell her.

'Russell is a carpenter, he made me a really splendid kitchen...'

Eva raised her hand in front of her face, a gesture for silence.

Mary continued, 'He's married with two children, Angelica and...'

'Stop! I really don't want to know.'

'But you asked!'

Eva thought for a moment, 'Yes I did, but not really, it was something like bad sarcasm. I didn't mean it.'

'Oh! I'll get on then.'

'Good idea.'

'Eva,' Mary paused, there was something about Eva, something so normal and girl-like, something strangely tangible in her very ordinariness, and yet... and yet she had done all those terrible things. 'Eva, do you think this place will help you?'

Blimey, Eva stared at her, 'I think it will stop me killing, if that's its purpose.'

'Does that help you?'

'It helps others live,' Eva smiled.

'But will you be better, will you still want to kill?'

'Does Boris?'

Mary looked out, as if a view of wonder rolled out further than she could focus, 'Yes. Yes he does.'

Jake

Jake marched into the office his head held high not in pretention but with an air of confidence today, but as he placed his briefcase on the floor beside his *new dynamic office seating with wheels* he felt less important than he had walking in. He perused his desk: the stapler was there; the hole-punch; the little pot of paper clips; the stand for pens, a variety of felt thicknesses on offer. *What a terrible scene.*

He switched on his computer and scanned the display. Flicking a shortcut icon, Jake read the description of the job promotion he had told his institution supervisor about, and a bundle of thoughts ran through his mind: could he really run the building? What had he been before, apart from a killer? Surely this information would be useful, what one could achieve or be capable of outside of death. His institution supervisor had not seemed surprised by his desire to seek promotion, and yet now, faced with the prospect, could he do it? Would he want to do it? He just wanted the car.

The stapler stared at him, the hole punch, the pens... these were things he had known of but not wielded himself, he must have had a secretary. He had in all likelihood run a building like this before. Did his current employers know this? Would the job be his because they knew he could do it, or would Rushton insist on it as a test? He was chained to the company, but not the position. *Damn them,* how was Jake to know what makes the man, what achievements they would really celebrate, when the world conspired around him. Society and all its hooks in your flesh. Jake started to feel a little normal, a little like himself: anger was a feeling he recognised, a feeling he understood above all this chaos.

Rushton

Boris looked at the clock, a white rimmed plastic affair in keeping with its place of residence. Simon looked at the clock because Boris had; Mary checked her watch, then swished over in her white coat (a coat that fitted slightly better than the previous white coat) and pressed her index finger into the plastic surround of the screen. It was time for Simon's favourite programme. Boris looked at the clock; Simon looked at the clock because Boris had looked at the clock; Mary checked her nurse's watch, lifting it from its brooch position pinned to her chest. A mottled cream with brown lino stretched out across the floor, meeting a once-scuffed white wall, redecorated with the refit to the office that overlooked the communal area: 16 paces long, 10 paces wide. Simon stretched out from Jake's old chair, his legs tucked under the table that blocked any easy access to the television. Boris looked at the clock: the little hand swung round, one second at a time, *tick, tick, tick*; still no *tock*. Simon looked at the clock because Boris had, again and again and again, one moment to the next, one cigarette break separating clock watching to the next cigarette, one moment lost to another. *How long had they been here?* Nobody asked the question, not even to themselves. Mary in her white coat (that fitted a bit better than Gill's old coat) glanced at the nurse's watch that hung at her bosom. Eva looked at Boris looking at the clock, then at Simon. She shook her head and tutted a little under her breath and then rolled two cigarettes, one for her and one for Simon. The day ticked on.

Horace

Horace sat, saliva building in the corner of his mouth, the wheelchair digging in a little. Horace was a sizable man, capable of lifting extraordinary weights. Rumour had it that he'd moved a car once. Wheelchairs were not made quite to his size, digging in a little, saliva building in the corner of his mouth, white coats: white, everywhere, no scuffs, no spilt-tea stains, no table, no television, no anything, just Horace, Horace in a wheelchair that digs in a little, saliva building in the corner of his mouth. His wife hovered over him, grapes in shaking hand, tissues in pocket, tears building in her eyes, white coats, white, everywhere. She crouched by him, the grapes now on the floor, the bleached white floor, chemicals everywhere, one hand on his knee, saliva building in the corner of his mouth, his knee numb to him, his mind numb to him, his wife numb to him. 'Horace,' the gentle tones of love squeeze from her mouth, 'Horace!' She lowered her head, the guilt of a decision made hanging over her now. She had heard of this new rehabilitation idea, this new institution; she had signed a form, several forms, allowing them to try, to test, to see... How could she have known what would happen? She had thought he needed help; the confusion in her mind when she had found the files, the office so neat, so creepy, the girls in the files so pretty. The fear of possibilities, the misunderstanding of a man escaping his world, just for moments, a fantasy that separates *him* from *them*, a game. She had signed him up, convinced him to try, sold the house to pay for it, wishing her husband normal, wishing for things she did not understand, wishing away a gentle man and bringing out a dangerous one. 'Horace!' The thick chemical air eating her words, drowning her breath, everything white, the wheelchair digging in a little, saliva building in the corner of his mouth, her husband. She picked herself up and stared up into the white that reflected the space all around her.

She picked up the grapes from the floor and, placing one foot and then the other, she first walked, then marched out of the building, over to her car, put on her seat belt and drove out of the car park, her destination: Rushton.

Rushton

Dr Washington sat rigid across from Horace's wife. They were waiting for the tea that had been ordered to arrive, an uncomfortable air stretched tense between them. Finally a man who didn't wear a white coat but always intervened stepped in carrying a tray, tea cups and saucers, a tea cosy with a bobble on top, a sugar bowl and milk jug.

'Thank you, John,' the doctor boomed a little, his voice reflecting his discomfort.

'Doctor, I'm going to get to the point,' Horace's wife sat with confidence, her back straight, her purpose absolute. 'I'm not here to criticise, I appreciate that it was all new and experimental. I appreciate also that I *asked* you to take Horace, even though your work was based on and meant for people who had killed. And now the risks of that decision have clearly come to an unhappy conclusion.' Horace's wife paused to take stock, sipping at the tea. 'Doctor, my husband is now one of the people you designed this process for, and I'd like you to try again.'

'Mrs Conway,' Dr Washington's hands hovered in the air, trying to bring calm to the room, calm to his own thoughts, 'Horace is a very different kind of killer to the sort we have here...'

'He wasn't a killer before he came here.'

'Yes, that is true, but Mrs Conway...' Dr Washington sighed, *what could he say?* He had taken on this challenge not knowing what to do with it, had pushed Horace, and made him a killer because he had already thought himself one. He had turned one kind of madness into another. *Wait: yes!* Horace was indeed interesting, more testing could be done, if one can turn a reasonable man into a killer, he must be able to turn him back; the power of suggestion. *Could it be that simple?!*

Dr Washington collected himself, 'Mrs Conway, I would be glad to try. In fact I am sorry we didn't approach you with alternatives. It was such a shock, Gill had been here from the beginning and we felt that Horace couldn't stay, but on reflection I think there is something we might be able to do. At least I would like to try and see what we can do. Trying is after all the only way of achieving. Failures are inevitable, and I am sorry that we failed your husband the first time round, but out of failures one can learn and adjust, no?!'

Horace's wife nodded furiously, 'Yes, yes, that's what I thought. Oh! Thank you, Doctor! Horace is a good man, just a little odd I fear – a little lost in a fantasy – but on reflection it was harmless, *he* was harmless. I want to fix my decision to bring him to you, and I think the only way to do it is to bring him back.'

'I think, Mrs Conway, that you are absolutely correct. I will start the arrangements immediately.'

And so it was, that cool, breezy day in an office with a bobble-topped tea cosy, that Horace found himself re-established into the institution that had made him a killer.

Simon

Simon hated cyclists. They never stopped at traffic lights correctly, never gave way to either pedestrians or other road users and they swore at him, even though he was a massive, very visible vehicle and they were in his blind spot, weaving stupidly around an indicating bus. Simon hated cyclists. Once, making a left turn, he had squashed one between his bus and a railing. The company gave him time off for stress, time he didn't need. Simon had liked it, time to recuperate after the shock of such a terrible thing to have occurred while on duty, an unfortunate accident. Which it was, that first time.

Rushton

Horace sat staring at the table, the table that blocked any easy access to the television, the television that had flickered with the movement of Jake's favourite programme and now flickered with the movement of someone else's programme. The chairs had been shuffled around slightly to accommodate a new guest, new to those now sitting round the table (the table that blocked any easy access to the television, the television flickering to the movement of someone else's favourite programme), but an old guest revisiting to those who had seen it all. Boris watched him; Simon was a little indifferent to him; Mary was a little afraid of him; Eva was fascinated by him, this being the man she had read about in the diary of Rose Heather Roberts.

Eva

Eva popped in the yoga video she had recently ordered and received from Amazon. A mat had arrived the day before and now she rolled it out, the curling ends face down to flatten out. She hoped for a stress release to aid her in the forever escalating killing spree in which she found herself embroiled. Her established fitness routine was just not cutting to the core of some anxiety she experienced. She desired a way to kill calmly; her current fitness routine added to her confidence as she out-manoeuvred her stronger opponents but did not help with the sudden outbursts she sometimes experienced, frenzied attacks. Many friends had talked of yoga's healing power for stress, how it had, in all its simplicity, calmed an inner beast of sudden outbursts. Outbursts not quite as dramatic as Eva's (she was quite sure of that) but outbursts nonetheless. She breathed in, deep and steady, stretching up her arms to extend her body to its maximum height, *in…and out.*

The Diary of Rose Heather Roberts – The Truth

Horace is always looking at the clock, what is that about? And why does Jake always look at the clock after Horace has? And why don't I want to do that? I mean it's not that I want to, it's really fucking dull, but I'm pretty sure they'd find it dull too if they knew what they were doing. Jake's cute though, he's got soft, floppy, surfy blonde hair and the most delightful blue eyes that sparkle. But he's not a surfer: he was an executive, smart suits kind of job, a clever boy. Killed his friend, I can understand that: I killed mine. He shouldn't be following Horace's lead, he should be the lead, he's a leader of men, he's a manipulating salesman, he's dangerous. I think I might love him a little bit. They're thinking about letting him out, but they shouldn't do that, he's a little bit smart, a little bit manipulating, a little bit of an actor, more than a little bit dangerous. The inspector knows that, I've seen it in his eyes, but then he's afraid of all of us, except Horace (he's just a bit odd) but then here he is, the clock-watching leader, the scary bulk, capable of lifting extraordinary weights… rumour has it he moved a car once. He looks like a mug shot, your typical kind of crazy women-killer. Saw his wife once, she came by, but didn't come in, saw her out the window and asked Mick who she was, he says she cried a lot, sad thing, Horace makes me sad. Life makes me sad. I have this fantasy, Mick's going to help.

Rushton

Horace stared at the table, the table blocking any easy access to the television; Boris stared at Horace; Eva rolled two cigarettes and passed one to Simon who had been staring at Boris, staring at Horace.

'Is that the guy you told me about?' Outside, Simon waved a thumb at the building, presumably in Horace's general direction.

'What?!'

'Horace, that guy you told me about.'

'I told you about him?'

'Yeah! You told me he'd killed the last nurse before Mary, can't remember her name now though, and that he was wheelchair bound and drooling.'

'I did?'

'Yeah! You did!'

Eva shrugged, 'Don't know what you're talking about, I never seen that man before in my life.'

'You never said you'd seen him, only heard about him. I asked how you knew, but you wouldn't say.'

'You've got to cut down on you meds, mate. I don't know anything about that man, what's his name?'

Simon threw his hands in the air, 'This place could drive a man to insanity!'

Eva laughed, maybe for the first time since her last kill. This could be fun.

'What's the name of the guy with the van, that guy you garden with?'

Simon looked at her, she was so changeable.

'Well? What's his name?' Eva asked again.

'Mick.'

Eva toked on her cigarette. *Mick.* In the outside world Mick would be dead already, but in here he might just be useful.

Inspector Jacob Rodgers

Inspector Jacob Rodgers held his breath as he listened to Dr Washington. Jake had been left the address book as a test, to answer exactly the questions the inspector himself was asking. Everybody wanted to know what he would do with this information, it could be the easiest way to see how Jake was getting on. *Could also be the quickest way to have someone killed,* the inspector thought. But however concerned he was about the consequences of leaving Jake with this possibly deadly information, he was more overwhelmingly concerned at the news that Eva Huddersfield had been admitted to Rushton.

Eva was the most frightening person the inspector had ever encountered; her calm demeanour even more chilling than Jake's, more chilling than Jack the Ripper. The doctor's thirst for knowledge seemed blind to the dangers of a woman who was, granted, an unusual and fascinating killer, such extreme behaviour was so rare in women. *But dear God, surely this can never, never be someone we release back into the world.*

Inspector Jacob Rodgers steadied himself against the back of his chair. The world had finally gone completely mad. *Where does humanity stop and idiocy begin? Why are we trying to find ways to understand and accept bad, even terrible behaviour?* Jacob found the local 'youths' difficult enough, their attitude and lack of respect tolerated, even taught. The more reasonable we become, the more horrible the individual who wants to be a wanker, anti-social behaviour programmes failing at every turn. *Surely we cannot extrapolate that to our killers.*

'Doctor, do you really believe you can change a killer's behaviour?'

'Inspector, I believe that all people have an equal chance of working for – and only for – the betterment of things; we must strive always to improve the world.'

'A true philanthropist!' Inspector Jacob Rodgers shuffled in his seat a little as he said it.

'Anyone can be a better person, given the right influences and guidance.'

'Or system conditioning?!' The inspector's eyes widened, the words questioning. 'What exactly is it that you do here, Doctor?'

'We correct behaviour and rehabilitate.'

'Yes, but how?'

'Inspector, our work here is extremely complex.'

'Doesn't look that complex: all I see when I come is people watching television or wondering round the streets.'

'That is your perception, Inspector, but I can assure you that much work is going on – Simon is working now, for example.'

'Oh I see, working!' The inspector twitched, something in the air made him uncomfortable. The doctor made him nervous, he somehow feared that if he said the wrong thing he might be taken away and re-conditioned himself, rehabilitated. 'Doing what?'

'Gardening.'

'That's what Jake did, isn't it?'

'Yes, it's good for the soul, re-connects you to nature and the beauty of things.'

'Give them a garden tool and a flower and they all turn into floating hippies with only love in their heart, is that how it works, Doctor?'

'I think that's enough, Inspector. If you don't mind, I have much to be getting on with.'

'I'm sure you do, Doctor, many pruning reports to write.' The inspector smiled, but only at himself, there was something quite odd about this place. 'I wonder, Doctor, if I might have a look at Jake's file, put my mind at rest about his progress.'

'I'm afraid Jake's file is confidential, as all the residents' files are. You must know that.'

'No harm in asking.'

'Well, good day to you, Inspector.'

'Good day, Doctor.'

Inspector Jacob Rodgers closed the doctor's heavy oak door behind him and lent against its solidness, paused and breathed.

'Hello. All finished with Dr Washington?' A guiding hand appeared seemingly out of the wall as the inspector opened his eyes.

'Er, yes.'

'This way.' A sweeping arm encouraged the inspector towards the exit.

'You must be the new head nurse of this block?'

'No, no, I'm a helper.'

'A helper?'

'Yes.'

'What exactly is a helper?'

'I help.'

'Help me to the exit?'

'Amongst other things, yes.'

'What sort of other things?'

'Breakfast, lunch, dinner, keeping checks, cleaning up, that sort of thing.'

'So meals, cleaning and showing policemen the door.'

A smile.

'What sort of checks do you do?'

'Here's the door.' Another smile.

'Checks?'

'Bye!'

And the door was closed. Inspector Jacob Rodgers looked round his surroundings: to his right, a short path that lead him to a gate in the wall and back to his car; to his left a long path that lead towards the town that formed part of the institution. Jacob stepped left.

'Hello, forgotten your way?'

'No, actually, I thought I might take a look around the place.'

'I'm afraid you can't do that, no unauthorised persons in the town. You'll need to get permission and be escorted.'

'Permission from whom?'

'Dr Washington.'

'I see. I am a policemen.'

'Rules are rules, no exceptions. Turn right please.'

Inspector Jacob Rodgers got to the gate, which opened automatically – as it always had – from either side. Once through, it closed tight, high and locked behind him.

I see.

Rushton

Mary sent for a caretaker. The clock watching thing was getting on her nerves, the nurse's watch hanging at her bosom was as much time keeping as was necessary. Pill times, favourite television programme times, meal times: these were all governed by her. The clock served only to get on her nerves, with all the constant bloody watching. The days' ticking stopped.

Jake

Jake got the promotion. He called his post-institution supervisor and handed back the car. He strutted to a tailor's shop and ordered a bespoke fitted suit, for which he purchased a quality brush, and opened an account with a dry cleaner. He went to work and began his journey up, up the trajectory of what was a rickety ladder for some, steep cottage stairs for others, but a sweeping wide, hand-railed stroll for Jake, who soon had a wardrobe of fitted suits and a growing list of accounts at restaurants, bars, shoemakers and banks. The more he climbed the angrier he got. Jake liked it. He laughed with friends about its idiocy, seethed at clients about their greed and manipulating ways to achieve it, all the while revelling in accounts and polished handmade shoes. Jake clapped his hands, *slap, slap* and smiled like he had never done before. Had Dr Rushton's New Wave of Rehabilitation actually worked? His uncontrollable hatred for society now felt focused, channelled into his joy at its benefits. He marvelled at his flat, now a balconied penthouse, contemporary suite. He brushed his suits and inspected his shoes back from the polishers. He had dinner parties, outside caters providing the three course culinary delights he wooed his friends with. He attended other parties, drank toasts to success. *Three cheers for business, hip hip...*

Rushton

Dr Washington sat quietly in his office. The sound of rain hammered down outside his window, a tumbler of whiskey and ice bobbed about in his hand. He could smell the wood, his robust and polished antique furniture. It complemented the whiskey. Jake's post-institution supervisor had visited that morning with news of yet another promotion and Jake's never ending success. Had the programme worked? Dr Washington wasn't sure… Was Jake a better person? His killings had been carried out to rid the world of people that he believed spoiled it; would Jake have killed his present self now, if he had met himself back then? Had they succeeded in making a better man, or just a lawful one? Does law have much to do with morality?

Horace

Horace murmured to himself. He lay on his bed, the sharp white sheets crumpling with his weight, and stared up at the ceiling. Something was different about it, this was not the room he had had before. Horace was sure of it. The thought sprung a coil in his mind: Boris, with his wild ginger hair, was not his brother.

Jake.

This was not his room, he was sure of it. He closed his eyes. The world not quite as it should be, his memory not quite in tune; what came before this room and the other room? *Which other room and why?*

He held his thoughts, tried to focus, but the colours and shapes behind his eyelids distracted him; *think, Horace, think.*

Rushton

Mary peered out from the office window, the one that looked out over the communal living area. Refurbished after Gill's death, the scuffs were no longer present on the walls, the spilt-tea stains long removed. Where was Horace? A man who didn't wear a white coat but always intervened tapped on the glass; Mary waved him in. Boris watched as mouths moved to shape words, lips expressing sentences, the air between the man who didn't wear coats but always intervened and Mary (with her nurse's watch that hung at her bosom), the lingering breath between them full of flavour: the food they had eaten, the words they were saying, the tone of their emotions, all mingled up in the space between them, invisible to the naked eye, but Boris knew it was there. He stared out their conversation, his eyes glazed with cruel intent. Eva watched Boris watching the man who didn't wear a white coat but always intervened and Mary (with her nurse's watch that hung at her bosom). Eva also stared out their conversation, her eyes glazed with cruel intent. Simon watched Eva watching Boris. He feared them both and in this moment – just for a moment – a flicker of a feeling, an angel's intuition tapped him on the shoulder; he knew why he feared them, knew the answers to the questions he had asked of Eva when she talked of Boris, when she had talked of Horace, of being like one and not wanting to end up like the other. These answers came in one moment: one tiny moment, a second of time filled with a wealth of information. He watched as they watched, and he knew what type of killers they were. Now only one question remained: what was he? He was the next Jake. He was the next one out of here.

Simon

Simon's mother tapped on the table, a sharp deliberate *tap, tap* with the bottom of her fork on the cloth. The cloth dulled the shock of it, softening the sharpness of the sound but not dulling the impatience. Simon pushed his sprouts around the plate, a plate that had red roses printed around its edge, red roses that distracted him from his food and clashed with the sprouts.

'Eat your sprouts, son,' Simon's father, a weary man with big hands and tired eyes, encouraged his son to eat his greens.

Simon squinted at him, searching for a strength, a strength that he could admire, but (as in his later years) he felt only frustration and claustrophobia: the smothering of his father by his mother, then the future beating of a girl whose name he would later first learn, then forget, only the death of her remaining between them. But at seven, as he squinted at his father, he did not recognise these thoughts, did not recognise the feelings he would later replicate. He ate his sprouts.

Rushton

Horace was discovered, without too much difficulty, lying on his bed, staring at the ceiling. Mary swished up to his side and placed a gentle hand on the exposed sharp white sheet at his foot end.

'Horace?'

Nothing happened: not a twitch, not a sign, not a breath.

'Horace?!'

He seemed chillingly still, but his skin was warm. Mary walked up the length of the bed and rested the back of her hand on his forehead. She wanted to sit down, sit by him like a visiting relative, read to him, as if trying to break through the silence of a coma. *Some say they can hear you.*

'Horace,' her voice was gentle, calm, 'how can I help you?'

What can be done to solve your riddle? Mary remembered Alice in Wonderland. As a child she had been fascinated by the questions confronting Alice, the riddles of the world, the strangeness of things, of people. Which character was Horace? What kind of kindness did he need? Each patient, each person in fact, from the doctors who monitored her, the caretakers that attended to her practical requirements, those who didn't wear white coats but always intervened, to the patients she monitored with the nurse's watch that hung from her bosom, they all had their own particular needs. Horace was no longer clock watching. Had she disturbed him by removing the clock, or was this the start of a revival? Despite the regularity of each day's events, the repetitiveness of it all, each person remained unpredictable. Each moment, so like the last, was a sort of surprise. And here, in this moment, with the back of her hand resting across Horace's forehead, feeling as if she would like to sit down and read to him, it was a surprise to realise how much she cared about this odd group of people with whom she had found herself working. What had she thought when she applied for the role? What opportunities did she think the position would offer her to help and change the way of things? And most importantly of all, was she fulfilling them? Was she living up to the expectations she had set herself? Was she making a difference?

Mary jumped up and started to sing...

Swishing round Horace's room, her soft shoes silent on the laminate floor.

'Mary?!'

'Woooh!' Mary spun round slowing her steps from the dance she had whisked up while she sang.

'Are you alright?' Dr Washington's frame filled the doorway, making the room seem smaller.

'Oh yes, I'm very well; Horace is fine, just resting.'

'Good. Is there something more you should be doing?'

'Oh very probably,' Mary smiled, a smile she had not felt for a long time. She felt it beam across her face: a smile of joy, a moment, a moment like this, a second of thought, as an angel taps on your shoulder, a moment of intuition. 'But there are more important things to do, Doctor, like helping the patients make the best of this institution, making your work here *work*, making all this worthwhile. My duties are bogged down with filing and organising, when I should be here, reading to Horace while he sleeps.'

'And dancing round his room?' Dr Washington whooshed his giant hand across the space in front of him, to demonstrate the extent to which she had been dancing.

'Oh most defiantly, Doctor! Lifts the spirits, don't you think? And Horace used to go to ballroom dancing lessons with his wife, I read it in his file, I think he'd like it.'

'Very good, Sister,' and Dr Washington was gone.

Back in his office, Dr Washington lent back in his *dynamic seating with wheels* and entwined his fingers, *here's the steeple and here's all the people.* He released his hands. *Very good sister, very good. Lift the spirits and get him home to his wife.* But then, Gill's death had served the institution well: no-one wanted to end up like Horace. Residents would think twice before killing again within these walls: Horace had given them a deterrent, greater than that of the law. So he had to be removed if he was to improve. *Damn it,* had he thought it through, he would never have returned Horace to this block, *think Washington, think.*

Dr Henry Washington picked up his telephone receiver and dialled a memorised number, arranged for Horace to be moved to the other block.

The circles of influence, yes, yes. Mary would be transferred with him to assist in his full recovery. They needed another Jake, *a cured,* one that gets out. Simon wasn't ready yet, and anyway he was too useful in the development of Eva, but he would be next. Dr Henry Washington felt a little pleased with himself. *Clever boy.*

Eva

Eva snapped open a Yorkie bar: she always broke them in half without unwrapping them first. She waved one of the open ends under the nose of Michael, a slender, well-dressed man, with a neat moustache and cuff links. Michael had been sipping a cappuccino at the cafe, two blocks from where he worked. A morning coffee and Danish before his day's stress began. Had he known that it might have been less stressful to go straight to work, his day would have been very different and would almost certainly have lead on to another. But on this particular day Eva had joined him, and so it was that this was Michael's last.

Michael pulled a little against the ties that held his wrists to the chair on which he had awoken to find himself sitting. The Yorkie bar worked like smelling salts, bringing him round and alerting him to a rather odd and difficult situation.

Eva smiled. 'Hello.'

Michael looked at her, questions in his mind but guarded on his face. Eva held in her hand an empty biro pen case, just the plastic bit, empty of its ink. Her favourite tool. Perhaps a better outlet for this delight would have been to become a nurse, or even a doctor: the draining of blood and piercing of needles a daily practice. She'd have loved that. But as it was, on this day, the idea of that had never crossed her mind, only the empty biro pen presented itself to her, both a comfort and excitable thrill. Eva smiled. Michael feared the worst as he watched his own blood jet out at surprising speed.

Eva wiggled the pen around in small swoops, directing the jet on the wall, writing out his name. 'Look Michael,' she said, 'that's you.'

He watched his name run down the wall, woozy now. Feeling faint, *tick, tick*... there's no *tock*... and Michael is dead.

Rushton

Horace had been moved the afternoon before, Mary with him, so a new ward nurse arrived this morning, the nurse from Orange Block. Chirpy and tubby, Yvonne marched in. 'Good morning,' she proclaimed with elaborate arm swings. *Dear God* the room breathed out. Eva hated her instantly. Yvonne kept a pocket watch on a chain, sheltered in the lower right pocket of her white coat, the white coat that strained at the bosom, the buttons double threaded and clinging on. A white coat that reminded Boris of another white coat, now gone and replaced several times over by other white coats. *Tick, tick.* But no clock hung from the wall any more.

The Diary of Rose Heather Roberts – The Truth

Shit man! Horace like totally bludgeoned Gill to death, terrible mess. Sort of surprised, but not surprised, this is a crazy place after all. Now he's one of us: a killer, rather than a dreamer. Bet it all goes wrong from here though, they'll take him away and dose him up, he'll be no-one now, a drooling mess in a white institution, more white than this one, he'll wear white, think blank white thoughts, stare into space at white walls, in a white wheelchair. Bye Horace. Shame. I wonder if I'm a shame, if someone looks over at me and writes a diary and says, 'Ahh! Imogen, such a shame! Like her, but she's totally cuckoo.' It always comes back to me in the end, don't think I don't notice. I know how self-obsessed I am, but it's all in here: I'm banging my head with my hand while I write this, pointing at myself, me, me, me, in here, in here, in here. I'm in here. I don't know how to get myself out there, it's all in here. How do I get out there with you? Wait... Who are you and why are you reading my diary????

Rushton

Eva held the diary out, she could hear the words, feel the presence, who was she to read this diary? *Shit man!* Eva threw the book down as if the cover burned her, but the page stayed open, the words staring out at her like eyes. *Who are you? Who are you? Who are you? How dare you!* Eva had watched many horror stories, indeed she had committed a few herself, but never had she been unsettled by anybody's pleas. She picked the book back up and turned the page; in bold letters, over drawn several times, three words bounced back at her, alone on the page, *I'M WATCHING YOU.* Eva turned the next page and the next. *WHO ARE YOU? WHAT YOU WANT?* Each page proclaiming another question, another statement, each more frenzied than the last. Eva slammed Imogen's diary closed and tucked it under her pillow. *Shit man!* Eva felt decidedly peculiar...

Someone knocked softly on the door, three short raps. Eva's head darted up, *what?!* 'What?' she called out.

'It's me, Boris. Simon and I were wondering if you wanted to come to the pub?'

'Be right there.'

Rushton

Simon missed the clock, not because he cared to look at it like Horace and Jake had, but because it was a useful tool for knowing the time. His favourite television programme started at a particular time and the new nurse that no-one really saw always switched it on, but how soon would that be?

Jake

It was all getting a little tiresome: he had made promotion; upgraded his stupid little car; bought some over-expensive accessories for his flat; re-established his sharp suits and pressed shirts, always in neat and orderly arrangement, nicely spaced in his wardrobe so as not to get crinkled. The next promotion would be easy and the next and then... *what?*

Flo: like a stream or a fast running river that salmon battle against to reach their spawning ground; or a waterfall that feeds the river and adds to its race; or a fountain that circles from pond to spout to pond again; or the cycle of the earth as it spins on its axis; or the flow of the universe itself. Flo-for-Florence rested a gentle manicured hand on Jake's arm, squeezing it a little. She felt his muscular structure beneath the jacket and through the highly pressed shirt. Flo-for-Florence liked it. Her voice breathed out, gentle and calm, like fresh air on a warm autumn morning, the beauty of the deep autumnal colours glowing and reflecting from the sun. The crisp chilled air, light and invigorating. Fresh and clear, her voice soothed him, intoxicated him. Almost as if in a trance, he listened intently to every word, his mind focused and responsive. 'Don't try to control it, but at the same time, you mustn't let it control you. There is a fine difference between knowledge and understanding. One can know many things but understand very little. You must see through the face of things and understand it, find the truth in it, be all-knowing in knowing nothing and understanding everything. See the world, Jake, see through it and into it, understand it.'

Jake nodded, felt the warm and gentle grip of her hand on his arm. He could feel the structure of his own musculature beneath the jacket and through his highly pressed shirt, could feel it being gently gripped by her beautiful manicured fingers. He felt his realness, his presence.

Rushton

Boris knocked gently on the heavy door of Dr Washington's office. The doctor's name plaque hung levelled at his sight line, embossed, gold and sturdy looking, reflecting pretentious authority.

'Come in.' A meaty voice sounded lost in the room beyond the door, as if its owner were much further away, down the corridor somewhere, echoing around wings of the building to meet his ears here, through the brick and dust; the sound of a lost voice from the depths of a wishing well perhaps, the haunting of his past.

'Come in!' A little louder now, more impatient, much closer. Boris entered the room and stood facing Dr Washington who sat, as always, behind his robust, official desk, his files flanking the side, his pen pot full, pencil poised in hand.

'What can I do for you, Boris?'

Boris took a breath and waited for Dr Washington to look up at him.

Dr Washington appeared to be marking school work, he was ticking sections of a written transcript and making scribbled notes in the margin, 'What is it, Boris?'

'I'm waiting for you to finish what you're doing and look at me.'

'I see.' Dr Washington was not keen on this line of conversation, 'If you wish to wait for me to finish, you can take a seat and wait, but I fear it may be a few hours. Better you interrupt me,' Dr Washington put down his pencil and lifted his head to eye Boris directly. 'So now I'm looking, Boris, how can I help?'

Boris took another breath. He wanted to sit down, calm himself, relax a little, but still he stood, the conversation running across his thoughts, the questions being answered by he himself, him alone.

'Boris,' Dr Washington's tone agitated now, 'what is it?'

'This place.'

'It's getting to you?'

'It's nuts.'

'How so?'

'*How so?* Is that a real question?! It's full of nutters.'

'So it is inevitable that it might be a little nuts,' Dr Washington hovered and turned his mighty hand over above the desk, 'do you not think?'

'Of course.'

'So the problem now is?'

'What's the point?'

'The point?! The point, Boris, is to make the world a better place, to re-educate the seemingly irredeemable, to make right the wrongs that people do, to make good your life and the lives of others like you.'

'I don't think it can be done.'

'It is early days, Boris.'

'It's been years!'

'It's a work in progress, Boris, one that will work eventually, with growing evidence and understanding. It will be a successful concept that we will leave as our legacy, for the future. All things take time to understand and make good.'

'It will never be done! The human mind is too complex, each one containing its own truth and mixture of desires and influence, we make it up as we go! Your truth is as nutty as mine and there're so many out there – not just in our block here – but *out there* in housing estates and streets, roads, blocks of other kinds: the world. The world! Full of people all thinking what they want to think at any given moment; what truths can we possibly understand? We work by order, by control, to place people, to organise people, give them something to do, some purpose...'

Dr Washington put up his mighty hand to interrupt Boris's flow, 'Boris, you are absolutely correct and that is exactly why we must create order *for you*, for everyone. Man observes patterns, works out what drives people, what pleases people, what makes them smile and so we find ways to provide that sense, provide it in order to keep order, as you rightly say. All people must adhere to this order so that we can all live contently. The people here are killers, Boris; this is not acceptable behaviour, not to anyone's truth, not even yours. So a way to change it must be found, do you understand?'

'You want to find peace on earth?'

'Yes, don't you?'

'What about war?'

'Oh for God's sake, don't be pedantic!'

'So it's okay if killing is done in the name of something?! I did it in the name of Boris – would it be different if I'd joined the army and killed in the name of… what? My country, the mission, the keeping of peace?'

'Boris, you're being ridiculous: the two things are simply not comparable.'

'And yet, unlike your normal answer to everything, you struggle to tell me how?'

'One man does not have the right to decide! There are circumstances in war when decisions are confusing, and yes, mistakes have been made, but a solider does not randomly kill innocent people, especially those they invite into their house first for a cup of tea!'

'Just innocent people caught in the crossfire.'

'Boris, if you want to make a statement about war, speak to your local MP or join a campaigning group that marches through the streets and demonstrates outside weapon manufacturers! If you were on the outside I would in fact encourage you to do that, if that is your feeling, but this office is not the place. It has nothing to do with what we are trying to achieve here, nor do I believe it has anything to do with why you came to see me.

'Boris, I do understand your concerns, it seems like an impossible task: some killers seem to be impulsive and out of control and so they will stay here, until we find a solution. Others have just had too much, snapped, if you like – Simon for instance – I do believe that he can be helped more promptly.

'Man has an obligation to find answers for all things, to make right the wrongs, to strive always for betterment. We need you Boris: you must stay focused and believe in the cause. You have come so far and are our greatest achievement. You should be proud of what you have learned here and of the better man you have become. These questions in your mind are good Boris, it is right to question, for without questions we cannot find answers. Think about what I have said: don't try to control it, but at the same time, you mustn't let it control you. There is a fine distinction between knowledge and understanding. One can know many things but understand very little. You must see through the face of things and understand, find the truth, be all-knowing in knowing nothing and understanding everything. You understand how to see the world Boris: to see through it and into it.'

Boris nodded. He did believe in the cause and had felt so sure and clear in the not so distant past. Boris took a breath, he felt the flow of it through his body, 'I'm sorry, Doctor – just a wobble – I'll get back to work.'

Dr Washington nodded. *Good.* 'And Boris, soldiers are trained and paid to work under a code of practice. They are brave men, not angry ones.' Boris bowed his head as he lent forward to close the door behind him, 'Yes, Doctor, I know. I'm sorry.'

Horace

Think, Horace, think.

Horace thought. He eased himself up and swivelled round until his feet hit the floor. He perched there on the edge of his bed. Mary would be knocking soon, Horace was sure of it. *Mary.* This was not the nurse he had had before, he was sure of it, just as sure as he was that this was not his room, sure also that the communal area – 14 paces by 9 – was a little smaller than it had been before. What was happening? *Think, Horace, think.* Horace felt a little dizzy. Gaps in his mind confused him… a wife, a daughter, ties, gardening, work… *Oh God!* That dreadful place where he had worked… *Come on, Horace, piece it together… What is this? What is happening?*

Horace scratched his side and as he looked, he noticed a mark. He checked the other side: it was the same, where had these marks come from? Grooves, red and indented, as if he had been sitting in a tight space. *The chair.* He remembered a chair, a chair with wheels, *dynamic office seating with wheels, no that's not it*: that was at that dreadful place he had worked, this was different, more recent. Time. *Think, Horace, think.*

Rushton

Eva swung back on her chair, rolling countless cigarettes, over and over, each one gently placed into a glass, all facing up, filters at the bottom. She pointed at them and explained, 'Don't want your grubby paws touching the filters.'

Simon looked away, his fear of her rising, his sanity evolving. All he had done, all he was doing, the questions and answers of his life funnelling towards a single goal: *get the fuck out of here, go back, drive a bus again, be patient with cyclists and forget all this ever happened.* The new nurse, whose white coat bulged at the breast, was not as present as the others had been: no-body checked their watch, but the clock had gone so there was nothing to check it against anyway. No-one floated around seemingly watching over them; pills were brought at set times but Simon was spitting them out now, just as Horace and Jake had done. Just as they all did. Very few residents took their pills, *lx* and *re4*. As Eva placed another roll-up into the glass a shadow loomed over the table (the table blocking any easy access to the television). Eva didn't watch the television; it was always Simon's favourite programme that was switched on, Eva didn't care what that was.

A godly voice broke her concentration, 'Come on, Eva.' A mighty hand reached out.

'No.'

But there's no discussion, no choice. She was taken away, just as Horace had been, just like Jake and all the others. *White coats.*

Simon

Simon leaned over and pulled off an end of day report. The ticket machine on his bus, after a day of chewing tickets and spitting out small remainders of ticket information amongst the blobs of ink, clunked out his report. His take over driver was impatient, and Simon even more impatient, as they both stared at the machine and its struggle. 'Good luck with that one,' Simon offered as some condolence for this next man's duty of ticket machine hell.

Back in the depot, Simon paid in his day's takings, the machine for that equally slow and frustrating. He battled with every note, pushing it into the slot, only to have it rejected back at him, 'Doesn't anything work?!' And then he trudged over to his girlfriend's house to bludgeon her to death, although he didn't know this on his way there.

Rushton

Dr Henry Washington sat back in his *dynamic office seating with wheels*, Inspector Jacob Rodgers playing on his thoughts. Tapping in a number he had listed in his contacts book, he held the receiver to his ear and waited.

'Dr Washington here. Just calling to check that you have it under control... I know, but he came to my office and I think that there may be new room for concern, keep a close eye on him and keep me informed, I don't want him making frequent visits. He has done his part as an officer of the law, which is to be commended – he is a fine officer, I would expect him to be curious – but his work is done, it is our work now. Dissuade him from digging, he'll be hard pressed to find anything but I don't want him trying... Good, good.'

Dr Henry Washington placed the receiver back on the body of the phone and breathed out, a deep, hard sigh, forced through his nostrils. He had much work to do.

Eva

Malcolm watched Eva work. He was impressed with her flirting techniques and efficient body disposal, but felt there was more she could learn. A quick-witted man might overpower her; it had not happened yet, she was fast, athletic, some training on her side, a martial art, though not one he recognised in its correct, disciplined form. Eva varied her moves: she wasn't mixing disciplines, but almost making them up. Malcolm pushed out his lips and frowned, strength building, as he strolled over to introduce himself to Eva. Twenty minutes of chit chat and they were off for a quiet drink at hers. But there is always room for surprises, even with the best laid plans; as Eva went for the jugular Malcolm twisted her hand, almost cracking her wrist.

'There is more you need to learn.' He said.

Eva snatched her arm back, 'What do you mean?'

'I've been watching you: you're good, but you could be better. I can help.'

Eva squinted at him, her right hand rubbing her left wrist. 'Who are you?'

'I'm the one you've been looking for.'

'Don't flatter yourself!'

'My name is Malcolm and we believe that you have potential.'

'*We?*'

'I belong to an organisation, one that has no desire to stop your special gift. We only wish to help you evolve it.'

'What organisation?'

'It's not important now, just know that we have resources. Resources that can be at your disposal.'

'Why?'

'Why not? I've been watching you; I've seen what you can do and what your weaknesses are. We can help strengthen what you do and eradicate weaknesses.'

'That's too weird. No.'

'You cannot kill me, your weaknesses leave too many holes. What can you lose by improving yourself, to get to a point where I cannot stop you?' Malcolm smiled.

Eva turned her head away from him, *too good to be true, has to be.* 'What do want from me in return?'

'You'll work for us.'

'No.'

'You don't know what we do.'

'I don't want to know, I don't work for anyone.'

'I'll leave you to think about it. You'll see me around if you change your mind.'

'I won't.'

'You will, you'll come around. They all do, whether they know it or not.'

The Diary of Rose Heather Roberts – The Truth

Creepy, this place is creepy, or maybe it's just this room: dark, dingy, door I've never opened, don't like it. My brain feels mashed, someone's messing with it. Jake's so cute, just wanna eat him.

Rushton

'Simon, how long am I gone when they take me away?' Eva felt a little confused. It wasn't unpleasant, her mind felt open somehow, as if things were starting to come together, but held at a distance, as if responding to a desire not her own.

'Two days.'

'What?!'

'Two days.'

'*You* don't go for two days.'

'Don't I?'

'No, half a day at most. Once you were gone all day, but never two days. What they doing?'

'Don't remember.'

'Me neither.'

'Do you feel different?'

'I don't know.'

'Me neither.'

'This place is going to fuck us up.'

'Maybe they're doing experiments on us.'

'I don't have any puncture marks, I checked.'

'Maybe they do brain experiments – show you flashing lights or something – then hypnotise you so you don't remember.'

'Whatever they're doing to me, they're doing to you too.' Eva pointed at him. 'I'm going to the roof, I want to see what this complex looks like.'

'You'll get caught! Anyway, they've got locks on all the doors, I tried already.'

'Did you? How far did you get and which way did you try?'

'End of the corridor, past Dr Washington's office, right at the end and through push button door, no security. At the end of that passage there's nowhere to go, you can see stairs through a glass panel, but that door is very secure, you need a pass.'

'What kind of pass?'

'Card swipe.'

'Does Yvonne have a pass, or whatever her name is?'

'Yes, she keeps it on a pulley thing attached to her belt.'

'I'm impressed, Simon.'

'I'm disappointed, thought you would have clocked all that already.'

'I've been distracted.'

'With what?! Nothing happens here.'

'Exactly! Doesn't that strike you as a little bit odd? Nothing happens: nothing. And yet we're changing... how? We don't take the pills, we don't do yoga, stress relief classes, nothing.'

'Must be when they take us away.'

'Of course, but no-one remembers what happens then.'

'Still, it seems to be working.'

'And that's okay with you is it? That you're changing by some secret method that you don't remember?'

'If it works, does it matter?'

'Does to me, I want to know what they're doing. Can't just mess with a person and not tell them.'

'Kept your victims fully informed did you? Told them all about what you were going to do to them once you'd lured them into your den?'

'I told them once they were there.'

'How kind of you, bet they were thrilled!'

'Point is they can't do that – I still have rights you know – they can't just go around making me forget.'

'Your victims have rights did they?'

'What is the matter with you?! Who cares about that? This is about us now, I mean what is this place anyway?'

'Dr Rushton's New Wave of Rehabilitation.'

'Exactly: who the fuck is Dr Rushton? Have you met him?'

'Don't think so, but who knows, I mean if they're wiping our memory...'

'Are you being sarcastic?'

Simon shrugged and smiled.

'I'm going to Dr Washington, I'm going to ask.'

'Go Eva.' Simon threw a fist into the air.

Eva strode with confidence. She would try for answers, and failing that she would reach the roof and take a look. After that she'd do some digging, some sneaking, and piece together the answers for herself. Eva knocked hard on the big oak door that blocked her access to Dr Washington's office.

'Come in!' A booming voice resonated through the wood. Eva stepped inside, her confidence a little depleted, the voice a sudden memory, a sudden influence on her calm, an instant authority to be respected.

Dr Washington looked up from his paperwork and smiled gently, 'Come in, come in, sit down.' His paddle hand pushed air around his head, as he waved her over to be seated. 'What can I do for you Eva?'

Eva sat down, but felt she wanted to stand. The chair engulfed her, her slight frame small against the robust dark leather of the armchair. 'I want to know what happens to us when you take us away. Simon said I was gone for two days. What did you do to me during that time, and why have you erased it from my memory?'

'Good questions, Eva, good questions. Shall I show you?'

Eva nodded, *could it really be that easy? Just ask and the answers are given...*

Dr Washington stood up, pushing himself against the broad oak desk as he did so. 'Come,' he said. Eva followed.

They strolled down the corridors, the card swipe doors swung open ahead of the doctor without him having to use one. Eva noticed a camera above each one, the doctor's presence noted before his arrival, the door activated by its operator; a light on its body flashed orange, then green. Dr Washington stopped and put his hand out to signal a change of direction, an open door to a room stood in front of her. Dr Washington nodded for her to go in. 'This is one of the study rooms. Here you learn history and science.'

Eva looked around. It did indeed resemble a classroom, cleaner and neater than the ones she remembered at her school, but nonetheless a classroom.

'Come,' Dr Washington took her to another room, very much like the first. 'Here you learn maths and English.' At the end of the corridor a door opened out into a hall, mats lined the floor. 'Here you improve on the art you were chosen for.'

'Chosen for?'

'Martial arts, Eva, your speed and ability is ninja worthy, you are one of our finest fighters.'

'I don't understand.'

'You are here to learn, to improve, your strengths evolved, your weaknesses eradicated. You are here for the betterment of things, to become a better person, to exceed all you would have been before.'

'Why do you make us forget?'

'Because you are not ready. Your mind is still that of an instinctual killer, you act on impulse. You are undisciplined. Here you learn, under hypnosis, you work hard and study well. If it were left to you, you wouldn't do it would you?'

'Got no interest in school that's for sure.'

'That's not for sure, because you do.'

'Only because you tell me to!'

'Exactly, but with enough education and training, you will *learn* to want to, to believe in its cause and its purpose.'

'What is its purpose?'

'The betterment of things, a better world.'

'What if I said I was in? No more need for hypnosis, I'll do it.'

'I wouldn't believe you. You're not ready.'

'What's in there?' Eva pointed at a door as they passed.

'That's the yoga room, but there are people practicing, so I can't show you.'

'Do I do yoga?'

'Yes, you do all these practices, you are a fine student, we are pleased. One day you will be a fine person, a useful person.'

'What other practices?'

'There's chanting and all aspects of calming management, business lessons, cooking classes...'

'What's calming management?'

'Well, breathing exercises and such like.'

'I want to remember.'

'You do, in a way. One day it will be all you know, without knowing it.'

'Was Jake a good student?'

Dr Washington gave Eva a slight side glance, they had all been told of Jake, he was after all the goal, the example of an achievable success, release. Having purposefully left Imogen's second diary for Eva to find he paused in this moment, awaiting her openness to declare the knowledge of its contents. Eva gave Dr Washington a slight side glance, *does he know I have the diary?* He pressed on. 'Oh the best! Jake is going to be very useful, he's moving up the ranks quickly, one day he will have influence to help our course. We have high hopes for Jake.'

'This is brainwashing.'

'This is correction. For the betterment of things, for the greater good.'

'This has to be against my liberties.'

'You are a killer. Your liberties have been given to me.'

'You're brainwashing me!'

'I told you that you were not ready to know.'

'Does Jake know?'

'He knows some, not all. His process is better served outside where he can grow using what he's good at. He killed when he felt wrongdoing, and that is a good thing: the intention to rid the world of the selfish. But it is not our belief that killing is good, so we just needed to alter his action, not his thought.'

'You're a cult!'

'No, we are an adjustment centre.'

'You're a cult.'

'No, we are not. We are here for the betterment of the world.'

'That's what cults say while they brainwash you! What's the difference here?'

'One day you will understand.'

'Yeah, when I'm completely brainwashed!'

'No. Is Boris brainwashed?'

'Probably.'

'But you're not sure. Boris has changed how he sees the world, how he wants to behave within it, he has chosen a better, more useful path.'

'Then yes, he's been brainwashed, because Boris is just like me.'

'A fine student, who can do great things to help the world. You just need redirection, you need to use your skills for better things.'

'Bullshit, you're a brainwashing cult! Oh my God! Get me out of here!'

'We are teaching you great things, Eva. You will grow into a fine person. Forget what you have seen for the moment, but remember its importance. The betterment of things always the goal, a fine world where you can make a difference and be credited with many great deeds. Hypnosis can only influence what you are willing to hear, what you are willing to become.'

And so it was that Eva was shown back to the communal area, 10 paces by 16.

'Hey!' Simon beckoned Eva outside for a smoke, 'What happened with Dr Washington?'

'Nothing.'

'You've been gone about two hours, something must have happened?'

'Two hours?! Really, wow! No, nothing happened, we talked in his office, cleared up a few things.'

'Like what?'

'You mustn't fret, Simon, this is a good place. We're being taken to a higher level, where all our skills will be recognised and used for a greater good.'

Simon stared at Eva, 'You're kidding right?!'

'No, I'm serious, I've learnt many things here... I feel full of useful knowledge.'

Simon shuffled in his seat, 'Shit, man!'

Inspector Jacob Rodgers

Inspector Jacob Rodgers sat back in his swivel chair. His lady companion had become a more established feature in his life, her calming and gentle touch, her kind and thoughtful words blurring the sharp edges of his reasoning. *Think, Jacob, think.*

Rushton

Simon tried to get to the perimeter, but he was always guided back by those who didn't wear white coats but always intervened. He was indeed locked in, restricted to certain areas. But then he knew that already. He had killed someone: of course he would be restricted. In all honesty, he felt he should have been locked up more securely. Why wasn't he in prison? *What the...* Simon was not all that keen on swearing so he pursed his lips and hummed the missing word... *is this place?* He looked around him: the not-so-yellow, not-so-brick road; the trees that lined it; the post office; the pub. He reflected on how he had lived before, flashes of memories. He looked around again: the not-so-yellow, not-so-brick road; the trees that lined it; the post office; the pub. *It's actually quite amazing,* how lucky was he?! Everyone here was really nice, no-one shouted at him, no-one really complained, not even Eva – with all her ranting, she was as curious and fascinated by the place as he was. He always got to watch his favourite programme, tea was served every few hours, breakfast, lunch, dinner every day and Simon had never felt cause to question its quality. there was something comforting and safe about this place. He didn't have to work, didn't need any money, yet still he got to go to the pub. He got to go to the pub! This place was magic. Simon wanted to stay. *There are blessings in the world, there is a greater good.*

Jake

Jake glanced around the office. Jake had been cogged, he knew it, one of many cogs, social cogs, the cogs of society working to ensure its continual rhythmic tick. His gaze settled on two individuals facing each other across a walkway, sharing a story and from the look of it (from Jake's view, with the shaking of heads and the squinted reaction to comments), not a happy story.

He remembered a game he used to play at school, a circle of friends. Darren whizzed through his memory cells, sparking little mini explosions in his head: the dark haired, dark eyed naughty kid that his mother had made him play with. He recalled the game, you had to throw on quickly, as if trying not to have touched the surface of the ball at all. You had to think quickly, pick out the kid not looking and fire without time to aim, the reflexes of the fast working brain. He remembered now his consciousness feeling like that ball, only he was the only player, throwing himself as quickly as he came, away to the next state of mind, the next Jake, passing the subconscious between the hands of the mind.

Today his gaze settled on two individuals who sat across a walkway from each other, sharing a story, and he saw the subconscious cross between them, he saw their beach balls being passed by the hands of their minds, fighting within themselves. He felt clear of it, as one, no longer separate from himself. Jake looked out and saw the world.

Darren was slightly shorter than average, but by no means short, and had been one of the first, the first notch tied to the pains of life. He had not cared about Jake, all those years ago, when he had kissed Jake's girlfriend, stray hand wedged up her shirt.

Rushton

Eva and Simon sat out the back, both puffing on a cigarette. Simon was more relaxed with his smoking now. Eva liked to watch him smoke. His lips puckered a little as blew out the fumes.

'Do you believe in God?' Eva questioned Simon casually, knowing that such a question couldn't possibly receive a casual or straightforward answer, especially for them.

But Simon kept his response simple and just said, 'No.'

Unsatisfied with this sharp response, Eva pressed, 'So what do you believe in?'

This time Simon responded in full swing, just as Eva had wanted, 'I believe in man's ability to find humanity and compassion, his ability to rise above himself. Jesus was a man who even when his people condemned him to death and hanged him from a cross, had only compassion in his heart, "Forgive them, for they know not what they do". That is the touch of God, the greatness within ourselves; we all have it in us, to be as righteous as Jesus was, to be better people, to find our compassion and love.'

Simon looked up at Eva before he continued, his manner implying a smile that his lips didn't reflect, 'God is not out there helping us,' he raised his hand and pointed into the atmosphere, the *out thereness* of things all around them. 'We're in here and we have to help ourselves, that is the teaching of God, to be better, not to worship a man who was better than us, but to *be* the better, to find strength in his actions, to guide us to be as good as he is.'

Eva tilted her head a little, 'You're a very interesting man Simon...'

Simon felt a little confused, no-one had ever found him interesting before. He looked Eva right in the eye and searched for the insincerity, for the flicker of mischief. *Ah! There it is.* Simon smiled and Eva continued, 'Does this mean I don't have to repent or anything?'

'Why? Were you thinking of doing so?'

Eva shuffled a little and shook her head.

'No,' Simon said, 'I don't think you do have to repent to an outside force or to please a clergy, but you do have to sort of repent to yourself. Forgive yourself, rather than hoping that you will be forgiven. And do better, make good your life.'

'Are you saying my life is no good?'

Simon sighed, 'You put empty biro cases into people's throats and drained their blood, that's not really very nice is it?'

Eva smiled, 'It was fun though.'

'Would it be fun now?' Simon asked.

Eva looked out across the smoking area, the gate that opened twice a week by the man with a van and considered the question carefully. After a silent pause, Eva quietly said, 'No.'

Simon waited for an explanation, a statement of reform perhaps, a confession asking for forgiveness, but Eva said nothing more.

'Right... Good.' Simon mustered, 'Sooo, you wouldn't kill again? You don't want to kill again?'

Eva focused and caught Simon's eye. 'You ask a lot of questions Mr...? What is your surname?'

Simon didn't answer.

Eva stood and turned with a posture of a determined exit, but then swung round full flurry and announced, 'I said that it wouldn't be fun anymore, I didn't say that I wouldn't kill again. Only now it would have purpose beyond my entertainment, I would be doing great things.'

'What sort of things?' Simon quickly asked, but Eva was gone, her determined exit complete.

Simon shook his head, as if trying to shake out a memory.

Horace

Horace thought. *Think, Horace, think.* He tried to remember. He reflected – every morning he had brushed his hair at the bathroom mirror, six strokes varying in manner had exercised his arms. Straightening his collar and shaking off any clinging threads from his attire he had prepared himself for work. Striding with long paces he had marched into the office. Horace had been a manager, but not of many: Horace was a middle man. As he remembered placing his briefcase on the floor beside his chair and settling back into the bulk buy *new dynamic office seating with wheels*, he had felt his middle man status: being neither here nor there. Felt his stress levels rising as he had strived to fulfil requirements, the boys above caring only about staff performance, the staff caring only for the rules inflicted from the boys above. The middle man, the glue that holds the two together, the messenger, the no-one.

At moments like that Horace had felt wearily average, he had argued in his head, re-grouped, justified, injected a hefty and much needed dose of self-belief. He had never wanted to be noticed. He had shied away from school performances, sports and groups, had never been particularly ambitious – in fact, scrap the particularly – had never been ambitious. Horace smiled. He had had his thoughts, his fantasies, secrets that separated him from them. *But wait…* Horace thought back, he could feel the details, be in the space, but something felt different. He kicked himself a little, mentally, for not having used that opportunity for better things, for not having appreciated his life, *but wait…* Horace pressed forward, watching the clock… Jake… his brother with wild ginger hair… Gill. *Oh God, what had he done?*

His mind was a rush, he loved his wife, he was sure of it. He had seen her first at a party, well, more of a gathering perhaps. A friend of hers and colleague of his were having a 'do'. What precisely that 'do' was in aid of no-one was quite sure, but as they mingled with a glass of wine in one hand and hors-d'oeuvre in the other, no-one really cared. Janis stood by an expensive, ugly-looking lamp, conversing with April. Horace knew April, she was the wife of another colleague with whom he had cause to interact over a photocopier not that long ago. He had met April (as he had met most of the staff and spouses) at the Christmas party; a drab hotel reception hall, lined on one side with a paper plated sausage and stick buffet, in which a slender girl and chubby boy decanted wine into plastic cups, laid out in rows of white, red and rosé. He had not spoken to April for long, he had not spent that much time bantering over the photocopier with her husband either, but he had met her and they had conversed and therefore he could legitimately go over.

Janis had eyed him with an intriguing gaze as he stepped into the frame, he had eyed her back, April had shuffled slightly and made a polite exit. Left to their own devises, they talked extensively about nothing in particular, their eyes each flickering over the other's more intensely as the evening drew on. Horace remembered the feeling of their touch as he passed her a glass, the softness of her skin, a slight twinge. He asked Janis if she would like to meet again, perhaps for a drink or dinner? Gleefully she nodded, shining eyes expressing a definitive yes.

As time passed and dates ensued, they married and had a child. Horace loved his wife, he was sure of it, he enjoyed her company, her manner, her charm, *her*. He remembered her gardening, remembered lunches on the patio, dinners in the kitchen, community work, his wife was a good person, a far better person than him... and a child, he had a child, he touched his neck searching for a tie. *The tie giver.* His daughter, how old would she be now? How long had been here? What had he been doing? *Think, Horace, think.* His mind a rush. *What must be done to be a better man?* Could his wife ever forgive him? Could his daughter? Horace breathed out, then in. *Steady, Horace, steady.*

Horace pulled himself up, his white t-shirt and jeans looser on his frame, his mighty mass slimming. He felt fitter, the weight he carried less lumbering. He breathed out again, then in, out, in. On the last out breath he moved forward, down the corridor and knocked on Dr Jefferson's office door.

'Come in.'

Horace opened the door and stood in the frame, he may have slimmed, but his naturally large build filled the space as if he himself were the door.

THE WHITE NOISE COLLECTIVE

'Hello Horace, what can I do for you?' Dr Jefferson seemed chirpy. He had a lighter presence than Dr Washington, partly due to his smaller frame and brighter smile. He was less imposing, less authoritative, but there was something else about him, a desire to give perhaps, a more open caring nature.

'I want to be better. I want to make right the wrongs I have done. I want to go back to my wife and daughter, but before I can do that I must prove myself, I must be worthy of them.'

Dr Jefferson smiled, 'Come, Horace, come.'

He took Horace down the corridor, through the security doors and into the training wing. 'There is accommodation in this wing, we can have you moved, so you can study and practice every day if you like?'

Dr Jefferson showed Horace around, as Dr Washington had done with Eva. Horace nodded, 'Today,' he said.

Dr Jefferson put his arm, as best he could given their size difference, around Horace's shoulder, tip-toeing a little, leaning against his mass a little, 'Are you sure Horace? You understand what you will be doing?'

'I don't think I understand anything else, Doctor. I must be better, I must show my wife and my daughter than I can be a better man, that the world can be a better place.'

Horace marched, his chest puffed out, his nose not in the air with pretension but with confidence and courage today. Horace was going to do better, be better. Dr Jefferson clapped his hands, 'I will make arrangements, Horace.'

And so it was, this average day, that two men marched together, noses in the air not with pretension, but with glorious anticipation of a new beginning, a new world.

Rushton

'You don't have to lie to us, Simon. I have a feeling you want to stay and I understand that, but be reassured that we will look after you out there, you will work for a company overseen by us, you will be working with others who believe in the cause. You will attend evening classes similar to those you have been doing here, but for a while you will still be free from the burden of it, you won't remember the action, just understand and feel its benefit. You want to be better don't you?'

'I am better.'

'There are no limits on how great you can be and you will be better served out there. The message can be passed to all people, not just criminals, though criminals are the ones we must reach with the greatest urgency, we must change things for the better. But all people should know and feel what you feel.'

'You're asking me to spread the word?!'

'Yes, but there are no words, it is an understanding, a feeling. You must find your own words.'

'Who are these others you talk of? Jake is the only one to be released isn't he?'

'Yes, but there are others recruited on the outside, some convicted of lesser crimes and others from law abiding life who we have reached.'

'How?'

'Groups, workshops, that type of thing. Outreach.'

'What type of groups?'

'Drug and drink groups, slimming groups, yoga classes, community groups, Simon.'

'This is a campaign?'

'Campaign! More of a philosophy, a movement for betterment.'

'A religion?'

'Simon, you have been here long enough to know its purpose. We are not – and that 'we' includes you – an organised religion of any status under the laws of religion. We are an *understanding*. Don't let us down now, on the eve of your release. I know you are ready, it would be wrong of us to keep you here when the world needs to hear you.'

'I want only the betterment of things, Doctor – you know that – I'm just curious about the network that carries that aim.'

'Very good, I understand that and the people working with you on the outside will help you identify with how that can be achieved, the betterment of things takes all people; without world change, there is no change… the betterment of things comes from within each person, so each person must be reached. Those who understand must help others to do so.'

'Yes, Doctor, I understand, you are completely right of course, I am sorry to question.'

'No, you are right to question, without questions, we cannot give good answers. To change the world the right answers must find their voice so that the betterment of things can prevail.'

Simon

Dr Washington shifted his suit jacket a little, so that he could feel its presence enveloping his body's breadth, he felt smart in it, important. Simon waited by the gate with his bags for the doctor. Eva watched from afar, she liked the way Simon leaned to hold himself up against something, he had a James Dean lean. He had a bit of the swagger too. Eva smiled.

Dr Washington strode over, blocking Simon from her view. Eva squinted, as if some magic power might allow her to see through him, but his bulk was too sturdy, impenetrable.

'Simon,' the doctor's tone held something of proclamation, a speech was about to follow. Simon braced himself to listen. 'Remember what you have learnt here, the goodness of yourself over others. The world is a difficult place, you must be strong to hold your beliefs, to stand up for the greater good. See the light that surrounds all things, know love, feel its presence. Don't allow it to be embroiled in passion or desire or need, to find it consumed by emotion and the desire to be loved. Feel its energy, let it lift you, engage with you, feel its presence all around you, out there in the universe.'

Dr Washington stretched out his arm to demonstrate the out-thereness of things. Eva smirked, she could just imagine the drivel he was spouting at Simon. He went on, 'It is giving and sharing in an absolute way, passion and desire are emotionally bound in a frenzy of want and need and are not the real essence of love in its richer involvement in life. Love is much calmer and more refined than that, it is the wondrous magic that breathes fresh air and light into our world.'

Simon nodded, 'I will try, Doctor. I will do my best to rise above the conflicts of the people and situations I face.'

Dr Washington put a strong hand on Simon's shoulder, 'I know you will, Simon. Keep your appointments with Gavin, he is our communication, he is there to steady you: a base, a friend.'

Simon nodded again, 'I will.'

Eva watched the shadow of Simon move away from Dr Washington and disappear out through the gate. Simon was gone.

Simon took a deep breath. He felt a little uneasy about the world that awaited him, not the ideas and cause that he carried with him, but the resistance and conflict of the society that had already pushed him to his limits. And he was a little uneasy about leaving Eva too. Although she was a far stronger person than himself, he felt a connection between them. He didn't really fear her, although he was often terrified by her attitude. She wouldn't harm him, he felt sure of it. The connection between them felt important for her progress somehow; Dr Washington had mentioned this also, that he was useful in Eva's progression, and yet now they were sending him out into the world away from her...

Simon loaded his bags into the boot of the taxi that waited beyond the gate and the wall. He glanced up as he bent his body to fold himself into the car. The wall was quite imposing from the outside, more redolent of a prison than it had ever seemed from the inside. Grey weathered stone towered up, sharp metal wire hung from the top edge, not visible from the other side, the gate double bolted and manned, the guard accompanied by a wise looking dog and clean maintained rifle.

The land through which the taxi started to roll seemed vast, acres of green flanked by trees at its far edge, tiny dots to the eye on the horizon. Simon swivelled round in his seat, he wanted to see the outer walls of Blue Block, but the grey weathered stone just went on and on, sweeping round so far that he couldn't make out a corner. Small huts broke the flatness of it at intervals; a movement, a shadow, told Simon another guard paced about outside them. There were no tower blocks or viewing platforms to rise above the height of the wall, there was nothing to see from this side. Simon turned back to face his destination, the taxi driver unfamiliar and inexpressive. Simon asked if he could smoke and only a quick twitch of the neck and a simple 'No' was offered to him.

As the trees got bigger, looming up out of the earth, another wall much like the last came into view. As they reached another gate, a guard stepped forward to meet them, raising his left hand, clasping a clean and well maintained rifle with his right, just as the other guard had. No words passed between any of them as he clocked the taxi driver and waved them through without questions. The gate swung open and more green spanned out into the distance. As they turned down lane after lane, Simon became increasingly aware that he would never know the way back. *What about Eva?* He would want to visit. He turned to the taxi driver, 'If I want to visit Rushton again, what's the address?' The taxi driver glanced briefly in Simon's direction, but did not acknowledge his question. Simon waited. 'You don't say much, do you?' The driver glanced again. Simon rolled his eyes.

Finally a village emerged out of the green and new colours flooded into to Simon's view: red brick, yellow signs, blue cars. They drove through and on, until the red brick turned to concrete and pebble dashing. Then the concrete turned to glass and steel as buildings grew in size and importance. The taxi indicated right and they turned into a picturesque tree lined street where they stopped and the driver got out. He opened the boot and removed Simon's bags. Pointing at a door and waving keys in the air he directed Simon to his new home.

A one bedroom flat on the first floor with a small balcony over the front entrance awaited him; on the side table in the hall was a pack, a folder of information listing his amenity providers, phone number and mobile phone. Instructions were also included: a date and time to be at a particular address, *come suited,* it said. In the bedroom wardrobe was a suit just for the occasion, hanging with a selection of shirts. Shoes neatly aligned and polished sat on the floor underneath. He lifted one of his bags on to the bed and unzipped it. One by one he folded or hung the clothes he had brought with him from Rushton.

At exactly 7pm, as the second hand ticked into position, there was a confident knock on the door, startling Simon a little. Simon answered, shook hands with a man, a fit, well-presented man, with bright eyes and healthy skin, who introduced himself as Gavin. A strong grip, but Simon could match it.

'How are you settling in?' Gavin asked as he stepped over the threshold.

Simon stood back allowing his entrance, his arm instinctively raised up to offer the space and direct the guest towards the body of the flat. 'Can I get you a drink?' Simon asked, 'Not sure what there is, I haven't checked the kitchen yet.'

'Whisky and ice.'

Simon went to the kitchen to find a bottle of Scotch with two glasses standing on the side. The freezer did indeed have ice, already prepared.

He handed Gavin the glass and raised his in polite gesture, not knowing what to raise it to.

'The future,' Gavin offered.

'The future,' Simon smiled.

'This is a really nice place.' Gavin scanned the room, pointing at a picture on the wall, 'That's a nice piece.'

Simon looked over, 'Yes, it is,' he agreed.

'Tomorrow you'll be taken on a small tour and shown the area. The time and date in the pack on the hall sideboard, I assume you've seen it?' Simon nodded, 'It's for your new position, your job. I understand you were a bus driver before, but we think you'd be better suited in outreach – troubled youths – there's a community building here that runs youth clubs and supports schools with difficult teenagers. You only have to wear the suit for the first day, after that it'll be casual jeans and t-shirts, smart ones of course, as you'll be a role model.'

'What sort of activities will I be doing with them?'

'You'll see. Don't worry, you'll be good at it. We have faith in you, Simon.'

Simon looked into his whiskey and swirled the melting ice round. 'Wow, I haven't had a real drink for a while, the stuff they poured at the pub didn't have any effect.'

There was no alcohol in it, that's why.'

'Really?!'

Gavin smiled, 'Really. But you don't have an issue with drink do you?'

'No, not at all, not that keen actually.'

Gavin smiled again. 'Right. Well, I'll leave you to settle in a bit more, there's food in the fridge that just needs heating for tonight and as I said, you'll be shown around tomorrow so you'll see where the shops are and you can sort yourself out. Bank cards are in the pack?'

'Yes.'

'Good, then you're all set.' Gavin shook Simon's hand again and was gone.

Simon looked around him: food in the fridge that needs heating; whiskey and ice; a community youth job; a suit; a flat. *Blimey, this is amazing.* Simon put his glass down and straightened his body, aligning it so that his feet were in a sturdy and correct postural position. Raising his arms up over his head as he breathed in, lowering his arms as he breathed out, he relaxed and reflected. *There is a better world.* He would be good at being better and helping others. *Love...* Simon raised his arms again, feeling the air filling his lungs... *and out.*

Rushton

Boris stared at the wall where the clock used to be. Eva glanced over at him and asked, 'What is Simon doing out there?'

'Doing?'

'Yeah, *doing*, like for a job and stuff.'

'Well it depends, I think, on different skills and personalities. I guess Simon would be placed in a practical position.'

'If I got out would they place me near him?'

Boris looked at her, really looked at her. As the autumn started to draw the days slowly in, the evenings seemed more intimate and their time in the communal area longer. 'Would you want to be?' he asked.

Eva shrugged, 'Yeah, maybe.'

Boris looked over at the silent switched off television, 'Do you miss him?'

Eva shrugged again, 'Yeah, maybe.'

Boris smiled, was the stony Eva starting to crack?

'Is there anyone else coming to replace him?'

Boris shook his head.

'Just us left then?'

Boris nodded.

'You know, I used to fix and look after my own motorbike, do you think they'd let me do some work around here? I've noticed that Mick's truck is sounding a bit cranky, I could have a look at it.'

'Motorbikes are a bit different from cars aren't they?'

'Not so, just a bit smaller and a more accessible engine. Wouldn't be able to fix new cars with built in computers and all that, but Mick's truck is an old battler, not so different if you've got a head for engines.'

Boris smiled again and gazed at Eva as if he had known her all his life, but had just seen the person for the first time. That realisation that parents must have of what their child has become, the truth and essence of a person beyond the tantrums and memories of a life shared. Eva looked up and caught his gaze. She smiled at him, a smile he had never seen before, a smile missing the malice perhaps, missing a secret thought behind it. She just smiled at him, a free and easy smile that he did not recognise, did not know to be hers. *A beautiful smile,* Boris thought and smiled back. 'I'll ask if you like, there's always work to be done. They've got an old lawn mower that could do with a head for engines. I'll speak to Dr Washington in the morning.'

'No, you don't have to do that, I'll ask myself. Thanks though.'

Boris's eyes widened, never had Eva said thank you. Come to think of it, never had they had such an easy exchange. And a smile, a shared smile. The warm yet brisk autumn evening felt cosy and calm, two people sharing a moment one night. Boris started to think forward to Christmas, as if he were in a family situation, *where would they put the tree...* he wondered.

Eva

Malcolm had first visited Eva the evening before: his assignment to recruit her, Dr Washington had sent Malcolm in the hope of recruiting Eva before she was caught; Inspector Jacob Rodgers was closing in and although Dr Washington had already prepared his request to take her the legal process would take time and he wanted to start work with her immediately. Today Eva stepped out in to the world with a new improved confidence, not knowing that Dr Rushton's New Wave of Rehabilitation awaited her; whether she refused it now or not it was to be her destiny, only a few months from this moment. She flicked a scarf over her shoulder, a light cotton affair, dusk blue with a row of small, tight tassels at each end. It brushed past her hair, which in turn tickled her neck. Eva swiped her hair out from under the scarf, catching the itchy bit with a polished nail. She walked with intention, but not the usual killer glide that made her enticing yet invisible all at the same time, as if a vision had passed you by; only the sharp eyed adventurous boys would hold her in their gaze until she became real. Others would see her and then forget, a mystic memory of a person that passed on the street, a vision, a witch perhaps, but no-one could be completely sure of what she looked like, *a vision* they would say, *just a vision*; no witnesses were able to stand in court.

Today she walked instead as if in a slight hurry, an important appointment awaited perhaps? A meeting? A lunch? Her boots shone, her coat was long and fitted, her hands manicured; Eva walked with intention. She never marched or strutted – she sometimes walked as a meander, other times her step was brisk – but most often she had her own special purposeful walk, the killer walk, the walk of ghastly intention. Today her intention was more honourable, she walked with a certainty, she was not dangerous today.

At a large modern office building Eva stopped to push through the glass revolving entrance. The other side opened out into a grand open entrance hall, sweeping stairs and lifts could be seen beyond the card operated stiles that secured the building. A huge painting hung behind the reception desk, lit up by a dozen LED bulbs strategically placed to illuminate its rich colours and deep layers of paint; it glowed out in fine glory. Eva liked it. But before reaching the tidy, red lipped receptionist at the front desk, Eva was intercepted by a broad man in a well-fitting suit. He put out his hand and introduced himself as Colin Davis. Eva took his hand, his grip was tight but she could match it. His eyes were soft, an airy blue, with dark eyelashes and well-groomed eyebrows lying smartly on his tanned young skin. A face guarded with secrets, his eyes revealed a weakness: a real secret is kept by not showing that you have one. Seeing them in his eyes made an entrance for Eva, *he does not protect his secrets well.* She knew then, in one single exchange, that she was smarter and fitter than him, but that she was not as knowledgeable of what would happen next. He was to guide her, introduce her, show her the ropes. She wanted the secrets behind his eyes. She gave a wistful smile, she knew how to get them.

Today Eva started a new job, full of people to play with.

The Diary of Rose Heather Roberts – The Truth

I went outside today. Love that air, when it's icy cold and brisk but startlingly refreshing, especially on a sunny day, when the brisk air slows pace and the sun's warmth awakens your senses. I sat for a while, in the park. It's like the Truman Show in here, everybody watching, everybody watching a life that is not your own, that isn't real. I feel better, but I didn't choose it. I feel compelled, as if an unseen force has made me think it.

Rushton

Eva wielded a spanner in the air as she searched for the right bolt. Dr Washington shook his head, not with disapproval but with amazement. Eva was a motor-fixing, computer-clever, people-leading ninja who could be beautifully seductive, sharply dressed or scruffy. He had to fix her, but he couldn't be sure if the changes he was seeing were genuine. She was highly intelligent, manipulative and calculating. Dr Washington watched her in a daze; he desperately wanted her in the fold, but he had to be careful.

Inspector Jacob Rodgers

A warm, soft hand, glided across Jacob's arm. 'You mustn't worry,' a gentle, equally warm and soft a voice conveyed reassuring words. 'The institution is backed by the government and sponsored by many well-recognised companies, there will be regulations and standards they'll have to meet. You concern yourself with too much, you did your job and removed dangerous people from the streets. It's out of your hands now, you must trust in the next step, managed by someone else.'

Jacob shook his head, 'I don't trust it, that's just it. There's something odd about it.'

'It only seems odd because it's new. In ten years' time, you'll be signing people over to it as standard practice.'

Jacob sighed, she was right of course: every year a new gadget out smartens the last, new ways of doing things, new ideas. If it didn't work it wouldn't be his fault and the institution would get closed down. It would only take one murder, one person may have to die to prove him right. But there had been one murder, *what about Gill?* Why had that not alerted the government to the strange workings of this institution? Horace had not hurt anybody before, why had they not questioned how he had become a murderer under their guidance? He quizzed this with his companion, her response was solid and certain, 'I'm sure they did, Jacob. Things happen, Horace was a very complicated case.'

She was either very trusting, on their payroll, or just trying to calm him. Which was it? Jacob felt a little paranoid, he nodded and decided to leave her out of his thoughts for now.

Rushton

Horace aligned his feet for the correct postural position; he breathed in, raising his arms, and breathed out while lowering them. Now that he had moved into the training quarter his practice was regular, every day. A healthy breakfast of bran and fruit awaited him and then classes, where he learned history and the mistakes humans have made over decades, mathematics, English, French and geography. He was taught ways of learning, his old mind resistant to an education he had long forgotten from school, but each day the art of learning became clearer and the studies easier, and as they got easier they became more interesting and before he knew it, he was healthier, fitter, smarter. It felt good.

Horace breathed in, a strong, steady breath, his arms raising without a twinge or the slightest stretch now. *And out.* He slept in a more comfortable bed than he remembered from the other part of the institution, ate better food, had conversations of interest and importance with people. Horace felt as if he had been punished, as if he had served his time while the white coats turned on the television and brought him pills, *re4*, or was it *lx4* and *re1*... Served his time in a place not as brutal as he imagined prison to be, but a place, nonetheless, that was empty. Now it was time to make good, to grow into a better person, to find forgiveness for himself by being a better man tomorrow. Then he would find his family and work for their forgiveness, be a better father and a better husband.

Horace learned defensive martial arts, how to fix cars (like his father before him). He learned how to read maps, build huts, plumbing, electrics, business and computers. His basic data entry from his stupid insurance job was way behind him now; he mastered Photoshop, Excel, ticketing platforms, web design. Horace knew it all.

Dr Jefferson looked on as Horace focused confidently at the lecturer standing at the head of the room. The lecturer glanced briefly in the doctor's direction, compelling Horace to do the same. Dr Jefferson nodded and they both resumed their focus on the subject at hand. Dr Jefferson was pleased, *this couldn't be going any better*. Horace was going to be a fine attribute to the institution and a great worker outside of it. Horace was destined for great things, his fantasies not so farfetched now, he was becoming the person that he always fantasised he could be. The empty envelope drops seemed silly now, but the confident man that delivered them was here, going on to do meaningful things, to make a difference and help bring about a better world. Horace was collected and focused, his mind steady, responsive, calm and in control. Dr Jefferson's only concern was that Horace seemed to be losing his softness, his bulk-like comfort which offered trust, a sense of kindness, despite his size. His kindness was more direct now, more assertive, his bulky muscular structure stood proud and confident. These were positive steps for Horace, there was no doubt of that, but there was an insecurity missing, the presence of which had calmed his stature. The loveable bear was now a towering power man. Would his family know him like this? If not, would they fear him a little like this, the confident man unknown to them?

Jake

Jake smoothed his collar, the laundry service did a fine job – sharply pressed tidy edges cornered his attire. But this evening it felt a little tight. He wanted to feel more at ease, a softer collar was required for his date tonight. Jake removed his jacket so that he could change his shirt, he had just the thing: a soft cotton open-stitched designer dress shirt, comfortable and stylish. He replaced his jacket and brushed down the sleeves, slipped on his shoes and made his way to the restaurant.

Jake had seen her amongst the guests surrounding a conference table two hours before meeting her at the hotel bar. A neat whiskey on the rocks sat patiently on the bar as she twirled it gently round on its own spot, mindlessly but with precision. Dinner this evening was an extension of that meeting, their drinks cut short by another date awaiting. Jake liked this one better, there was something elegant about her, something secretly seductive, something more he wanted to know. He had asked his questions wisely and unearthed her thoughts on the way of things quickly, the way of things as she saw them. Jake had been pleased that she believed in the betterment of things and that the key to life was love. He hoped that she would not cloud his judgment on passion and desire. He wanted her, but he wanted her understanding and camaraderie in his endeavours more. Jake had been seeing the world for some time now: he could see others' pain and misguided behaviour, he wanted to help realign people, to bring about better things. His will to do that found no boundaries in boredom (as he had in his climb up the company ladder), found no anger in other people's stupidity – he felt smarter than them maybe, a little wiser perhaps, but never arrogant. His mind focused only on helping that person see the light, the corrective for their unbalanced selves.

Jake did not preach, he had nothing to preach about. It is only an understanding that set him apart, he could only teach by example. Jake had to be the better man, had always to behave in a way that was good and honourable. That wasn't to say that, should such a companion be full and real in his life, his desires could not find a place. He wanted to have some passion and he wanted to have fun too.

Jake shook himself down, a slight wiggle dance, *relax, Jake, relax, she's going to love you; you're attractive, smart and very well groomed.* Jake smiled as he saw her. She wore the perfect dress.

Rushton

Boris looked up at the wall where the clock had once hung. He missed it; the clock had been a strange point of stability. With Simon gone and Eva in the midst of a transformation so phenomenal that it couldn't possibly be true, Boris didn't really have very much to do at the moment. So he had started to read more, many books varying in content and style. Eva was a little impressed, she had taken Boris for a one-genre kind of man. She watched him reading out of the corner of her eye as she sat rolling cigarettes, which she placed always with the filter at the bottom of a glass so that no grubby fingers could touch the filter tip, the end that went in her mouth. She used to roll until she got bored and then smoke until they were all gone. Now she counted: today it was 15, last week it had been 20. Boris watched her out of the corner of his eye as he pretended to read his book.

Perhaps he should stick to less indulgent books, he's obviously struggling, takes an age before he turns the page, Eva thought, plucking one of her 15 rolled cigarettes out of the glass and rising from her chair. Boris read with speed to catch up from where he had left off, so that he could turn the page while Eva was out smoking. Eva returned, swiping a book of her own from the shelf as she passed, a hardback faded grey bulk of a thing. She rested it across her legs and flipped it open. *Quantum Physics*: pages and pages of tiny writing and complicated diagrams. Boris almost tutted out loud, *ridiculous.*

Horace

Horace's wife held her daughter's hand across the space between their two chairs. 'He'll be coming home soon, not sure exactly when, but soon.'

Horace's daughter frowned. She had been twelve when he was first taken away, she now boasted a legal right to drink and a bag packed for university, eighteen and on the cusp of womanhood. 'I don't want him coming here to live with you after I'm gone,' the tie-giver spoke quickly, her nerves a little frantic.

'It will be alright,' her mother reassured her, but they were only words, the truth of *alright* was yet to be seen.

The tie-giver held her mother's hand tightly, 'I just think it would be sensible for him to stay nearby, you could date again, get to know each other again, so much must have changed between you and in yourselves, Mum. I just think you should get to know him again as a new person, just like I will. I'll visit him when I'm back in the holidays and here with you, we'll all go out together, but please don't rush into it, you've waited this long, be patient now and take it slowly.'

Horace's wife breathed slowly out, her daughter was right of course, she missed her husband but knew that a different man would be coming back – a much better one, they'd told her. She hoped she would like him as much as the last one. She hoped that he would forgive her for putting him in that place and turning him into a murderer, she hoped the better man who was to return would understand her fear of what she didn't understand when she found the files in the garage. She hoped a lot.

Rushton

As the autumn faded and winter took hold, the trees across the grounds from Eva's window looked like stalks: distant sticks poked into the ground where a line of green, then golden reds, yellows and oranges had been. Eva stared at them, making shapes and images, as one might do with clouds or star formations. She saw a bent old man with a walking stick and a conjured dog-like being, as if a man was transforming into a wolf, bent over, with long back legs and grotesque feet, the snout brisling, the teeth growing. A queue of sticks all waiting at the gate of the Rushton Institute of Rehabilitation.

Today she was to fix the van. After watching her with the lawn mower, Dr Washington had approved her desire to work on mechanical objects; the more versatile his people the better. Skills were essential and Eva had many – *if* he could change her, *if* this transformation was real then she would be a greater asset even than Jake. They were both leaders of men, both smart and convincing. Both feared by Inspector Jacob Rodgers, both uncompromising, an attribute only if guided by the right beliefs. Dr Washington flicked through the reports on Jake, pleased with his progress. It was working. Dr Washington picked up the telephone receiver and pressed only two numbers, on speed dial. Dr Jefferson picked up on the other end.

'How's our Horace doing?' He asked.

An excited, 'Marvellous,' was boomed down the line, Dr Washington smiled. *Marvellous indeed.*

Simon

Simon had been a bus driver for nine years before which he had been an electrician for industry, wiring new office blocks. Having worked for the most part alone, Simon's already limited knowledge of the interactive skills one learns at school had reduced further in the intervening years. Simon had not been popular at school, although not picked on either. He had generally been ignored, a trait that would follow him through life. But now, free from Rushton and yet protected by it, Simon felt a new power of interaction unfolding in him. Troubled teenagers, what a thing to ask him to do! And yet he felt confident and a little proud of moving into something useful, something that might make a difference and help bring about a better world. *Arms up... and breathe.*

Rushton

The atmosphere of Blue Block was strangely relaxed. Now that Simon had gone and the need for television switching had ceased, and with the clock long since removed so no watch checking was necessary, the nurse that no-one really saw was absent as usual. Boris had become resigned to the whole idiocy of it all as he watched Eva become a super human, bordering on comic fiction. With the smiles that passed between them, comforting and alluring, Boris was content to allow the show to go on.

Dr Washington strutted, as best he could (given his size and manner) smartly up and down the corridors, smiling to himself. The air as it came into winter rang of spring, with a dappled, glowing light filtering through the institution, breathing fresh air and calm. Boris felt at home and wondered around straightening items and dusting surfaces. He looked around him, the place lacked personality, it needed something: a throw over the chairs perhaps; a vase of flowers; a funky side table; books; more tasteful paintings; and most of all – to set it all off and incorporate the style in his mind – it needed one of those long armed lamps with a big shade hanging between two chairs, he'd seen one in Jake's favourite programme and fixed it in his mind.

Boris stared out across the room and sighed, he realised that it was the only time he had really felt this way, the comfort and safety of a home, a place he had never created for himself and one that had never been provided for him, until now. Boris suddenly wanted children, he looked at Eva. *No.* He shook his head, *don't be ridiculous, Boris.* But maybe someone, maybe it was time for him to seek release, seek his exit from Rushton. After all, he had been the first to actually be rehabilitated – in fact, he was still the only one that he believed it was true for – and yet he was still here. Perhaps it was time for Boris to build a home for himself and someone, time to buy in to the requirements of society, time to be a useful member of the outside world. He had been a useful member of this small world, inside; could he not extend that further now?

Boris turned a corner to find Dr Washington strutting towards him. 'Doctor,' he announced, startling Dr Washington out of his happy stride.

'Yes, Boris?'

'Doctor, I'm wondering if it might be time for me to move on.'

'Well, the Orange Block could do with someone like you.'

'No, I don't mean out of Blue Block, I mean out of Rushton. I'd like to have a home and maybe a family, I'd like to be a useful member of society.'

Dr Washington looked deep and hard into Boris's eyes, 'You are a useful member of society, Boris, your work here is essential to our success. There is no greater good you could be doing Boris, this is your home.'

Boris looked a little sad and Dr Washington acknowledged it, he put his arm around him, a show of affection. Boris had not known this from the doctor before or – come to think of it – from anyone for a long, long time. 'Boris, there are of course many great things you could do in the outside world, but your work here is very important and you are exceptionally good at it. You have allowed our work here to transform people's lives, Jake, Horace, Simon and even Eva potentially – she is coming along in leaps and bounds. I'm not sure we could do our work here without you, Boris. If you'd like to make it more to your taste and add a few items of furniture, I'm sure we could stretch to arranging that, in fact, I'd be happy for you to go out into the world and choose the items for yourself.'

Boris smiled, a step into the outside world! He nodded furiously, 'Yes, yes, I'd like that.'

'Consider it done, I will arrange for a van to take you next week – in fact let's not wait – I'll try to arrange it for tomorrow.'

Boris beamed. Dr Washington smiled along with him, hoping that a step into the chaos of the real world would frighten Boris back. He was, of course, totally institutionalised. He had been here far longer than many, if not most of the others, from any block: Boris was one of the first. Dr Washington had no doubt that Boris would not find the outside world to his liking. But he was right to want to make his surroundings more his home, this was his home and should reflect him more. 'Your room Boris, is there a different bed, side table or wardrobe that you would like? Your room is absolutely your space and I think it only right that it reflects you better.'

Boris thought, he was sure there was, but couldn't imagine one, 'I'll take a look and decide,' he said.

'Very good, Boris. I'll arrange a budget on a card for you to take with you.'

'Thank you, Doctor.'

'My pleasure, Boris.'

And the two men parted, Boris to his room, where he pondered on furniture ideas, not really sure what was available to him, or how designs had changed. Perhaps he would wait and see what he liked. Dr Washington strutted to his office where he picked up the receiver of his telephone and arranged a van for the next day.

Eva

Well fitted jeans and a dark tidy coat. He skipped a little as his dog danced around him, waiting for the ball in hand to be thrown out for him to chase and retrieve. Eva watched, her peripheral vision finely focused after many years of use, clearer and more concentrated than a rabbit, Eva watched as if she were looking across the park away from him. Every detail of his movements, his arm swing as he threw the ball, his little skip as his Rhodesian ridgeback danced about him, his soft eyes as he smiled with real joy at his pet.

Eva's new job was going well. She made a fine executive, her manner, style and charm well received amongst the people with whom she worked, but the fun had not yet begun. She needed time to build these bonds and allow influence to take hold. Eva had in mind a new game of manipulation and life-fucking, more long-term than her usual antics with empty pen encasements. So, a little uplift was needed in the meantime. She smiled gently, turning her head to face the soft eyes of the pet owner. He smiled back and they collided just as the Rhodesian ridgeback returned the well thrown ball... a slight stroke of the doggy's head, a kind comment about the breed... they walked together a little way, chatting wistfully about the park and weather. He liked her. Of course, that was Eva's magic, that everyone liked her, and here in her suit and long fitted coat an executive strolled with him. A computer man himself, well paid, well liked, but not ambitious beyond his mark. His life a relatively simple one, a man and his dog. A girlfriend expecting their first baby, the decisions to make, a little out of his comfort zone, the decider of marriage, the commitment he had found himself in. But Eva had no feelings about any of that. She observed his coat as it crumpled a little with the bend of his arm, the ball flying once again and 'Roger' the trusty hound bounded off to fetch it.

'He could do that endlessly,' Eva's new target commented.

She smiled, 'Is he good with children?'

'I guess,' he shrugged, 'never had an incident, he is a soft old dog.' His eyes went out into thought, a memory perhaps, as he recalled many a fine day out with Roger or perhaps he reflected on the question, *how will Roger feel about the baby?* He didn't want to neglect his loving dog when the baby came. His rounder's arm had found a new purpose, long after school was out, his hound looked at him with joy and love so easily every day; the excitement of his obedience and the joy as the ball always came back, to have an animal do as you ask, the self-respect that brings to you. How the simple things mattered, bringing the world together with a sense of contentment. How uncomplicated it all seemed as the ball flew and Roger fetched.

How simple it was too for Eva, the little joys, the excitement as the blood sprayed out, spelling victims' names across the wall. They smiled together at simple pleasures, their thoughts a world apart and yet the same in feeling and presence. What a good father he would have made, Eva thought.

The park was nearly empty and spanned a view in every direction, they were alone as they strolled past a toilet block. She thanked him for the walk, grabbed him by the arm, pulling him smartly in to the building and cut his throat. Roger barked, his owner in need of him, he jumped up at Eva, his teeth on display, his loyalty clear but the situation confusing. The Rhodesian ridgeback called Roger was scared, he whined a little for his owner who lay slumped on the floor, blood oozing out from his neck, but growled at Eva, his jumps in the air ignored. He edged forward a little, his intention more aggressive now, he sprung up to make contact, something his dear owner now lying on the floor had trained him not to do, but fell suddenly and hard to the ground. Not even a whimper pronounced Roger dead.

The Diary of Rose Heather Roberts – The Truth

There's no children here, it's like a weird suspense movie I'm sure I've watched. People walk around so stiffly.

I see colours and light differently now, there's a strange calm, feels natural to me, yet not me at the same time. Like something I would have been, should I have caught that other train. But my life is not that other train, I caught the 10.57 and I lived it, that other train's life is lost to me, this feeling is unnatural in the mechanics of the journey I chose. I liked being who I was, I liked my sadness, it was fitting, my father was owed it, he deserved someone to feel sad for his loss, my mother understood that and yet I hated her for it.

That's better, guilt for my mother now.

Rushton

Eva smiled at the thought of Boris with his home improvements budget off out for the day on his shopping trip, what a funny manipulating place this was. She rolled cigarettes and placed them filter end down into a glass, a glass she wiped clean herself. Her training was going well and her resistance to the mind games was becoming easier now. The hypnosis wasn't quite getting through as smartly as it had before. She'd been observing, focussing in each moment as they enforced their will throughout the day, *clever boys*. Eva had first thought that they were hypnotised only at the end of each training day, but no, it was constant and in short bursts throughout the day, every day. The same games she used to play with her co-workers, the power of persuasion, enticing her will into the desires of the collective. Eva was confident that she would most certainly win this game, smugly believing that she outwitted them all.

Inspector Jacob Rodgers

Jacob sat quietly in his car, an empty take-away coffee cup propped up on his dashboard. A newspaper sprawled out across the steering wheel to stop people from eyeing him suspiciously. Inspector Jacob Rodgers turned the pages slowly, briefly scanning their contents: pictures of government officials dominated the debates, tax cuts here, war intervention there. Jake stepped out from his flat and brushed himself down to straighten his attire, his coat a little bunchy over his three piece suit. He lifted up his collar against the wind and started down the street. Jacob watched, the corner of his sprawled out newspaper twitching, then folded the paper in to a neat shape and stepped out of his car. Brushing himself down from his crumpled position in the car, his coat a little bunchy over his two piece suit, he strolled down the street after Jake. Inspector Jacob Rodgers had heard wind that Eva was being considered for release. The news had shocked him: there could be no greater wrong in the inspector's mind. He had to prove that this was all a mistake, before it was too late; Jake was his only hope to do that. He willed Jake to slip up, to reconnect with his past and rekindle the desire to kill. He would be there and then, maybe, no-one would have to die.

Rushton

Boris returned from his shopping trip with a large lamp that curled up and over, dangling from its shiny chrome stand in the air between two chairs, two chairs that sat in front of the occasional table guarding any easy access to the television, the old spilt-tea stains long removed and new spillages wiped away briskly by a person who didn't wear a white coat but always intervened. Boris stood back and admired his purchase. Eva shuffled her seat away from it a little. Then a box was opened and instructions laid out with all the little bits required for a new side table and its assembly. Boris rubbed his hands together and asked for a screwdriver; a women who didn't wear a white coat but always intervened nodded and galloped off to fetch one.

Boris picked up the instructions and started to digest the information with much interest, nodding and humming he read on till the screwdriver arrived and then set about with all the little bits required for its assembly. Eva smiled and smirked at Boris's triumphs and embarrassments, only once involving herself to suggest where a thing might go, an interjection quickly dismissed by Boris's waving hand and assurance that it was all under control. A remarkable 40 minutes later a new occasional table was introduced to the room, an 80's glass and chrome affair, presumably purchased to match the lamp.

'Oh God,' Eva recoiled a little, 'really?'

The shabby corner table with its damaged veneer suited her better, or perhaps not *her* per se, but the place and its purpose: what a suitable institutional table it had been. A box of books was unpacked to fill the void on the shelf and cover a bit of the white walls that surrounded them on all sides, a continuous whiteness with only small breaks composed of ugly art. Ugly art that now came down to be replaced by larger, brighter prints. Eva was a little more impressed by the prints he had chosen. The awful new table (although awful) *was* lighter, perhaps more cheery, the glass bounced light around the room and the chrome legs glinted. New chairs and side tables were all assembled and placed. And then, to finish, a huge rug was thrown down, a little fluffy under foot; even through Eva's boots she could feel its soft warmth.

'How was it out there?' Eva enquired as Boris straightened books and aligned an ornament.

'Mad,' he replied simply.

'Mad?'

'Yeah! People everywhere, cars and things.'

'Things?'

'Yeah! Things! It's chaos out there. Nice and calm and safe in here.'

Eva smiled, mission accomplished, *Boris won't be leaving here anytime soon.*

Jake

Jake thumbed the address book that had been so strangely left amongst his belongings from his former life. Names and places flashed past, all unknown to him. He sat back in the chair on which he was sitting, relaxing a little into its back and allowing the book to fall on to his lap. The book fell open to the most creased page, where the spine had been cracked a little in its over extension. The book relaxed on the page listing *F*. Jake glanced down at it and then looked a little harder until the names came in to focus. *Derek Faulkner* caught his scan. He perused the address, but no recollection sprung to mind. The address had been changed, the old one crossed out with over lapping lines almost obscuring the details, Jake looked harder, something seemed important. The name glared at him, *Derek Faulkner, Derek Faulkner,* he knew this and it was important.

Rushton

The light faded from the windows and the new dangling lamp hovering from its shiny chrome stand between two chairs was switched on, as if the Queen had come to illuminate the Christmas extravaganza of lights lining a shopping street. A girl who never wore white coats but always intervened clapped gleefully. Boris stood proud, perusing his arrangement and choice of furniture. Eva sighed, *yes, yes, very good.* Eva had no feelings about it, one chair or a different chair, she sat in them all the same. Although she did concede that the new one was a little more comfortable and its wider diameter allowed her to curl her legs in. She leant over its arm, dropping her cigarettes into a glass, wiped clean by her herself, resting on the new side table. Eva liked the dangerous sound of glass hitting glass, she picked up and replaced her glass on to the new side table more times than necessary. Boris flinched each time; one day it would break. He jumped up and fetched her a coaster, he had forgotten purchasing them but remembered now why he had included them in the shopping spree. He whipped it under Eva's glass and sat back down a little more relaxed. Eva smiled, it was never going to be his home while others influenced and used the space, touching and rearranging his furniture and design.

Horace

Horace sat on a bench in the park. A dog walker crossed his view at the far end, a red lead dangling from the walker's hand as the dog ran free ahead of him. Horace recalled the sensation of sitting in this way in his distant past, but his mind was different now, his purpose in the park greatly altered. *How silly* he thought, the games he used to play with himself, when now he would be doing them for real. His training was going well, he was being educated and guided towards better things. In the outside world he would infiltrate to spread the philosophy of the right way to live and be. He would know of others in the know, others working around him and with him, winks and acknowledgments would pass between them, all striving to make the world one, of one greatness. His wife must already know, she sent him here after all and she was a good person, charity work and community minded, she was already a better person of the highest order. He must check on his daughter, but believed he's wife's influence good enough to ensure a goodness in her too. What a happy place he would be returning to and what great things he would achieve, helping to make the world a better place! He would finally be the man he had wanted to be all along: a functional, influential person, respected by his peers, a wink and a nod between like-minded good people, people whom he could trust. He was going to be a part of the system, no longer a man lost in its workings. He would help shape the future of mankind.

Rushton

Dr Washington picked up his ringing receiver and answered the call with a sturdy, 'Dr Washington speaking.'

A soft, but slightly out of breath voice responded, 'Inspector Rodgers is following Jake, what should I do?'

Dr Washington took a deep intake of breath. Inspector Jacob Rodgers was becoming a nuisance.

'Follow him, make a note of times he goes home, how often he has to pop in to cafe or somewhere to use the facilities, when he eats, that sort of thing. I want to know when he's watching and when he's not.'

'Okay.'

And the line went dead. Dr Washington kept the receiver in his hand, pressed the disconnection key with his other and then dialled a number. A light, tender female voice answered. Dr Washington told this women to work harder with Jacob. She protested, explaining that he was fixated but that she had managed to calm his urgency about it. Dr Washington disagreed and told her about him following Jake. She fell silent, but after a short pause, she asked for advice.

'We must get him into the programme, you must work on changing his view, he must see the world more as we do. He is a good man, he uses his position in the police with good and fair judgement; his heart is there, but his mind is too untrusting.'

The women responded with appropriate noises, 'I will try.'

'No,' Dr Washington interjected, 'you will *do*.'

Simon

A man stepped out into the road, two fingers pulsing towards Simon in a V shape, challenging him, *come on!* Simon watched him with clear and sober eyes, his foot twitching at the brake pedal. This man was relying on Simon's integrity, in his goodness as a human being not to switch to the accelerator pedal and pound the bus forward into his weedy little body. They hovered there a while, the man's fingers still pedalling towards him, goading Simon, egging him on. Simon's eyes glinted, he released the brake and eased his foot onto the accelerator, *let the battle of man versus bus commence.* Simon was unable to understand the man's combat, what was it that he thought he would win? What honour or challenge was there in defeating a bus driver to not run his arse flat into the tarmac? *Come on!* The man darted out the way, waving his arms in the air.

'Shit man, you could have killed me!'

Simon slid open his cab window and folded his fingers towards the man in the same gesture that had been shown to him, 'Come on then, if you think you're brave enough!'

Then a cyclist swerved around the front of Simon's cab, just missing the front corner. Simon's heart pounded, his head swirled, causing him to brake suddenly and a passenger to fly forward. He cursed the idiots who relied on his good driving skills to always miss them, none of them taking responsibility for themselves. Simon felt as if people were endlessly throwing themselves into his path, testing his skills, testing his patience, believing the bus company liable, the payouts possibly high, 'Dare to hit me,' he heard their silent mantra. But accidents happen and the CCTV fitted to the bus would absolve Simon of any misdoing, so he dared to risk it, to show these fools that the responsibility was theirs, *come on then, keep your headphones in, don't look when you cross the road, come on, wave your pointy little fingers at me, call me a wanker one more time.* Simon revved his engine, *COME*

ON! And then there were all the other road users in their polished little cars!

Simon waited, giving way to oncoming traffic, parked cars narrowing the road preventing a two way stream, but an impatient car overtook him into the path of another vehicle. The two cars stared at each other for bit, Simon edged the bus forward, blocking the overtaking car's space to reverse back out. *Now what you gonna do? You fucking little prick.* Simon smiled, he loved his job more this way. He revved his engine again and shouted out the cab window, 'Get out of the way!'

The overtaking car driver sat bubbling with furry, not at his own stupid actions, but at Simon; of course, it was always the bus's fault. *COME ON!* A queue of cars was now building up behind Simon's bus, preventing him from reversing out of the way. They sat, all waving arms at each other, oncoming driver blaming the overtaking car, the overtaking car blaming Simon, the cars behind beeping and trying to overtake the bus as well. The road was now fully blocked in all directions. *All because one prick couldn't wait, all because one prick, like so many others, thinks buses sit on roads for the hell of it.*

Eventually the oncoming car reversed, slowly, moving with caution – he had a long way back to go. The overtaking car edged along with him, followed by a stream of cars behind. Simon was left there for over half an hour while they all did their thing, as if the bus wasn't even there. *Who's the wanker? You fucking wankers!*

Simon waited and allowed the reversing car to come back again; the driver stopped by Simon's window and complained to him about the other cars. Simon squinted, he'd seen this driver before; the other week Simon had not given way, already committed to the road ahead and this very driver had stuck his fingers in the air at him for making him wait. Simon shook his head, 'You're all morons,' he announced.

The man, already cross from the situation, started shouting. Simon drove off, leaving him red faced and screaming far behind. At the next stop a couple got on, a little wobbly on their feet, unkempt and slightly inebriated. They asked for a free ride, 'We're only going to the next stop.'

Simon asked why they couldn't walk for such a short distance and so the barrage began, 'I've got a bad knee, come on, I can't walk that distance I'm not well, only wanna go two stops.'

Wait, they'd said the next stop, how many stops did they really want? Simon insisted they pay and so a tiresome rummage in their coats and bags ensued, pulling out one penny at a time, the full fare possibly there to be discovered deep in the endless bottomless pockets, if everyone had an hour to spare.

'You know it all depends on how you treat us you know, we're reasonable if you are,' the man explained.

'No,' Simon said, 'it all relies on you getting what you want, if anyone says "No" you kick off and rummage around for ages, asking all my other passengers to be reasonable and patient; that doesn't make *you* reasonable, it makes you a nuisance and a bully.'

The queue behind backed away from the door as the kick off began.
COME ON!

Rushton

Dr Jefferson perched on the edge of Dr Washington's wide leather arm chair, the one reserved for guests. He sat with his hands pressed together, his elbows on his knees. 'Horace is doing extremely well. It's all coming together, Henry, the chips really work...'

Dr Washington raised an urgent hand, 'Don't speak of it! We don't speak of it, you know that!'

Dr Jefferson lowered his head and nodded, 'I'm sorry but I'm so excited, it's really working and what Horace has shown us is the other alternative, how the chips can work the other way...'

'STOP!' Dr Washington's hand filled the air with very clear instruction.

'I'm sorry,' Dr Jefferson said again.

'Horace's mistake is not to be repeated, there is to be no testing on the alternative. There *is* no alternative that is of use to us or anyone. Do I make myself clear?'

'Yes, Henry, I know, but it was useful to see it wasn't it? So that we can be careful and understand fully what's going on. His time at the clinic taught us much about how this works, when the chips are working on the wrong part of the brain.'

'You say that word again and I will fire you here and now!'

'But, Henry, maybe it's time to open up about our work here. I mean, the results are amazing, they are all switching to the good, it really works! Are we to pretend that it's all on therapy and influence?'

'Yes we are! The work we do here is organic, changing people's behaviour based on influencing their thoughts and helping them to see the betterment of things.'

'But that's not entirely true. Of course we are doing that and the results are based on them changing their own behaviour and becoming good citizens for themselves, but we cannot ignore that these... things...

are in place, helping them, like the influence of Ecstasy, helping them feel good, so that the change is fluid and comes from a place of euphoria.'

'Exactly, they are making changes for themselves. That is all that matters.'

'But Henry, these *things* alter their mind pattern, re-circuiting the brain waves so that they no longer feel the anguish and trouble of life, literally re-channelling how the brain works – we cannot ignore that.'

'Yes we can! It does not remove their free will, it does not prevent them from feeling or thinking, it simply cuts off the process of anguish just as you said, but unlike Ecstasy it does not cause the patient to think he can fly, nor is it a drug with long term repercussions with varying differences to individuals – it is not dangerous – it only helps the free mind understand goodness.'

'The *free* mind?'

'Yes, free from the influence of negative feelings and anger, the emotions and influences of humans that cause distress and wickedness. Now enough of this! It's working, that is all that matters. These people are learning to channel their natural selves in positive ways, they are still themselves, working from a place within themselves. All we have done is remove the anger and then taught them new things, things that encourage them to understand goodness. Education, so that they can be useful. Meditation, so that they can be at peace. Yoga for flexibility and stamina. Do I need to go on?'

'No, Henry, I know what we do and I know why, I just think that...'

'Stop!' Dr Washington's hand filled space once again in the air. 'We do not have a remote to these things that you speak of: we do not control, only influence and help. What use can come of disclosing these things? The real work and the main influence comes from the teachings that we provide here. Decisions are made by the subjects, and them alone.'

'What about the hypnosis?'

'What about it?'

'Isn't that less of their free will and more of ours?'

Dr Washington eyed Dr Jefferson curiously, 'You know as well as I that hypnosis is required to teach them while the chip settles in, it is important that they are not overwhelmed, we don't want to make people crazy. It is an influence that stops eventually, when they are ready.'

'And who decides when they are ready?'

'We do... You know all this! What is your point? Have you lost your nerve?!'

'No, Henry, I don't disagree with what we're doing, I just think it would be wise to be honest about how it is done. We don't know yet of any long term effects, we don't know if the chip has a life span. We hope – and of course we have spoken of this before – that if it does the influences and person that they have become will be so much a part of who they are that should the chip stop it won't change anything, but we don't know yet and we must be prepared to talk about it.'

'We are keeping a close eye on everyone. Subtle changes in thought and behaviour are being documented, we have people everywhere checking. We will know if things start to alter.'

Dr Jefferson shook his head, 'We cannot know if the inner workings of the mind change, it is for the individual and let's face it: how will they know?! They won't know what's happening to them! One day their feelings will start to change and maybe the anger will seep back as the euphoria depletes.'

'They will understand better things by then and the anger will be gone, their previous misgivings gone. Only good can prevail when you have been that way for so long.'

'We cannot be sure of that, Henry. We can hope for that – I desire it as much as you – but there is more research to do, more time to study the long term effects.'

'We are studying, monitoring their every move. Testing them, checking them. What more do you suggest?'

'I think we should tell them.'

Dr Washington paused for a moment and then calmly asserted his counter argument, 'If we were to tell them, they might re-find their anger. No one would appreciate a chip in the head, altering the way it sends messages so that only happy, good feelings can be passed around. What we are doing is for the greater good – and never forget that the people here lost their rights when they chose to kill, when they chose to be dysfunctional, causing only wickedness and horror in the world.

Horace was different of course, but his wife insisted… it was perhaps a mistake to feel her sadness and take on her need, but the results have been most educational, just as you said earlier. The chip failure that caused Horace to become a killer gave us important knowledge. How else would we ever have known without witnessing his confusion about what he was and what he had done circling in his mind, creating anger and frustration in him that did not exist before? But there have also been significant failings in our teaching of him: we should never have told him he was a killer.' Dr Washington shifted slightly in his seat, 'Perhaps it was inevitable in some ways, Horace didn't need his anger turned around. But then of course it was utterly unexpected – the chips were designed to only work in one way. You know the process was fully scrutinised: the scientific team was questioned and the basement laboratory was revaluated for order and process. A full investigation, at the end of which the government cleared us, allowed us to continue, despite endless discussions and many questions asked.'

Dr Washington paused, scrutinising Dr Jefferson's face, looking for weakness. He had fought for this, he had studied his whole life for this. He would make the world a better place, he would leave his legacy, he would fix it. He continued, 'Man is ultimately good. Our recruits on the outside have not required such an intervention, they work for the cause because it is right. *I* work for the cause because it is right.' He leaned back in his chair.

Dr Jefferson nodded, of course the cause was right, he had no doubts of it, he wanted it all to work as much as Dr Washington, he wanted a better, safer world, he wanted goodness to prevail. *So... so what if a few people, the minority, who had all killed, needed special influence*, it was the right thing to do. Dr Washington was right; Dr Jefferson nodded his agreement.

'Good,' Dr Washington proclaimed, 'we are not to discuss the chip again.'

Dr Jefferson nodded again.

Eva

Eva had been only nineteen when she first killed, a quiet academic man only nineteen himself. He had made a rare adventurous effort to put down his studies and attend a local bar. He sat stiffly on a stool, perusing the room with uncertainty and shyness. Eva ordered a drink and sat next to him. Needless to say he never completed his studies or ventured out again.

Three years on from her first kill and still eight years away from Rushton, Eva sat on a park bench, a take-away coffee resting beside her. The winter had been unnaturally long, the worst winter since records began, or so the reports said as they did every year in one way or another: an extra week of rain or an extra sunny spell, each year brought its own report of weather unprecedented in the last however-many years. But this year it was cold, seemingly endlessly so. It frustrated her a little, she preferred warm days when a jacket could slide down her back and her tight white t-shirt presented to the on-looking football players in the park. But still, she improvised: the cosy layers of warm jumpers and snaking scarf all had their own alluring nature. She found a way, whatever the weather, no matter the season. She clutched her coffee, clasping it with both her hands and sipped gently from the small opening in the lid.

'Want a finger of Kit-Kat to go with that?' A man stood a short distance away from her, fumbling in his pocket to retrieve the aforementioned chocolate treat.

Eva looked up and smiled, 'No thanks, not that keen on wafer. My mum used to pack me off to school with those multi-pack wafer things, can't remember their name now, used to swap them for fruit with the other kids.'

'Fruit eh! Healthy.'

Eva smiled again, a little broader than before, 'I practiced martial arts, energy foods have their place, but not at school when all I'm doing is sitting, bored out my mind.'

The man grinned, he liked the idea of a fit martial art physique 'Do you still practice?'

'Oh yes, do you want to come back with me and I'll show you a few of my moves?'

The man smiled broader still, now there was an offer he didn't get often, if ever. 'Sure,' he announced with confidence, putting the Kit-Kat back into his pocket.

How many would that be now? Eva had lost count, the number not important to her, the last one yesterday, this one now, and only the now really mattered.

Rushton

Boris realigned the books, someone had fiddled with them. Eva smiled, 'It's not about how they look up there you know, they're there to be read, to be moved.'

Boris shuffled. He agreed, but there was something he didn't like about it, it wasn't that people (of which there were few now, with only Eva left as a resident) were using them, reading them, it was just that they had been fiddled with, seemingly for no reason: just fiddled with. Eva moved her hand down and pushed the coaster that had been placed next to her away, her glass clanged against the glass of the table. Boris's ears pricked and his head spun round like an owl, almost disconnecting from his head. He glared at her and she smiled, 'Come on, Boris! Relax!'

He sighed, 'It's not mine to have as I would like, is it?'

'No, but your room is, why don't you go play with that?'

'Don't need to, nobody moves anything in there.'

'Then you like it being moved, keeps you busy, something to fuss over.'

Boris sighed again... 'What about a sofa, instead of chairs in here?'

'Not sitting that close next to me, mister.'

Boris's smile beamed into teeth, 'Oh come on!' he said, almost wanting to go over and tickle her, 'We can snuggle up when the cold sets in.'

Eva stared, straight faced back, 'Don't be silly, Boris. That is never going to happen.'

'Wow! You sounded really posh then.'

'I am posh, don't-you-know,' Eva's voice raised an octave and she smiled a genuine smile.

Boris continued to beam back, 'Okay, I'll get some soft blankets instead, how about that?'

'Nothing too girly, I don't want anything flowery or pink.'

'Why don't you come with me, we could go shopping together?'

Eva froze. Outside: *go outside with Boris, on some kind of family shopping outing, what the fuck is going on here?* 'Okay,' she said.

Boris's eyes widened, 'Really?'

'Yeah! Why not? Day out might be nice, spend most of my time with you anyway, might as well be outside.'

'I'll ask, not promising, I'll ask the Doc.'

'No need to promise, Boris. I'm not a child who is going to slam doors if the trip to Legoland gets cancelled.'

'Right, sorry.'

'And don't apologise! How did you get in here?! Dangerous killer excited by shopping trips.' Eva shook her head, 'They've really stuck it to you haven't they!'

'Says she, reading a classic, all curled up on her chair... like the blouse by the way.'

Eva looked down at her shirt, 'It's not a blouse.'

'Oh well excuse me, looks like a blouse, very pretty.'

'Very funny.'

'When you two have finished bickering, dinner is served in the dining hall.' The white coat's voice came from somewhere, Eva looked round, but it had already gone.

'It's more of a room than a hall.' Eva argued.

'Does it matter?' Boris questioned.

'Well yes, in a way, you wouldn't describe a glass as a mug would you?'

'What? A glass and a mug are clearly different.'

'Well so is a hall compared to a room.'

Now that there was only the two of them, they sat opposite each other every day for breakfast, lunch and dinner; this evening was no exception.

'When we getting more company?' Eva shouted out into the hallway but no-one replied.

'Stuck with me then,' Boris teased.

The table was set rather elegantly, complete with cloth, wine, polished cutlery and (for the first time) an ashtray, subtle and unused at the edge of the display, inviting them to spend a longer part of their evening there. Eva, not usually one for rules, looked about her as if checking that it was okay before sparking up one of her pre-rolled cigarettes plucked from the glass, the glass now sitting on the table with them. She waved her napkin over her lap and asked, 'What's going on here?' Boris shrugged.

'Okay Boris, tell me your story. What you doing here? Is it because you can't be trusted on the outside?' Eva lent forward, ready to buy into the evening and engage Boris in conversation.

'I don't know.'

Eva frowned at him, 'What don't you know?'

'Well, I'm not sure anymore that I would kill again. I was sure before and told them not to let me out, but I think I was scared in hindsight. Scared of the world outside rather than it needing to be scared of me, and now they won't let me out because I'm too useful in here. I've shown my worth, I guess.'

Eva considered what Boris had said. She took a long drag on her cigarette, released its vapours gently and sipped some wine before responding. 'We all have a purpose and yours is to stay here and keep me company, it's not so bad is it?'

Boris was quick to respond, 'No, not at all, I like it here with you.' Then he stopped, feeling the silliness of what he was saying. Eva would just laugh at him. But instead she smiled sweetly, 'You've done good work here, Boris, you are a good companion and you have been that way for many before me I'm guessing.'

Boris repressed a smile, he wasn't entirely sure why, but he knew that he didn't want every compliment to show such quick, unchecked emotion in front of Eva. 'I've been thinking though that I'd quite like to go outside, live out there again.'

'Thought it was all crazy cars and stuff out there.'

'It is,' Boris looked down. He felt the anxiety of it, but wanted to challenge his fear.

'You know, people work better in different environments, perhaps this is yours, your niche. The betterment of things must come from everywhere, this is your *where*.'

Boris nodded, he had heard these things from Dr Washington.

'Do you train like me?'

'Train?'

'When they take me away, teach me things.'

Boris considered, 'Used to, but not anymore, I was one of the first that arrived here.'

'So you've learnt all the stuff?'

'Oh, there's always more to learn, I just stopped when I said that I wasn't to leave. Guess I don't need to know all that to stay here.'

'What about the meditation and yoga, those things can help wherever you are, whatever you do. Do you still do things like that?'

Boris paused, he felt the conversation building up to questions he would be unable to answer honestly. 'Yes I do... that stuff still.'

Eva tilted her head a little. *Is he telling the truth? Why would he lie?* 'Do you remember the stuff you learned?'

'Yeah! I can pass in French and German, I got a couple of books in those languages to keep in practice, we could speak in them if you like, you know, to practice.'

Eva smiled, 'It's okay, I like English best.'

Boris smiled back, 'Me, too.'

'But I might have a look at those books, if you don't mind me touching the shelf display.'

'It's okay, I was being silly, they're there to be read, they have to be touched.'

'I told Simon once that I wouldn't kill for fun anymore, but that I would kill for a higher purpose, I don't feel that now. How come you still want to kill? What are they doing to me that they're not doing to you?'

'They're not. It's just that I don't...'

'Don't what?' Eve shuffled a little further forward on her seat, the answers were coming, *be patient Eva, let him fall in to it.*

'I did all the same things that you're doing. I just feel different, that's all.'

Eva lifted the bottle to pour Boris some more wine, but he took the bottle from her, 'It's my job to pour, it's a bloke thing.'

'Oh! I *love* the bloke thing!' Eva joked as she relaxed back into her chair.

'Do you really feel different now... about killing I mean, that you don't want to?'

'Yeah! Totally! I feel sort of euphoric... love and light... you know.'

Despite being a statement and not a question and despite Boris knowing that, he answered anyway, 'Yeah, I know.'

'Then why do you still want to kill?' Eva persisted.

'I *know*, but I don't feel that way.'

'Why? I mean why hasn't all the teaching done that to you?'

'It has, in a different way – I feel it in a more natural way: I understand what I have done and I am endlessly sorry, I want to be a better person but for a long time I was still aware of my inner self and the desire to kill – the anger, I guess – that wouldn't go away. But now it's starting to, all by itself, fading into a deeper part of me, but no-one knows for sure what might come back if I was released.'

'What do you mean by "natural way"?'

'Okay guys, smoking in the building is over, you've had your extended dinner, love.' The white coat ushered Eva off but lead Boris by the arm, 'You're coming with me, your turn to help clean up! We're a bit short staffed this evening.'

Eva watched him leave, *secrets!* What was it that separated him from her, separated him from them all? *What natural thing did he mean?* Eva wasn't one to be brainwashed easily, certainly less easily than she imagined Boris would be, and yet he was here before her and her turn-around was quicker, what was his resistance over hers? *What were they doing to them?*

The Diary of Rose Heather Roberts – The Truth

Eva picked up Rose's diary gingerly. It was not in her nature to be nervous, but there was something about Rose's diary that made her wary. It tended to shout at her and, unable to put out her fist or wrap her hands around its throat to silence its onslaught, she felt vulnerable in its presence. She took a deep breath, held it, and then with unusual speed threw the pages into view.

I went outside today. Love that air, when it's icy cold and brisk, startlingly refreshing, especially on a sunny day, when as the brisk air slows pace the sun's warmth awakens your senses. I sat for a while, in the park. It's like the Truman Show in here, everybody watching, everybody watching a life that is not your own, that is not real. I feel better, but I did not choose it. I feel compelled, as if an unseen force wills it.

Eva looked into the air, *I feel better but I did not choose it, compelled, as if an unseen force wills it.* She flipped the page.

There's no children here, it's like a weird suspense movie I'm sure I've watched. People walk around so stiffly. I see colours and light differently; there's a strange calm that feels natural to me, yet not me at the same time. Like something I would have been, should I have taken that other train. But my life is not that other train, I caught the 10.57 and I lived it, that other train's life is lost to me, this feeling is unnatural in the mechanics of the journey I chose. I liked being who I was, I liked my sadness, it was fitting: my father was owed it, he deserved someone to feel sad for his loss. My mother understood that and yet I hated her for it. That's better, guilt for my mother now.

Eva stared at the page, *colours and light differently, a strange calm, natural, yet unnatural to me.* Eva flipped back a few pages to where it had started to make her nervous and read the extract again.

Shit man! Horace like totally bludgeoned Gill to death, terrible mess. Sort of surprised, but not surprised, this is a crazy place after all. Now he's one of us, a killer rather than a dreamer. Bet it all goes wrong from here though, they'll take him away and dose him up, he'll be no-one now, a drooling mess in a white institution, more white than this one, he'll wear white, think blank white thoughts, stare into space at white walls, in a white wheelchair. Bye Horace. Shame. I wonder if I'm a shame, if someone looks over at me and writes a diary and says, 'Ahh! Imogen! Such a shame! Like her, but she's totally cuckoo.' It always comes back to me in the end, don't think I don't notice. I know how self-obsessed I am, but it's all in here, I'm banging my head with my hand while I write this, pointing at myself, me, me, me, in here, in here, in here. I'm in here. I don't know how to get myself out there, it's all in here. How do get out there with you? Wait... Who are you and why are you reading my diary????

Eva considered, *banging my head, I'm in here, self-obsessed.* Eva had not felt these things, yet somehow she understood them. Imogen had fought back, she had been fighting whatever it was they were doing to them, pushing it out, trying to get her sadness back.

She read the next page.

Creepy, this place is creepy, or maybe it's just this room, dark, dingy, door I've never opened, don't like it. My brain feels mashed, someone's messing with it. Jake's so cute, just want to eat him.

Eva's thoughts ran over the bits that stood out to her. *Someone's messing with my brain, messing with my brain, messing with my brain. Unnatural feeling of calm, compelled as if an unseen force has willed it.* Eva slammed the book shut, she wanted to get up and go to Boris, go to Dr Washington, go outside, scale the walls and find someone who could or more to the point, would, answer her questions, the main question and the only one right in this moment; *what the fuck is going on?*

Rushton

Dr Jefferson watched Horace, his broad dominating mass gentle on the mat, gliding his body into downward dog. Yoga practice seemed natural to him now, his moves flowed with a grace. Dr Jefferson could see Horace's calm, his body moving and his mind still as he worked on the floor, holding his positions with ease.

Dr Jefferson shook his head, as if trying to avert a memory, he was not completely happy with the conversation he had had with Dr Washington; he understood the other man's point, and of course he was totally in agreement with the cause, but questions and doubts haunted him. He worried to himself, *Imogen, what had happened to Imogen, why had she killed herself, how had this process failed her? And Eva, if Imogen was strong enough to find herself again in the depths of her mind beyond any mind altering techniques, what would Eva do?* She was something else, the biggest challenge of this institution and yet the most important. They had tried to recruit her willingly before her arrest, before Inspector Jacob Rodgers had concluded on his leads. With the right training and guidance, Dr Jefferson mused, Eva could change everything. She and Jake had the very ideas they wanted, the anti-society, anti-bullshit beliefs that fuelled their very own, plus they had skills – many skills, executive abilities – placing them in positions of importance, of influence, fighting techniques and a steady calmness around all that they did. An unnerving calmness when they were free to do as they pleased, but a useful tool in the world as they wanted it to be. To turn it all around and change the world: what an ambition! But it could really be done, were the causalities of their attempt worth it?

Is it fair to say that the loss of a few is outweighed by the gain of the many? It was easy to argue in the affirmative, and yet Dr Jefferson wasn't sure. There were glitches. His face crumpled with doubt and concentration, *perhaps Imogen can be excused, she killed herself after all, there was no harm to others... and*

Horace, well Horace is becoming a fine man, the very man he was sent here to be, all his own desires and fantasies coming into their own.

Was Gill's loss outweighed? Was one person's redemption outweighed by one person's death? Had they noticed any signs? The research carried out on Horace after Gill's death had taught them much, but would they know if it happened again? Horace had not been progressing then as he was now but the process had been new, they had had no real idea how long it would take. They had clearer timescales now, they watched more closely, lessons had been learned. But Dr Jefferson still had doubts, someone like Eva could hide herself from them, she was something else. A mistake with Eva, having trained her beyond what she was already capable of, was frightening.

There must be no mistakes with Eva. Dr Jefferson turned on his heels and made his way to the basement; a new chip was being developed, one that could switch off the part of the brain that caused question, as well as redirecting the parts that created anxiety and hate. Eva had lost her rights, every time she plunged an empty biro into the throat of an unsuspecting victim. If this new chip was to be tested, Dr Jefferson reasoned, it should be on her.

Dr Jefferson arrived at the basement, two entrances faced him, the one on the left allowed access to the main laboratory where the original chip's research and application was housed, the entrance on the right guarded access to the new chip's development suite. Dr Jefferson stepped right and punched in a five digit code, followed by a fingerprint recognition system. It flashed red, his access denied. He tried again: no response. Dr Jefferson creased up his face, Dr Washington must have removed his access after their recent disagreement. He banged on the door, but the steel was too thick for his efforts to be heard from the other side. He pounded harder, *hear me, God damn it!* One scientist inside tilted his head up, did he hear something? He concentrated but heard nothing more and carried on.

Dr Jefferson stepped left, a light flashed green, access granted. Dr Jefferson nodded, neither of the doctors liked the new chip, it was not part of their principles to turn soldiers into robots, that was not the intention of their work, research was purposely slow, but for people like Eva, Dr Jefferson found new enthusiasm. He wanted to go to Dr Washington, but knew his visit would be futile. He decided, instead, to speak to Eva.

Inspector Jacob Rodgers

Inspector Jacob Rodgers looked over to his female companion, *where had she come from?* She was so understanding about his job and the hours that he worked, never had he been made to feel so important so easily, her touch so calm and loving; her understanding put him at ease.

He didn't want to doubt, to be paranoid, but this was so unusual; relationships in the past had barely got past dating as he missed dates, was continually late and never bought gifts. On occasion he had forgotten their name or that a date had even been arranged, but this women seemed to appreciate his job, seemed to be interested and accepted lateness and missed times as a reasonable part of his vocation. *Who is she?* As he was considering these questions she had been watching, her smile touched his senses: she was a beauty.

'How is it going at work?' She asked, 'Any developments?'

Jacob paused, he felt suddenly hushed by an inner force, *don't tell her anything!*

'Oh it's fine,' he casually expressed.

She looked inquisitively at him, 'Really?'

Questions hung in the air, so he reaffirmed his position, 'There's nothing to worry about, I'm plodding along at the moment, no big cases in, everything's fine, really it is.'

She nodded, a little disappointed perhaps, there was very little else that they talked about, her interest in his work seemed to be the focus of their connection.

'Any more progress on Jake?' And there it was. Jacob's eyes widened, *Jake, Jake,* she had made many suggestions and shared her thoughts about Jake: *he* was the focus of their connection, the point of reference and conversation. Jacob made a decision to lie, 'Oh I've given up on worrying about Jake, I'm sure you're right, the institution has it under control and of course, like you said, the government are involved, it's being monitored and checked… I think I was being over-cautious, but it's not my problem or area now.'

Stop Jacob, stop, there's lying and there's over doing it. He held his breath and tried not to say any more.

His companion smiled and nodded thoughtfully, 'Good, I was getting worried about you worrying; I didn't want it to become an obsession, especially when it's out of your hands now.'

Jacob tensed, *obsession!* That was not his type, *people think inspectors get obsessed because they put the hours in, but killers loose on the streets require the hours – you can't go home and waste time faffing around doing the washing up while a killer stalks his next victim. You have to find him and if you know where he is, you have to stop him.*

Jacob finished up his meal and made an excuse to leave. His new companion made no fuss to keep him there, no subtle pleading, just a knowing nod and a soft kiss as he straightened his coat.

Jacob got into his car and headed straight for Jake's flat. He looked around: the building opposite Jake's place was up for rent, an office floor; Jacob wrote the number down. The lights were off in Jake's flat but his car was parked outside. Jacob sidled over and looked at the tyres, no mud, few bits of gravel stuck between the groves. He peered through the window: nothing. He looked up towards Jake's flat, and as he did so a light came on. His instinct was to duck to the body of the building, out of sight under the window, but he remained standing where he was, looking up. Jake came to the window and looked down, a phone in his hand. Jake nodded and the inspector felt as if he knew, knew who Jake was talking to and why he had come to the window. He called his lady companion; the line was engaged.

Rushton

Dr Jefferson called the white coat that no-one really saw, she picked up the receiver from the office that overlooked the communal seating area, 10 by 16 paces in size. She nodded, said she would have to clear it with Dr Washington. Dr Jefferson announced a very firm 'No!' insisting that he must see Eva and that there was no need to involve or interrupt a very busy Dr Washington. The white coat that no-one really saw frowned, she wasn't sure, but agreed to send her over.

Eva knocked on Dr Jefferson's door, less austere than Dr Washington's, the plaque indicating his name a little smaller, the door less heavy and – she observed on entering the room – his office less imposing. Dr Jefferson sat behind a light glass desk, his swivel chair plastic and without arms. His files lined a bookshelf against the wall.

'Ah, Eva, thank you so much for coming over, I hope there was no bother getting in?'

'No, none,' Eva stated.

'Good, good. Come in and sit down.' Dr Jefferson gestured with his hand, as Dr Washington always did, towards the chairs opposite his desk. Eva sat.

'So, how are things going?'

Eva looked around her, 'Okay.'

'Just "okay"? Do you have any questions?'

Eva considered and decided that perhaps Dr Jefferson was different, perhaps he could answer some of her thoughts, some of the thoughts that she shared with Imogen, 'Well,' she began, 'I am a little curious as to what is going on. I feel – how should I put it – as if compelled by an unseen force. I feel good, but it is not my feeling really, it's a mask over myself, a feeling not completely instructed by myself. As if compelled, you see.'

'Compelled, I see.' Dr Jefferson mused, 'Like an unseen force has willed it?'

'Yes, exactly like that.'

'Do you not like to feel good?'

'Well, it's a different kind of good – a calm – a while ago it was more euphoric, now it's a calm, a balance in my mind, but it is not me who controls it.'

'Controls it?' Dr Jefferson thought out loud, 'Does it feel like control?'

'In a way.'

'Your thoughts are your own Eva, you still have the power to make decisions, to consider, to question, do you not?'

'*Still*? What do you mean by *still*?'

Dr Jefferson shuffled, he had momentarily forgotten how quick Eva was, he must be more careful with his words. 'Well, you say you feel different, calmer, and this is a good feeling. You feel good and yet you question it, but you still have the ability to question, so what unnerves you about this good feeling?'

'That somehow it is not my own, that it has been implanted into me somehow.'

'How are you getting on with your studies?'

'Good. I actually enjoy them, it is wonderful to learn new skills, languages, practices.'

'Do you not equate the calmness to these practices, the yoga, meditation?'

'In a way, yes, but there's something else… something I'm not doing. When I meditate my mind finds focus and peace and yet there is so much of it that is different, as if I am not working through it all for myself, that it has been done ahead of meditation, like I said, as if I have been compelled to feel this way. But it isn't my own.'

'Do you still have negative feelings about men?'

'No, that's just it! Where has that gone?'

'Well, perhaps with all the work you have been doing here that feeling has dispersed as you have learned new things and expanded your mind. Do you think it might be possible that you have just rediscovered yourself with new focus and purpose?'

Eva considered, 'Maybe, but...'

'Dr Jefferson!' A booming voice filled the room, accompanied by the crash of his office door being strongly pushed out of the way of the incoming Dr Washington. Dr Jefferson's head darted upwards towards his co-worker. 'What are you doing with my patient?' Eva swivelled round to see Dr Washington's raging red face boring into Dr Jefferson's.

'Eva and I were just having a quiet chat, Dr Washington. Why don't you join us?' Dr Jefferson waved his hand towards the other chair opposite his desk and next to Eva.

Dr Washington seethed with fury, he never sat that side of the desk, *he* was in charge. 'Eva! Get back to Blue Block and don't ever visit this block again without my permission.'

Eva smirked, she liked this, perhaps her mind was more hers than she thought, the subtle mind games she played with Simon and now the joy of this distress between colleagues. She did not move.

'Eva!' Dr Washington turned to look at her directly, 'Let's go!'

'Actually, I'd like to stay a while.'

'No, go back immediately, I will follow shortly.'

Eva got up languidly, taking her time to leave. She winked at Dr Jefferson as she slid round the door frame.

'Dr Jefferson, what the hell do you think you are doing?'

'Eva feels compelled by an outside force, she is aware that her mind is being altered somehow, we must be careful, Henry.'

'Eva is a stunning student, she's coming along fine. Her feelings about this do not affect her achievements.'

'Henry, the new chip that removes questioning, maybe we should consider this for her.'

'No! That is a side line, funded by the government from the military budget. It is to be used on soldiers and soldiers alone.'

'But I have to say I disagree with its use in that way, it is not what we believe in, it is not why we're here. The government is wrong, we need our soldiers to question.'

'Concessions always have to be made, the government have their own agenda and we need their support.'

'But, Henry...'

'Enough of this! If you no longer wish to be a part of the work here, I will happily accept your resignation, otherwise leave it alone.'

'Eva is potentially very dangerous.'

'We will turn her around, she has come so far already, I will work on the hypnosis a bit more if it will bring some peace to you.'

Dr Jefferson nodded miserably, something was better than doing nothing.

Eva slid down the corridor almost at a jog, *a chip that removes questioning, government agenda, what the hell?* She slipped past the office that overlooked the communal area, 10 by 16 paces in size, and knocked gently on Boris's door.

'Hello,' muffled its way through the cracks, 'it's Eva.'

'Come in.'

'No, let's go out.'

Boris came to the door, 'What's up?'

'Let's go out: pub, cigarette, anything.'

'You okay?'

'Please, Boris.'

'Blimey! A please from the mighty Eva!'

'Don't push it, I might be different now, but I'll still break your scrawny neck.'

Boris put his hands up in surrender, 'Okay! We can go out, but not the pub.'

'Why?'

'Don't fancy it. Come on, we'll go for a walk.'

Once outside, Boris guided Eva around the paths to the park, 'Keep away from the trees.'

Eva looked around her, 'What for?'

'They have listening devices in the trees, in fact they have them everywhere but the park's the hardest to cover, so if we talk quietly they shouldn't hear us here.'

Eva's head twitched about, taking in her surroundings, 'Listening devices?'

'Come on, Eva! You're a killer, don't think you're not locked up in some way.'

'The walls I understand for that very reason but listening devices?! I'm starting to feel like I'm in a spy thriller.'

'You are.' Boris smiled, 'So what are we doing here, what's the matter?'

'I overheard the doctors, they said something about a chip, a chip that removes questioning and a government agenda.'

Boris took her arm and led her a little further into the centre of the park, 'That doesn't have anything to do with us, they're developing some kind of implant that the government want used on soldiers, so that they can control them more, real spy thriller shit for sure. But you've got it all mixed up, you still question, don't you? You are now, so trust me, it has nothing to do with us.'

'But there is something to do with us, he said a *new* chip that removes questioning –Dr Jefferson wants to use it on me – but aside from that, if there's a *new* chip, then there must be an old one. Boris talk to me, tell me, what is going on?'

'Okay,' Boris breathed. 'The reason I'm still here is because I don't have a chip. I'm the big experiment to do it all natural but it's taking years. I've learnt from my mistakes and I'm sorry for what I've done, but there is a part of me that I don't trust, a part that might switch and kill again, I can never be sure. You, Jake and all the others have been implanted with a chip that works like Ecstasy, changing the brain waves to bring a euphoric feeling: calm and peace of mind. The rest is all your own work – with the programme, the training they're teaching you and hypnosis of course – to ease you into it.'

'Brainwashing! I knew it! It's a fucking cult!'

'Eva,' Boris smiled broadly, 'it's not a cult, it's a belief. The doctors believe in the greater good, they want to change the world for the better. The chip doesn't alter who you are, it doesn't stop you from thinking or feeling or questioning, it just redirects brain patterns so that different parts of the brain talk to each other, to remove the killer in you, to help you feel love more, to be a better person. I'm afraid I agree with that.'

'Dr Jefferson wants to use this solider one on me. What will that do?'

'I don't know really, it isn't part of all this, it's something the government want and this institution needs government support.'

'That's what Dr Washington said.'

'Well, there you are then.'

'But Dr Jefferson...'

'Dr Jefferson is not your doctor, Dr Washington is and he won't use these new chips, he doesn't really believe in them.'

So Eva had been wrong to trust Dr Jefferson more than Dr Washington, *and yet he seemed...* she didn't know.

'Eva,' Boris's voice was soft, he rubbed her arm, 'it's going to be alright, you're doing so well here, they're going to hone all your skills so that you can be fulfilled by yourself. When you're training don't you feel really cool, learning language and martial arts? You have so much potential. Eva, you are amazing, you really are, you have so many skills that could be put to good, real life use. You and Jake are the forerunners of this whole project, you are going to the change the world and make it a better place.'

'Fuck that! What's the point of a better place if it's not real?! You can't tell me that a chip in the brain makes any of this real.'

'It does; have you ever taken Ecstasy?'

'Yes.'

'How did it feel?'

Eva tried to recall, 'I don't know, kind of floaty, kind of colourful.'

'Did you kill anyone while taking it?'

'No, I don't believe I did.'

'That's because it alters the brain waves, removing certain connections that encourage negativity and anxiety in your mind. That's all this chip does, it isn't changing you as a person per se. And then the training helps direct your new focus, equips you with new skills and enhances those you've already established with its teachings.'

'What's the hypnosis for?'

'Helps to keep you relaxed, it just helps you not to become overwhelmed by it all, helps you to ease into it.'

Eva shook her head, 'I've been reading Imogen's diary—'

Boris interrupted, 'How? Where did you get it?'

'It was in my room, well, the first room I was in, I guess it was hers.'

'Yes it was her room before you; what does it say?'

'Lots of things, it talks about this feeling of being herself but not herself, as if someone was messing with her mind, which of course they bloody well were. She killed herself, Boris – and Horace, what the fuck! Didn't stop him did it?'

'It doesn't work for everyone, nothing does, what system do you know that works for everyone? It's impossible. But it's working for you – you mustn't give up – don't get fixated on this chip, it isn't doing anything to harm you. Don't you like feeling more love and light?'

'Don't get any smart ideas, it's not going to make me get all jiggy, jiggy with you Mr Boris, whatever your surname is.'

'*Jiggy, jiggy?*'

'Don't be naïve!'

'You mean sex.'

Eva raised an eyebrow, 'Bravo.'

'Sex is not necessarily an expression of love.'

'Oh don't start getting all deep!'

'This is all deep, in a way.'

'Too bloody deep! Messing with brain waves, altering my focus...'

'They're rehabilitating you in a way that prisons fail to – it's the way forward – it could be an incredible thing for the human race.'

'What about the people on the outside? Not Jake who came from here but the others. There must be others, there was a Malcolm who came to my home, tried to recruit me, I remember him now. Dr Jefferson said they'd tried to get to me before that inspector arrested me. Do they have chips?'

'No, an average person on the outside doesn't need it, they buy into the belief because it's right and they work for the cause because they believe in it.'

'What if I wanted to believe in it, would they take the chip out?'

'No, you need to see beauty more, you need the chip so that you can see beauty more.'

'There was beauty in the flow of blood, beauty in the art of it.'

'Do you still feel that?'

'I know it, like a childhood memory of someplace I saw and thought was amazing, but I don't feel it, I don't want to recreate it, like I don't want to visit that place again.'

'There are many places of beauty to visit and many beautiful and wonderful things to do.'

Eva breathed steadily *in, then out.* Her practice with her at all times, she translated Boris's words into French, then German, how knowledgeable she had become! 'Why did they let Simon out, what changed? It seemed sudden.'

'He recognised thanks, he appreciated what good things were happening for him, how his life was better now. He wanted to stay you know.'

'Really?'

'Yeah really, but Dr Washington felt that he was ready, ready to use this change in the world.'

'Has he? Is he?'

'I believe he is, working with troubled teenagers.'

'I miss him a little.'

'Good, you're feeling a little love.'

Eva's face screwed up like a young child.

Boris smiled, 'Love isn't just full on you know.'

'Stop it with the love crap!'

'You're such a child sometimes! What happened to you?'

'Oh! I know it all comes down to the mother.' Eva waved her arms in the air, 'Psychobabble bullshit. Life's a bitch and then you are one; what can I say?'

'And you still are a little, so don't worry, you are still *you*.' Boris smiled again.

'Not entirely, as we have just been discussing.'

'But you are. Don't you see? You are the better part of yourself, the person you were meant to be, the one that can achieve great things. You're super clever and super agile, you have so much going for you. Don't you feel better focusing all that energy and talent into a better place, for a better purpose?'

'Well...' Eva looked down, never had anyone been so encouraging, never had she been believed in as she was here. Maybe they were right or maybe she could just pretend they were right and outsmart them all. Eva smiled and Boris knew why.

'You can outsmart us, all of us. Dr Washington is a man, just a man, you could run rings around him if you truly wanted to, but you don't have to live under his control. He is guiding you, that's all; he has no intention of ruling your life. You must let go, Eva.'

'From what I saw today he could do with this chip himself, red raw he was, furious. Little love and light going on there.'

'He is passionate about this, that's all.'

'I want to see the research, I want to see how this chip really works, I want what's happening to me properly explained.'

Boris nodded, that seemed fair, 'I'll speak with Dr Washington.'

'Why, shouldn't I?'

'If you like.'

'What about the drugs they give us every day?'

'Well, in the beginning they were painkillers, from the operation. After that they're just vitamins and protein. They know that everyone will stop taking them eventually, when they start to question, after the operation for the chip has worn off. It's the placebo effect: when you stop taking the pills you believe you're outsmarting them, understanding things with a clear head, so that the feelings you get from the training you believe to be yours and yours alone.'

'Clever boys!' Eva sat on the grass, the cool air circled around her. 'I am lucky I suppose, this place is definitely better than prison, although I was kind of looking forward to the bitch fights... would have broken a lot of bones by now.'

'Yes I'm sure you would have.' Boris sat beside her on the ground, the grass soft under his hand, he stroked it in arcs around his legs. 'Nature is beautiful isn't it?'

'*Amazing!*' Eva lifted her voice in sarcasm and lay flat out looking up at the clouds hovering over their heads, the breeze so light – even up there – that they hardly seemed to move.

'Do you not see its beauty?'

'Oh stop and just lay here with me!'

Boris reclined and stared up with her into the distant sky.

Jake

Jake was feeling a little peculiar, Derek Faulkner played on his mind. His new lady companion played on his mind also. Things were going so well, but there was something unnerving about it all, something that was not his doing, something in the way he was that was not himself. He was enjoying his job, he liked the idea of climbing the ranks to be of influence at the top, to spread the word, but the word of what? Goodness, was he to be a prophet? He scratched his head, *ouch!* There was no pain but Jake felt a small lump, the psychology of which made him squint. He rubbed it, how had he got it? He could not recall an incident but he struggled to recall many things. *Derek Faulkner,* why could he not remember? *What have they done to me?*

Rushton

Dr Washington ushered Boris into his office with his waving paddle hand. Dr Washington was smiling, Boris had not seen this often and felt a little unnerved.

'Boris.'

'Yes, Doctor.'

'Please, sit down.' Boris sat, his knees together, his hands perched on the edge of them like a child in front of the headteacher.

'You have done well; your conversation with Eva was good.'

Boris looked confused, 'How do you know of it?'

'You have a microphone on your jacket.'

Boris looked down at his shirt.

'Not your shirt, your jacket. But don't worry, you have done the right thing. Eva wasn't going to stop until she knew some truths and you explained them very well, I'm pleased with you.'

'Thank you, Doctor, but...'

'Please don't worry Boris, each person is a new test for us. Eva is exceptional and we run each person with their own rules, Eva needed to know, it will be fine.'

Boris nodded.

'I do hope though Boris, you were intending on coming to tell me of this conversation, had we not recorded it?'

'Yes, Doctor, of course.'

Dr Washington smiled again, 'Good.'

'Doctor, Eva spoke of Dr Jefferson wanting to give the new chip...'

'Don't worry', Dr Washington interrupted, 'I won't allow it. Dr Jefferson is getting nervous but please be reassured that I will play him your conversation, I'm sure he will be as delighted by her responses as I am.'

Boris nodded, 'Good, I don't like the idea of them.'

'Me neither, but as you know, to retain government support we must fulfil this line of research. But I have no intention of ever using it on my people here.'

Boris nodded again.

'That is all, Boris. Thank you.'

Boris stayed in his chair, his hands twitching against his knees.

'What is it, Boris?'

'What happens to Eva now? Now that she knows.'

'Nothing, she carries on the same, a few more months in training and we might even be considering letting her out.'

Boris's head darted upwards, desperate to shout out a massive *NO!* Eva was playing games, Boris was sure of it.

'You seem nervous, Boris.'

'I don't think Eva's ready.'

'You said that about Jake and he is doing exceptionally well.'

'For now, yes, but I am still nervous about him, I think long term effects and questions will change him.'

'He has a girlfriend now, keeping a close eye on him. We'll know if anything changes.'

Boris shook his head, 'It's the girlfriends that start to make them nervous.' Boris had no idea how he knew that, he just felt it, like that would be how he'd feel. But he did not have the chip, he could not really be sure how any of this worked. He just didn't like it.

'How so?' Dr Washington enquired.

'I just think it would, because they'll be perfect... supportive, loving, understanding. I'm sorry, Doctor but life's just not that easy, it'll make him question, make him nervous.'

Dr Washington smiled for the third time during their exchange, 'Sometimes life is that easy, Boris. In the better world, it will all be that simple and we must up keep the feeling of it. Jake must believe that the world is becoming a better place.'

Boris nodded, 'But won't he feel that she's fake?'

'Fake?'

'Yeah, that she's just there being supportive, what about passion? Surly he will feel that it's not quite real.'

'But it is real – a women from his office asked if she could do this. She fancies him, wants to be with him, and after a few dates it seems that Jake likes her too.'

Boris put his head down, 'Right.' It was all so contrived, but Boris knew that the doctor would find an argument for it, *as long as everyone's happy, why does it matter?*

Horace

Horace studied hard, now living permanently within the training facility of Dr Rushton's New Wave of Rehabilitation. He woke early every morning, meditated, went to the main hall for yoga practice, then to a classroom to learn (depending on the day) mathematics, English, geography, history, French, German, science.... Lunch consisted now of a finely balanced menu, fulfilling all the necessary requirements of the body, specially designed to Horace's profile and build. Then more classes in the afternoon filled Horace's day, followed by marital art training before late evening meditation and a light snack. Horace slept better than he could ever remember. He soaked up everything they taught him, he was becoming their finest prototype.

Dr Jefferson was very pleased, he almost clapped his hands with joy, the real success was going to be born from Orange Block: he was going to release to the world a man who would do great things without fear of reprisal. The real success would be his, and not Dr Washington's. Horace was the one, not Jake and especially not the very volatile Eva.

Dr Jefferson held all the same concerns as Boris: Jake had been released too early, with the consequences of that rash act yet to be learned; and Eva, she scared him even now – perhaps more so now. The more they trained her the more dangerous she could potentially be, but there was no convincing Dr Washington.

Dr Jefferson called Horace into his office. Horace strolled in, his mass now refined, his body flexible, agile and toned. Still huge in the doorway, his body filled the space. Dr Jefferson gestured to him to sit down. Horace sat.

'How are you feeling Horace?'

'Very good, Doctor, I feel amazing, and I'm learning a great deal.'

'Very good, Horace. Do you have concerns that you would like to ask me about?'

'No, none, everything is perfect. I want to learn faster so that I can go home to my wife.'

Dr Jefferson smiled, 'Soon, Horace. You are coming along better than we could ever have hoped. Your dedication to the cause is outstanding, we are very proud of you.'

'Thank you, Doctor.'

'You will of course carry on your practices after release, so it is not necessary to learn everything here.'

Horace smiled, breathed in, he felt a rush, a rush of pleasure, *to go home!* To be the man he was supposed to be, to show his wife and daughter how all this time and anxiety had been worth it.

'I know you are in a hurry to see your wife again, but how do you think it might work between you, after all that has happened?'

'I'm not really sure, Doctor, but I will do everything I can to make it right. I must prove myself and regain my family's trust.'

'Do you think you might like to see her here at Rushton before your release, to see how it feels?'

Horace thought, he would very much like to see her, but *here?* he wasn't sure. 'I don't know, Doctor, I had in my mind the vision of knocking on the door of our house and offering my hand to her, maybe taking her out, to get to know me again.'

'I see. You will need to get to know her again too and your daughter, who is now at university.'

Horace's eyes widened, 'Really?! University!'

'Yes, you have been here many years.'

Horace looked down. He felt sad for the first time since he had made this decision to change his life and the whole world.

'Don't feel sad, Horace, she is a fine women, you will be pleased.'

Horace nodded, 'I'm sure she is, my wife will be taking great care of her.'

'And I'm afraid your house is long since sold.'

'I see. Where does my wife live now?'

'In a flat, not far from where you were.'

'I see.'

'You'll be given your own flat, close by. If it works out between you, which I'm sure it will, you can make your own arrangements. Your wife has been informed of your progress and is anxious to have you home.

She feels a little responsible for Gill… you do remember what happened with Gill?'

Horace stared unblinking and wide, 'Yes.'

It was your wife that put you here with us, Horace, when she found all your files in the converted garage; she sold the house to pay for it.'

'Is she still paying for it?' Horace seemed a little startled.

'No, it has since been removed from her concern – financially I mean – since Gill we fund you. We were responsible for you, after all.'

'I see.'

'How do you feel about that Horace?'

Horace considered, his eyes softened and he gazed a little around the room as he thought, 'It all worked out for the best,' he straightened in the chair, 'I couldn't be more grateful for where I am now in my state of mind, and physically I'm fit and agile. This institution has made me the man I always wanted to be.'

Dr Jefferson smiled, 'I'm glad you feel that way, Horace.'

'I'm going to make my wife proud of the decision that she made.'

Dr Jefferson beamed, 'Then you better get on with it, Horace! I believe you are due for martial arts in a moment.'

Horace stood, 'Thank you, Doctor.'

'My pleasure, Horace, my pleasure.'

Rushton

Dr Washington worked extensively with Eva; he could feel the turning point close ahead. She had responded well to being told the truth. He allowed her to look at the equations that made up the footprint of the chip, the initial research on Ecstasy and then the chip development that honed in on the principle of that effect, funnelling it into precise, controlled redirection of brain waves. He showed her how it did not take away who she was, how the brain worked as it had before – her memories, her calculations, her personality – how it enhanced but did not change her good emotions. Eva read intensely and quickly as if she were learning the deactivating instructions for a bomb, set to go off in five minutes and counting. A mistake in the understanding of these instructions would allow the bomb to go off, any missed information could be crucial. She took in every detail, closing her eyes every few seconds to compartmentalise the information, so that she could recall it later in clear order. Dr Washington had taken on board Boris's fears of Eva's ability and possible desire to outwit them, so he used hypnosis on a deeper level, trying to reach the calculating, game-playing aspect of Eva's free will, tweaking it gently but often, trying to persuade it, *the betterment of things, for the betterment of things.*

Simon

Simon loved his new position. He had missed his vocation, had missed himself. Simon felt fulfilled and happy as he strolled into the pub to meet Gavin; Dr Washington had been clear as they parted, "Keep your appointments with Gavin, he is our communication, he is there to steady you, a base, a friend."

'Hey, Simon, how are things going?' Gavin sat at a table by the far wall, two pints in front of him.

'Really good,' Simon responded as he sat opposite his companion and in front of the second pint.

'Any problems?'

'No, none.'

'How's the flat?'

'Really nice.'

'Made any friends?'

'Not really.'

'Do you not want to, or are you finding it difficult?'

Simon focused his eyes on Gavin's ballpoint pen, ticking boxes and writing short notes on a page of paper in front of him.

'I... haven't thought about it. I love my job, I get on really well with the guys there, then I go home and rest.'

Gavin nodded.

'Do you have any questions?' Gavin asked without looking up.

'How's Eva?'

'Who's Eva?'

'From Rushton, she was in my block.'

'I'm afraid I don't know.'

'Dr Washington said you would be my communication to him, can you find out for me?'

'Sure, Simon. I'll ask.'

Simon relaxed, he had not been aware of his tension until the answer he wanted rang through his ears.

'She is important to you?'

'Yes, I suppose she is.'

Gavin nodded again and scribbled something down.

Rushton

Dr Washington was feeling confident, things were going well. He put down his pencil and relaxed back into his large leather desk chair and entwined his fingers, *here's the steeple and here's all the people.* His forefingers tapped gently on his lips as he considered the potential consequences of releasing Eva.

He was startled out of his contemplative state by his ringing phone; it seemed urgent, the hand piece rattled and jumped upon the main telephone body. He swiped at it, 'Dr Washington here.'

He listened carefully, his hand clasping the hand piece with increasing tightness. Inspector Jacob Rodgers just wouldn't go away. 'Well it is clear that you are failing; I will send someone else.' Dr Washington sighed as the voice on the other end spoke of what they had done and said to dissuade him.

'But it's clear that it is not working.' He responded with authority.

'He's obsessed,' the voice pleaded.

Dr Washington paused, then asked, 'Is there anyone he trusts, a work colleague perhaps or a friend, preferably both?'

The voice considered, 'He talks about a guy called Jim.'

'Very well, then suggest you all have dinner, say you'd like to get to know his friends and that it would be good to get away from work. Check this Jim out and let me know if you think we can reach him.'

'Yes, Doctor.'

'Very well.'

And the phone line went dead.

Eva

A few months had passed since Eva had been told the truth. She had been dedicating a lot of her time to meditation, controlling her thoughts and being one with herself. It helped her identify the chip's altering pattern in her brain, focusing her concentration in smaller and smaller circles until there was nothing left, only silence and a fuzzy warmth dancing over her body.

Dr Washington consulted Dr Jefferson about her release, a thoughtful meeting had taken place where Dr Jefferson took on board the changes that had transpired since his fears about her had surfaced. He nodded positively and congratulated Dr Washington on his work. Dr Washington in turn congratulated Dr Jefferson on the incredible chip he had designed, without which his own work would be impossible. The two men, lost in self-indulgence and the sight of a working project that would put their names in the history books, agreed to release Eva.

Now, at the same gate where Simon had stood, Dr Washington relayed his speech once more to Eva; she nodded in response, 'I will, Doctor.'

Then she was gone, through the gate, across the land, through the second gate and beyond, back into the world.

Rushton

Three more people had been moved in to Blue Block, one of them just before Eva's departure, but neither she nor Boris had paid much attention. The new arrivals watched the television and shuffled around, just as they all had in the beginning, while the operation from the chip calmed, heavy painkillers dulling their senses. Boris dusted his new decor, waiting for them to stop taking their pills and for his work to begin again, Eva playing on his mind.

The Diary of Rose Heather Roberts – The Truth

I have this fantasy… I hold a gun to the temple of my enemy (of course this enemy is me, you have figured that out now, haven't you?) I can feel the trigger, the power of a strangely simple yet deadly invention that rests in my hand awaiting my own death. So many people have died at the hands of such a weapon, so many innocent; am I innocent?

Rushton

6.02am and the white coat that was rarely seen (otherwise known as Yvonne) ran full pelt down the corridor clasping her oversized self, trying to hold together the undersized white coat that clung to her, double stitched but desperate. Her pocket watch bounced around, banging against her thigh, the tightness of the coat no match for the pleated pocket big enough to comfortably contain a pair of shoes. She punched a red alarm button as she went, one of a series buttons installed every 20 feet along the walls following Gill's demise.

When she reached a new inmate's room (otherwise known as Sam) Yvonne pulled together her early nursing training, *keep it simple, just remember first aid first and foremost*. She tried to turn Sam on to her side. Sam was choking on her own salvia, but Yvonne struggled as Sam's fit tensed her muscles, throwing her rigid body out of Yvonne's grasp. The alarm had summoned a medical crew of two and a security guard troop of five, once again precautions put into place after Gill's unfortunate murder. Yvonne stood back and allowed the crew to take over.

The security guards stood in a ready-for-action posture, a little stunned, a little nervous, their mouths visibly agape, slightly on edge as if they felt there was something they should be doing but had no idea what. Yvonne shuffled them off, beckoning one back to help carry Sam if need be and just for precaution. Sam was taken to the infirmary, sedated, prodded and monitored.

6.22am; Dr Washington summoned Yvonne for a debrief, his coat only half off over his shoulder, his briefcase slightly skew from its usual indent on the carpet. Yvonne spoke softly, there was always a calm that came over her in his presence. 'Sam had a fit. I don't know why, she has no history or records that could explain it. Perhaps she's reacting to one of the drugs?'

'No, that's not possible.'

'I'm sorry to disagree, Doctor, but isn't it always possible? All drugs have the potential to affect one person in an unexpected way. You wrote a thesis on it yourself, the dangers of drugs and the argument that there must be other ways.'

'It's not possible because we don't give them any drugs.'

Yvonne looked around her – the pictures on the wall, the bookcase, Dr Washington's coat stand – as if these things held answers, as if they might help her find the clues that separated the pills she gave them every day from this statement.

'The tablets you give them, Yvonne,' Dr Washington interjected her thoughts, 'are vitamins and a protein.'

Of course, what else would they be? Yvonne relaxed and felt her clasped hand uncurl; she had until that moment not been aware that she held in a fist. She felt cross with herself, *be aware, concentrate, Yvonne, think.*

'In which case, Doctor, I'm afraid I am at a loss to know why this has happened.'

'Did the support crew arrive promptly?'

'Oh yes, Doctor, very quick, and with five security guards.'

'Very good. I'll visit with Sam shortly. Please don't worry yourself with it, I'm sure she'll be fine.'

'Yes, Doctor.' With which Yvonne turned on her heels and left to carry out the rest of the day's duties.

Inspector Jacob Rodgers

Becoming increasingly paranoid, Inspector Jacob Rodgers started to find cause in every case he ran – some connection, some minor detail that related to Rushton and those around him. He felt as if he were being watched, as if the world had suddenly focused on some strange collective understanding that he had failed to see, as if he had missed the news broadcast that day, as if the world around him had some shared secret kept from him, a conspiracy.

Rushton

Dr Jefferson knocked clearly and energetically on the hard, thick door of Dr Washington's office.

'Come in,' boomed through the gaps, around the hinges and into the soft, small ears of Dr Jefferson.

'You've heard about Sam?' Dr Washington spoke before even the muscle flex of inner consciousness twitched at the idea of speech for Dr Jefferson.

'Yes,' he replied simply, still pushing at the door to silence their conversation from the corridor.

'What do you think?'

Dr Jefferson gathered himself, 'I think it was probably the chip.'

Dr Washington's eyebrows rose and eyes widened, 'Go on.'

'Well... she has no history of anything that could have caused a seizure, but she is still on the painkillers from the operation... It may be that we have an incomplete file on her or that she never reported it to a doctor. However, we did carry out a medical check here before the process began and there was nothing to suggest, well, anything medical really.'

'So?'

'So, it must be the chip.'

'So?'

'Well... given that no-one else has suffered the same reaction or anything near it, I would say that it was a one off. I'll take a closer look at her and see if something was amiss with the operation.'

'Very good.'

Dr Jefferson had already turned to leave when Dr Washington stopped him with another statement. 'We've been asked by the government to extend our work.'

'Extend? Extend to what?'

'Mankind.'

'I'm sorry, did you just say *mankind?*!'

'I did.'

A silent pause of great magnitude sat between them, the two doctors alone in Dr Washington's grand office, surrounded by criminals and people in white coats, holding the possibility of a better world in their knowledge, in their research, in their dreams. Dr Washington took Dr Jefferson's hand and shook it enthusiastically. They'd done it, they had achieved their ultimate goal, they were going to be able to reach the world, to make their beliefs in its betterment normal practice: they were going to make the world as they believed it should be.

Dr Jefferson broke the heavy yet excited silence first, 'How exactly do we intend to do that... *mankind?*!'

'Not overnight, Dr Jefferson. In time, constructively and consistently, but we are to expand our intake of people here with immediate effect. Funding has been given to build more facilities, smarter ones that people might volunteer to reside in. The government wants to advertise its benefits and send people on long term unemployment.'

Dr Jefferson stood with his mouth agape at Dr Washington as if he were mad.

'Why are you staring at me like that?' Dr Washington asked a little contemptuously.

Dr Jefferson dropped his head into his hands. His knees felt a little weak but he stood fast clasping his mind, trying to find a good reason not to expand.

'What is it, Dr Jefferson?' Dr Washington pushed.

'What have we done?! In the world I knew before all of this there was a saying that you cannot please all of the people all of the time. That saying exists because people disagree, they have different opinions... what if we have brainwashed them?'

Dr Washington straightened up, 'But you can please *most* of the people, *most* of the time. They will still have freedom of thought. This is what we wanted! World peace! Isn't that what most people want? Everyone says it, from beauty pageants to politicians, a world where we are all fulfilled, where we are at peace with ourselves.'

Dr Jefferson wanted to agree, he had worked for this his whole life alongside Dr Washington, it had been a joint desire, a joint hope for the world. 'What about Sam? It's a one off here, with small numbers to be comparing it to, but if we expand that may happen more... We need more time to get this right, to be sure that it is right, to be sure that it works. We don't yet know if Jake will turn, if the chip has a life span and what the consequences of its failure might be. It's too soon.'

'Nonsense! We have folders of research spanning years, how much time do you need? This is what we've worked for.'

Dr Jefferson bowed his head. There was no argument to be had, it was indeed what they had worked for, dreamed of, and now it was within their reach: the funding and the approval to change the world. Dr Washington took Dr Jefferson's hand again but this time thrusting a crystal glass with a thin line of brownish liquid into it. *Clink*. Dr Washington tapped his glass against Dr Jefferson's and announced, 'We've done it.'

Jake

Jake pulled in to a service station to consult a map; he scanned the page already marked with the address which he was seeking. The roads intertwined and crossed each other in a disorderly fashion. He used his index finger to follow the path, located his position and his destination and connected the two. He placed the map back onto the passenger seat and pulled away to resume his journey. As he drove, he tried to conjure some memory of his surroundings, did he know that wood or that building, did he recognise the town names? Why had Boris remembered himself, his past? Why had Horace killed Gill? Why was he going to work every day? Did he really like Evelyn or was she part of the... *the what?* What was he a part of?

Rushton

Dr Washington slumped down into his chair, a fabric coated chair softer than the one in his office. His wife hovered over him with a cup of tea. He nodded his gratitude and she nodded back, a small, sweet smile lighting up her eyes as she sat down to resume reading her book.

'Dr Jefferson has doubts.'

Dr Washington's wife glanced up from her spy thriller, 'What sort of doubts?' she asked gently, unconcerned.

'He thinks we should test it longer, make sure it really works.'

'Do you agree?'

There was a pause. Dr Washington considered the question, more deeply now in those few moments than he had while Dr Jefferson had been speaking of it or in all the time in between then and now.

'Caution of this kind could affect funding, could affect the government's belief in our success and conviction. I think we would be unwise to turn down the very thing we have worked so hard to achieve. I believe it works enough to change the world for the better, any alterations later can be dealt with; we are keeping a close eye on everyone, if things start to sway we can intervene.'

Dr Washington's wife smiled, not quite as sweetly as she had before but with honesty and respect for the man she knew as her husband, 'Then perhaps it's time for Dr Jefferson to be parted from the task; he has been of great value but perhaps his work here is done.'

Dr Washington put the tea down and rose from his chair, a few steps and he repositioned himself with a glass of whiskey, tall and straight, and took a deep breath, 'Yes. *We* did it, now *I* must complete it.'

Horace

Horace was the next to be released to make room for the new recruits. He was set up in a flat just around the corner from his wife (as promised) and placed in a role that utilised his new-found abilities in language. They had adorned him with certificates of excellence, tastefully framed in solid wood, which he proudly hung from the wall in his wide hallway.

His wardrobe made him smile as he admired the suits that hung there, the shirts of varying colours neatly ironed and hanging to the left of the suits. The tie rack. Horace paused and as he ran his hand down the length of a tie he remembered his daughter. He brushed himself down and went to the bathroom.

Horace brushed his hair at the bathroom mirror, six strokes varying in manner exercised his arms. Horace was a geezer, *Sha!* Straightening his collar and shaking off any stray threads clinging to his attire, Horace prepared himself for the long awaited visit to see his wife. Striding with long paces he marched into the hallway, his scent altering the air. Horace was not walking with arrogance but with love and pride in his heart today.

Rushton

Dr Jefferson settled down in the wide worn-out leather arm chair that had been handed down from grandfather, to father, to him. He kept it here, in his cabin, a place away from the rush and thrill of the world, a place he came to relax and find solitude. The two doctors had agreed to take a few weeks off, to rest before the expansion work began, before the world was to begin its journey in the footprint of their beliefs and research. He unfolded a national paper and scanned the headlines for interest, each depicting another disaster, sometimes in nature, but most commonly among people: another attack, another murder, another mistreated child, another fight – a fight for the individual, as well as a country. Court cases, taxations, strikes: mayhem everywhere.

He rested the paper on his lap and sighed, Dr Washington was right, they could only improve on the nightmare that currently existed. Even if something *did* change or a chip failed, they were monitoring everyone, they would know and be able to intervene. He went through it in his head again: *worst case scenario and someone does change unnoticed and does something awful, how much more awful would it be than the news I read now? We have the ability to make it better, if only for some. Some is surely better than none: we must continue.*

Dr Jefferson folded the paper up and reached for his glass, but just as his fingertips brushed the cut crystal a gentle but clear knock startled him a little. Dr Jefferson paused. His cabin was miles from anywhere, it was his solitary retreat, his private location. *Who would come here?* Perhaps a broken down car further up the track, there was a small village a few miles away. He raised himself and headed to the door. Another light tap. Dr Jefferson pulled the blind from the glass of the window next to the door to view his unexpected guest. *Eva.* Dr Jefferson went to the door with a sudden haste and opened it wide, 'Hello,' he found himself saying with unnatural vigour.

'Hello,' she said gently in return, a slight smile softening her eyes. 'Can I come in?'

Dr Jefferson moved out of the door frame, 'Of course, come in, come in,' he waved his arm in broad gestures towards the interior of his cabin.

Eva perused the surroundings and, with a little glint in her eye, began her evening seduction.

Simon

Simon had been given Eva's phone number. Dr Washington could see no good reason not to allow it; they were good for each other in a strange way and he thought that their connection may have its advantages in the outside world. But he felt the situation was sensitive, and not wanting Simon to turn up on her door step he agreed to pass on her number so that she could decide if she wanted to carry on their companionship or not.

Simon held the scrap of paper with her number on it in his hand. He stared at it as if he were about to ring for a long awaited job interview, the job he wanted but at the same time doubted his ability to do. Anxiety and nervous tension built in his blood, pushing it faster around his veins, his hand shook a little. What would she be like outside of the Rushton walls, would she play games with him? Would he be able to control or even deal with such games? He dialled the number, one determined digit after another and waited for the calling *burr, burr, burr, burr.*

'Hello?'

'Hi, is that Eva? It's Simon.'

'It's Simon.' Eva announced out beyond the phone. Simon strained to hear the voice in the background, the voice that Eva was keeping company, but he couldn't make it out.

'How lovely!' She continued.

'I'm out, got my own flat and started work with teenagers.'

'How lovely!' She said again, 'Of course you know that I know that already, you did leave before me.'

'Yes of course, I just heard that you were out too and I wondered if you wanted to meet up, maybe a drink or something?'

'I'd love to. I'm on a business trip at the moment but I'll save the number that you just called with and call you when I get back, just be a couple of days.'

'Great!'

Simon sat for a moment looking at the phone after the line had disconnected, and so it was left.

Rushton

Dr Washington marched into his office a week ahead of his expected return. There was much to do. The white coat that clung uncomfortably around the frame of Yvonne tip-toed in behind him. Dr Washington turned and jumped a little when he saw her, his nerves a little on edge. 'Yes,' he announced, 'very prompt.' The white coat that no-one really saw composed herself to consider her words before speaking.

'The expansions,' Dr Washington began, 'new people will start arriving at a higher rate soon and I think it necessary that you should start recruiting some more help.' He pulled out a file from his neat and ordered collection flanking his wide dominating desk, flicking through he stopped at a page, 'Yes,' he mused out loud, 'I will send you a list of people to contact, we have people already lined up who are in the fold. The ones at the top of the list have requested to join us, contact them first. New beds are arriving in two weeks, each room will be doubled up and the training process fast-tracked a little.'

The uncomfortable white coat finally formulated a question, 'Fast-tracked, Doctor?'

'Yes, is there a problem?'

'Well, it's just a very sensitive thing, are we wise to fast-track something we are still discovering?'

'It is not for you to question what works and does not! But to put your mind at ease, the new people will not all be killers, not even criminals; some of them have just been long-term unemployed or are volunteering for our work here. Their progress will be quicker and easier to manage.'

'Very good, Doctor.'

Eva

Eva smiled to herself, what a wonderful life she had found herself in! What a lovely cabin surrounded by such beauty! She made a strong coffee on the wood burning stove and stepped out to sit on the veranda looking out across the land, breathed deeply to take in the fresh, clean air that circled her head. *Lovely.* When she was finished, she glided back into her car and started her journey back to the city, calling Simon en route to arrange their rendezvous. As she disconnected the call, she glanced over at a car that was headed towards her, travelling in the opposite direction: an old silver Honda. Inspector Jacob Rodgers looked tense, sitting forward in the driving seat, willing his car to travel a little faster as if an urgent appointment was soon to be missed. Eva smiled, repressing the desire to wave languidly out of her window. She plucked a pre-rolled cigarette from the cup holder instead and lit it just as their vehicles passed, lighting her face. Inspector Jacob Rodgers turned at the last minute to catch her profile, his right foot plunged to the floor, *damn car, go faster!*

Rushton

The Rushton Institute of Rehabilitation was a frenzy of activity. Well-established recruits in Orange Block were planting and developing more vegetable plots to feed the many that were due to join them. Blue Block busied itself with bed assembly, and the old chairs that Boris had removed from the communal area were returned to provide more seating, arranged in a separate semi-circle, back to back, against Boris's new modern area, squashed in the 10 by 16 paces space. Boris felt unnerved but knew that his work here was going to be more important than ever; he was after all a part of the foundations, the foundations of things that stood to change the world. He had doubts about how quickly it was all moving but believed in the cause, *the betterment of things*, a better world, and placed his trust in the doctors; they knew what they were doing.

The Diary of Rose Heather Roberts – The Truth

Bang, bang. Soon, very soon.

Rushton

Dr Jefferson had not returned to his post. White coats from Orange Block had called Dr Washington, 'Not to worry,' he had said, 'Dr Jefferson is extending his holiday.'

Dr Washington breathed heavily through his nose, *hold it... and out.*

Inspector Jacob Rodgers

Inspector Jacob Rodgers had called Rushton and asked for Dr Jefferson. Told that he was on holiday in the mountains, he got in his car and headed for Dr Jefferson's cabin.

Jim, Jacob's long term friend and colleague had not been invited into the fold but – convinced by Jacob's lady friend – found himself concerned for Jacob's state of mind, his obsession with Jake. He had pleaded with Jacob not to go to the mountains but had been hit by a wall of obstinacy, 'Not you as well!' Worried for his friend, he had decided to follow him there. Standing on the veranda of an empty cabin he now tried to reassure Jacob that he was wrong.

'No!' Jacob shouted, 'This is wrong! I saw Eva on the road here, something is wrong.'

'Eva? But there's nothing here.'

'Damn it!' Jacob rushed in to the cabin and pulled off files from the walled shelving and flicked through, searching, searching. A click sounded, as if a timer had moved into position. Inspector Jacob Rodgers turned around to see the wood burning stoves fire ignite into a blaze, engulfing a tall locked cabinet. He ran outside to the shed shouting at Jim, 'You get the fire! I'm going for the cabinet!' Inspector Jacob Rodgers arrived back with a crowbar.

'Jesus, Jacob! What are you doing?! You need a warrant for that sort of thing!'

'Just get that fire out!' Jacob wedged the crowbar in and pulled, forcing the cabinet open; he scanned through the paperwork.

'Look!' he waved a sheet out to Jim, who was trying taps but couldn't get a flow of water, the fire increasing, forcing him back.

'They're putting chips into people's brains, altering the brain wave patterns!' The fire was raging now; Jim had failed to find any control. He called the fire brigade, out of his depth. Jacob left him, running to his car to speed as quickly as the Honda would allow back down the track to the road.

Jim sighed, Jacob's girl was right, this had become an obsession.

Jacob drove nonstop back to the city, crashed into the door of Simon's flat, 'What is going on?!' he demanded, a little red in the face, a little crazed.

Simon put his hands out in front of him, 'Okay! Okay! Come in.'

Jacob rushed in, scanning Simon's flat for evidence. 'Where's Dr Jefferson? He's not at Rushton or at his cabin.'

'I don't know,' Simon was a little nervous but was not lying.

Inspector Jacob Rodgers stood inches from Simon, 'Where?'

'I don't know!' Simon's hands guarded his face.

'Where's Eva?'

'I'm meeting her tomorrow; she's been on a business trip.'

'Business trip... where?'

'I don't know.'

'Tomorrow: where and when?'

'I haven't seen her since her release, I'd like to see her alone. Perhaps you should make your *own* arrangements.'

Jacob lunged for Simon, 'Don't get cocky with me, boy! Where and when?'

'It's none of your business! Hit me if you want.'

Jacob paused, he wanted to, but how would that help? His face roared with anger as he left Simon's flat.

Simon called a number, who called another number. A circle of information was passed, eventually ending with a call to Jim. Jim disclosed his worries and said that he thought Jacob might be becoming unhinged. Further calls were made.

Rushton

The white coat that no-one really saw and didn't fit all that comfortably turned on the television, just in time for Sam's favourite programme (now recovered from the unexplained fit), she was obviously important. 16 paces long, 10 paces wide, this is their space. The white coat so far had not let her down, except once: a long weekend when another white coat had arrived, a coat that didn't quite fit the same. Sam was sure that it was a different white coat, she asked a person who didn't wear a white coat but always intervened; the person looked up – he saw an inmate, a complex, intricate soul – he looked down. The weekend passed and the coat that didn't actually fit as well as the replacement coat was back. Sam watched the television: a black box flickering with amusements, laughter coming from an unseen but up close audience. When the favourite programme finished, the old white coat pressed her finger into the plastic surround of the screen, Sam watched, awaiting the inevitable day when only a stub might reappear. Quad didn't care, Quad didn't exist, and the man he related to no-longer lived there. Sam had once overheard a question, these were her thoughts: *Do I want large chips? What does that mean? Long chips? Fat chips? More chips? Not sure if I want chips? Do you get more chips? How many more chips do you get?* Sam looked up at Boris, he had wild ginger hair; they were not friends, Sam was certain of it.

Jake

Jake, a tumult of images collated into an intricate montage of assumed memory, a dizzying mosaic of simulated involvement.

The only one – well, the only one in Blue Block – to have lost moments in his memory, the chip playing with his brain.

Rushton

White coats, those who don't wear white coats but always intervene, new beds, vegetable plots, chairs, an institution set for progress, for the mind altering progress that was going to bring about a better world. Dr Washington sat smug in his enormous chair, ahead of his broad, imposing oak desk. *History.* History was being made and he was the one that was going to carry the rewards, an OBE, *oh yes*! Dr Henry Washington had earned his place in history.

Horace

Horace looked at his wife. His little eyes welled as his heart beat faster to see her. He reached out his hand and took hers with a soft, careful touch, folding his other hand over them both, embracing his wife in a moment expressed by hands alone. She bowed her head, fighting back the tears that had been building for so long. She must find her strength to embrace the new world that awaited her. *The betterment of things*, a lifelong mantra for her through her charity work and friendships, now held bigger possibilities. This man she loved, this man – her husband – was going to join her efforts, the world had begun its journey to better things. Dr Washington had proved his place, the little people who worked in his name were going to be a part of the whole, the world was going to unite and breathe a sigh of relief as mankind finally found its unselfish and forward-thinking purpose. Man's intelligence so vast and beautiful but so often unforgiving and single minded had finally found the answer. She clasped Horace's hand in return, looked him straight in the eye, forgave him everything and knew that from now, from this day forward, they worked together with a single goal.

Rushton

The uncomfortable white coat ran down the hallway, not due to a medical emergency this time, but an emergency nonetheless. Inspector Jacob Rodgers pounded on the institution door. How he had got through the gate and over the land was a mystery, but there he stood, fists ablaze at the reinforced glass that protected the white coat from the air outside. Equally frenzied bangs resonated through the thick door of Dr Washington's office. The sound was so urgent that Dr Washington pushed his paddle hands down on the wood to raise himself up from his leather executive chair. Opening the door himself he enquired, 'What is it?'

'Inspector Jacob Rodgers, Sir… he's at the door,' the white coat pointed down the hall towards the communal area, 10 by 16 paces wide.

'What does he want?'

'He's banging, banging on the door… he seems a little upset. I didn't ask what he wanted, thought I should inform you before asking questions.'

'Very good, thank you, I will attend to it.' Dr Washington moved along the corridor, a little slower in pace than the white coat that really didn't fit all that well (a little snug around the hips and belly). The white coat's pockets bounced, something filled them, making the large expanse bulge and bounce against the leg as Yvonne rushed back towards her glass outlook (the one that overlooked the 10 by 16 paces communal area, now double seated, half with Boris's modern ensemble and half with the old tired seating of times past).

Dr Washington reached the door and eyed Inspector Jacob Rodgers with caution. He pressed a button and his voice burst into Jacob's ears, 'What do you want?'

Inspector Jacob Rodgers kept pounding, 'Let me in! I want to see Dr Jefferson!'

'Dr Jefferson is not here.'

'Where is he?' His question cushioned by the glass.

'On an extended break.'

'I've been to his cabin, he's not there.'

'Well, perhaps he chose to go somewhere else, I am not his keeper.'

'Eva killed him and you told her to!'

'Inspector, I suggest that you seek help, this has gone too far. You are clearly in need of assistance and care.'

'Damn you, Doctor! I know what you're doing and I'll get you!'

Dr Washington pressed the button one last time before turning away, his eyes directly focused on those of Inspector Jacob Rodgers, 'You are mad.'

A security guard moved in, plucking the inspector from where he stood and marching him to a vehicle that would take him far away, for now.

Simon

Simon had followed Eva's rather convoluted instructions to find himself outside the Red Lion pub. He looked around; the streets a little dirty, the area run down and strange faces staring at him from street corners. He took a breath and entered. Eva sat on the far side, a pint already half-drunk, talking to a man: he seemed intoxicated; Simon couldn't determine from this distance whether it was from alcohol or Eva's witchy spell. Simon went to the bar first and ordered two pints, requesting 'Whatever that girl over there is drinking,' knowing the barman would remember what she'd ordered. Simon plonked the two pints down on the table in front of her, 'I thought you'd be a spirit drinker.'

Eva smiled, 'Did you? Why?'

'Don't know really, hardcore maybe.'

'There's hardcore control over toilet visits with beer that shouldn't go unrecognised.' She raised an eyebrow jokingly, Simon smiled.

'How lovely to see you out of that other environment,' Eva continued.

Simon nodded with agreement as he swallowed his first sip of lager. The intoxicated man now left, deflated, and shuffled off.

Eva bounced on her seat, 'So, what you up to these days?'

'Well,' Simon started slowly, one sip quickly followed by another, the lager a need in this moment. 'I'm working for a youth group, troubled teenagers.'

'How very!'

'Very?'

'Very good,' Eva smiled again, a smile beyond the moment.

Simon looked around the pub, 'What we doing out here?'

'You don't like it? Bit down for you?'

Simon looked at Eva directly, 'Down for you, I thought.'

'Don't be silly, I'm an experienced soul, I love places like this, brings out the broad in me.'

'The *broad*?'

'Yeah, the broad, the tough and tumble, the broad, broad shoulders.'

'Ah! I see.' A silence fell between them. Simon scanned her, as if looking for a wire. 'So, what are you up to these days?'

Eva laughed, 'Business my boy, big business.'

'Inspector Rodgers came to my flat, asked after Dr Jefferson and you. He wanted to join our meeting today but I told him to make his own arrangements.' Simon threw it in, trying in some feeble attempt the element of surprise.

Eva cackled, 'How lovely! That man is so cute, so very inspector-like in his stupid rain mac.'

'What did he want?'

'How do I know, the man's nuts,' Eva circled her temple with her finger.

'Is he…? He caught you didn't he?'

'Ah, Simon, you have respect for a man that catches the criminal, but be careful, the world is a bigger place, your role in it a bigger thing. We have been given a new challenge, a new start, Inspector Rogers' place in it no longer applies.'

Simon took another sip, his pint almost finished. Eva jumped up, 'Another?' she pointed at his near empty glass.

'Why not?'

Eva smiled as she floated off towards the bar.

On her return Simon started talking before she'd sat down, 'He's still the law, isn't he?'

Eva sat gently, pushing Simon's pint across the table towards him, 'No, he isn't. The world is changing, the betterment of things is the law now, of which – my dear little man – you are a part. You are the new law of goodness now.'

Simon considered. He was happy in his role with teenagers, he was making a difference that would make the world a little better.

'Totally better,' Eva had this unnerving ability to read one's mind.

'And what are you doing in this better world?'

Eva smiled with a little breath, her chest bouncing, her figure to die for. Simon took a breath, *in through the nose, out through the mouth.*

'Influence, my brother, influence! I'm turning business marketing into a positive thing.'

'You're selling stuff.'

'Selling stuff but also spinning a little wisdom.'

Simon smiled, of course, those days at Rushton; her wisdom, her magic… Who better to market the world?

Rushton

There are rare moments in life when one ponders on the significance or insignificance of time spent, the worth of one's actions. Dr Washington sat for a moment and concluded that he was indeed doing absolutely the right thing. And so onward and upward the work went on. The brain child of Dr Rushton was to become the legacy of Dr Washington.

Eva

Eva's mother had cradled her new born baby gently in her arms, smiled sweetly at her, coo-cooed a little, tickled her a little, sung soft quiet songs of nothingness. Stroked her head, changed her nappies, wiped her delicate little bum and somehow missed the knowledge that all along she nursed a child who would become first a curse and burden to society and then a founder in a new beginning in a new world, far better – in some opinions – than the one she grew up in. There is certainly reason to agree, a life of betterment, a life of a shared vision in goodness, of a shared belief working towards a better world of fulfilment and happiness. Eva sat now on the edge of her own sofa, her memory not long enough to recall that first moment her mother held her in arms of love. She remembered only annoyance, and as she flicked through a photo album that 'they' had seen fit to pack amongst the boxes that awaited her in her new flat, her mother conjured only memories of weakness, *bang, bang.*

Rushton

A letter had arrived. Dr Washington, although used to mail, stopped when he saw it. A slight smile on his otherwise intense face didn't lighten the mood but rather compounded its intensity. He opened it quickly, read it quicker, and called a number.

Dr Jefferson had relieved himself from his work and chosen not to return to the institution (the letter read), he would however continue with its objectives in a private way. He no longer, in short, wished to continue at such a high level at his age, especially with the impending outreach of their work moving to the masses and the workload increase that would come with it.

Arrangements were made for his replacement on Orange Block.

Dr Washington sat back in his mighty chair, behind his mighty desk and entwined his podgy fingers. *Here's the steeple and here's all the podgy people.*

The Diary of Rose Heather Roberts – The Truth

I watch the world in all its complexity but do I know any more? More than what? What is it that one looks out for? I hope for peace and yes, you can laugh, whoever you are, rudely reading my diary, a peace within, within the chaos, the chaos of one's mind. Psychology, what a thing! Practiced by the privileged, what the fuck do they know? They are still surprised when they meet a person who holds an alternative view, cocks! Isn't it them that are supposed to understand, they are supposed to see outside the box, so that they can explain the unexpected? They know nothing of any view but their own.

Rushton

It's a rush, Dr Washington breathed smartly but thoughtfully, deep into his lungs, as he stood proud in the park overlooking his work. A new building was being erected, diggers and cranes hummed and jarred the day's air with noise. Orange Block was to remain single roomed, reserved for the killers they had worked so well with. Indeed, his own office was to move there close to the hub of the action, to take charge of the chip operations and be close to the back office, so to speak. Burly men had been employed to move his heavy oak desk, boxes had been sought to move his files and books. He wanted to beat his chest, to cry out with enthusiasm. Blue Block was to take petty criminals and the new Purple and Yellow Blocks, when completed, would take on the unemployed and those who volunteered. The world was going to see, the world would understand only what *he* wanted it to.

Inspector Jacob Rodgers

Inspector Jacob Rodgers burst into Downing Street having gained entry by showing his official identification. Such access would have ordinarily been a little more difficult, but although the Inspector considered his conviction alone to have facilitated his entrance, he had actually been expected. His rain coat now floated in the breeze, the security guard left clasping its bodiless cloth having lost his grip as Jacob ignored a request to wait in the lobby. 'Prime Minister, please! You must hear me out!' Jacob blundered in.

The Prime Minister held up his hand to halt the oncoming guards that raced to his protection.

'Inspector Rodgers, I believe?' The Prime Minister's voice was clear and calm.

Inspector Jacob Rodgers flung his body over to double up, breathing heavily.

'Nancy, will you fetch the inspector a brandy? Please, Inspector, take a moment to collect yourself.'

Inspector Jacob Rodgers stood straight and awaited his drink, collecting his breath and thoughts, 'I'm sorry to burst in like this.'

'Most people go to their local MPs or write to me, Inspector.'

Inspector Jacob Rodgers nodded, *of course*, 'I understand,' he said, 'but this needs a more direct response from the top and I thought my letters would go unnoticed or ignored.'

'I see,' the Prime minster gestured for the inspector to sit.

'I'd prefer to stand.'

'Very well.'

'It's about Dr Rushton's New Wave of Rehabilitation.'

'I thought it might be.' The Prime Minster took a sip of tea and checked his watch.

'Prime Minister, I believe you are making a grave mistake putting a chip into people's brains,' the inspector shook his head, the sheer idea of it was so wrong, surely.

The Prime Minister interjected, 'It doesn't take away people's sense of self.'

Oh God, the inspector stared in horror, here he was bringing important information to the head of his government which he thought would most certainly end with an investigation and the eventual closure of Rushton, only to discover that he was in on it.

'It takes away what it is to be human, Prime Minister. It blocks emotions – are we to be robots?'

'Only *negative* emotions. Don't you want the world to be at peace, Inspector? Are you afraid for your job?'

'Prime Minister, please! You cannot place the sanity and function of the mind into the hands of one doctor.'

'There are *two* doctors, Inspector, who have made it their life's work to find answers to the human condition, to implement a way of making the world a better place. They are the founders of something that will save mankind from itself and bring about a sort of true paradise on earth.'

Inspector Jacob Rodgers stood opened mouthed, wishing he'd accepted the seat as his knees gave way a little beneath him. But he pressed on, he was not to be defeated yet; he feared Dr Washington.

'There is only one doctor now, Prime Minister. Dr Jefferson's cabin has been burnt down and he is not at the Rushton Institute. I believe Dr Washington has had Dr Jefferson killed and started the fire to get rid of the research.'

The Prime Minister smiled, Dr Washington had been right: the inspector was indeed a little mad and could perhaps benefit from the Institution himself.

'Dear, dear, a conspiracy theory indeed. Dr Jefferson felt that his work at Rushton had come to a natural conclusion, he left the institute of his own accord. The chip works, there are no improvements to be made, the correct re-direction of the brain waves has been achieved; he felt that he had accomplished his life's work and that Dr Washington was better suited to carry on with the practices that support it.

I am sorry, however, to hear about a fire, Dr Jefferson must be very sad about that. I'm sure that they have copies of the research.' The Prime Minister took another sip of tea before continuing, 'Inspector, I fear that you have become obsessed in a quest to prove Dr Washington wrong

413

without knowing all the facts, because he makes you uncomfortable somehow. Please be reassured that he is well educated and a fine man, working only for the betterment of things. I think you should take a break. Your superior informs me that you have been neglecting other cases to pursue this line of enquiry regarding Dr Washington's practice, and your girlfriend says that you talk about very little else and that you are pre-occupied...'

Inspector Jacob Rodgers intercepted, 'I'm being set up. She's not my girlfriend, she works for Dr Washington, she's a spy.'

'I think you'll find she works as a history lecturer. A spy? Really, Inspector! Dr Washington may well be a brash man on occasion but he is not in the business of hiring spies! You must pull yourself together and understand that I cannot take the advice of a man who has clearly lost perspective. Inspector, if you were in a more grounded state of mind, you would have pushed for an appointment with me, you would not have burst in like this – I mean no offence – but you are behaving in a rather dramatic fashion over the legitimate research of highly educated and informed doctors of Neurobiology and Psychology, the research of two gentleman with more letters after of their names than you use to spell yours.'

How can this be ignored? How can this be? They stared at each other for a moment before Jacob continued, pressing his point, 'How can you say that you are not altering the human condition by taking away people's right to feel bad if they want to?'

'These steps are necessary for the betterment of things, all people will be fulfilled and at peace with themselves; that is a gift, Inspector.'

'And ultimate control! I didn't take you for a dictator.'

'We're talking about world peace, Inspector. I would have thought that a police inspector would be grateful to see the end of all those murders and crime scenes that you encounter, is that not what you want for mankind?'

Jacob shook with anger, 'Of course it is, but this is not the way.'

Two security guards moved forward a little; they'd been hovering behind, poised to restrain the inspector from a possible launch at the Prime Minister.

'What *might* be the way, Inspector?'

'I don't know.'

'Well there you go! In the absence of a better option I'll take this one.' The Prime Minister smiled again and finished his tea, 'People are born fundamentally good, all this does is remind them of it. Why don't you stay at the Rushton Institute, Inspector, and see for yourself? It will answer some of your questions and perhaps help to put your mind at ease.'

But this was not a question or request; before Inspector Jacob Rodgers had had time to consider this option an order was given, a car was called and he was bundled in.

Rushton

It was early morning and the sun poured a soft light across the room. Inspector Jacob Rodgers awoke to strange surroundings. He breathed his first conscious breath of the day, a slight disinfectant smell tickled his nose.

'Good morning, Mr Rodgers, or can I call you Jacob or Jake?'

'Jacob.'

'How are you feeling?'

Jacob looked up, he tried to move his head but it seemed pinned to the pillow. He narrowed his eyes to see the figure connected to the voice, he squinted at it. *White coat.*

Jake

Derek Faulkner. Who are you? Who are you? Who are you? Jake narrowed his eyes as he waited for the door to be answered. He rubbed the frown flat from his brow, pressed his temple as if trying to summon the memory from his mind, willing it free from its hiding place. Somewhere deep in his own brain lay the answers to his questions, his own truth, the knowledge of who it was that he awaited to answer the door. He tided his shirt a little, shook his shoulders free from tension. He felt a flicker of recollection, not from the house but from the process, as if calling for a date. Jake focused on the door, willing it to open; he rang the bell again.

The door eased open. A man of well-proportioned build stood in the frame. Jake watched his lips moving through the darkness of the night and the pitted light of the orange street lamps. Nodding appropriately and smiling eagerly the two men shook hands, swiftly followed by a welcoming gesture to enter the house.

'I know who you are,' Jake strolled in.

Rushton

It had been a few weeks since his head had first been able to lift from his pillow and Jacob was making fast progress, he had stopped taking his pills already, he wasn't going to let them control him any more than they did already. He smiled to himself about that, out-smarting them so soon. *Clever boy.*

Horace

Horace took an evening stroll. He breathed lightly but deliberately as he walked, his pace steady, his strides long, but as he turned a corner he stopped directly: a couple of 'lads' (as Horace thought of them) were kicking another 'lad' who was holding himself in the foetal position to protect his vital organs.

'Oi!' Horace shouted, 'What do you think you're doing?!'

The lads paused their onslaught to eye Horace with some viciousness, 'What's it to you? You wanna be next?'

Horace thought, quite vividly, perhaps he'd even said it, *'Don't be so ridiculous why would I want to be next, who'd want to be next?'* Then he remembered all at once, a flashing vivid scene, from a film perhaps or a boxing club, where one might well want to be next... but he was pretty sure that the lad on the floor was not in a fight club.

'Leave the kid alone,' Horace announced with some authority, his mass shadowing both their shoes now, the street light behind and to the left of Horace, their faces lit up to him, his features darkened, shrouded in shadow, his eyes piercing, his size intimidating.

The lads flicked their heads left and right respectively to check out their exit, a sideways dart was the only escape; backing up would first trip them up over the boy still curled up on the floor and then against a wall, a scruffy looking wall at that, many a lad had urinated there. The lad to Horace's right put up his hands, the other lad glanced at his mate then back at Horace, more worried than before. They ran.

Horace knelt down, 'I'm not going to ask you if you're alright because you don't really look it. Come on, I'll get you a cognac, let's get you up.' With which Horace swept him up, like he used to with the tie-giver sometimes when she had fallen asleep on the sofa he'd carry her to bed cradled in his mighty arms. Only he didn't cradle this chap quite the same; Horace put the lad's legs down, patted him on the back, 'You'll live.'

The boy looked at him, a question in his face but then gratitude, he smiled gently to himself and followed Horace's support into the pub. A large cognac later he was more himself again, 'I'd better go now but thanks, man. That was a really decent thing to do,' he scratched his neck just under his ear and winced, 'Thanks for the drink as well, man. Glad you were passing.'

'I'm glad too,' Horace said, 'I can teach you.'

The boy looked at him, his eyes carrying a question, 'Teach me what?'

'To protect yourself.'

The boy's questioning deepened, 'I'm okay.'

'You didn't look okay; I can help you in many ways.'

'You part of a cult or some sex ring?'

Horace looked horrified, 'No!' he announced with absolute certainty, 'Why does a good deed have to be wrapped up in cults and sex rings?! Do you really not trust that good people are just out there?'

The boy scratched his neck again, 'It's just weird, that's all.'

'Well it shouldn't be, should it?'

'No, I suppose not.'

Horace handed him a card, 'Take this, if you change your mind call me on that number or email me.'

The boy nodded. 'Thanks.'

'No problem.'

Rushton

Boris eyed the inspector; he had heard of him and remembered his visits with Dr Washington. He had been the arresting officer of Jake, Horace, Imogen and Eva. He was notorious. Boris shuffled his chair a little closer to him, 'Hi,' he said.

Jacob looked at him, squinted, tried to recall, but nothing came to mind.

'I'm Boris,' Boris put out his hand to be shaken. Jacob looked at the hand, considered, and took it.

'Nice to meet you,' Boris continued, 'I've heard of you.'

Jacob's eyebrows rose.

'Jake, Horace, Imogen and Eva were all here.'

Jacob's eyes widened to meet his brows. He had many questions, he didn't know where to begin, perhaps slowly; gain Boris's trust, become friends and ask questions later.

'Nice to meet you too, Boris,' he stated with a chirpy leaning to his voice.

Simon

As work at Rushton extended, rumours in society had started to circulate of an organisation. What this organisation was nobody knew. But Simon knew, he was in it, along with the ones who didn't wear white coats but always intervened, the gardener that had dug, first with Jake and then with himself. Horace's wife, *how had she heard of it?* The 'do gooder' of her community, the organisation of betterment, the organisation that wanted to make the world right.

Some say can't be that bad, but fear comes when the truth is unknown, what organisation that is doing only good things would hide itself? Simon reflected on his life; it was far better now than it ever would have been without Rushton, he was grateful for it and believed in the betterment of things, things *were* better and he was doing good things, helping teenagers find a better life for themselves. An organisation, of course, it had to be, otherwise the support network wouldn't exist, it had to be organised. Simon dismissed the rumours as stupid, *people fear what they don't have absolute understanding of,* but what was there to understand? It was a good organisation; he didn't think it hid itself, after all he knew about it, he lived in it, he was *living* it.

Rushton

Tick, tick. The new gleaming clock face hung high on the wall above the office that overlooked the communal area, 16 by 10 paces in size. Jacob looked at the clock; Boris looked at the clock because Jacob had; the white coat that was around more now checked her watch.

Eva

Eva sat on the edge of her robust, heavy wood bed. The always crisp and clean bedding crumpled a little under her slight frame. She had all her washing laundered for her, domestic chores were not her thing and as she climbed the marketing ladder the more she passed these chores on to other businesses. Her bedroom seemed bisected by the sun starting its decent through the buildings surrounding her own, the light cornered the room, cutting it almost exactly into light and dark halves. Eva sat on the dark side, the light side a wall, as if she were a vampire restricted to the shaded half of the room. Eva had decided to take Imogen's lead and write her own account of events at Rushton and beyond, notes of her thoughts and feelings on the matter. She poised her pen over paper.

She began... *Beautiful and structured by etiquette is the world of psychotic manipulation....*

Rushton

Dr Washington stood at the entrance to Orange Block, the hub of their work. Well, *his* work now. He smiled and straightened his attire as he waited for the security door to grant his entrance. The smell inside was different to that of Blue Block; his nose twitched, connecting to his mind, trying to label what it recognised. Dr Washington walked into his new office, his strides confident and determined. He sat carefully, using the desk to assist his weight as he negotiated his chair, worried that the wheels might spin away from him as his weight descended. At rest, he leant back and entwined his fingers, *here's the steeple and here's all the people.*

The Diary of Rose Heather Roberts – The Truth

The shadows flickered across the room, an eerie feeling around me but not really within. My mind busy with all kinds of esoteric activity. I am calm in this space but then I stand and leave the room and the feeling comes, a feeling I knew somewhere else, somewhere beyond this place. A fantasy. Bang.

From the Papers of the Late Dr Rushton

When I was seventeen, the most serious girlfriend I had had to date dumped me. Admittedly it had only been a six month affair but at that age every day was an experience, stretched out to fill space for me. It had been a hard kick that made my head pound and my heart ache. My dad was a bastard, pushed and shoved, made me hate him and love him all at the same time. I found it hard to understand my emotions about him, so I focused on this girl; she was cool and thrilling, easy on the eye and sexy. I'd watched her for months, until one day in the school playground she approached me, making me jump right out of my skin. I tried to gather myself, so I didn't look like the idiot I believed myself to be. She spoke sweetly, I could feel the physical heart that pumped my blood around swell and pound; I tucked my hand under my leg so that she couldn't see me shaking, the blood rushing too fast now. I remember I felt a little dizzy. From then on we met up, just for a walk or coffee, sometimes she brought vodka and once or twice a smoke but not the skunk, mind numbing stuff, some kind of home grown. She said her brother got it.

She dumped my company for the cooler, more popular boy a year above us. I left school that day, went home and raided my dad's drawers and secret hiding places. I found an outrageous amount of money – hundreds of pounds – and a credit card. This was a moment when I remember smiling, really smiling. I called up a travel agent and used the card to book a ticket. This was how I discovered that escape by travel really works. Well, the travel of the mind, for I'd only got as far as the bar at the waiting lounge and all the stresses of my life melted away. Everything before that moment seemed meaningless, lost in the past, only the future mattered now. It was as easy as that. Escape by the mind can exclude all the heartache and betrayal that you knew before. I turned on my heels and went back to school, clear now of a future. I studied hard and forgot Miss Cool and her even cooler boyfriend; I ignored my dad and kept out of his way. My name is David Rushton and I am the founder of an institution that I believe can change lives and make the world a better place.

It took only this one day to realise the potential of the mind. Since then I have studied many theories on the matter but none that concluded with an answer, an answer to the human condition and how to turn it around, how to make the world a better place by embracing the fundamental goodness of people. How to right the wrongs that people commit has been misunderstood, the things they do due to circumstance or upbringing, so often pushed and pulled, forcing a spark that changes their direction. I know a better way, an absolute way. So I introduced an idea: to add a new spark, a new direction, to turn it all around and help people find their goodness and work towards the betterment of things. To make the world a better place, by making the people in it better people.

And so it was that Dr Rushton's New Wave of Rehabilitation found its roots. Dr David Rushton died and left his work to two highly educated and respected doctors, Dr Henry Washington (Psychology) and Dr Jeremy Jefferson (Neurobiology). Together they developed ways to fulfil the dream of Dr Rushton, always, without falter, for the betterment of things.

Rushton

Jacob looked at the clock; another new resident namely Spencer looked at the clock because Jacob had; Boris tapped on the glass that encased a new school of fish; Yvonne checked her watch.

The days tick on...

Printed in the United States
By Bookmasters